P S I - F I

Where the **P**hysical, **S**piritual, and **I**ntellectual facets of humanity synergistically combine, as they do in everyday life, to create a dynamic, mysterious, and ingenious futuristic world in **FI**ction.

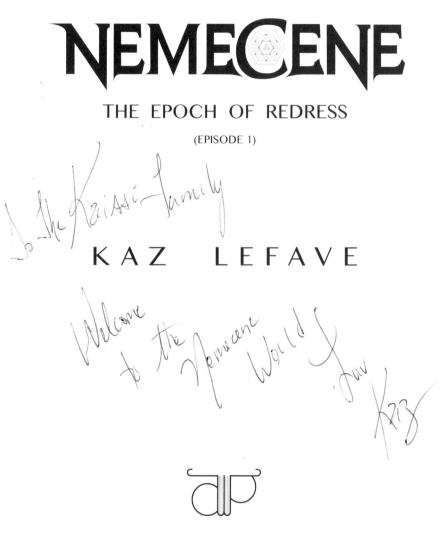

NEMECENE

THE EPOCH OF REDRESS

(EPISODE 1)

KAZ LEFAVE

To The Kziassi family

Welcome to the Nemecene World! Luv Kaz

AGUACENE PUBLISHING, INC.

NEMECENE

THE EPOCH OF REDRESS

KAZ LEFAVE

www.NEMECENE.com

An Aguacene™ publication
Published 2011-2017 by Aguacene Publishing, Inc.
Toronto, ON, Canada • publish@aguacene.com

Distributed by NBN (National Book Network, Inc.)
15200 NBN Way, Blue Ridge Summit, PA, USA, 17214

Printed in Canada

ISBN-13: 978-1-988814-00-1
ISBN-10: 1-988814-00-6
10 9 8 7 6 5 4 3 2 1

FSC
www.fsc.org
RECYCLED
Paper made from
recycled material
FSC® C103567

Paper:	FSC® certified
Cover:	Supreme Recycled Silk 100lb, 55% recycled with 30% post consumer waste, made without the use of chlorine gas, manufactured using cogeneration energy
Pages:	Roland Enviro Print 50lb text, 100% recycled, 100% post consumer waste, processed chlorine free, manufactured using biogas energy
Press:	Variquik PC15, web offset

Cover art by RUKE. Edited by Sylvia McConnell. Page layout by Karen Lefave.

NOTES ON THE TEXT

THE NARRATORS

Each chapter is organized into three sections, each section consistently assigned to a single narrator.

Section I - N A T H R U Y U
Written in the third person in Nathruyu's voice from an out of body point of view.

Section II - E L I Z E
Written in the first person as a running dialog inside Elize's head. If she does not think it, hear it, see it, taste it, feel it, smell it or sense it, neither do you.

Section III - K E E T O
Written in the first person as diary entries to his mother. One section represents one journaling session.

THE TIMELINE

The novel, as a whole, moves forward in time, although sections may overlap as the different narrators offer their experiences during the same time period. A note at the beginning of each section states when that segment begins relative to Chapter One, which starts in the late evening on day 1.

Flashbacks and fanciful musings are enclosed between the following symbols:

$$\blacktriangledown \ \blacktriangledown \ \blacktriangledown \ \text{and} \ \blacktriangle \ \blacktriangle \ \blacktriangle$$

Gaps in the story, where the text jumps forward in time are preceded by the following symbols:

$$\times \ \times \ \times$$

GLOSSARY ENTRIES

Since the characters are living in the *Nemecene* epoch, they are intrinsically familiar with their futuristic world, its technology, and its language, therefore they would not naturally explain the meaning or significance of words, foreign to our 21st century society, as they relay their story to you.

I encourage you to read the glossary at the back first, in order to immerse yourself in their world.

THE MYSTERIOUS *they* OR *them*

Who are *they*? That's a well-guarded secret. In fact, only one person knows the answer to that question and I'll give you one guess. ;-)

Feel free to share your theories with me and each other by following *Nemecene* on social media. The answers shall be forthcoming … in due time. Muahahaha.

For my children Siobhan and Jeremy, my parents Art and Norma, my sisters Laura and Kylen, my dear friends, and the one water which connects us all.

A WORLD IN A WORD

Water is so much more than life ... If you only knew ...

Welcome to the dynamic, engaging, and ingenious futuristic world of *Nemecene*, a 9 + 1 episode series designed as 3 trilogies and one grand finale, where the physical, spiritual, and intellectual facets of humanity evolve towards a deeper understanding of who we really are.

Inspired by the works of Masaru Emoto, and the current ocean crisis facing our planet, science fiction fantasy author Kaz Lefave has foreseen a future where humanity's fate lies in our understanding of what or who water really is. She believes that a deep fundamental disconnect between our species and our life source is at the core of the pain we have inflicted upon Earth and, ultimately, upon each other. The Nemecene™ World encapsulates her talents as visionary and storyteller to bridge that gap by engaging, inspiring, and empowering science fiction fantasy lovers to create lasting positive global impact through fun.

What started as a tale of psychological demons became a philosophical journey into the meaning and origins of life. Emoto's water crystal photography, the North Pacific ocean garbage patch, Plastic Island, and African women walking 8 hours to collect dirty water for their village, were the images bubbling out of the internet soup. The canvas that emerged through the splatter of revelations was a world map showing over 400 oceanic dead zones plaguing our coastlines. As global warming continues unchecked, the prospects are frightening. Shock sparked one question that revealed Kaz's purpose.

What if all these zones, these anoxic dots, connected, like the bonds in the water molecules they infect? The Holocene epoch would end, and a new one where Earth decides to right the wrongs of her nemesis, humanity, would ensue. Such is how *Neme - cene* was conceived —a future where our oceans have died, choking the life we know, as noxious gases from her oxygen deprived depths cover the planet in hydrogen sulfide.

While vested interests debate whether our personal choices impact the climate, characters Keeto and Elize are faced with a choice of their own, one which will affect the world in a way they too could not have possibly imagined.

Science, spirituality, deception, humor, adventure, murder, numerology, cosmology, quantum physics, dance, fashion, art, consciousness, sacred geometry, and more all come together in a world where the theory of every thing and the theory of no thing collide.

"Science fiction is when we see into the future of our planet.
Fantasy is when we believe humanity will survive."
— Kaz Lefave

MEET NATHRUYU

*She moves through time with the balletic grace of a
tantric ninja*

These gemstone eyes are watching you and they will leave you wanting, either for more, either for less, but wanting nonetheless.

In Nathruyu's world, there is no first person narrative and no third person detachment, since such a distinction only exists as an illusion of the mind. There is only a visceral experience through the entity that animates her flesh. If her narration seems obscure or her vocabulary provocative, they are. Every word is an intention designed to suspend time through the void in which she glides. Nothing is by happenstance.

So keep a dictionary handy and feel Nathruyu's pace as she expresses herself through rhythm, and sometimes through rhyme, for this is the voice that defines her kind.

MEET ELIZE

Her restless tough-girl attitude betrays her splintered mind

Keet is such a pup. Honestly. There's nothing mystical about my nightmares. It's a scientific fact that dreams are just our brain's way of processing things. And in my case, it's simply trauma nothing more. Keet's afraid I'll get lost in some mental void like Mother and that Father will commit me to the GHU. That's where Mother died. Wipe that image. No more tears. Good. So we're keeping everything hush. Crazed, eh? Anyway, I hope he's wrong. Better keep the voices to myself. Everybody hears some. They just won't admit it. It's not considered normal. Right. Normal. At least, we'll be gone soon and maybe even … Crap! No. Not now.

Breathe, Eli, breathe. Here he comes. Breathe. Act normal.

MEET KEETO

*His courage hides inside the cocoon of an
armchair archaeologist*

Time has not filled the void you left when Eli and I were just nine years old. As I cloister myself here, sprinkling the pages of another journal with my emotions, I image that you see through my eyes, and write through my quill. It is this insanity that keeps me sane while my days spent digging for answers to questions that constantly change consume my sheltered life. If only your spirit could materialize into the Mother I need you to be once again. But reality reminds me otherwise. My only hope is that connecting with you, in these quiet and sometimes not so quiet moments of reflection, will uncover truths that liberate us all.

But will they come soon enough?

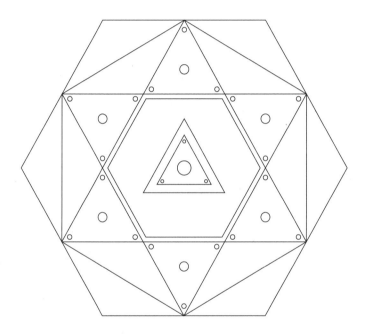

CHAPTER ONE

NATHRUYU

Day 1: late evening

The hour is late and Nathruyu's pace has slowed, carving silent impressions in the earth while she glides over ash and stone, with the cool air tempering her gait and the warm moisture from her lips betraying her presence as she moves. Haste is the nature of her pilgrimage, yet it is not to come easily. She softly passes amidst the perils of darkness, but had an alternative to travel with the sun been possible, she would have gladly selected it. Circumstances, however, had changed, and the change was swift.

Her muscles inflict grief on her already weary thighs, as she marshals the strength within and strives to gain the summit before the moonlight divulges her path. Welcoming as daylight would be for her on this terrain, it could only endanger her mission and risk her just rewards. She drags the load of her conscience with her as usual and trusts that the chosen will prevail and their story will be told. Such is Nathruyu's plight.

The top of the ridge brings a grateful repose. A solitary field of fragrance spreads before her to the hamlet below. She must remain wary of her balance and awake to the night as she negotiates the floral thicket sloping down to the closest cover lest she announce her passage. *They* will be looking for her, as before, as beyond, lamenting what she has done, but the truth must override, and the sacrifices shall be made, for all cry foul when a decision seems cruel.

Carefully, she guides her body through the underbrush, its tentacles claiming the hem of her coat as it floats over the landscape, reminiscent of the countless small hands begging for time as they sink into the void. She forges on into the valley, unconcerned, for the branches, like the timid, freely bend to her sway. The distant tranquillity assures her that her silhouette is not plainly visible against the steep violet tapestry. Her choice of dress has succeeded in masking her well, leaving her immediate approach unencumbered, and despite the drop in ambient heat, her legs have managed to garner speed. She attains her destination with a few minutes to spare and borrows the light to move swiftly in the shadows of the village.

Here she pauses, contemplating the scene she is about to influence. Several events have transpired since their initial encounter, and there is no guarantee that expectations will not follow. Her best hope of breaking the dubious bond of trust between the twins and their father is to listen closely for clues and hence uncover the pursuit to unfold, then tail them and fulfill her and their destiny. Failure to comply is not an option. The phase has begun in which she must justify the means and usher the twins to their appointed fate.

As she points her feet in the direction of their home, she removes her multi-panel coat, shakes any lingering twigs onto the ground, inverts it, and promptly slips it on again. The backdrop has refashioned, as must her camouflage. Her eyes scan the surroundings for trouble and she proceeds prudently towards her target, perking her senses for signs of interference. The desolate track blows a cloud of dust with her every step, relinquishing but a hint of her trail, each puff a reminder of a past she remembers quite vividly, a past bathed in the powdery residues of an experiment gone terribly amiss.

▼ ▼ ▼

It was early morning when the storm hit. Although it appeared to breach the threshold without warning, it was known in advance to some. Regardless, the extent of the carnage eclipsed all expectation. The arrogance of a smattering of handsomely paid bureaucrats, touting the virtues of their equally anointed scientific advisors, chose to repeat the shortcomings of their 21st century ancestors. Even after a dozen or so ill-fated attempts at circumventing the instinctive retaliation of Earth's intricate ecosystem, from shading the ice sheets of Greenland with enormous reflective tarps, to desalination and glacial harvesting projects, to cooling the seawater off the coast of South Africa, politicians recklessly persevered with futile efforts. After trillions upon trillions of combined personal hours spent laboring to patch a spoiled habitat with feeble intellect, the planet was drained of her vitality and had just a single avenue accessible to her.

The road to recovery was onerous, and the prices demanded en route even more so. City after city was engulfed, land after land was swept into oblivion, species after species became extinct, and child after child was orphaned, often dying of starvation or disease. The battle for sustainability was also fierce. The oceans rebelled, sometimes gradually over the course of months, other times violently, in barely a few hours. As much as the pride of man could not admit accountability, he was somehow able to harness his courage and do everything in his capacity to survive. Cities graced with advantage were fortified and transformed as countries united to evacuate others not as blessed, rebuilding more modest towns at greater elevations. Unfortunately, ventures to preserve the heritage of the people fell short, and crucial historical records were lost.

Nevertheless, on that fateful morning of the ocean's ultimate wrath, history repeated itself, as it often does. When the wake of the first wave subsided, broken nations sought to regain their prosperity, as they previously remembered it. Concluding that the planet had adjusted itself and was starting to stabilize, the ambassadors of the new order presumptuously declared the rehabilitation complete and embarked on a mission to repackage faulty public policy and sell it to the masses. The glaciers had obviously melted and the impact had been thoroughly absorbed by the hydrosphere, they reasoned, therefore fossil fuels were not likely a recurring hazard. Evidently, the rash conclusion that the earth had finished her metamorphosis was false, and a radical age of human conceit emerged, unleashing the most formidable catastrophe in their abrupt saga.

Temperatures were progressively rising, and a 21st century concept that was formerly dismissed was attracting an audience. After a brief reprieve, hardly lasting a hundred years, global warming resumed its destructive agenda, and intelligent simulations from reputable institutions across the globe predicted a grim prospect for the near-term world economy. Forever seduced by the delusion of human brilliance over nature's perfection and subjugated by the whims of an unrestrained ego, society found that the captive sparkle of its disillusioned existence had suffocated and perished. Plans to use geoengineering to reverse the damage caused by the resurgence of greenhouse emissions became the recycled trend, and in this revision, the chosen poison was stratospheric sulfate aerosol, a solution aimed at producing atmospheric particulates meant to reflect the ultraviolet spectrum, thus mimicking the effect of volcanic eruptions.

▲ ▲ ▲

The pungent imprint of the aftermath is still faintly discernible as her tattered silk brushes the ground while she surreptitiously sweeps across the inner courtyard of the cluster, leaving tiny puffs of yellow-tinted dust that harbor the memory playing in her mind's eye.

▼ ▼ ▼

For decades the toxin lay dormant, patiently expectant. Meanwhile, the few who staked a claim to the patented technology raped the earth of its coal and profited from its ravenous consumption. The oil wars of the 21st century switched to futuristic carbon wars under the guise of freedom, sovereignty, and religion.

▲ ▲ ▲

The blatant hypocrisy of those hungry for dominance haunts her journey, as she sprinkles her path with tears, reliving the agony of the innocent, who unwittingly bore the consequences of a breed that had learned nothing from the mistakes of its forefathers.

In the end, the inevitable manifested, and the supply of black gold dwindled. A vocal minority assembled and lobbied the world leaders to brace for a violent climate shift, but their recommendations were left unheeded. Fortunately, this forward thinking union gathered supporters and successfully raised fortunes to construct enclosed havens in the high meadows of the disjointed continents.

▲ ▲ ▲

The rings of multi-family dwellings and dedicated generators, mostly intact in the hills, are testaments to these endeavors, some of them still boasting a fully functional emergency biowall, whilst others waver in disrepair, making their masters vulnerable to reawakening sulfuric activity, albeit no longer a crippling threat. Nonetheless, of all the inhabited circles amongst the vast collage of mountain glens, it is this circle, the one in which she faithfully travels, that holds the key to the future.

The fluttering breeze caresses her tensing cheeks and temporarily relaxes her as she detaches herself from those distressing thoughts. That day belongs to the past. The day the blistering winds off the coastal waters propelled the fireless smoke onto the awaiting shores was the ocean's final fury.

▼ ▼ ▼

Centuries of burning, to manufacture immense quantities of sulfur dioxide artificially injected into the stratosphere, suddenly stopped. The fuel was spent. The arising sulfuric acid and drizzle, designed to scatter the sun's nourishing energy and chill the atmosphere, disappeared from the straining ecological system. A brutal backlash shortly ensued that infected the planet with a debilitating fever. The formless gases, enjoying their reign for years, malevolently hovering atop the tallest peaks and destroying the ozone layer, digested the insulating blanket protecting Earth's beauty from cosmic radiation, and many magnificent creatures vanished. Life expectancy dropped sharply for those fortunate enough to have outlasted the worst.

▲ ▲ ▲

Easing her stride, she succumbs to a rush of conflicted emotions as she recalls the senselessness, the transgressions, the horror.

▼ ▼ ▼

With the resultant slowing of thermohaline circulation,

causing a further increase in oceanic dead zones, the deep recesses of the seas became toxic and cloaked with a thin green shroud, infused with whatever oxygen was available. Contaminant spewing algae indiscriminately replaced fish and marine mammals and periodically stirred from the depths, releasing lethal hydrogen sulphide bubbles to the surface and carpeting bordering shorelines with a film of golden powder. The chemical cesspool living in the air, land, and water incited a chain reaction, leading to the cataclysmic anoxic event that very nearly annihilated their great civilization.

Savage gusts of wind, encouraged by the burgeoning thermal gradients over endless expanses of territory, took siege and enlisted the noxious vapors into their fray, affording them no chance to convert to their more benign format. The gale force stream strengthened with the unseasonably cold dawn sky and syphoned in the deadly mix of ever-present sulfur dioxide and mist, to give birth to a charging front of dense fog tainted with yellow death.

The tempest grips her. Motionless at the fringe of the plaza, Nathruyu struggles to center her spirit. She feels powerless, her body frozen in the face of a stealth airborne demon, as she watches her children gasp for their last breath and slump lifeless to the ground, in a puddle of malignant cinders, their twisted forms blanketed in blonde ashes. The features of the terrified swarms hopelessly scrambling to outrun the accelerating poisonous mass live locked in her soul, and the bravery of the ones she failed to protect, crushed in the panic, further strengthens her will. Her limbs, burdened with the weight of child after child sinking helpless in her arms, desperately groping for her, ache with regret. Kneeling in the midst of a field of torment, she offers peace to the brave and comfort to the fearful. Her eyes weep the tale of her anguish, and her flesh becomes stone in its path. As the storm's assault disperses, all that persists is the tarnished wreckage of ignorance and deceit.

▲ ▲ ▲

Nathruyu arrives at the gate with a deep, cleansing sigh, poised to embrace the forthcoming business and her latest challenge. Examining the kitchen area for contours, she places one hand firmly on the garden fence and leans into it for an instant, calm as the starry heavens. The building turns dark, and with a graceful swoop of her balletic build, she nimbly sails over the pickets and tucks herself quickly and quietly in the space between the hedge and the outside wall of the house, a significant distance ahead. She waits.

Soon, the Ministry hounds will come, and the trials along with them. Although they cannot audit her daily activities, her general whereabouts for the latter three months are not a mystery anymore. She has been diligently cautious not to lead them to her cause, for fear of disrupting the larger intent, but private forces inside the Ministry are at work, hampering her ability to conceal her motives and spinning a web she must test faith to confront. Safe behind the broad blooming shield of the hedge, she grabs the opportunity to draw in its intoxicating perfume and to meditate on her crusade in light of the recent awareness. The generous petals of her shelter rejuvenate her skin with a pale rose brush and fill her blood with a radiating flush. The hunt is in progress, and she must accomplish her task before they arrive.

She closes her eyes and delays a moment to reconnect with her purpose. There is a tenet bigger than life that she must honorably uphold. She cannot grant her resolve the scantest weakness, no matter how callous and heinous her actions are judged to be, and she must continue, detached, for if she were to falter, her diligence would have been for not, and the cycle would commence anew.

▼ ▼ ▼

To the unenlightened, the children appear to nap when she collects them, holding them close to her chest as she carries them. Away from their bed, she retreats, gliding in utter silence, anticipating their treacherous voyage and forgiving their confusion. Pressing soundlessly past the ears of that which cannot hear, she takes them to the place where all manner of suffering will finally cease. They are so delicate and fresh in her care, cleansed of the madness and whole again. She sways from side to side, with them nestled in time, their bodies still toiling with all that is new, but soon shall yield to the essence of truth.

The corridor she travels is narrow and temperate, her coat framed by the naked tunnel as she hurries onward. The flapping of leather upon granite grows louder on occasion, waking her passenger slightly. The drowsy eyes watch her fleetingly, then drift back to a dreamless sleep. She must keep her secret until it is complete, or *they* will know and seek out her charge, reinfecting the child with the illness from which she has been saved. Too many young minds have been programmed and controlled, the few taking liberties from and with the many, but the era is looming when the children shall choose. Until that epoch, she dutifully obeys her directive, in spite of barbaric rules of what is right and what is wrong. Notwithstanding the remnants of compassion enduring in her physical being, it is her conviction, above everything else, that will conquer the weak and ill-informed.

She crosses the hidden doorway, and into the open she flies, painstakingly ensuring no injury befalls her precious cargo. The bundle is marginally responsive. Her lustrous long hair shimmers in stride against the setting sun, as the solar crest sinks below the horizon and they race to the river bank. The girl's absence duly noted, Nathruyu prepares for an overnight vigil, since they are frantically searching, and, as always, effective sanctuary during the following days is paramount to her survival. If the hounds pick up her scent and intercept the process, there will be no semblance of clemency for her carelessness, for a transition is marching steadily forwards, and souls shall be laid to rest. Even if her agility should facilitate an escape, the girl must not return with images that can speak. She has seen too much.

▲ ▲ ▲

She opens her eyes and gazes at the hillside, the neighboring structures mere outlines etched into the rustling slopes. The hunters are there, by the water's edge, and eventually they will share the valley with her.

As Nathruyu hones in on the noises in the house above her, groggy footsteps, a cupboard door squeaking, dishes clanging, she cocks her head, and concedes that it must surely be difficult for them, trying to find their way in obscurity with limited sight, but there is no assistance she can provide. She must not allow them to detect her until their hearts are ready to accept who she is and what she has done. Elize is especially fragile at the moment, and any additional complexity might derail her and compromise her critically needed focus, which currently lies fragmented in her mind.

A chair screeches, and then she hears someone walking towards the window, pausing for a bit with the fingers of one hand peeking around the trim. Nathruyu interrupts her lungs. The lumbering is clearly Keeto's, rummaging around the cabinets for something to feed his developing body. He hesitates, then pushes himself back, slams a book shut, and mutters his displeasure. The stars have not yet invited the moon to shine, and, exasperated, he collides with a stubborn stool.

As her ears follow the plodding of his slippers, she ponders the irony of consciousness. Before there is darkness, there must be light, and without darkness, there cannot be light. If only they believed and would acknowledge the truth, she would not be running from misguided righteousness, because vision would reenter the spiritually blinded, and her deeds would be revered on the stage of redemption. The twins must make the leap.

The room falls quiet as the thumping fades, and she

concentrates her attention on a faint glow in their father's study further down. Silently, she springs from her handy refuge and lands near its source. As this also surrenders its light, she gently positions herself beneath the ledge of the open pane, depressing the soil underfoot with the slim heel of her shoe, and stays with her hand the whispering leaves of the bushes, alert to the distraction they may have provoked. Her heartbeat skips when she hears hushed movement in the house, and then the boy's tenuous voice.

"Hello? Anybody there?"

E L I Z E

Day 1: late evening

Where is it? No, no, no… Aw don't run out of charge. Crap! I can't see a thing anymore. Ouch. Oh, I hope no one heard that. Someone's in the room. Crap crap crap! Just drop to the floor, Eli, and stop breathing and maybe they'll just go away.

"Hello? Anybody there?"

Sounds like Keet, but not a hundred percent on that. I sure hope it's not Father or I'm busted. Think fast, girl, you've got to sound convincing, just in case.

"Hello?"

There it is again, a little more faint. Ah, it's Keet and he's sounding a little scared. Hehehe. Time to have a little fun. I'll throw the light in the corner by the window and see what he does. Good, he's heading there. I can sneak up behind him now and grab his ankle.

"Eek!"

Got you back. Oh, this is priceless. I wish it wasn't so dark so I could see his face.

"Eli, you little witch. I almost lost my meal on you, and it would have served you right too."

Retribution at last. "You know you could have turned on the light." Sometimes Keet is in another dimension.

"I did but the generator is down. The whole circle is dark. What are you doing in here anyway?"

"I'm looking for Father's flashes. I know he keeps them

locked up somewhere in his study, but I can't seem to find the box."

"That's because it's pitch black."

Well, isn't that just stating the obvious? "I had a light, pup, and it stopped working. Anyway, I know Father has a late meeting scheduled. I checked his planner. But just to be extra safe I decided to practice my thieving skills. You never know when that can be handy." Sooner than later I figure.

"If you take them now, he'll know they are missing. He'll get suspicious and we'll be forced to rethink the whole plan."

"No, he won't. The last time he looked at them was three months ago. That's when his viewer mysteriously went missing." Hehehe. My doing. "He hasn't bought a new one yet, so I'm sure he thinks he left it somewhere in the house and that it will turn up. You know how he gets. It's a wonder he has any brain cells left by now."

"You took the viewer? Are you bent? That was never part of the plan. Where is it? We have to put it back!"

"What's that story you read me once? Oh, yeah. Don't be a mother hen." Come to think of it, his mouth does look a little beakish. "I hid it somewhere safe. It's best if you don't know where, just in case." He knows what I mean. He talks too much and his brain is left trailing. The real truth is that now I can't remember where I put it. I don't want to alarm Keet so I'd better not tell him about the memory lapses. He already has enough to worry about. Everything is not in place yet and we're running low on options. "Can you help me find the flashes then?"

"I caaaaaan."

Here he goes again. "Ok. *Will* you help me find them?" I really think it's time for him to grow out of this. "That's it! Grow! I just remembered. I hid the viewer in the fern pot by the window. Right over…" Where is it? Calm down, girl. The maid must have moved it to a brighter room.

"Oh no, Eli! Now we're doomed! It's only a matter of time before Father's scary friends throw me into a dungeon and torture me for hours and hours. And my dying words will be: 'It's in the fern! It's in the fern!'"

"Rip!" I can't believe I said that out loud. "Well, now that you know where it is, we'd better dig it up so I can hide it somewhere else."

His eyes just lit up. He's excited now. "Dig? Where? I don't see a fern anywhere in this room. I don't even remember a fern ever being in this room. Are you sure you planted it in there? I mean, you might be confusing it with—"

"I am *not* confused." Honestly, does he think I am a complete scatterbrain or something? "It is in the fern pot. I wrapped it in a waterproof bag and buried it in the dirt." So fitting. A little grave is exactly where it belonged. Until we can get our hands on those flashes, it might as well be six inches under. "We've got at most thirty minutes now to find everything before Father gets back." Ok. Focus.

"We planned to look for the flashes tomorrow, Eli, remember? Let's stick to plan for once."

He's wasting time and he's supposed to be the organized one? "I'm not a greenberry, Keet. Let's just do it and you can cross it off your list tomorrow. Ok?"

I feel like my hands are going to explode. Slow down.

The blood's pounding too hard under my skin. Oh no, it's happening.

"Eli. Breathe with me. Slow down. It's all right. Think this through. Is it so important that we do this tonight?"

I can hear my thoughts again. "Yes. If we don't find it and the flashes tonight, I'm afraid—" I can't control it. The voices are back. Why won't they leave me alone? "Shut up!" Did I just say that out loud again?

Keet looks concerned. Go away. You don't belong in my head. Why can't I gather my thoughts anymore? Ok. I *am* confused. Are you happy now? Good. Give me some quiet so that I can find the fern then.

"Wake up." He is shaking me like a rag doll now.

If only he could toss the voices out my ears then I'd squash them like bugs when they hit the floor. That'll shut them up.

"Ok, ok, I'm here. Just thought I heard Father slide in." That sounds plausible. He'll buy that one. Well? Yeah, it worked.

He's walking towards the entrance and checking the glass. Wow. I never realized how tall he is. Most of the time he is just pouring over old books and researching all sorts of old stuff, like he's looking for something, but he's not. He's just obsessed with bones, fossils, old garbage, anything buried actually. Brrr. It's getting cold in here.

"No one there. Let's work fast then. I'll dig up the fern." Good he's smiling again. Just say the word dig and he's on it.

"And I'll find the flashes."

He's good at finding things. For some reason he just knows where things are even if he didn't put them there himself. That's why I had to be creative with the viewer. I can concentrate on the flashes now.

Father was in here last season. I was peaking through the frame and watching him. I remember asking him about the flashes years ago, but he denied that they even existed. He said it must have been one of my dreams, it didn't really happen. But I know better. He's hiding them from us, so I haven't mentioned them to him since. There is something in there that he does not want us to see. I see it in his face every time he visits them because I am watching him. He is careful to keep them contained and out of view by anyone but himself, so I never actually see what he does. Just a faint reflection of images in his eyes.

Think back to last time, Eli. I'm there.

▼ ▼ ▼

I can see him sitting straight up in his chair, looking apprehensive as he unlocks the box and pulls them out. His hands even seem to shake. Then when he finally manages to snap them into the viewer he becomes more tense, frozen even, until the scene plays out completely and then he sighs deeply. For years, it's been the same routine. Only his clothing is different, the suppleness of his skin, the gray in his hair. But the memories don't change. And he is relieved. Yet this time he says something.

"Soon."

What does he mean, soon? Watch him carefully, girl. I must know where he is hiding the box of flashes now. I don't want to find out what "soon" means. Behind the wall? No, he just grabbed something else. Now he's bending under the desk. Crap! I can't see his hands! Get up and turn around so I can see. He's going to the far end of the room. Shhh! I hope he didn't hear that. It's quiet now. Something heavy sliding on a hard surface. And again. He's back in view now and the box is gone. My heart is sinking. Wait! He's brushing off his shirt. Looks like dust. That's a clue. No. It's more like ash. Juicy! The fireplace!

▲ ▲ ▲

"Indie strikes again!"

Who's that? Oh yeah. It's Keet. Good. That means he's found his little treasure. And not a moment too soon. His great quest gave me time to poll my own memory flashes and now I just need to feel my way through the darkness. Best get on the ground to keep from bumping things. Am I near the window yet? What's this? Oh yeah. The light I got Keet's attention with. That was fun. It's still broken. I guess throwing it wasn't such a good idea after all. Where is all this darkness coming from? Father says rodents are getting into the generators, but I don't buy that. I know the ins an outs of our circle and there are no rodents around. I've even asked Jenny next door. She says it's "soul suckers" watching us, but we of course can't see them because they are invisible. Sweet girl Jenny but not too bright. Quite dim actually. Must be the "soul suckers". Hehehe.

"What's so funny?"

"Creeps! You jumped me! Just thinking about Jenny next

door and her ghouls and goblins."

"Well, it is very dark you know." I can hear him chuckle.

"Oh stop it. I found the flashes. They're just… Did you hear that?" Oh no. The lights are on and Father's here. Hurry. . Grab the box. "Keet. Over here, quick. Wipe the floor. Get all this ash off me. And get the light by the window. Let's go. My room."

This is close. I hope he didn't see anything through the frame. I'll just put the flashes in with the other stuff we're collecting and get the board game out. It's always set up in some random fashion ready for when we need a quick cover. Keet's already in position. "Your turn. Ha! See if you can handle that one, pup." Father's lumbering up the stairs again. Just need to slow down my heartbeat now and we're juicy. His head's at the door.

"Remember I'm going to the plant tomorrow. Leaving early. Heading off to bed now so keep it quiet, ok?"

"Sure thing." It's late anyway. Keet is quiet. It doesn't happen often, but it does happen. Mostly when Father is around. "We should get some sleep too. We can check the flashes tomorrow when he's gone. We're almost there." It looks like relief on his face, but I can't be sure. At least he can focus back on the plan now. It feels great to curl up and just shut the voices out. Best not think about it. I can't sleep through the chatter. Sleep now.

✂ ✂ ✂

It's still dark. What time is it? 3:33? Father will be up soon.

I hear voices and this time they're real. They're coming from outside. I have to get closer to hear what they are saying. I'd better check on Father and Keet just to make sure they're asleep before I go down. I think the voices are coming from the gate. No one up, quickly and quietly now.

"She was here."

"Are you sure?"

"Yes. The green hedge. This is the place. We must advise."

Who was here? What place? Advise who? There's a third voice, but I can't quite make it out. Something about "them". And "found". Maybe if I peek out of the corner here I can see their faces. I can also open the frame and catch them a bit better. The mechanism is smooth so they shouldn't hear anything from my end.

"Their father is an elder. He works for the URA. It makes no sense."

Heartbeat, slow down. Muscles, loosen up. Brain, stop spinning around. And stomach, I already had my dinner, I don't need to taste it again. They're talking about us! What's the URA? Father doesn't work for the Unification; he's a technician for GenTech. He fixes cooling reactors and generators. Fear, control yourself. Is he the one sabotaging the circle generator? Maybe he knows what we just did, and he told them because they want the flashes. Maybe he is supposed to report back to them after he checks them and he hasn't been able to do so because I took the viewer. Ok, imagination, time to take a break now and let me focus on the facts. I'm starting to sound like Keet. Father wouldn't be leaving us tomorrow if he knew these creepy guys were around. He doesn't even let us go out of the house without a tag. Focus.

"She has been here. I've been talking to the others. They say the generator is wavering, especially these past three months. This must be the place."

"Very well then. We advise and wait for instructions."

"The GMU will catch wind. They will investigate and he will be warned."

"The choices remain. We prepare. We advise. Then we act swiftly. Agreed?"

"Agreed."

"Agreed."

The third one seems unsure. He knows something the other two don't. And worse yet, all three of them know something I have no clue about. And that's not juicy at all. I need to get in closer. I need a more detailed image in my mind. I certainly have the heightened emotional state necessary to put a big red dot on this one. The drawer. There's a lens in it. I can use that to zero in on their faces. Just a profile is good enough. That's it. They look nervous. The third one is sweating and dripping all over the place. The other two are also sweating, but not as much. I still can't make them out. Whoa, it's getting warm in here. Now I'm sweating. Oh, I'm not feeling very well, where's the floor. It's moving up the wall. Stop rocking. I still don't have a proper breadcrumb to follow. Ouch. That's going to leave a mark. Face down on the floor. Great! Stop. Did anyone hear that? No. Good. No movement from above. Now back to the creepy ones. They're gone! Sit here and listen. Make sure they're not coming in. Don't think. Don't let your brain make any noise.

No voices, no steps, no creaks, no temperature rise, no triggers. No balance either. I'd better just sit here awhile until I stop shaking. Let's think about this for a bit. They want something that we found. Well, Keet and I have been "finding" a lot of things lately so maybe it's not the flashes. Think girl. What have we been hoarding for the past three months. They did say three months, right? But that's just how long whoever-she-is has been watching us. Yes, it must have been within that period then, because no one would have been watching us to tell. *She* must have told someone who passed it on to them because it doesn't sound like they're together on this one, based on their tone.

Well, Keet found some old books in the basement. He was pretty ecstatic about that, ancient civilizations and the like, especially *The Rise and Fall of the American Empire*, *The Chinese Indo-Brazilian Federation*, and a whole box of even older ones. That's why I call him pup. He's always digging for bones. Ah, there's a giggle. I'm feeling more relaxed now. I found some of Mother's old things. Father tucked them away under the sliderpad. He has a stack of stuff under there so I spent a couple of hours a day for a week swallowing my tears and choosing with my heart. I miss her. Mostly they were items we had as babies. Even though I have no recall of them, I just know they were the treasured ones. And then there is the jewel she used to wear. We found that tucked away in an old box in her room. No one ever went there. Father kept it barricaded. I sent a crabbot through the window though. And finally the flashes. We'll have to go through them all one by one.

It's almost four. Get upstairs now! Father will be awake

soon and we've run out of time. Keet's going to hate me for this, but we're off the plan again. I'm not waiting for them to "act swiftly". We'll beat them to it. "Wake up. Shhh. We have to go." My body is shaking again.

"What? Where? What's wrong?"

"I'll explain later. Grab everything. Fake the lump. And hurry." He's wide awake. My panic is showing through. "This is it, Keet. Together."

"Together."

Outside finally. Wait.

Something's missing.

"Where are you going? Eli! You'll wake him up."

"I forgot my dreamcatcher. I'm not leaving without it. It's her last gift." The tears are welling up in my eyes. He understands.

"Be the silent storm. Go!"

Open the door a third. Block it with my bag. Up the stairs. One. Two. Three. Four. Five. Six. Seven. Eight. N….crap. Skip it. Ten. Quick quick quick. On the mirror. Got it. I can see Keet outside. He looks scared. I have to be strong for him and keep it together and that means focus. What's that? Freeze. Listen. It's too quiet. I don't like this. Phew. There it is, he's snoring. He must have just dropped his glass. Surge like the flood, girl, and don't look back.

"Got it?"

"Got it. He's still out."

Keet's doing well, considering... "Fly like the wind. We have twelve minutes."

And never look back.

K E E T O

Day 2: late evening

As the mist slowly lifted off the horizon, I sat there in amazement and in a kind of numb state of shock. We finally did it, the months of secret planning and sneaking about have finally paid off and not to mention of course Eli's keen sense of adventure. She truly is the spirited one in our little family.

I wonder what Father was thinking at that very moment. But do I really?

It was a long trip I must say. You would have been proud of us, I can feel it. Luckily, Father was in his usual stupor by the time we squeaked out the back gate—I can always count on him for that. I don't remember whether things were different back then, before your accident, whether you too choked us with fears, but somehow I sense that you didn't. Father seemed to always want to keep you from us; he said you were sick and dangerous, and that's why you were in the hospital. But Eli remembers what happened. She dreams and sometimes she tells me. Mostly all I notice are her bloodshot eyes in the morning after a night of sobbing. We would have taken you with us...if only.

Flip, there goes my fountain again. I still cry when I miss you. "Sorrow is for the weak-hearted" is what Father used to say. I was never good enough or strong enough. Well, maybe he was right. Eli is the natural leader, the bold one, yet I know her true heart as if we were one. Just like I know you despite the little time we were allowed to see you, talk to you, be with you under the watching eye of the GHU. Why did they keep you under such tight surveillance in the psychiatric wing?

As Eli and I descended into the valley, my heart sank with the change in pressure. The trip on the transport was smooth for the most part, but now and again a sharp jolt would wake me from our adventure and fear would set in. Thanks, Father, for that. Would they find us? Would they hunt us down like criminals, like the ones who flee the GHU looking to cheat the inevitable? Would they be waiting for us in Eadonberg? Were they watching us even as I sat gazing into the morning fog? Paranoia claims many victims, and Eli and I are leaping into a new world. Our destiny awaits us in Eadonberg, and you're coming with us, in my heart.

Eli was able to sneak a few catnaps along the way. A welcome break for her I am sure. I for one was unable to relax; plunging into the unknown is not something I do well. In fact, it's not something I do at all. Anyway, there she was, curled up in a ball like a kitten basking in the sun. At times I even thought I could hear her purr, and then the same jolt that would call my attention to my surroundings would catapult her out of her seat. Perhaps she was feeling the darkness through the mist as was I. It wasn't an absence of light as it clearly was daylight, but rather a thickness or weight that was pressing down on us. And so it was with a heavy heart that we left our home, a place of grief, pain, and sorrow, yes, but all that we know and understand in this world.

That last toss, however, had a force so strong as to shatter the window behind us. As I fumbled to check whether my restraints were still intact, I felt a dust storm forming at the rear. It was at that point that I realized what had been causing these reality reminders. The valley had reached the wetlands where the silhouette of a cooling plant was clearly visible against the lime green horizon. The fog had lifted somewhat and was casting its last shadow before the final scattering. Everywhere trees were stripped of their green coats and painted with a yellowish powder. Smoke bombs of sulfur controlled the landscape, and any life form within its grasp for that matter, and we were no exception. Our great escape from a prison of memories had instantaneously transformed into a flight from death. A thick cloud was rolling towards the transport as we raced for the tunnel ahead. This section of the route was normally protected by a biowall but recent cosmic activity had altered the frequency generator's output and was causing sporadic drifts. We were just unfortunate enough to have been caught in one of them.

One final thrust of the accelerator pushed us into the tunnel and we were safe, for a while. Had we known what was awaiting us in Eadonberg, perhaps we would have been content with our lives as they were; I probably could have endured, but I am not so sure about Eli. She has been so lost and confused since you left. She is showing signs of the illness that afflicted you. I feared that if she stayed and continued to fall deeper into it, I would have become incapable of covering for her, and Father would have suspected her condition and have sent her away as he did to you. I cannot bear to, no, I refuse to lose her to that same fate. So there I was, on a path to confront my own fears as we sought out the answers in Eadonberg. At least, that was the plan and Eli's acceptance into the Bioengineering program at Schrödinger University was the break we were looking for. The movement through the tunnel was lengthy yet smooth. It gave Eli and me some time to calm our senses and observe the other travelers. After all, we had to make sure we had not been followed. Casting furtive glances around at our immediate neighbors, Eli was able to gather useful information. Even though she may appear at first glance to be a rather "nervous" girl, always on the go, she has an incredible eye for detail when the situation calls for it. And this was indeed one of those situations.

Looking back at it now, I wish I had taken more notice of her flinch as she scanned the far end of our section. Under normal circumstances I tend to just chalk it up to her natural tendency to fidget, and that is exactly what I did in that moment. By the time I realized something or someone had caused her to instinctively widen her eyes for a brief instant, whatever it was was no longer visible as the lights grew dim, the ambient temperature dropped, and Eli squeezed my arm for what felt like an eternity.

Some time passed before we could see daylight and leave the tunnel behind, plunged in darkness. Eli was breathing naturally again, yet she remained visibly shaken. I searched her eyes looking for the cause, but all I could see was that all too familiar emptiness after one of her nightmares. She brushed the incident off, in her usual tough girl way, and came up with some random lame explanation, which I pretended to accept. So that is where we left it as we continued the trip in silent contemplation.

When we arrived at our destination, we fumbled our way through the crowd and started looking for an exit. There was a sense of urgency in our pace which seemed to draw attention to us, especially from the direction of the three GMU officers against the scanning wall. It was my turn to quicken my oxygen intake as visions of a clampdown and a quick shove into a transport back home polluted my mind. Surely Father would have noticed our flight by now, but it remained a question as to whether the authorities would give our disappearance any priority. After all, recent events of a more global concern were no doubt more pressing, or so I hoped. In any case, we never got the opportunity to find out. Just as the three officials started towards us, they were distracted by something else which pulled them into a fast pursuit in the opposite direction. As fate would have it, our opportunity appeared and we used the ensuing commotion to slip past the sensors and lose ourselves in the traveling mass.

At last, it was time to test the months of twilight research and memorization against the physical terrain. The underground network we had used to gather painstaking details about our new home ensured we could find our way around easily enough, but the reality of actual experience proved to be quite a different story. While others were going about their daily routine, buzzing around from here to there, in and out of converted 21st century office towers, I was engulfed with a sense of awe and amazement at what I was witnessing around me. I could see Eli busily working with the maps in her mind to get us headed in the right direction, although the wonder in her eyes was also unmistakable. As was the case on the journey inward, if we were not careful, our emotions could betray us, so we tucked away our excitement, shared a quick lock-and-nod, and made our way straight to the hovertrain heading to our final destination. This was not a time to linger.

What happened next is still a whirlwind of memory flashes. I remember navigating a maze of corridors, leading us outside onto what appeared to be a bridge on the edge of the world. Peppering the city, as far as the eye could see, were glass and concrete islands growing out of the water like the groves back at the cooling plant. Some were mirrored, reflecting all that passed, some were beautifully carved with remnants of color from days gone by, some were several stories tall, while others mere platforms with purposefully manicured gardens surrounding crystal structures. Looking down into the depths of the canals, my eyes could vaguely outline the glow of a glass building below the garden directly ahead of us. A rush of heat flowed beneath my skin as I realized what I was looking at, as I realized what had transpired here. Below the city lay a murky graveyard of foundations which were once buildings in their own right, long, long ago. All but the top floors of the highest structures were submerged. The city was all it had claimed to be and more, a testament to the focused resolve of a peaceful civilization determined to survive on a dying planet.

We started walking along a crossway towards a gathering of people standing on a solid surface extending along the main street, if that's what you want to call it. It was more like they were balancing on a floating stone carpet rolled out across a stagnant river and tethered to its bed by an intricate series of hooks and chains. The invisible barrier surrounding the city kept the dangers of the looming horizon at bay, a seemingly sheltered haven of life. We were safe from the natural dangers of the outside world yet vulnerable to the more sinister ones within. And it was precisely those hidden dangers that we had voluntarily thrown ourselves into, although if anyone were to ask us, we would say that the choice was not ours to make. Something other than Father's suffocating tyranny has drawn us to this place. I can sense it though I cannot see it...yet. All I hope at this point is that personal experience will uncover the real truth behind the childhood ghost stories that scare the mind and trap the heart, and more specifically for me, your story, which has been haunting Eli's nights for the past nine years and is now creeping into her waking hours.

As we reached the platform, a rush of hot air skimmed the top of my head and hovered for a moment. I looked up and saw the hull of our ride sucking up its passengers from rings etched into the surface around their feet. Eli on the other hand was looking down, scouring the ground around us, and quickly pulled me towards her when she realized I was straddling the edge of a bright red circle. One split second later, and I would have felt more than just a tiny zap between my legs. Ouch. A buzz through my body followed by a cool sweat gave me a little shake. I shudder to think of what would have happened had I been half caught in the lift. I would have needed to seek medical attention and become an easy target for authorities while lying helpless in the belly of the GHU. I guess the extra three minutes Eli has had on this planet have given her a wisdom I am lacking after all. Once I caught my balance, I looked sheepishly at her, expecting her usual snare face, a funny little contortion she makes when she gets annoyed at me (it's somewhere between a sneer and a stare), but her eyes were fixed on where I had been standing. I touched her shoulder lightly and she jumped as if woken from a trance. It was the dream again, I know it.

We had missed the hovertrain and were left alone in the center of the street, in full view of anyone who cared to notice, trying to look unfazed. Since we only had a few minutes to wait until the next ride and the platform was filling up fast, I signaled to Eli that we should plant ourselves immediately on two free spots at the head of the markings. As I rushed for one at the front, I almost smashed right into a woman vying for the same spot from the opposite direction. For a split second, she gazed deeply into me with her gemstone eyes and sent me a sweet smile. I felt my heart racing and the day's third flush of blood rushing through my veins, and when she turned to walk away, leaving the hovertrain marker free, the grace in her step took part of me with her. Did I know her? I checked to see a reaction from Eli, but she had already stepped into the ring and activated the holopost beside us. My mind was still with the mysterious stranger as I searched for her without success amongst the other waiting commuters. She must have floated like an angel to her destination, I thought, as my heart recovered and my attention returned to Eli's laughter. She had noticed my awkward moment and has no doubt stored it back in her calculating little brain for future fun and games at my expense.

The highlands we had come from were not as sophisticated as the main cities, so although we had heard of holoposts, we had not as yet actually seen them. Our form of communication technology was sheltered inside buildings and private homes because of the brightness of the skies around us, whereas in Eadonberg and other cosmopolitan areas along the lowlands, haze and cloud-cover dominated the air space, providing a more effective contrast for the images. Eli reached into the middle left frame where Stew Uber, the creative genius behind VLine Clothing, the most innovative fashion house in the Unification, was showcasing his latest collection. I was more interested in the little black VLine strips hiding the provocative bits of the female models that momentarily flashed between each click of the designer's remote selector. As he punched through a sample set of different looks, he explained how the woman would have an attractive jewel, either on her wrist or around her neck, with full control of several parameters, one of which was the density of the virtual fabric to simulate different transparency effects, along with warmth, color, and drape. Each customization option could be purchased separately making the VLine products affordable for everyone, a simple yet elegant concept, and a first in fashion history. In fact, VLine clothing would feel as natural and comfortable as if you were wearing nothing at all, with no laundry to do, zero impact on our fragile environment, and most importantly, saving our most precious treasure, time.

Time. The emphasis he placed on that word kept echoing in my mind as a grim reminder of our fate. Half our lives had already passed, yet we were but young adults just starting out on our own. Floating atop the ruins of our ancestors, the tragedy that befell them seemed all too real to me. With their careless misuse of resources and lack of respect for the gift of life, they stole a long and fulfilling future from their children and dragged it down with them to their watery grave. Even though centuries upon centuries have passed, the wake of their recklessness remains, and we are left squeezing every piece of our dreams into a highly compressed time capsule. We turn to our elders, the few who have somehow managed to cross beyond the dreamless state, for guidance, hope, and meaning, sometimes finding comfort in their teachings, while other times falling into despair. I feel as if not even they have the answers, least of all Father who has spent his life filling ours with lies. Lies about him. Lies about us. Lies about you.

Eli had moved onto a news channel when my thoughts returned to the present. Transport number 369, scheduled to arrive in Eadonberg at 4:14, had crashed through the biowall at the GT-45 cooling plant earlier today killing all passengers on board. We stared at each other in disbelief... How could that be? We had been sitting in that very transport and had arrived safely. An example of another government mistruth aimed at scaring the public off travel no doubt, keeping them confined and experientially ignorant. Regardless, the hovertrain would arrive shortly. The ring around our feet lit up along its outer loop, giving ample warning, which I had somehow missed the first time, and we were sucked up the invisible shaft. The second half of our journey had begun.

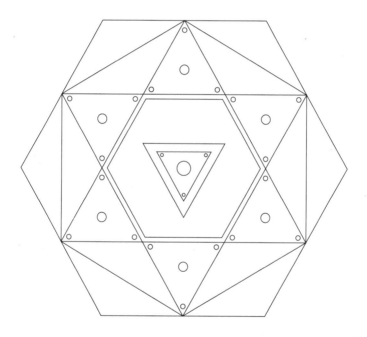

Chapter Two

Day 2: late afternoon

She brushes the crimson powder from her chest and allows her legs to guide her towards the glowing garden. The twilight vigil in the highlands has left her admittedly drained. Keeping the weary travelers within range of her influence, she sneaks into the relative privacy of a vacant sajadum to spy upon her quarry from behind its smoky amethyst walls, as they retire for the evening across the shimmering lavender divide. The nourishing power of her adopted sanctuary provides the reprieve that she so desperately hungers for, giving her the requisite stamina to stay bound to her all-consuming purpose. Balanced at the threshold of a void, her awareness disengages, and she relaxes, and as the world beneath her sighs, her body releases its cares to the skies.

▼ ▼ ▼

Years have passed since the Great Smoke of Ages, and Earth, once again, has learned to adapt. With the help of a few, with the wisdom of millions, the air was reclaimed, and a vision reframed. A global consortium assembled, and decades of peace and prosperity ensued, made possible by the support of the enlightened ones, the elders, who evolved to fully understand the true and just nature of this perfect harmony of chaos that they considered home. A tremendous current of change swept the northern shores as nations united to integrate their daily lives with the ebb and flow of the planet's rhythms. Simple luxuries, for which millennia of human suffering had taken place, duly transformed from their excessive reliance on scarce materials to a more symbiotic style of innovation expressing a sublime beauty, unsurpassed by the monoliths of the past.

A reclusive group of citizens, whose mystical culture had survived the first flood, came to the forefront and lent their minds, bodies and spirits to this rebirth. The Coalition leaders held a discreet council and awarded these champions the highest distinctions, granting them unlimited access to all resources, regardless of cost. They bred creatures, grew organisms, wove cloth, brewed potions, mixed powders, rebuilt cities, harnessed light, but the most significant technology they bestowed upon mankind was the web of self-perpetuating cooling plants that presently dot the coastal lowlands, safeguarding its inhabitants from certain annihilation. The testament to their feats of ingenuity endures as history, taught to the children in prose and in rhyme, but the tale illustrating their sudden and mysterious disappearance has yet to be told.

▲ ▲ ▲

Balancing at the threshold of the void, she falls out of consciousness.

NATHRUYU

▼ ▼ ▼

She surveys the diminishing lands from her rocky perch, alone on the summit of a wind-polished peak, the hot mountain climate thinning her blood as the network of blue flames, floating throughout the German Islands, dance inside their crystal domes. The heat that licks her flesh is a product of drafts rising from the chemical marvel below. An intricate grid connects the luminous balls to their ocean source, delivers refrigerant to the underground mesh of tunnels and tanks, and rhythmically pumps bursts of chilled water into the sea through a series of pipes. Like the wisps of her gown swaying in the wind, the flux paints a snake on the ocean's bed, re-carving the line of the ancient Gulf Stream. Expectant she stands, waiting for the final switch to be thrown, as hope's song fills the breeze with its bliss. The green sludge starts to disperse, and jets of cool air gush effortlessly from strategically placed vents as far as her eyes can see.

She closes them now and savors the moment, a heart-warming instance of faith in humanity, which, at last, has succeeded in recycling toxins from centuries of neglect, birthing a circle of life through its death. The fragile stasis is revived. Beholden, she gently cups her cheeks with her hands, slides them by her temples and along her hair, and, with a cleansing sigh, etches into her memory the likenesses of those who were saved. Then, with a vastly overdue lightness in her gait, she wraps herself in an extra layer of fabric and embarks on the dusty winding path out of the mountains and along the valley to partake in the celebrations.

▲ ▲ ▲

The morning arrives. Her body rouses. The fog is thicker than usual today, which she welcomes quite graciously, for it allows her greater freedom to cover her tracks, as she nimbly negotiates the system of footpaths stored in the files of her brain. This city has been a friend and a foe, she knows it well. Sightless in the white nothingness, she can still successfully navigate the bridges and scaffolds, even playfully skip from ledge to ledge, if she pleases. The advantage is hers as she devises her route, comfortably outpacing whatever may hunt her, or whoever might judge her in an ill-favored light. As she commits to the moist shroud forming around her, she pauses for an instant to recruit her full senses. Her ears scan for hints of others about, and she directs her skin to slip its way stealthily around any potential collisions, while her finely tuned nose uses the subtle stench of the city's water-filled foundation as a protective railing. She surges on, straight ahead, then left, then right, and instinctively stops outside the arches of the marble gate.

Her journey faces a detour as she is sucked into a mirage of a cantankerous crowd.

▼ ▼ ▼

The protesters have confirmed the decision, and the mob grows restless. They no longer approve of the lenient stance the courts have recently taken concerning the likes of this beastly woman, for however benevolent and tolerating their society has become, they will not abide such inhuman assaults upon the innocent children. As she strains to decipher the fantastical action in the mist, the sordid affair elicits accusations from the surviving brood, pointing their pale fingers at the maiden chained on center stage. There was no denying the trauma that the fortunate few who were found had suffered, but the plight of those who went missing had never been determined, leaving questions unanswered and evidence circumstantial. Her mouth blows mute words, lost to the bellowing cry of the vengeful horde, and before she is able to conclude her rightful defense, the scene vanishes into the suspended brume.

▲ ▲ ▲

Nathruyu's thoughts converge as she regains control of the present. Meandering the black alleys of the subconscious realm only serves to jeopardize her work and undermine all the sacrifices to date. As she tears away from the distressing interlude, she begins to shiver, and intentionally hastens her pace to induce the proper heart rate she requires to warm her extremities. Since there is much to adjust before the twins appear, maximum dexterity is critical for a smooth and timely departure. Soldiering on to another obscured crossing, she hops to the left, then along the stone bridge, then straight, to the manicured surface of the campus oval.

On a previous occasion accessing the suite, she had entrusted the secrecy of her visit to an esteemed collaborator. Lamentably, yesterday's abrupt events had forced a new schedule, and the Ministry insider was nowhere to be seen, having been unable to orchestrate an appropriate distraction. Although an easy passage has been denied, the poor visibility, due to the prevalent weather patterns, promotes the opportune environment for her approach to proceed undetected. As it was in the highlands, she trusts her agility to land soundlessly in the safety of the lush orchard, and once she acquires solid footing, she promptly accelerates to the northeast wing of the residence complex.

Feeling with her eyes up the side of the building, she contemplates the options presented to her. In short order, the low clouds will commence their return to the sky, unveiling her soaring form as they lift, a marbled goddess bequeathed to a king. Many shall question the permissions assumed by this exotic intruder. By approximately midday, the sun will have dried every droplet of sweat clinging to the blades of the thirsty foliage, and by mid-afternoon, the haze will relinquish its grip on the horizon, and dusk shall be free to embrace the stars. Such is the cycle that governs the coast, ending at dawn, to begin anew.

The tips of her shoes peek through the lawn, and, steadfast, Nathruyu whisks herself toward the grassy strip separating the east and central sections, brushing the flanks of the walls as she speeds. The dormitory is built as a square of nine towers adjacently attached to one another via enclosed passageways jutting from each floor and establishing external links between the structures, like the rungs of a giant ladder, one tier apart. Her chosen ingress looms high above her, as she lengthens her thigh muscles, springs clear of the dense turf and grabs the first link, while the soles of her feet dangle at the cloud cover's brim. Her silhouette becomes a pendulum, fleeing the edge of a rising curtain and oscillating over the chasm exposed.

By each stroke of her arms, the tick of a clock brings a past to the task. The pictures that stir against the ascending white screen occupy her and threaten to end the story too soon. As she gracefully pulls herself up, defying the lies of gravity, she scales the links, enlisting the tail of her long flowing coat to counterbalance her weight, as she swings up to the crest. The initial image passes by quickly, simply a frozen sketch of father and child, he looking at her and speaking wonder from his eyes, and the next, as she spans the first gap, is of a gentle touch massaging her back. The second passageway breached, the frames move on, showing the face of an infant tearing as she reaches for her, scared, whilst the third portrays a jubilant grin as she invites an imaginary friend in. The visions keep coming, a notch for each year, until they subside as they arose, and her fingertips finally guide themselves to the top.

As she clings to the eaves, prepared for the crowning swing, she steadies her lateral momentum and humbly acknowledges her unscathed ascent, but the recent flashes still playing in her mind cannot be erased by the ease of her climb. Sentiments of loss and despair overwhelm her as she places a trembling hand on her heart, and the musings persist.

She extends her arms, striving to stretch out her fingers to catch theirs in hers, but they are too distant, and she regretfully retreats, barely persuading her features to fashion a last reassuring smile as she recaptures her composure and remembers the roof. Her delay has divulged the hem of her diaphanous dress, so she flies for the sunshaft, carved into the tower's core, and dives for the bottom of the bright tunnel, just as daylight finally emerges through the fog and the angled mirrors at the rooftop aperture pick up her reflection.

Crouched at the base of the well, she sprawls across it and listens for movement. A voice is intensifying and a platform materializes beneath her. As a clearly distracted young man enters the chute singing and jiggling his hips to the beat of his verse, she inches herself upward, fixing her softly focused eyes beyond him, squeezes over from the rear, to select the ninth level, and calms her breath while she teases the nape of his neck. The lift engages, and up the converted shaft she rides. Her good fortune is holding. The student removes a slippad from the pant pocket under his shin and feverishly starts reading and marking sentences, while he wiggles out at the fifth level, boldly dancing down the hall and towards one of the connecting hallways. Her lungs relax, knowing that, as of yet, her trespass has gone unnoticed, and after a sweeping inspection of the target area, she exits and confidently strolls in the direction of the indigo door, at the northeast corner of the branch.

Every click of her stride quickens her pulse, as she is enthralled by anticipation of the adventure to unfold. Years of watching and waiting under the guise of a friend have met their end. She waves the door open and marches in. There is little more lurking around corners, and bushes, and posts. Whatever must come to fruition, whatever she must uncover in the recesses of her psyche, it is time for Keeto, Elize, and herself to get introduced properly, and to weave a different blanket of deceit for those who once protected her from an untimely demise. Yes, Elize's whereabouts must remain a secret, and her brother's as well, until the key she harbors within is released.

Nathruyu glides to the window and stares dreamily at a clay rooftop in the distance, carefully patched from seasons of wear, while the bustle of students below, rushing for class, splashes the courtyard with color and animation. The vista from here to her post is direct as she immediately recognizes its slanted panes bouncing the sunlight. The line of sight to the medical lab is also unobstructed, completing a flawless triangle of treachery above the heads of an unsuspecting community. She secures the perimeter of the frame using the emitter she carries close to her skin, and revises the procedure for the balance of the room. Scrutinizing the zone furthest from the prying eyes of outsiders, she seizes the local controller, summons a stepping stool to extend her reach, and processes the suite, specifically the joins amongst the frequency-proof walls, ceiling, and floor. On the way down the first wall, she programs the shelf from attack, then seals the three others, and attends to the flooring. The fortress secure, blocked from interference and illicit attempts at stealing her well-earned prize, she solemnly wanders to the middle of the unit.

This is where it all begins.

Closing her eyes, she raises her arms away from her sides, shaping a cross with her limbs. Placing a curved palm up, and a flat one forward, she gathers the invisible particles of life from the space traversing her and funnels them through the tips of her sensitive fingers. The tingling builds, causing her hands to float rapturously up to the sky, as they climatically come together, pointed at the heavens, then drift gracefully back down, lovingly entwined, caressing the river of consciousness bisecting the frontal plane, to rest fulfilled at her breast, fused as one. In tranquillity she rejoices, the chatter of her organs willfully silent, whilst her ears perk to the presence of her voice.

"Soon."

Fatigue engulfs her as she kneels to the floor, assuming the pose of a penitent whore. Her hips on her heels, her head to the ground, she lays her arms back and swallows all sound.

▼ ▼ ▼

In and out of an anxious sleep, she seeks the source of her repose, surrounded by light, surrounded by night, she takes the gift from his hand and bows to the man. A net of turmoil entangles her being, for she is unsure of the method they aim to employ. "The risks are too great," she hears her tongue say and offers her shell to hold them at bay. She rises, and the three join hands as they pray for the fresh ones, whose souls are so readily seduced by empty promises and then tragically squandered by those who corrupt them. Collecting the special box as she withdraws, she inserts it in a hidden pouch between the inner layers of her generous cloak, and leaves the precious jewel on the table where it shines.

▲ ▲ ▲

The confusion melds and forges her course as she diligently

labors in the dark to expunge any signs of her offenses, but privately she fears that they will not abandon the search, and that, one day, someone will lead them to her, someone who knows, someone who saw, perhaps even someone she has mistakenly trusted. Spent of energy and suitably sheltered, her tall quivering body molds to the shape of a fetus, and she submits to the burn of the afternoon sun.

✄ ✄ ✄

She wakes to feel the shag tentacles of the carpet tickling her lips. It is almost nightfall and her vitality is wholly restored, making it ripe for her to assume her place. A finishing seal around the entrance, and she hustles right to the lift, in plain view of anyone who wishes to chase the delicate echo of her fluttering down the corridor. She braces herself mentally for a likely confrontation with internal security, and ups her intention to escape safely onto the clearing. The lift makes a single stop, but no one is there, then it continues on downward and retracts, revealing a muscular man carrying a loaded belt. As she dares to press on, concentrating to conceal her angst, the guard pushes his hand forcefully forward, and firmly signals her to halt. Panic sets in. She is trapped in a cage in a building that wants her. Were he to compare her imprint to previous records, he would find something highly suspect, which could reveal more than what she is prepared to, at this juncture.

Just as she appears to agreeably step one leg back, with open fists innocuously poised and slightly uneven over her head, yet covertly selecting an effective strike point, the cause of his advance whizzes by her. The cleanerbot is doing its rounds, and if she had stepped out, she would have surely tainted it with her blood, a fate much worse than getting caught. She ceremoniously thanks her valiant knight for saving her ankles and rouses her singular, sweet, penetrating smile that never fails to disable the knees of men as he traces her curves with his eyes. Unexpectedly, she wields a provocative kiss as a diversion and uses his weakened body as a shield, while she visually shadows three officials heading to the medical lab. She then swiftly flees from the lobby, out the main gate and off the island, swooping amidst the shadowy walkways as the darkness beyond the setting sun nips at her heels.

E L I Z E

"There. I'm done for the night. I should head back before they lock up, right, Eli?"

"Well, it's about time! We didn't leave prison to live cooped up in a tiny dorm together, Keet." In all honesty though, it feels scary to me as well. This is the first time we'll be apart since forever. He looks hurt. "Besides, I don't want to be around when you bring a girl home, yuck!" That should lighten his mood a bit. Good. A chuckle.

"You mean, juicy!"

"Ugh. That's just wrong." We share a much needed laugh. The visual on that one still weirds me out though.

"I'll leave my journal here for the night, if that's ok. Just until I get a protector set up. You should get one too. You're safe from outsiders, but you never know what your neighbors are into. I certainly don't want—"

"No one is going to steel your journal, pup. It's not like they can trade it for credit." They'd be more interested in Mother's jewel. But it's safer here. The university has several protectors stationed in each building, so for tonight at least, keeping our valuables in my dorm is our best choice.

"Just the same. It's important to me." His tone has changed.

I take his hand and reassure him. It's been really difficult for him growing up without her, so he relies on me for comfort. But it's time to let go now or I'll smother him like Father has me. We exchange a warm hug, he hesitates, and then fills me with pride.

"Maybe it's time to stop calling me pup."

Indeed it is. I lean over and kiss his check. "Good night, Keet." He smiles and leaves me alone with my thoughts.

Come on, girl. He's less than ten minutes away. But I still can't stop the tear rolling down my cheek. Well, it's a dry night tonight anyway. It could use a little humidity. Sigh. "Ok then, time to figure out how the sleep surface works." Well, that didn't take very long. I'm already talking to myself. Now where's the controller. Let's try this. Maybe not. In the dark again. Ok. Turn them back on. Good. Now how about this. Aha! Oh. Wait! No no no! Stop! Ouch. There it is. Phew! Caught it before his journal got baked. Why does Keet insist on using such a Neanderthal system anyway? Slippads are so much more practical in my opinion. No need to fuss with those key and lock things, like… Juicy! The matter beam pulled the clip out. I wonder what…

Don't you dare, girl. It's not right. That's an invasion of privacy, and if his constant babble is any indication of what goes on in his brain, then I don't even want to know. So where am I going to put this; the virtabed replaced the virtadesk. There has to be a place in here somewhere where I can store solid stuff. Beside the window. The shelf box is real, isn't it? Let me check. Crap! I guess not. What a mess! Well, at least the floor is smart. It's a little unnerving to have a floor that catches things, but I guess I'll get used to it. "Thanks." Did I just talk to a carpet? I have to get out of here and go find some people. It's good enough. I'll put the journal here and just make sure I don't click the shelf off again. Even if I do, at least I know my friendly mat is on the case. Maybe I'll need to strap the binding though. Wouldn't want Keet's secret life story to fall into the prying hands of some shag now, would I? Hehehe.

Before I go, let me give Keet a quick comm just to make sure he made it back to his crypt ok.

"Miss me already, eh?"

Oh, just let it ride. "I see you haven't been thrown in the dungeon and tortured by the likes of Father's creepy friends, yet."

"Rip! The walk was uneventful. Just the way I like it. You off to dream now?"

That made me queasy. "In a bit. The room is a tad too lively for me at the moment. I'm going to check out the shared space for a change." Something's wrong. "What?"

"My journal."

"Don't worry. The wall box has teeth." Seriously, it does. "Nobody's going near it. I'll bring the controller with me." Lost a pup and gained a cluck.

"Juicy! You have to show me how it works later."

That'll keep his mind occupied. He'll spend all night researching it and showing *me* how to use it. Works for me. "Talk to you in the morning then."

"Sure." He sounds pretty ok. Not that I'm being clingy and all. Just making sure he's loose.

I have quite a nice view from here. The field is so green, and look, there's a pond over there with stems, some benches, a few I-don't-know-whats. I'll check them out in the daylight.

Time for some exploring now. Ouch. Oh yeah. Forgot to clean up the avalanche. The flashes. Just a quick peak before I go. Stick one in the viewer and...nothing. Crap! The viewer is burnt. I really have to figure out this furniture. Life in the highlands may have been backwards, but it sure was simpler. Meanwhile, I also need to find another viewer. Maybe the shared space has something I can borrow. Ok. The secure band, the controller, and a flashpack and I'm out.

"Hey lo." Hmmm. That was awkward. Do I have three heads or something? Here's someone else. Let's try again.

"Hey lo." Stop. There's a reflection. "No. I don't have three heads." Someone found that funny.

"Hey lo. New here?"

And they look at *me* funny? What's with the head mop. Is that hair? Ewww. I don't even want to ask. Come on, girl, say something. But I can't stop staring at his… "Eek!" Not exactly what I had in mind, but it's something.

"Sorry about that, lass. It's a bit of a jumper the first time. Hey...lo? Zafarian."

Oh. He's greeting me. I think. So hold out my arm like this and whoa. What the? Did he just touch me? Yep. That's nice. Sure. Ok. I really didn't want to feel his squiggly stuff against my cheek, but I asked for an adventure, so here he is. Friendly smile at least, not like the two flatfaces over there. He's kind of cute too in an odd, freakish sort of way, like a snotty-nosed kid who knows how to wipe, but still hasn't figured out how to put his clothes on, or what is actually considered clothing for that matter. And the shoes. Wow! This boy's got a style of his own! I haven't actually said anything intelligent yet have I.

Um. "Your hair." Well, at least it's better than *eek*.

"Yurheir? Funny name."

Why does he keep smiling at me like that? Maybe I should just keep walking then. Really, girl, get a grip and say something smart.

"No. I mean. Your *hair*? It's…it's, well, moving."

"Yeah. Trip, ya fig?"

"Huh? Oh yeah. Long trip. Just got here this evening." Ok. Now he looks confused. But still smiling. I'd better smile back and introduce myself. "I'm Eli. And you're name again?"

"Zafarian. But my friends call me Stitch or Zaf. You choose."

"Ok, Stitch." Couldn't have been more fitting. "So where on earth did you get a name like Zafarian, right? I mean, it's pretty bizarre." Well, he's pretty bizarre.

"Yeah. I'm trip with that. I swear my parents were smoking weed when they named me."

"Smoking? Weed?"

"It's a plant they used to grow on the roof and it smells like piss. That was before the garden police caught wind of it… quite literally." He smiles again.

"The garden police?" Maybe this guy's been smoking it too. And why would someone smoke *anything*, especially something that smells like a toilet?

"Yeah. That's what my man called the neighbor. It's like this guy never saw a vegetable before, my man used to say."

Vegetables? Who is he kidding? Even our circle doesn't grow those. They haven't been around for centuries. Every kid from the highlands knows that. "And *your* dad did? Come on."

He starts to laugh and pokes me. "You're cute."

"You're strange." He laughs even harder.

This is getting a little awkward. What do you talk about with someone who smokes pee, wears random pieces of everything stitchable, and whose hair can't lie still? Hehehe. I can just image what Keet would be thinking right now.

"And yes. Now the ice has been broken, it has. Shall I give you the grand tour then?" He offers his arm, but I'm not falling for that again. I'll just hang on to this elbow rope thing. He laughs even harder and walks me down the first hall.

"You're in branch J. Remember that. Up there in the corner is where you'll see the marking if you get lost. I'm down four levels and across three branches. It's a bit bending at first." He taps his secure band and then heads towards a dimly lit tunnel. "I was just heading over to the viewing room. My man sent me some flashes of his new garden. Always planting stuff, yeah. It's across two links then straight down. Section V. Watch out for the sentinel." He is pointing towards the archway, but I don't see anything.

"Ahhh! Hey! Help me down! Stop laughing!" He is completely hysterical, and I'm dangling in mid air by some… Ohhhm gee. "Stitch! Get over here and do something! The thing has eyes, big eyes, and I don't like the way they're looking at me."

"Pica trip! So that's how they work. Pass me your arm. Whoa!"

And what's that stench? Oh oh. Something's wrong. He's not laughing any more, in fact he looks pretty serious and it looks like his hair is trying to peel back off his head.

"Ok. That won't work. Ummm. Try to tap that button on your band. It doesn't look too keen on letting me help you, so you'll have to reach it on your own. Just tap it once. Oh rat. Hurry!"

I can't reach it. It's swiping at my other arm. Hey, something's grabbing my band. Ouch. Juicy! On the floor in a puddle of... Ewww. Is that...? "Whoa! The thing was about to eat me?"

"Not quite. Just hold you for a while."

A stern-looking man is standing right above me and scowling at my new freaky friend. "The sentinels are not pets." He helps me up and checks my band. "Miss Elize." He turns around and seals the arch with a tap of his belt and the beast disappears. Just his eyelashes are faintly visible through the ceiling.

"And Mr. Zafarian!" Right. I didn't like that tone. Sounds like Stitch might be a little too familiar with this guy. "I'm not surprised to find you involved in this little incident." He's taking a slippad from his belt now and writing something. "Miss Elize. I see you are new here. First night in fact. Well, now you know to use that pretty little bracelet on your arm, am I right?" The man hands me back the band and Stitch gives me a visual nudge.

"Yes, sir. I'll be more careful." Then off he goes without another word and heads into the lift shaft. I hear Stitch laugh again and I turn to him in disbelief. "Mr. Zafarian!" Oh, do I ever owe him for that one. He set me up!

"Hey lo, miss Elize, lass." And he howls even louder. "You should have seen your face. Pica trip!" He comes over to poke me. "You're cute."

"And you're bent." I am definitely not amused.

"Welcome to Monster Hall." He leans over and whispers in my ear. "I wouldn't have let anything bad happen to you anyway." He pulls away again, smiles, and stretches one hand out towards me, palm up. "Chumbuds?" I am confused.

He grabs my hand and lays it face up like his, then he makes a fist with one hand, slams it onto mine and covers it with his other hand palm down. Hehehe. Looks like a knuckle sandwich. He notices my mood lightening, then holds out his hand as before. First fist. Then slap. I hope that doesn't mean we're now bound or something.

"Trip! Back to the tour?" Just like that? No apologies? What would Keet say just about now. Oh yeah. Frodo's not in the Shire anymore.

"My rump is covered in slime, Stitch. I'm going back. Maybe later."

He leans over. Creeps, those things are moving again. "Tomorrow after reg then? I'll pop up threeish. You trip?"

"Ummm, yeah. I guess." Another big flash of teeth and he's off, shadow dancing.

Sure. Can't wait. Keet just has to meet this dweeb. Should be fun to watch.

Quickly, back to my space. Enough adventures for the day, please. Better tap this button here and run, just in case. Nothing stays still in this place. Funny. Just like me. There. Back in the sanity of my own cell. There should be an instruction slip or some sort of welcome to the twilight zone package for newbs. I need my wits about me, especially out there.

Freeze. Lights off. There's something moving by the bench. Oh no. It's looking at me. Hide. Stay hush here for a while. That's it. Just bring that heart rate down. Don't let it happen. Ok. Count. One. Two. Three. Breathe. Four. Five. Six. Seven. Eight. Again. Just a peek. Nice and easy. You hick! Nothing's there. I must be suffering from sleep deprivation. I'm starting to jump at trees now. It's this wobbly city that's jiggling my brain around with its obnoxious walls, slobbering doorways, chomping book shelves, sassy rugs. Yeah. I'm talking to you down there. Honestly. As if the voices weren't enough, now I'm seeing things too.

Maybe Father was right about Mother and she did lose her mind, she did become a danger to herself and to us. Sometimes I just want to make it all stop, and I do mean everything. The hope is that this floating maze will somehow offer enough mindplay to keep my brain so busy that there's no time for anyone else in there. That is, at least until we can find some answers. Keet seems to believe Mother had them. We just need to find Dr. Tenille and he'll tell us. I just need to make sure I become one of his crew and then… I wonder if he'll remember me. So stay focused, girl, and forget the crazy museum curator. Nothing is getting past those hanging drool buckets. It's all in your head. My eyes sure are getting heavy. I'm not awake enough to fuss with the controller tonight, so I'll just lie down here on the shaggy one. Too warm for a cover anyway. Nice. Feels like thousands of little hands holding me up. Deep breath in and…

✂ ✂ ✂

Air, air, I need air. I'm so cold. I want them to stop! What's happening to me? They're not going away, they're getting more and more real. Look at me. I'm drenched in my own sweat, and ouch, my eyes. They're raw. Calm, I need calm. Can you at least give me that? They were hurting Mother again. That's enough. I have to tell Keet while it's still fresh. I need to find a way to get past this, it's always there, in the background, eating away at me, burning inside me, tormenting me. Maybe he can make some sense of it, he's the only one I can trust. I'm shaking still. Grab the comm.

"Hey lo. It's a privyrack, that shelf. You can choose the bite setting by… Are you crying? What happened? Eli, please talk to me. This happens every morning, doesn't it, I know it. You try to hide it with your eye gel, but it still shows. It's the dream again, isn't it? Mother. Please let me in."

How does he know it's about Mother. I've never said a thing to him or have I? Sometimes I say things out loud, but surely I would remember telling him.

"They're hurting her, Keet. She is lying there looking at us and they are hurting her."

"Who is hurting her? Can you see their faces. Anything. A mark, a voice, a scent. Close your eyes and try to remember. It's ok. Who's there with you?"

She's turning her head and looking straight at me. The room is dark, there are shadows, I feel cold, she's breathing, I can see the mist.

"Eli? Please. Talk to me."

"I'm losing her. She's fading, and you're crying. Keet, we're both there with her, but we can't move. There's something holding us back. Don't go. It's quiet now. She's gone. It's all gone. I can't remember." Once again. I never remember and I relive the same pain over and over. I burst into tears. I can barely make out Keet's soothing words on the comm.

"It's just a bad dream, Eli. That's all. I know it feels real, but it's not. We'll figure this out together. I promise..."

"Ok." That's all I can muster up between sobs.

It's just so frustrating that I can't recall enough so I can just let it go. I even lose part of my days sometimes, especially when the voices drift in. All I am left with are feelings. Awful feelings. Maybe if I wrote things down like Keet I could piece it all together. Like that woman, there was something dreamy about her is what he said, or did he? Wait. A dream. My dream!

"I'm ok. I have to go. Let's meet after reg. Around threeish."

"Be careful."

Now where's that journal? No one will know if I read it.

K E E T O

Day 3: early evening

It has been just over a day since we arrived, toting with us little more than the weight of our own torments while the bulk of our treasured effects traveled separately with the itinerant merchants from the strongholds. The information we had gleaned beforehand, or rather paid for handsomely, has proven its value a thousandfold, and the expediency with which they had successfully smuggled the articles we had spent months choosing and collecting honors their craft. If Father had suspected an alliance forging between the fringe element of the Unification and his maniacally monitored children, I imagine he would have removed what little freedoms we had sporadically enjoyed. Although lawless according to the tenets of the ever constricting societal norm, I have found the Gadlins to be more respectable than most, at least in the matters of propriety and loyalty. Once they pledge to complete a task, they do so with speed and proficiency, a quality worthy of consideration for future use.

As I reflect upon today's events, I am writing from the comfort of a virtachair in Eli's dorm, at the northeast corner of the complex. Between occasional interruptions from her prying eyes and more than occasional eruptions from my ailing intestines, I am feeling slightly more challenged than usual as I attempt to focus my thoughts on our second series of new experiences. The one that immediately presents itself is of course the much anticipated yet disappointingly horrid smoked flyer we had for midi. It came with root fingers and sweet jam that tasted more like rot fingers and toe jam. The main itself probably hadn't flown for weeks which might explain why it was attempting to do so in my stomach. Nevertheless, I find it amusing to watch Eli snare in my general direction every time she catches a whiff of the unfortunate fowl, as she unloads her share of the past from her keepsakes.

Her conversation grows suddenly sparse when she reaches the items she selected from the hidden sliderpad vault. I can hear the heartbreak imprinted in your crystal hair tresses as she fondles them gently between her trembling fingers, releasing their delicate melody. A single tear is all it seems to take for her to saturate the silk band you used to wear around your neck, with its dangling constellations suggesting an obscure fascination with otherworldly superstitions. Although I am the one who inherited your love of legends and mystical beings, it is curious that Eli shares a special fondness for this side of you, a side which she has denied any access to her waking mind. Logic is the only path she has chosen to follow, which I do believe leaves her broken and confused. I feel the conflict within her and the undercurrent of fear which plays out every night in her dreams. And now, released within the confines of an oppressed society, she clings to a reality which no longer makes sense.

She's becoming more chatty and my attention shifts to her words. "I saw her in the hovertrain," she tells me. Not entirely sure who she is referring to, I ask for clarification. "Your angel. The one who sucked the fluids from your brain yesterday on the platform, disabling your motor control system. Hehehe." Well, I knew that was coming, although I'm not sure what series of thoughts lead her mind in that direction. I momentarily disengage from my memoirs to notice her crouched down in the corner across from me, painstakingly rearranging the jumbled threads of her dreamcatcher. She appears intent on her task, though sharply cognizant of my defensive stare, as if she subconsciously knows someone is watching.

The exotic stranger. She did steal a bit of my heart, that I will admit, but turning me into a puddle of mush? Well, that's a bit of a stretch. Besides, it wasn't like that. The feeling that came over me I mean. There was joy, kindness, and a deep connection beyond the physical, something which Eli would never acknowledge. But you understand.

"Don't despair, jelly knees, you'll see her again." She says that with so much conviction that I wonder if she's hiding something, or maybe she's just toying with my resolve.

As I re-immerse myself in the events preceding yesterday's close, I realize that Eli is probably right. She likes that you know...likes being right. Although with a strong enough case and irrefutable evidence (just the facts please), her synaptic network of overactive brain cells short-circuits and makes room for new members. It happens. This particular hunch of hers however is not a subject for discussion. The city is quite populous but bounded, so I must agree with her position. It is just a matter of time before our paths cross again, and perhaps we may even share a few words. Having a friend on the inside might ease our transition.

I had begun recounting the details of our defection during

the final third of our transport ride in anticipation of a certain change in my late night ritual. The unpredictability of what the second leg of our trip would bring prompted me to take advantage of any pockets of calm that presented themselves along the way. With respect to the deluge of sensations flooding our bodies as we experienced the exhilaration of our escape, I had managed to quickly outline a cursory account of our inaugural flight in the relative safety of the hovertrain as we traveled deeper into the city center.

The first drop proved to be a popular one, with more than a third of the passengers disembarking and just a few jumping on, leaving the area around us clear of unwelcome witnesses. The subsequent malfunction as the craft sped to the next platform offered the opportunity I was waiting for, and I started writing impetuously. The words seemed to flow from my pen like a wave of pristine images, crystal clear in my mind as if captured in time. I remember feeling a cool breeze brushing my shoulder and the sweet scent of myrrh as she walked passed, filling a seat near the front. I kept my focus on the page, trying to ignore her penetrating gaze, while Eli, as evidenced by her comments tonight, had no doubt taken special note of our secret admirer.

I had just scripted what became the closing thought of the day, when the power returned and I caught a glimpse of the fluttering tails of her silky black coat gliding down the exit. In an instant, she was gone, and we were one stop away from a much anticipated rest, her perfume still tickling my nose and directing me back to a flash of a little boy sleeping peacefully in your arms.

The exit vent will take some getting used to. Just as the hovertrain's arrival gave warning of the impending lift, the fare collector buried in the armrest of each seat signaled the goodbye plunge. This time, Eli was the one caught off her guard when she sprang back into her body while I simultaneously dropped out of mine. What a rush! I can see why the Gadlins steer clear of the local transfers, wanting to avoid a painful retreat into a violent past. Although the shafts into the dungeons were long in comparison, their cells' RNA houses the spirit shattering memories of their distant kin. Fortunately, the wayfaring ways of their people keep them safe from further harm and preserve the belief structure of their ancestors.

After the blood had returned to my limbs, I reached for Eli's hand and we darted towards the hostel which was to be our refuge for the night. Although evening had not yet settled in, neither of us had slept since the morning prior, notwithstanding Eli's feeble attempts through the outlying islands. The provisions we had packed were plentiful, so after we had secured a pass to our room from the glassy-eyed elder who welcomed us in, we quickly devoured our meal and fell fast asleep, cushioned on the soft warm surface of a large magnoform. We were so exhausted in fact that we had not even noticed the frame in the outside wall until the next day when we headed for the Museum of Antiquities.

By the morning fog, our senses had fully absorbed our new surroundings and we proceeded towards the doorstep of my first career. As I stood mesmerized by the sheer density of the brume, someone tapped me from behind and started peddling his wares. I politely declined and continued walking along the building scaffold, yet was unable to escape this person that I could not see. Eli kept giggling as I repeatedly attempted to swat his invisible hand while he tapped and he flapped, trailing my steps as I became increasingly irritated. "It's a versal shame, young man, not to give this a try. I guarantee by the roots of my hairs that one swig of this ale will relieve all your cares." It's all he kept chanting. When the fog finally lifted enough for me to confront the assailant, my jaw dropped to my chest as I realized we had been flanking the side of a holowall. By this time, Eli was getting excited and begging for us to stop and have some fun with it, but my appointment was near, so we left the play for another day.

We reached the city's core with a few minutes to spare, so we took the time to marvel at the architectural masterpieces that lay before us, framed against the trailing haze of the rising fog. The buildings had been raised from the depths of the sea, refurbished, then sealed to protect the intricate stone carvings interspersed throughout their facades. The yellow stains caused by the Great Smoke of Ages and which marred the fabric of the city landscape were nowhere to be found. It is inspiring to see that the lore of our past holds a commanding position in the ranks of this urban life, and humbling to stand witness to the extraordinary artistic accomplishments of our creative ancestors. I could have lingered for hours, lost in the stories of the epics I had read, but the curator was waiting, and Eli was waving. Off we scurried through the arches of the museum's marble gate.

There was no hiding the surge of pure adrenaline raging through my body as we breached the threshold of the Great

Hall. The colorful canopy of painted scenes high above our heads kept our eyes fixed skyward, to the peril of my shuffling feet. A hop and a skip saw me falling into the arms of my new mentor. "Crap!" is all I could muster as he frowned.

"Genius is the word we use here. Mr. Keeto, I presume?" My face flushed as I apologized profusely, to his and Eli's great amusement.

"And this young lady would be…" turning to Eli, he bowed as she answered. His demeanor was rich and his clothing impeccable. A man of few words, "the exhibits do the talking" he would say. Room after room, corridor after corridor, there were artifacts of irreplaceable value, most of which I have never even heard of, despite my meticulous research, but the chamber that stole my breath, at the center of my new world, was a forest of books as far as the eye could see. There were rows upon rows of wooden towers diagonally arranged around an immense circular table, where privileged scholars spent their waking hours absorbed in acquiring ancient wisdom. Eli's only comment was "So where are you going to set up your sleeper?" We all laughed and the curator showed us to my quarters.

In the far reaches of this enormous library, there was a small door which led to the back terrace. At the end of a marble bridge there were nine small stone enclosures forming a circle around a floral centerpiece connected like the spokes of a wheel to the base of each pod. The third unit on the right is where the curator led us, pausing at its entrance and handing me the key, an actual physical key, complete with ring and all. As he bade us a formal farewell, I turned to Eli and beamed. Although the tiny homesteads were clearly reproductions of the museum's unique architectural style, the stone cast faux-marble finish provided a convincing facsimile of family mausoleums, a titillating berth for my overactive imagination, and embodied the perfect atmosphere for you and me to reconnect.

The interior was dim. A narrow slit above a one-meter niche built into the facing wall provided little chance for light to enter. Eli poked her head around the corner, then walked gingerly into the center of the room, closing her eyes and perking her ears. Whatever compelled her to listen attentively is still a mystery, because once she had finished and opened her eyes, she denied ever having taken the stage. I quickly dropped the subject and made a personal oath to observe her more closely in the weeks to come. The air became cold with the fear that drove me here, so I steered the conversation towards the far corner, where my transfer chest lay. I ran a thorough scan to verify the contents and nodded in approval of our trustworthy Gadlin hires. My mission accomplished, we dedicated the rest of the day to getting Eli settled. I filtered through the contents of my satchel spread over the bed and flung the bag over my shoulder as we left for the campus.

On our way back through the archives, the curator stopped us and voiced a concern. "Best reach the complex before dark, just to be safe." There was talk of miscreants about, mutilating bodies in the medical lab at Osler Hall, across from the J tower of Van Billund Hall, the residence complex. They hadn't targeted the living yet, but blocking their path could prove unwise. Impeccable timing, considering my new base is a 16th century tomb. Eli leaned slowly into me, stiffening her stance as she tugged on the sleeve of my linen shirt, drawing my attention to three officials we could see through the marble gate, who were making their way across the Victory Bridge and towards the facility.

What secrets hide behind the cultured facade of the Central Core? We decided to risk the advent of dusk rather than test the influence of Father, who we now knew worked for the URA. We found a barge where we could sample the delicacies of the lowlands, bringing me to the source of my current digestive discomfort. As we patiently waited for the triad of officials to leave, we followed the crest of the sun as it sank into the toxic depths of the tide. With such a harsh reminder of the earth's power, our immediate concerns are insignificant in retrospect.

When I finally managed to coerce the last bit of food into my groaning belly, the vendor was already half-packed, nervously struggling with his controller. There was a certain urgency with which he worked that caused us to sharpen our senses and move towards the ramp. As we reached the railing, he stopped us gently and said, "No, not that way. They are coming. I will take you," and he led the raft through the murky channels towards the oval forest ahead.

I surveyed the wonder before us, with its polished walls glowing slightly as dusk paints the sky, and caught a glimpse of some activity on our original path. Our guide continued in silence, shrewdly scanning the bridge before pressing on past the trees on the right. For a moment, I questioned whether this man could be trusted. And how did he know where we were headed? From what I could tell, we had missed the main entrance of the campus and were held captive on a virulent course. But the air about him was crisp, and as we rounded the park and spotted the back entrance of the complex, the stranger uncovered a large box he had been sitting on, and bowed. It was Eli's chest, in perfect condition. We had intercepted the secret voyage of our precious cargo and concealed our passage in doing so as well. Our Gadlin accomplice has stayed true to the call, once again. Too bad he can't cook.

The perimeter was well protected. A campus security escort promptly appeared as we landed the crate. A curt cordial exchange, and our ferryman drifted back into the shadows, avoiding a challenge from the approaching footsteps. While Eli presented her provisional registration, I leaned against a spiral lamppost and stared into the distance. The site is enormous, looking more like an actual island than a floating stage, for that is what it really is. The water's edge is nothing like the clear blue ocean so eloquently described in the stories you read us, stories where silky soft beaches beckoned the lonely traveler smoothly and safely into her warm salty vastness, which brimmed with life, creatures of all sizes and colors, sharing a perfect world in peace and serenity.

I awoke from my dream with the whistling of stars and the voice of Eli anxiously calling me into the pathway running alongside an ivy covered wall. A storm was coming and we needed to hurry in case the frequency generator controlling the biowall started to drift. We raced to the back gate where the caretaker ushered us promptly into the building just as lights across the city started to flicker. Catching our breath, I was impressed at how easily Eli had dragged her baggage behind her on the cobbled surface. Not only tough in spirit, my temerarious twin. She threw me a snare. Did she hear that?

Another protector checked Eli's permissions and directed us to the reflective shaft in the center of the tower, where a porter waited to shuttle us up the lift. He shook his head as he struggled with Eli's effects. "It's the shoes," I explained, rubbing my shin with my foot and suffering another one of those l... ...*ooks*. Sorry for the scribble. Her fault. So...she's finished unpacking. "What? No shoes?" Ah, I was bracing for that slam. I lifted my pen just in time.

Eli now seems ready for our adventure. But am I?

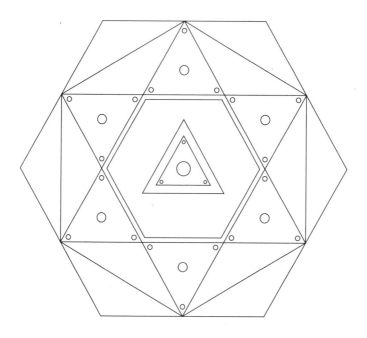

CHAPTER THREE

N A T H R U Y U

Day 25: dawn

Eager for rebirth in the golden source, her serene silhouette stands perfectly still against the evolving Eadonberg skyline. Shimmering ripples in the distance announce the sun's arrival, cleaving darkness from its path and eclipsing the dissolving stars. With her breath arrested and her gaze transfixed, Nathruyu remains statuesque as the rays assail the coastal lands, looming unprotected behind her, and trigger the onset of another potentially volatile cycle. The last three weeks had been pleasantly uneventful, allowing her to observe Elize adapting to new surroundings and affording her the luxury of introspection. Her recent homecoming has heightened *their* awareness, which she must ultimately turn to her favor, for tonight will challenge the soundness of her plan and expose previous sacrifices to harsh judgment from all who bear witness.

As the pressure builds over the water, the mesmerizing sparkles dance eastward across the orchard and fill her lungs with the morning's first deep draw. The freshly ionized air reanimates her momentarily halted heart, gradually re-inviting her blood to the surface and feeding it, as it seeks the heat. As usual, her senses marvel at the exquisite artistry of Osler

Hall, the medical lab and the pinnacle of Gadlin design, which dominates the campus oval and now lies in stark contrast to the morbid enterprises within.

The contortion of shadows between the two outer towers, coiling around the center one like a wide-based double-helix cylindrical pair, each thread piercing an enormous stepladder of twenty-seven distinct crystal disk-shaped floors, greets dawn with a mosaic of textures. The third shaft follows a straight axis up from the ground, tunneling every third tier of the middle sinusoid structure of twenty-seven smaller overlapping pods, and fuses seamlessly into the other two, an open mouth swallowing the sun.

Sliding her eyes south past the citrus grove and then west towards the brim of the city, she sees a flicker inside the J branch of Van Billund Hall. There is activity. Elize is frantically gathering her materials for the day. She springs from the building predictably flustered, disappears quickly under the floral covered walk, and reemerges, half-dressed, short-winded and still grappling with her trailing jacket. This morning, however, from the clarity of her rooftop perch, Nathruyu notices a slight change in Elize's daily routine, for she delays a little longer than expected in front of the Victory Bridge. She knows. Swiftly retreating behind the terrace stairwell, Nathruyu cautiously peeks one eye around the corner, as the mitered edge of her coattail flutters in the converging draft. It is too early to reveal herself.

The pulse through her veins distracts her and incites a gust of flailing silk which lures Elize's unease up to her. The evanescent impression of a presence sends Elize scurrying into the oncoming fog. As the powdery wall rolls across the maze of pathways and channels, cloaking the objects en route in a dense white cloud, Nathruyu resumes her watchful stance and releases her fears to the drifting mist. Elize has clearly changed her agenda and the habitual jaunt to the Snack Shack, prior to her lectures, is forfeit. Urgency commands her to the task. If she and he are to be as one, this evening will unfold as foreseen, regardless of this late indiscretion, or even a certain trepidation penetrating her thoughts. She has long coveted him from afar, forbidden to thrust him onto her aching breast until her obligations have been met. She must constantly weigh her loyalties against a relentless desire.

A solitary tear struggles to make its way to the decorative tiles of the roof, but her quivering lips divert its stream, leaving it broken and vulnerable, as her tongue seizes it to quench her drying thirst. Only the tripartite spire of the twisted towers remains visible above the thickening brume and casts a pointy finger in the direction of their abandoned home, as if reminding Nathruyu of her priorities. As the foggy film interferes with her spying, the gruesome incidents preceding the twins' voyage replay in her mind and taint the atmosphere with the blood of the innocent. She calls out to the shadows, but the dead have no ears, and as much as she would welcome absolution, her part in the whole binds the guilt to her soul. Nathruyu is whisked back to the eve of their arrival in Eadonberg, twenty-five days ago.

Some students have arrived, but most are at home, collecting the bits of nostalgia they will be relying on for comfort during the demanding training ahead. The twins are no exception. Keeto has planned their departure for tomorrow night, but their lives are fated to a different schedule, one which Nathruyu is skillfully able to accelerate by virtue of her fortunate discovery.

She has managed to impair the sensors at the east wing entrance of Osler Hall and infiltrate the access tube, unbeknownst to the blinded sentinels. She has also deactivated the movement mechanism to ensure a private escapade up the spiral chute. The inner surface has no protrusions nor depressions of any kind, not even a single crack in the polished concave lining to slide a razor along, forcing her to manually de-tune the entry panels at each pod as she breaches them, and then to leverage the transient thin apertures they present in order to transmit her momentum up the levels. After a dozen or so surges, her slender fingertips freeze, tenuously curled around the slit on the southernmost floor, with the point of her boots barely clinging to what little friction her weight can produce. There are murmurs at the cusp of the next curve, blocking her ascent.

Considering that it is not possible to invade the upcoming section without forcing the stored sunlight in the tunnel through the slot she will need, her choice is evident. An inoperative flume will raise an alert, and the second line protectors will flush from the walls. It is not her intent to entice them to stir at this juncture, so she widens the gap where she stopped, slips silently into the sombre space beyond and realigns the frequencies. She braces for the wrath of the awakening sentinel.

As Nathruyu performs her evasive dance with the disgruntled beast scowling down at her, she keeps a mindful ear to the shuffling of feet above. Timing her steps to the rhythm of the creature's dives, she humors it long enough for the talking to taper, and then, confusing her attacker, hastily reenables the lift, reestablishes her course, and collapses the hole after her. An instant's reprieve, and up the bend she soars, guiding her body to the frigid cell, devoid of light, hairy defenders, or any other apparent signs of security. As she trespasses further in the cold vault, her temperature steadily drops. She is reminded of the perils inherent in lingering and quickens her pace towards a diminutive figure left supine and inanimate on the elevated platform.

Dusk has only just acquiesced to the moon as it funnels the solar reflection through the semitransparent architecture and bathes the shape of a person in an amethyst glow. She reaches for the tools, artfully concealed between the layers of her clothing, and tempers her breathing to stabilize the explosion of conflict inside. Brushing the soggy bangs from the girl's forehead, she finds evidence of their tampering and plunges her into a deeper phase of suspension. Her brain already prepped for the impending modifications, she firmly cups the back of the girl's neck, locates the void at the base of her skull, and burrows into it. Nathruyu nods in approval, then systematically rolls the flaccid youngster to an appropriate angle, frees her hair from the site, and leans over her as she slices, catching a red spray with her chest. As she feverishly bores her thumb into the wound, she searches the cavity, sharply aware of the gravity of her actions, and confirms her suspicions.

The distant sound of the matter generator, forming some virtachairs, echoes from the shaft behind her as the familiar tone of his voice draws dangerously near. Driven to forsake her unwitting donor, she creates a temporary rift to the outdoors, glides her lean frame through it, and steps gingerly onto the flat top of the adjoining pod. There she waits, anticipating a code three lockdown once they discover the growing crimson river she has released, draining from the slab and pouring into a viscous pool around their feet. The surprise interruption has betrayed the desecration and has thwarted its completion, putting the child unnecessarily at risk and compromising her plotted exit strategy. She kneels and lays an inquisitive hand on the cool translucent quartz, anxiously trusting that their attention will stay drawn to the patient while they strive to dam the flow of blood. As she labors to abate the crescendo of tremors overtaking her nerves in order to avoid transmitting them via the ceiling, she redirects her focus to the vibrations emanating from their agitated dialog.

As per instructions, a state of emergency seizes the building, and GMU operatives stealthily assemble and fortify the boundaries of the university property. Nathruyu's options are scant. She shrinks her stature and holds fast to her coat, as she pastes her ribs to her thighs, bringing another palm and one ear to the conversation below. He is reprimanding their carelessness and a defiant tongue is countering as the more obedient two clamor for something.

"The girl is lost. Salvage what you can and protect it."

"She is here. The wound is fresh."

"No. There is no time. Tonight you must travel."

"And the units? They are waiting."

"Cancel them. No disclosure. We must keep this private."

The man who is noticeably in charge motions vigorously at the attending ones and urges the upheaval onwards. Her body naked to the encroaching blackness, she challenges the limits of her reserves and strains to identify the cause of the chaos. The ransacking continues awhile, and she notes the leader's impatient displeasure at the results.

"Enough! She has taken it. Clean up this mess and find them!"

His features are hardly discernible behind the clouded screen, but his outline against the moonlit backdrop is unmistakable. Nathruyu knows whom he is referring to and whom he is compelled to hunt. The operatives having withdrawn as directed, she retreats inwards and harnesses whatever energy she can contract to overpower the lethargy in her slowing muscles. Boldly, she jumps onto the lower level, an audacious grin cocked over her right shoulder. Meeting his delicious frustration as she pauses to lock eyes with him, she revels in the opportunity to once again crush his arrogant taunt, before winding her laughter down the outside of the tower.

▲ ▲ ▲

Nathruyu gasps for oxygen as she sways in the onshore breeze, reliving the angst of her narrow escape. The efforts to conceal her transgression have thus far succeeded, but soon... Soon, the truth shall slash the fabrication, and *they* will combine their forces to pursue her and to vindicate their involvement, exposing the girl and the unfortunate sentry who fell at the perimeter. Without this vindication, the grim dark road to the highlands and the resulting events leading up to her present devices would have remained latent, a hereafter never to be manifest. But until such date, she must advance, impelled by the promise of unison.

Today, Nathruyu conspires to revisit Osler Hall and complete the procedure on someone else, using the orchestrated meteor showers as a camouflage. While the ringleader burdens himself with seemingly random blasts from the heavens, she will recapture the advantage and claim the mark. Coaxing the sunshine through the mist, she raises her arms to receive it, settles the flux enveloping her and calmly extracts its essence. The current begins, as before, inducing a rejuvenating interlude that refreshes her cells for the forthcoming physical trials and the mental acumen they demand. This time, there will be no surprises.

✂ ✂ ✂

She rouses to the gentle brush of a feathered hunter, playing in the swells of the afternoon gusts, then swooping past her and into a remote memory, a sobering reminder of her ultimate fragility. The views to the south are clear again. The cityscape features the diverse endeavors of the crowds below and showcases the one she has specifically arisen to partake in. From the raised entryway of a medi clinic beyond the Snack Shack, where Elize has curiously sequestered herself while eating her favorite treat, a refined and attractive lady, with the timid child in tow, fluidly matches her gait to the frenetic tempo of the homeward-bound masses. Nathruyu watches closely as the duo glide forth, unnoticed, by the canteen and the narrow scaffold abutting the museum. Delighted by the newest selection and thrilled by her assured success, she sinks into her refuge and emerges a few minutes later outside the marble gate, confidently trailing the woman and the girl across the wide-open corridor bisecting the central canal.

Ingress onto the island happens easily, as the spirited escort drags her young friend along, forcing the straggling child to concentrate on her rebellious sandals rather than the approaching stalker. Slipping into the heavily guarded crystal helix purports to be more onerous, but as fate would have it, the sandal flies off her soppy foot and slams its heel across the bridge of the greeter's nose. The dumbfounded expression on the man's profile switches to a bellowing laugh, as he dutifully hoists the harmless weapon from the landing where it had dropped. Nathruyu furtively monitors the teasing game between them, fueled by the beauty's captivating allure as she nonchalantly sneaks towards the scanner and steals a guest tag from the security desk as she saunters by. Posturing at the lift and sporting a borrowed slippad, her ribcage giggles at the spellbound official attempting to impress his audience with his feeble wit, ignorant of the blatant trespass she has staged right in front of him. A final toss of the woman's head and a flirtatious titter concludes the banter, and the offending footwear regains its rightful place, ready to shuffle on. Once they satisfy the sensors, the sapphire blue splendor of the lobby's gemstone inlays highlights the reason for his infatuation. She could not have solicited a more fitting distraction, for eyes such as those reduce a man to repose.

Nathruyu carefully inspects the fidgeting child, understandably agitated in the burnished halls of the vestibule. She imagines they told her some innocuous assessments were necessary for whatever ailment they had conveniently fabricated, but a toll far more mortifying awaits her.

Tap tap tap goes the child's nervous shoe, reminiscent of the soothing beat of the antique timepiece he used to wear, whose lullaby chimed as he draped his arms around her. The details of his blissful face disperse behind her sunken stare. The visions always come to Nathruyu in fragments, wrapped in sentiment that she fails to digest, feelings clawing at her core and hanging there, precariously, surrounded by an acid-filled abyss. The future was perpetually resisting them, she vaguely recalls. As the nausea creeps up her throat, her discomfort is painfully obvious to her enlisted accomplice.

"All will be well soon, my dear," reassures the blue-eyed charmer as she crouches to the girl's height and smiles, subtly glancing up at Nathruyu as she coddles her companion.

An archway develops and a staircase of benches materializes, good for three passengers, and straps them in for the tilted and swirly ride up the tower. When the tube re-carves a doorway, they exchange parting words, the pair enters the destined level, and Nathruyu continues on to the next tier. Once inside, she disables the controller, stows the examination beds, and proceeds to generate a one-way portal in their stead. Assuming a background position, suspended face down above the rifted stone, she records the last lucid moments of this frightened lamb. The sedative spreads rapidly and the child now lies alone, unconscious and primed for the dreamless sleep lurking beyond.

Skirting the secret window with the tips of her limbs, she embraces the coolness of the waning light and paints frosty twinkles from her breath on the scene. The ravenous torrent within overwhelms her, and she flings her emotions across the oceans, hoping to rekindle her primordial and sole passion.

Separate yet together, she still feels his warmth inside her, as it was in the beginning, eternally chained to one another in erotic bliss, their bodies writhing in ecstasy, but the bitter reality of his fading scent saturates her with lonely tears. The anguish of his sensual form, seductively extended beneath her, seeing but not touching, their carnal appetites denied and forcibly contained, devours her flesh at every passing of the stars. Each morning as the earth reappears, she laments the rising sun, and yearns for the day when night will persist, and they shall be one again.

A bright flash and splintered glass shatters her lustful dream, as she wakes to the present and rejoins the room. Quietly sweeping the haze blurring the scramble below, she unveils the particular physiques of her own stalkers, their torsos sloped over the table where their test subject rests. She can scarcely distinguish the contours of their hands, busy at work under the heads partially obstructing her sight. The sudden blackout, aggravated by the sweat trickling down their faces, hinders their progress. Nonetheless, in roughly a minute, the assault is finished, the gash is sealed, and the girl is adrift.

Their suits drenched and their fists soaked in her scarlet

juices, they store what they took, and immediately vacate the area. Nathruyu races to beat their return. She promptly rifts the uniportal and drops, grabbing one edge with her hands and swinging her legs underneath, to land nimbly aside the vitreous facade, then pauses, scans the trees in the orchard, and smiles. She has come. Into obscurity she recedes, and the chase is on.

E L I Z E

Stay loose girl. Toes, stop twitching. Sigh. Why is this taking so long? I really don't want to be here. What am I going to do when they find out? How on this planet am I going to explain this? Ok. That's it. I have to get out of here. I'm sitting here trapped in a sick ward.

"Excuse me, my appointment is at, or was at, three." Whoa! Have I been here that long?

"Your name?"

"Eli Simone." Oh oh, she's frowning. This is not a good sign. Someone must have given me the wrong date, or worse, what if they already know... I'm in deep...

"Oh yes, Elize. Dr. Phelophelus will see you at 4:50." That does not qualify as a smile. "You were rescheduled." That one even less.

I wonder if there's a special school they go to learn that, or maybe it's Darwinian breeding techniques. You know. Survival of the clueless. Be careful, girl. Ill-thoughts breed ill-deeds, Keet would say. I'm messing with spooky Karma now. Boo! Who says being trapped in a room with a bunch of diseased people can't be fun.

Ok. Back to my seat and… Crap. Where did it go? "Hey! Come back here!" These newer models are just too neurotic. Keet finds them cute, but I'd rather be sitting on the floor instead. Well, a solid floor at least. Yeah. Solid. Not like the shaggy one in my room. "Ok. I promise not to fidget." Just don't go taking off on me.

I can't help it. He'll know right away that I don't have a working biochip and then I'm busted. Think, girl, think. I need to come up with a really good excuse. The trick is how not to get flagged and then sent to the Ministry for tracing. Then it's over and Father will find us, once they run the DNA check. What's that kid staring at anyway? I think I'm pretty well dressed normally now. I've had three weeks to figure out what works and what doesn't. What if I just stare back. Geez. She's relentless. Does she know me? That's enough. I'm going to get on the comm with Keet. We were supposed to meet beforehand and figure something out. That was the plan. Better switch to hush mode.

"Where are you? You're hush."

Here comes the storm. "I'm at a medi clinic waiting to see a doctor."

"Are you ok? What happened? Ohhhm gee. We're busted! What happens if they find out, I mean, when they find out you have no—"

"Shhh. Don't panic." That's why the hush mode. "Well, not yet anyway. We still have a few minutes to come up with something. It's just part of the student requirements, remember? I've been trying to get out of it but then the counsellor nabbed me and—"

"And now you're busted. I completely forgot about it. The archives. I get so lost in them. They're revamping the entire cataloging system you know. It's absolutely riveting! The artifacts I get to handle. I mean, some of the things in Mother's books are actually real!"

"That's all juicy, Keet, you having fun digging around, but didn't you put it in your strawberry?"

"It's a—"

"Yeah, I know, pup." Oops. I slipped.

"Eli, I thought you promised to stop calling me that. I'm an adult now you know, just like you." He sounds annoyed. Rightly so.

"Sorry. It just slipped out. But seriously, why do you even use that relic anyway? There are better systems."

"Sure there are, and then the Ministry knows your every move. But wait! I can get a bioCal now, so I can buzz your new and improved biochip. Muahahaha."

He can't be serious. "Rip. Very funny. *Not* helping. I can't focus. Keet?" Breathe. Everything's loose. "Better." It's quiet up there now.

"Just a rib. It might be ancient but it's well cloaked, just in case. Anyway, at this age, it's a big operation, so they can't just do it right there. They'll put a tag on you for sure, but we'll work with that. Let me comm our special friends. Don't worry."

Hey. There's Caroline from registration. She seems healthy enough. I wonder...

"Way, Eli. Got caught. Sucks. What about you? Counsellor's on the prowl these days, yeah?" I thought everyone from the lowlands had perfect biochips. She's born and raised here. How could she... "Who are you talking to?" She squeezes in to peek and one eyebrow goes up.

Oh, right. Still on hush with Keet. "It's my cousin. Hang

for a sec, Caroline." I'd better just comm out before he starts asking too many questions. "Ease, Keet. Just a friend from school who walked in. She's juicy."

"Niiiiiice. When do I get to meet her?" Yuck. That joke's getting old. And she heard that.

"You bet I am, girl!" She winks at me and lowers her voice. "You still trip for the daze tomorrow?" Hick! I hope he didn't hear that.

"Did she say daze? Eli? Don't think I don't know what she is talking about. I don't think it's safe to start—"

"Whoops. Gotta go. My seat's making a move, so I'm next."

"Juicy! You're on a crabseat. They're so cute. Especially the way they just scooch along, and they're so comfy."

Comfy? Who's he kidding. Snappy more like. They're called crabseats for a reason. "Sure. See you tonight. Off now." Phew. I'll deal with him later. Now back to Caroline.

"Hey lo, Caroline." She giggles. "You slacked on your scan too?" That should give her a hook. Let's see if she bites.

"Neah. Caught with my head down. They're so anal, yeah? I just had a draining night and they think it's contagious. Crazed! What's your story?"

That reminds me. I'd better think of one fast. There were scanning stations set up at registration, but I managed to slip through them, until now. She'll be wondering how I did that.

"The scan showed an 'exception' they called it. Oooooo." Let's add some little wavering fingers for good measure. Great. She's caught on the line.

"Must be coming from your language center." A snicker

and more giggles. I like her. She's loose. It's her first time with us highlanders, so I sound really funny to her. I don't mind. I can always use it to flip the topic when I need to, just like now. "You'll pass, Eli. The GHU has to come up with all sorts of excuses to keep themselves busy. It's Ministry, yeah?"

"Yeah. Same plan for tomorrow then?" She nods, and my throat goes dry. My turn.

The seat takes me through the scanner in the center of the office, then parks itself in front of the doctor's desk. He's staring at his slippad and looking a little concerned. Toes, stop it. Maybe he thinks the scanner's broken. He's still scouring the slips for something.

"Miss Elize? That is your name. Elize Simone from…" He's squinting now and pursing his lips. "Blarney Way?"

Hick, the minute I open my mouth he's going to know I lied on my application. He lifts his eyes slightly, so I just nod then. Make believe I have a sore throat. Quick thinking. He starts flipping the slips. What do I do now?

I should be starting to sweat already but I'm not. I'm feeling chilled. He's looking full up now. That's it. Here comes my stomach.

"Set it over there, please."

What? Oh. Someone just walked in with some food. The last thing on *my* mind at this very moment.

"Working through meals again, Dr. Phelophelus?"

"Always a pleasure to see you, Nepharisse."

Well, she just brightened his mood. I can see why too. She's quite stunning. Beautiful deep blue eyes and a mesmerizing smile. He's like a giddy school boy. This is too funny. He's in la-la-land. Hey. Just the distraction I need. Ok. Think fast, girl. Yes. Show time.

"Thank you for the prescription, Dr. Phelophelus. I'll get the patch right away." If I hold out my hand, palm up, and stand, maybe it'll work. Come on. All you need to do is sign the slip and hand it over. Nepharisse walks past me and gently touches him on the shoulder. Seriously. He looks like he's going to pass out. Wonder where his blood is going. Hehehe. How salacious!

"I think the girl needs the slips for school, Terence." Perfect! That's exactly what I was hoping I could dupe him into doing while his brain is floating around somewhere else. He signs the top one and then hands me the whole pad. Juicy! She's looking straight at me, her hand stroking his back. There's something so calming about her, I feel like... Legs. Let's move before the doctor wakes up. Let's dart right past the scan and head for the exit. Better hide this in my bag.

"Way, Eli. Slow down a bit. I think he likes you."

Huh? Sure. Cute. "Go back! I'm done." Those crabseats, I tell you. "Thanks, Caroline."

Don't want to be around when he starts looking for his slippad, and it'll be dark soon. Famished finally. Just a quick something before I head back. Should still be enough light. Besides, things have been pretty quiet lately. Don't think I need to be quite so paranoid.

Good. On the left. The Snack Shack. "I'll have a two hundred in a maple bake." That should sink down there for the night. "Oh, sorry. The white one please." The red flyers tend to drip everywhere and they leave stains, dark red ones.

Like dried blood flakes. I need to drop my slip off to the counsellor tonight and I'm already on his "special" list. He might be thinking I'm the one getting creepy in the medical lab and that'll dump all matter of crap on me. "Thanks, Ashton." Mmmmmm. Now *this* is what I call a flyer bake.

I should probably check the notes while I finish this. Let me find a corner somewhere…there. Quick look around and… no sniffers. I'll just shift the bake to the right, grab the notes with the left and go easy on the mess. Let's see what kind of medical history I paid for. Elize Simone, 18 years old, baptized Unified. Sure. In your dreams, Pramam. Father factory worker…natural causes, mother transport operator…natural causes, no siblings…orphaned age 17, education credits…. Next slip. All updates in order, no major drifting. What's this? Age 9, MPD afflicted? Explode details. Defects found, biochip patched, noted as per procedure B4UC-F8. Defective biochip? Odd. Maybe Keet has access to the procedural archives. I wonder who these entries belonged to. Shudder. It's just creepy thinking about it, but it was the way to disappear.

What about the rest of the notes? Maybe there's something here on that gawking kid. Let's see, she was just after me, ahead of Caroline. Here she is: Mashrin Tamehr, 9, recently orphaned…transport accident…emotional drifting. Aw. The poor girl. If only I knew. And here's Caroline. Interesting. Seems like my fun-loving friend is having a little trouble staying upright recently. Oh no. She's being tracked. She needs to read this, and I also might want to rethink dazing with her too often. Avoid complications. Time? Oh oh. I'd better get back before the counsellor opens a case on me. Pull off my official scan, release and tuck it in my jacket, then back in the bag for the rest. I'll hand it to my snarly little privyshelf for safekeeping when I get home. It's Keet.

"I found a mick who can hack into the medi files. It'll cost us plenty, but we can disable the tag and change the logs. He'll meet us at 7:20, tonight, at the ivy wall. You yay with that?"

"Wow! You're blistering, Keet! No crisis. Everything's juicy." It's getting warm.

"How? Why? You didn't do something bent now did you? Where are you?"

"Of course not! The doctor had a little problem with his blood flow. Hehehe."

I have to take my jacket off. There. Around my waist is good.

"What's that supposed to mean? He's still alive, eh?"

"Unless she killed him after I left. Heart attack maybe?" Give it a silent pause. Ok. Enough torture. "Don't panic. He was just distracted by a woman. You know what that's like now, don't you?"

"Rip. Guess his biochip isn't working either then." Good whip!

"I'm walking back now to drop it off. Won't be too long. I'll comm you. We can meet the hack at the ivy anyway. He might be someone to keep handy." Equilibrium tends to rule and the balance has been tipped in our favor so far. It's just logic.

"Ok."

Faster. The top floor is dark and that means the counsellor's leaving. Crap. Run for the gate. Phew. Beat the autolock. I see him at the window and he sees me, and he doesn't look very pleased. Oh well. Let's get this over with.

"Miss Elize. You have something for me I presume...for your sake."

What's with the nose, señor. Any higher in the air and I'd see his frontal lobe. Assuming he has one of course. "Yes, in my...right here in my..." Crap crap crap. It's not in either pocket. Crap! "It must have fallen out when I ran for the gate. It's not far, I'll go get it. Please, sir, I really do have it." Oh, he's changing color now. Not good. What do I do?

"Well, don't just stand there. You have until I lock the front door to receive my charity."

I never thought my eyes could get so big. I'm a hurricane. Thank the itty bitty baby prophet. Just grab it and... Eyes really big now! Heart, get ready. I'm soaked. Muscles, time to fire now, let's go. Don't like standing here in front of these three. Listen, I'm begging, please, don't start. I don't need you in my head right now. Breathe. Calm down. Maybe they're on their way somewhere? Say something.

"Miss Elize!" Relief. It's the counsellor. He's broken their focus.

Run.

"Here it is, sir." I'm shaking so hard I can barely hand it over. His features soften and he brings me inside. I'm almost crying I'm so scared.

"Best stay here for a few moments while they go about their business. You've had an eventful day I am sure. The door is already locked, all you need to do is shut it behind you. I must leave. Avoid Osler Hall on your way back to your room and you'll be safe." He rubs my shoulder and smiles warmly.

Maybe I misjudged him.

"Thank you, sir."

He's gone now. I can't hold myself together anymore. Be strong, Eli. Deep breath in, open the door, all clear, time to go. What were they doing here? I thought the break-ins had stopped and the lab was off curfew? Certainly nothing has happened this past week. The techs would have mentioned it, especially for the ghoul factor. Well, that's as close as I want to get to them ever again. Staring at me like that. It was just...my skin is still crawling. Let's get this jacket back on so I can stop shivering. This city must have a defective thermostat, unless I caught something at the sick fest. Clear that thought, girl. No GHU in my near future, thanks.

I'll have to take the path through Rubrique Court if I want to avoid the lab. I should be able to sneak a peak at it through those trees over there and still keep cover. All the lights are on. What was that? It sounded like shattering. The lights are off now. Every single one of them all at once. I wish I had night lenses. I can make out some shadows, away from the windows. Looks like they're leaving. Shhh. My comm.

"On hush mode again? Where are you? You were supposed to—"

"Shhh. Listen. Someone's at the window, in the medical lab. I can see. No. Wait. They're gone. Crap. I have to get out of here. Where are you?"

"I'm at the back gate." He's early.

"You were supposed to wait for my call."

"I did. It's already 7:20. Our mick won't be hanging around

for too long I wager. Should I go through the woods and meet you at the front?"

"No. You bent! They'll be here any minute. I have to get to you. Stay at the gate. I'll head into the Social Studies sector and cross Rubrique Court then come around the other side. I'm switching to one-way." I can't have the chatter right now.

No one ahead. Scan the windows. No one there either. Ok. Go! Ears, stay sharp. Just need to reach that dark nook over there and then check again. Made it. Wait. I heard something. I think I'm being followed. There it is again. There's the archway into the sector. I can't see anything out there. Probably just a rodent. Head through the arch and ok. Get my bearings. Which path leads back southeast around the residence complex? There, between those two buildings on the left. The lights just went out. Listen. I hear footsteps. They're definitely behind me. I have to get through those buildings. Just move. Fast. I'm still on one-way, Keet's probably beating the comm just about now. Better say something. There's a tunnel on the right, I can hide there for a bit.

"I think I'm being followed. I'm almost at the northwest branch. Shhh. The footsteps have stopped. I can make it to the security zone if I run. Almost there. Don't worry."

"She has come."

No! The voice! It's them! Too much echo. I can't tell where it's coming from. If I stay here, they'll find me. I am so cold. Here I go. Deep breath in. Surge like the flood, girl. Take the tunnel, right down the steps, and "Ahhhhhhhhh…"

K E E T O

Day 25: late evening

I don't even recall what events unfolded earlier today. My nerves haven't come down yet from Eli's last words, echoing in my brain. All I could hear was her panting as the cold air came down upon her, and then her final scream. That's when I started running as fast as my legs could carry me, along the outside wall of the campus, begging for a break in the fence so that I could find a way to reach her, our childhood playing in my mind as painful sobs came shooting out my lungs.

The comm was still active and seemingly functional in one-way mode, but part of me wished that it had not told me the story I am about to share with you. She was being followed, that much I knew, but who or what exactly was following her still obsesses me. I heard her body hit the ground, tripping on something hard as far as I could tell, just as her shrieking voice flew out of her hand. The sound of it whistling through the darkness, reminiscent of the night we first breached the back entrance by the ivy wall, has come to represent the flare of emotions fizzling into the depths of my very soul. The echo of scurrying feet in the distance and shadows of a conversation I could barely hear paralyzed my ability to think as I tried desperately to comb the forest for a manageable climb. My leap into the courtyard would surely alert the protectors, I imagined, but the eventuality of a capture was a risk I had to take.

As I neared the perimeter, I clipped my comm to my shirt collar and dug my fingers into the knots of the closest tree, straining my ears all the while to filter whatever I could from the air. At this point, I could barely see. My eyes started to swell from the salty flood, but my hands inherently knew where to reach, leading my body and pulling me swiftly up the trunk. As I looked onto the clearing beside the Social Studies sector, the unsettling conversation continued resonating from within the confines of the arcades formed by the tunneled entrances into the square, whispering evidence of their crime. "It is done, we must leave now."

I cannot relinquish to mere words what I felt at that moment, only to say that I took your heart in mine and suffered a puncture so real as to send me clutching my chest as I slumped to the ground. Expecting the intrusion to immerse the courtyard in light, I sank to the shadows and steadied my breath. But darkness remained, and an eerie stillness took hold. The voices were leaving, their presence diminishing in the distance, as they hastily retreated into the void, and the peaceful song of the night flyers calmed my senses.

I was three steps from the main arches when I heard it move through the comm. At the time I had not attributed the soft fluttering to anything other than those winged minstrels dancing in the wind, but once I had reached the area leading to the northwest branch of Van Billund Hall that Eli was referring to in her last words, I stepped back in horror as I stood directly in the path of a tall dark creature, numbing my trembling body as it advanced. It was holding a limp bundle in its arms underneath a layered cloak, then as if powered by the power of a million stars, my strength returned. Eli!

Nothing in the universe could have thwarted the fury I unleashed onto this monster, as I surprised my legs and shot straight for it. Startled and off-balance, it dropped its captive and fled the scene empty-handed as the light returned to the pathway. The air was still cool, and I could see no mist escaping the lifeless form on the granite stones. Swallowing whatever fear remained in my tightening throat, I knelt beside her and brushed the blanket from her face. The confusion that followed left me scrambling for answers. Under the veil of darkness, it had been impossible for me to distinguish precisely the stature of this girl, but as I huddled beside her, it was clearly that of a child, no more than nine.

As my relief turned to fear once again, the realization that Eli could still be in danger consumed me. Could the voices have taken her? Or was she lying somewhere near, unconscious and bleeding to death? "No," is all I could hear my heart say, so I left the girl covered and vowed to find Eli. As I stood, I noticed a three-story high passageway. I went towards the arched tunnel, guided by the weak signal of her ditched comm, and down a few steps is where I found it, and a few steps further I found him. Stitch was leaning over Eli, looking intently at her head, wiping the wound with the sleeve of his shirt. He then removed his jacket, covered her legs with it to keep her warm and greeted me with a quiet "Hey lo."

He started to explain that he had been on his way back to his dorm from Osler Hall, when he had heard some noise in the sector, people talking. He then saw three figures obviously engaged in a serious discussion just outside the arcade, but when he started towards them, they ran off in the opposite direction. He had noticed that one of them had been pointing to the covered passage, so he headed down the steps where he saw a dark figure holding something wrapped in a blanket and crouched over Eli. The night flyers had been disturbed and were trying to find their way back to their nests. Apparently, he doesn't recall much else of what happened next, just that he found himself walking towards Eli and then the dark creature was gone.

By the time Stitch had finished his account, Eli was stirring and mumbling to herself, visibly disoriented. As he proceeded to lean her against the stonework behind her, I butted in and intercepted his advances. The way he was handling her and looking at her made me instantly uncomfortable, and I instinctively took charge like a protective father. As I gently cupped her face in my wood-chafed hands and lifted her gaze towards my bloodshot eyes, she appeared lost in a trance, muttering nonsensical sounds I did not recognize as words and staring right through me at the fallen girl beyond the steps, whose long silky hair was strewn against the cold slab. "This is a dream." She reached for my hands and pulled them down sharply, squeezing them tightly as she closed her eyes and started to lull her breaths into a smooth rhythm.

The robotic tone of her voice and her vacant expression really troubled me. The first time I remember feeling that look was the morning we had wakened after the accident, the first morning you were no longer with us, when Eli turned to me as dawn lit her face and drowned the sheets with her relentless tears. It seems like tonight, however, the well has run dry, and all that is left is the emptiness of over three thousand nights of torment. I wish I had the power to turn back the clock, but I don't. The closest I can get is to sit here, in the serenity of my crypt, and rummage through my splintered memories of you for some guidance. I've been cowering from the lashes of my own personal tyrant and blaming others for my suffering, the Unification, the Ministry, the GHU, and especially Father. I've been romanticizing places and people and things from the past and ignoring my role in the present. I can feel that Eli is pulling away. She sees me seduced by the charm of the archives and is becoming careless with her guard, downplaying the urgency of her health scan, plotting to attend an illegal daze, and vulnerable to the questionable motives of a peculiar stranger.

While Eli sat locked in her catalepsy, Stitch offered to gather her things which had randomly scattered during the fall. I watched as he brushed off each item and carefully placed it back into her bag, pausing for a moment as he read the letterhead on a slippad. Before he could flip past the first slip, I pretended that I heard something rustling further down the building and told him to hurry, so that we could attend to my "cousin", who was still suspended somewhere in her head. He hesitated at first, most likely questioning the truth of my observation, then promptly picked up the remaining bits before handing the heap over to me. I could sense a mutual distrust tainting the space between us, a distrust which would best be dealt with under more favorable circumstances, so I let the exchange pass and redirected my attention to Eli.

It took repeated reassurances from both Stitch and me to drag her back from whatever horrid place her mind was visiting and convince her arms to drape our shoulders as we eased her up the steps and into the corridor. The young girl had not moved, and to my surprise, nor had anyone moved her. The campus protectors were nowhere to be found. Hadn't they heard the scream? the voices? the confrontation? It's as if none of this had actually happened. They had not strayed from their routine, patrolling the deserted halls of the buildings around us. But the evidence lay at our feet and around our shoulders, and now that I knew Eli was alive, albeit shaken, I was secretly grateful for our mysteriously enduring good fortune, almost as if someone were watching us and keeping us safe.

Eli had regained control of her body by the time we reached the child and was frantically motioning me to hand over her satchel, as she fell to her knees and started to tremble. As Stitch and I competed for her arms, trying to help her back up, she brushed us aside and reached for the blanket obscuring the girl's face. The lingering weakness in her limbs caused her to buckle, but the pressing need to disprove her suspicions overruled. With the gentle stroke of one hand she slid the girl's hair away from her delicate forehead, and with the other, slowly tugged on the blanket obscuring her face to reveal the unspoiled features of an innocent child. Suddenly, as if stung by a knockout stick, she sprang forcefully backwards and looked up at us, wide-eyed yet sad.

She scoured the contents of her sack, oblivious to our dismal attempts at extracting her thoughts. Even the alarming signs of someone's impending approach failed to distract her from her task as I pleaded with her to cover our tracks and flee. Stitch stood weighing the options and battling with his own crazed conclusions. Evidently the only one who grasped the severity of our situation, I grabbed Eli by the armpits, pulled her up to her feet, flung her bag over my shoulder and ran straight down the path pointing out of the sector, leading my straggling companions away from the suspicious scene.

After we had reached the back of the sector, facing the northwest branch of Van Billund Hall, we encountered a snag between us and our final destination. The patrol schedule along the west side, where the entrance lay, was not amenable to unannounced visitors, especially one with a fresh wound on her head. As I dragged the others behind the shelter of a hedge, I reached inside for that space where ingenuity breeds. The conversation near the girl was funneling towards us, which made it simple for us to anticipate the resulting distraction when the alarm sounded, and the protectors across the island started to rally into their sweep formation. We hadn't a moment to lose, as it takes a dozen minutes or so of organized chaos for them to get themselves and an army of sentinels ready. Eli had crossed a sentinel before, I remembered her telling me, and I wholeheartedly shared her determination not to relive the experience. By the look on Stitch's face at that possibility, I could see he concurred.

I signaled to them to head for the east, staying low in the bush, but Stitch took the charge and wove through some holes in security, gesturing at us to follow his lead. He had done this before. Once bordering the complex, we headed in the direction of Eli's branch, taking cover twice under the links while security marched past. I could see the medical lab from the questionable safety of our second stop, but noticed nothing to suggest the transgressions Eli was to describe to me later in her room, except perhaps the secrecy of our companion's behavior as he casually reached inside his coat. Onwards we went, straight through the front door and into the lift, while the greeter was distracted by a rattling under his desk.

It felt like the lift would never arrive. Eli and I were both staring at her suspicious friend, no doubt juggling the same questions I had in my mind as he assumed his usual habit of bobbing to a beat no one but he can hear. What on this planet had just happened? Did we just nonchalantly walk in plain site of hundreds of heavily armed brutes and fanged escorts? And exactly what had he been doing in Osler Hall after hours? Heading back to his dorm? Sure. He would have seen Eli enter the sector in that case. Was he the one who was following her? Even if he wasn't implicated in her assault, I still question his intentions.

Which brings me to Stitch's part in all of this. As the lift was ascending, I noticed we had missed his floor and were heading directly to the ninth level. When the ride stopped, he hurried us along to Eli's room. We opened the door and he followed us in, securing the exit quickly behind him. "You were supposed to meet me at the ivy wall."

If my teeth were not bolted to my jaw, with pretty healthy bone I must admit, they would have been play toys for the shag. Eli, obviously impressed by his ability to render me speechless, which on occasion she also manages to achieve, just coyly looked over at him and smiled. The real Zafarian had just introduced himself.

Even before Eli had invited him to join us at the Snack

Shack for a midi break on our third full day here, I had felt a pretension about him that in my mind could only point to mischief. The incidental familiarity he had with the branch protector, in a not so positive light, was the origin of my immediate dislike for him, not to mention his flirtatious demeanor towards Eli, according to her version of their initial encounter, of course. Although he had only known her for a day, he seemed much too comfortable poking her when she said something he found "cute". Yeah. Sure. I don't accept his lowland upbringing as an excuse for impropriety as readily as Eli does. Perhaps that is what bothers me most, the ease with which she has been adapting to this new culture and connecting with people, others not me, while I bury my head in the bowels of the archives, surrounded by clones. Why am I so afraid to live?

As I challenged him, still reeling from the bomb he had just dropped, he simply listened openly to all my concerns, assuring me that the events of the day would only exist between the three of us. My defenses finally relaxed. I realized that while I was preoccupied with saving my sister from the dubious ploy of a would-be suitor, the real threat came from the injuries she had sustained in the dark, most pressingly, the foreboding images which induced the haunting emotional display we had witnessed in the arcade. Having put aside our differences for the moment, Stitch proceeded to satisfy my curiosity by providing the answers to a barrage of questions concerning our narrow escape.

He had spent most of his childhood pulling apart every imaginable device that had survived the unfortunate karma of entering his parent's household. I find that a strange choice of words; karma…as pertaining to an non-sentient object, but for Stitch it was how he viewed all aspects of the universe, from the buildings to his toys to his clothes…and did I mention his hair? In any case, the boy is a complete genius and entirely bent! I guess the two go hand in hand. He also has a more mischievous side, as I had suspected, which prompts him to flaunt his cunning in the face of authority, sometimes landing him in restraints, which he always seems to get clear of, both physically and on the Ministry records, which was in fact the very skill we were looking to inquire about on this very night at the ivy wall.

As much as I still mistrust his intentions, his exceptional resourcefulness and fondness for Eli, coupled with his history of flouting the rules, make him a great addition to our little criminal unit. Besides, he had already taken a big leap of faith by exposing his craft to us, and now he has committed to helping us solve the case of the dead girl on campus.

While we sealed our pledge with his awkward chumbuds salute, Eli retreated to the corner of the room staring aimlessly out towards the city skies, her open bag on the floor beside her. Fearing a relapse in consciousness, I went to her and called out to her softly, gently releasing her hold on the slippad. Her skin came alive and she managed a smile, then she sharpened her gaze and pointed a finger to the slip in my hand. "Mashrin Tamehr."

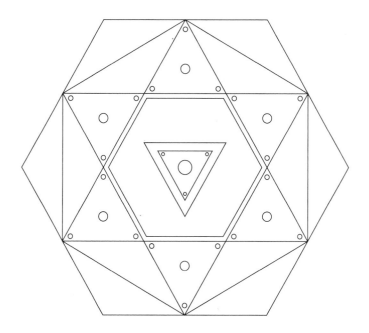

CHAPTER FOUR

NATHRUYU

Day 25: early evening

She chases the lights that frame the cobbled crust of the orchard path, and races to her old refuge at the east end of the campus oval, momentarily melding with the ominous shadows of the moonlit medical helix. The black offers Nathruyu no reprieve as her legs labor to reach the trellised gardens of O'Leary Hall before the alerted protectors assemble the sweep. The rocks flare down the blazing heavens and point a fiery finger in her general vicinity, signaling her presence and threatening the effectiveness of the city generators, a drift which could actually work in her immediate favor. She must trust that he has reacted predictably to the earlier disturbances and refocused his search on the twins' home circle, far away from the newest trespasses. A confrontation with his prize canines, at this time and place more so than at any other, would jeopardize much more than her simple freedoms. As she inches her body around the limestone structure, she slumps onto the backyard portico and contemplates her latest entanglements.

She was not supposed to stumble upon her, and furthermore, there is now proof of Elize's inadvertent fall. Her mind desperately scours its hidden recesses for vindication as she envisions harsh retribution for her carelessness. Straying from the agenda was not a privilege afforded to her, yet there she cowers, paralyzed by the cascade of events she has heedlessly allowed. Her weakness, her transitory lapse of resolve, in conflict with her profoundest commitment, had veered her off course, and risked the young captive wrapped in her well-intentioned betrayal. She had not expected to cross an individual lurking at the ivy wall behind the triple towers, nor had she anticipated his eventual pursuit.

Contemplation turns to apprehension as she relives the latest ordeal in her mind.

▼ ▼ ▼

The subconscious impulse that ushered her to the south gate has vanished and her thighs engage back to her original line, dividing the grove. The intended focus regained, she sails amongst the whispering leaves and ferries Mashrin to Rubrique Court within instants of today's rendezvous.

The detour has compromised her schedule and compels her to improvise amidst fluid circumstances. Stretching her ears for the oncoming footsteps, she gauges their likely trajectory and lays the innocent messenger across the most direct route. She feels the frantic pace of her heart as their cadence draws closer and corners her into a nearby passageway. Confident however that the bait is well positioned, her silhouette scales the rugged piers and hangs precariously outstretched from the ribs, where she waits, a conspicuous intruder in an overcrowded nest of night flyers.

Their sanctuary unnaturally breached, the sightless rodents

morph into a turbulent cloud of wings, as if evading their fiercest predator, drawing Elize's attention from her scurrying feet and the motionless bundle in front of her and up toward the anxious eyes of a nightmare. Terrified and disoriented, her attempt to run out of the tunnel sends her tripping on the blanketed child, ejecting the comm from her nervous grasp as she plummets to the ground with a chilling shriek and in the process grazes the jagged corridor with her head.

Nathruyu's throat tightens. Her predicament is severe. Elize's stability is already in trouble, and this untimely disclosure might plunge her into a heightened emotional trauma, a state where the boundary between memory, fantasy, and reality collide, and cause her to fight demons she has not, thus far, sufficiently evolved to comprehend. Swooping from her perch, she gathers the flaccid girl and moves Elize gently onto the granite slab. The notion of being on the brink of fulfillment, yet, once again and by her own doing, torn from him, overwhelms her as she fears the worst. She leans over in despair and caresses Elize's wounded flesh. A few moments stretch into weeks, and weeks into years, and she journeys backwards to the seat of her affliction.

As a girl, she too had been chosen and had tolerated things outside what her youthful spirit was designed to handle, barely returning from the void after her selfless deed. The irreversible decision, deemed cruel and unfair to a child's limited intellect, entrusts the children exclusively to her, negates secondary influences on their evolution, and eternally binds them to her destiny. In Elize's case, the initial days had been harrowing and exhausting. Nathruyu had toiled over her stubborn recovery, cleaned her wounds and wiped her endless tears, for such a generous gift demands many concessions. It is the versal law, the law she lives by, the law she dies by. It is the law that reaffirms her convictions whenever she strays, and the one she ultimately obeys, however reprehensible are the exploits her submission may require, even those contributing to the current rash of atrocities, and culminating with Elize, broken once again, in her care. Nonetheless, ages later, she delves for signs of life in the child cradled on her hip. She is still afraid, but hopeful, and just as relief flushes her veins, the stranger who blocked her at the ivy wall, appears before her, stunned.

▲ ▲ ▲

The shame behind the images replaying in the dark solely serves to distract her further from untangling this self-inflicted mess. The girl's loss upsets her overall plan, and consequently, she must devise a clever ruse to revisit the site, undetected, and conclude the job. She verifies that the stolen vial is retaining its heat, buried inside the pockets of her garments, wobbles to her numbing feet and braces her shoulder against the landing's pillar. Her lifeless reflection in the protruding pane catches her off balance. Dizzy with cold, her body heat diminishing rapidly, she can hardly discern her sculpted features carving the gray backdrop. Where could this glow be coming from? Fearful that the source is emanating from the interior, she stares beyond her sunken reflection and into the opposing window. Had she not witnessed the counsellor exit the north gate from her vantage point in the lab? The brightness dims and her semblance fades.

The voice booms louder, somewhere trapped between her temples, unmistakably stern as he utters these cutting words: "Remember your place." Disjointed loyalties have interfered with her obligations in the past, prompting her to challenge the morality of certain actions whilst defending the depravity of others and subsequently provoking his reproachful quip. The previous occasion on which she had relaxed her vigil, she had been apprehended and had eluded prosecution purely by secretly indenturing herself to the presiding chancellor, who shortly thereafter passed, dragging the selfish deception to his grave. The J branch of Van Billund Hall, nevertheless, remembers. This time, capture would endanger her health, eighteen years of patient monitoring and countless sacrifices, which grievously pales in comparison to the suffering she would continue to endure in the name of her insatiable desire.

What must be done must be done. Tottering at the edge of unconsciousness, she pulls her shivering form to the middle of the garden and siphons the energizing fragrance of the blooming vines. A sense of clarity revives her. If she gauges her approach correctly, she can stay ahead of the sweep. At first, they will retract all but a minimal contingent of defenders and sentinels from their stations, then summon them to the orchard. Once arranged in concentric arcs, they will fan out across the island, scan every unfortunate creature in their way, and flag their biochips as suspect, so that they can legally infringe upon their rights and record their slightest moves, till the investigation is complete and the barbarian unmasked. The cooling tunnels will serve her best. As she follows the carpet of wilted petals that extend from the thatched gazebo where she stands, she disappears via a narrow subterranean tube, skillfully disguised as a common sun catcher.

The predicted maneuvers have started. She follows the vents below the chancellor's office, relinquishes the painful flashes of her recent experiences and continues underneath the grove, headed for the intricate mesh of ducts feeding Rubrique Court in the Social Studies sector. The synchronized march of the human-beast pairs produces a concert of deafening rumbles throughout the entire ventilation network, urging her to stagger more quickly in the vibrating shafts and imposing a premature evacuation from the catacombs, while her muscles squeeze the leftovers from whatever force she had garnered for the trip. Mindful of her present vulnerability in the face of a trained operative, she surfaces straight behind the archway patrol and stops to postpone her breath prior to hazarding a strike. She surmises that an ambush is the most advantageous tactic given her impaired physical capacity, and stealthily drops her opponent to his knees. Something about the unexpected attack from Keeto tonight has weakened her and left her uncommonly drained in his wake despite her diligent preparations in solitude that afternoon. The energy they had exchanged had been palpable, delighting her as it apparently did him and suggests that maybe the forceful introduction to adventure is an invitation for something deeper, something enticing.

A speedy calculation gives her three seconds until the first row of militia overruns the square. She throws herself onto her rigid victim, tears off his belt and disables the monster diving menacingly from the keystone, then darts for this evening's crime scene, the weapon secured diagonally across her chest. Her memories have no recollection of a supervised ingress to the court, an emotionally charged piece of knowledge she is not inclined to forget. Turning to the left passage where Mashrin had lain, her mouth gapes. The girl is gone and merely two explanations logically fit. Either the boys and Elize managed to filter through security with Mashrin using a fanciful story for the weak-spirited guard, or, the hounds have her. She defers assessing the probability of each scenario to concentrate on foiling the forthcoming brigades and flies out of the arcade, disturbing her diaphanous-winged siblings one last time.

As Nathruyu gains the northern portion of the residence complex, the answer to her question is hauling the spoils of her bittersweet victory back to the medical lab. She dashes amongst the grass strips between the branches, her elusive mark visible from afar, and formulates her assault. The hairy limbs of the front line abominations punch through the trees, their masters in tow, and precede the supporting units to the clearing. Soon, tranquillity will replace the outer chaos, as hysteria chokes the commons. She is conflicted anew. The twins are subject to identification unless they are observing the fray, sealed inside Elize's room where no frequencies can penetrate, blinding the sensors to their hideout. But were they to emerge, the GHU would come, and a fresh cycle would commence.

She chances exposure and takes advantage of the protocol permissions check the GMU officers are requesting from the three officials. Cautiously peeking out from the open recess separating the east and center sections, she spies a fleeting pair of eyes above the ledge of the ninth floor window, then retreats to the shadows, appeased. Elize is safe, and she is conscious, but the numbers Nathruyu must currently surmount between her and the triple helix are excessive, and their imminent arrival does not afford her enough time to scale the links. She must circumvent them by fancying a temporary rift and promptly seeking out the underground grid to glide beneath them. As she seizes the emitter stored next to her skin, she encounters an atypical tackiness to its hilt, like a viscous film stuck to a substrate. She retrieves the device, creates a transient hole in the facade beside her, infiltrates its insulating air pocket and forges a uniportal on the indoor panel. During the gaps in the flickering darkness of the emergency lights, she manages to glimpse the color smeared on her hand. The sound of her jolting against the interior framework, when she realizes what passenger she is bearing, diverts the warden from his post. Elize's blood.

As he sniffs out the source of the interruption, walking warily towards her, she mentally reviews the events since Elize's concussion. On which side did she carry the girl? Did she brush the stonework at the administration building? What about the sentry at the arch? Revealing herself too soon, fumbling her mandate, and now this? The atmosphere grows thick with regret, strangling her lungs, as her brain spins inside her skull. The blood in the Ministry's custody might bring the twins' father to the lowlands, thus shattering her fragile web. Keeto and Elize had only just begun. She needs more time.

The man's tensing brawn now mere centimeters from her, unbeknownst to him effectively contained by an illusion, overtakes her senses. As he smooths his palms along the barrier isolating her and feels for undulations or a crevice, Nathruyu loses control of her whereabouts and mirrors his fingertips with her own, painting a crimson masterpiece with Elize's blood. Imagination sends her back to her forbidden love for a second interlude this evening, a portal to her past, to her present, and, plausibly, to her impending future. The guard's ear now pressed to the level of her breast, he hears her heaving from beyond the illusory divide. He traces the border of the viewing membrane and drives his rod in, wedging the encumbrance free and liberating her hungry gaze. Startled, he gropes for the alarm on his waistband, but foolishly releases his grip when he recognizes Nathruyu's signature smile. Another provocative kiss, his stance wavers, and she bursts into the vestibule and out the entrance, deserting the pandemonium in the student lounge.

Once in the field, she realizes she has lingered too long. The GMU swarm is engulfing the towers, which is fortunate, but the girl is missing, again. Distressed over the red stain from Elize's injury, she escapes for the trees to think. There, huddled under the citrus canopy, she fills the stillness with her thoughts. Frame by frame, her soiled hand travels the distance from the arcade and back, leaving no detectable token of its mischief. Her dominant arm had clutched the girl, while the other had delicately attended to the gouge at Elize's hairline. Nathruyu's waning temperature had kept her skin cloaked, and her dwindling self-control had enlisted the strongest offensive against the patrol. But as irony would have it, only succeeding the discovery, and her sober awareness of it, did the residue manifest itself. It was smeared on the underside of the fractured panel.

Nathruyu can still taste the salts on her lips, as if the precious droplets of life imbedded in the creases of her palm were flooding the speckled sky, gradually reducing to crystal dust as they bleed. The scented trail of the wound plays tricks with the landscape, transforming the encircling waters into a scarlet river. Sometimes they screech, sometimes they cry, whilst others whimper and cling to their damaged bodies. But Elize was different. Quiet and contemplative, she simply watched as her splintered world dissolved, only to divulge itself in fragments. She strained to survive in the obscurity of her dreams, dreams that fail to recall the most gruesome elements, perhaps for posterity's sake, in order that she might maintain a veneer of sanity in her waking hours.

But there is no mistaking this particular hue. It exudes a shade of its own, easily recognizable to those who know, to those who have seen, and to those who are looking, quite specifically to the one Nathruyu is constantly fleeing. She must rub out the incriminating blemishes and destroy any hint of their existence before she touches anything else, in order to avoid complications and thwart suspicions should they arise. Elize's true identity must remain private.

Opportunity arrives in the guise of the retreating corps, their partners relegated to their appointed nooks at the extremities of each catwalk, and undoubtedly reprogrammed for more interactive responsibilities. Once the rear of the finishing wave invades the secure zone, she curls in tightly and whisks past the pond as the thirsty blades rip her coat.

The lobby, she notices, is still harboring the crimson painting she had abandoned, its artistic swirls flat up where they fell, and her surrogate lover is collecting the debris. As it was in the highlands, she dutifully waits to confirm where his inner dialog is leading him. He slowly lifts the coveted chunk by its edges, careful not to deface their work of art, leers at it, sighs, leans it tenderly against the exterior wall and repairs the rupture, invisibly preserving their memento in the empty space.

Contented by the outcome, she regroups and consumes the evidence with her tongue, like a hunted feline licking its tattered paws before the crowning sprint. And then she hears it, the methodical clicking of chiseled nails against stone, expectantly pacing between her and her target. His canines are here. Someone is supplying him with aspects of her deceit that he cannot conceivably foresee. Something curious is watching her, yet choosing to act vicariously. The howling begins. Next, they will locate their evasive prey and catch an extra morsel from the vial in her clothing. She estimates the steps to the nearest sheltered hatch and concedes defeat, for the moment, and instead commits to the seaward side of the buildings, absconding into the soil precisely as the hounds barrel around the final corner, at the south central wing. Relieved at their confused grunts, she pauses underneath them where they cannot follow, and when she hears them thump to the ground, weaves through the maze in the direction of the main corridor. By the time he finds his comatose pack, she is out and over the surrounding channel, reentering the labyrinth at the foot of the Victory Bridge and heading to the museum to lure an awakening adventurer.

As she nears the generator beneath the floral pond, she sheds the defiled layers of clothing covering her sensuous figure and thrusts them deep into the burning gases. There she will rest till the morning fog, naked and waiting.

E L I Z E

Day 25: early evening

"What are you looking at?" Sounds like Keet.

"Hmmm?"

"Are you here? Eli?"

I think I am. "The trees are moving and there's no wind." Something is bothering him. He's glued to the slip. "Crap!" It's the creepy ones! And they have her. Ouch. Have to remember not to move so fast. Won't be taking the hovertrain for a bit that's for sure. It feels like my brain is a scrambled mess. "I'm ok." Keep low. And where did he pick up that mothering instinct? "Get down! They'll see you."

"Who?"

"*Them.*" I'll pull him down to my level so we can both peek over and motion with my head at the sweep. Ooooooooo. Motion. Not good. I think I'll just sit back down here.

"Crap." So he gets it.

They're organized now, and they're fanning towards us.

"You're still bleeding, Eli. Hold still."

Yeah. I'm trip with that. Ohhhm gee, I'm hanging with Stitch too much.

"We should get you to a doctor... Stop. Just hear me out, ok? We'll get Odwin to set it up."

We don't need the mystery Gadlin for this one. "Why don't we just ask Stitch? I mean, Mr. Zafarian." A bow for effect. "Looks like he's plugged in." To what I'm not quite sure. Hey, maybe that's what drives the hair.

"No bloody way!"

Wow. That was direct. Assertive in fact. Like tonight. He just took charge and got us up and moving. And later, he kept digging and digging at Stitch. Well, the digging part I expected, but not the tone. What's he sniffing in those archives anyway?

"You don't trust him."

"Not one bit. And don't you go telling him anything either." There it is again. That tone. "I mean you haven't told him about us, have you?"

We need to lighten up here. "No, my love, our affair is secret." Hehehe.

"Eli. This is reaaaaaally serious."

So I found a body, got a bump and now we're cornered. Right. But something tells me there's more. He's staring at the slip again.

"Do you realize you haven't stopped staring at that thing since Stitch left?"

And he looks up at me with a puzzled look on his face. "Don't you remember?"

What is he talking about? Of course I remember what happened. But he's still staring at me with this you-belong-in-jar look, like I'm some sort of specimen at a carnival freak show.

"Her. You *know* her." He is pointing at the girl's picture.

"Yyyeah. And? I saw her at the medi clinic. I told you. Hick." Now who's the slimy one.

"You babysat her last year, her parents we're out of town for the night. She stayed over with us because Father wouldn't ever let us out, remember?"

Yeah. I remember his paranoia. That's why we left. But the girl? No way. I know I've had lapses recently, but not a whole day! Ridiculous. He's been spending too many late nights in the books.

"Keet. I have *never* seen this girl before today." My turn for stomping. Now back off! And you too in there. Shut up. Stop talking to me...oooooo my head. Go away. Breathe.

"Eli, Eli. Focus over here. Let's work this through together."

Ok. Calm now. Concentrate on his eyes, follow his breath. What if he's right? What if I dropped my own internal flashes when I hit the ground? Maybe I do know her.

"So...what are you saying, Keet?"

"I'm not sure. It just seems a little too random that *you* should be the one to find the body. Our town isn't that big."

He's right about that. Not many kids her age there either. And those three creepy guys showing up at our gate, at the transport station, running into them earlier, following me, and now taking the body? Could they possibly be connected?

"But you're the only one who remembers her. It's just a coincidence."

"Father knew."

Right. Now *he's* the creepy one. I know how he feels about Father, but honestly, he's not a murderer.

"Father doesn't even know we're here." That sounded plausible enough. I'm starting to wonder whether I even know where *I* am anymore. Everything still feels so unreal to me.

"I hope you're—"

"Shhh." They're in the building. That wasn't just another

meteor blast. By the size of Keet's eyeballs, I can tell he heard that too. They're force switching the doors and they're on this floor. If I weren't so dizzy I could think straight. I can't let on though. Keet's worried enough as it is. Let's just move behind the closet and...holding hands is good. The death grip is a little much, but no one's watching. They're getting closer.

"Hey. Let go! You need council bypass for this. I know my rights." That's Shaplo.

"Quiet. The only permissions I need are right here. Turn around. Any struggle and I'll tag you with resistance as well."

Keet and I are looking at each other in horror now. Neither of us dares to even whisper it, but we both know what is happening out there. Everyone's getting tagged suspect. Whoever is on campus right now and non-Ministry will be clamped, and that means Father will find us. My lips are bleeding. I've felt this way before. Terrified, waiting for my turn, not wanting to let go. Keet's welling up inside. He closes his eyes and grabs my other hand. It can't hurt. Do the same. Complete silence.

✄ ✄ ✄

Is it over? It's blacker than black. Oh. My eyes are still shut. Hick. Where's Keet? Where am I? Quick, the base of my skull.

"Eli." It's coming from the doorway. "Eli." There it is again, a little louder this time. "Wake up." He's scanning the hallway with his rump in my face. Maybe crawling wasn't such a good idea. I sure hope he's been eating fresh.

"Hey." Definitely not a good idea.

Elize

"Sorry, tough girl."

Giggle. My guess is they missed us, and that was sarcasm.

"What happened?"

"Well, they came to get us and you turned into a fireball monster and sucked their brains out. It was most impressive." Now that deserves a snare face. Come on. "Rip. You passed out, tough girl." And blanked out as well no doubt. "Welcome back. We're juicy. Don't know why or how, but no tag."

"We have to get you out of here, Keet, before they put the sentinels back. You'll need to take the roof and go down the outside of the links. You ready for the circus?"

He's not looking amused. "You're bent. Do you know how high that is?"

"It's one floor up. We can grow some steps and bust through the ceiling. Maybe the privyshelf is hungry. There'll be extra drooling monsters at the lift I'm sure."

He's thinking about it. "And once I get out, provided I'm still in one piece, what do I do next?"

Oh. He's not going to like this one. "We need to call Stitch. Yes. We don't have to tell him anything, just that you can't be trapped on the oval with the rest of us. You'll lose your job." Head moving back and forth, puckering his beak, squinting his eyes... Good.

"Ok. That's all we tell him."

He's really nervous. Give him a huge hug. "You'll make it look easy." He's not convinced. So on to Stitch. Grab the comm.

"Hey lo, Stitch. Perk. Keet needs to flip a pass. The shoe will stick to him something fierce if he rides."

"Ta, chum. Everything's just tripping down here, yeah?"

Oh, crap. That was rude of me. "So sorry, Stitch. Need to clip. You trip?"

Keet is completely lost. "What language are you speaking?"

"Shhh." I'm missing it. "Sorry, Stitch. Keet's dunked." I am so loving this. "The back?... Yeah. Who? Yeah. He will. Ta. We're trip."

"Lie low, Eli." How did he set that up so fast?

Keet's shaking his head. "You'll have to translate that for me later. Right now, just give me the facts." Hey isn't that my line? Juicy. He's a fast digger.

"Back entrance by the ivy wall. Our friendly chef will be waiting for you in fifteen minutes. You can make it if you clip, I mean hurry. Stitch said to comm when you're safe." Lock and nod, and he's off. "Oh and don't let him feed you." Unless he wants to knock his colleagues out tomorrow. Hehehe.

I'll need to cover this hole with something later. Oh no! Quick...or actually slower is better...to the window. Phew! They're leaving. I can just see them...there. Last one off the... What's that? Oh, give your head a shake, Eli...or maybe not. When will this throbbing stop? I must be seeing things, there's nothing moving down there. Shaggy time. Yep. You have a name now, oh tentacled one. How fun, the puppies are playing catch with...

✄ ✄ ✄

Moan. Groan. Is this what a daze feels like? Just a little groggy, but the pounding is over at least. I'm awake right?

Here it comes again. Brace for the flood. I feel so nauseous, so helpless. Why do they make me watch? I want to run to her, I want to make them stop. She didn't do anything wrong, we were just on vacation, all four of us. Why did they take us there...

✂ ✂ ✂

It's so cold and dark, can't someone help us? Please. They're hurting her. No. Mother. Stop. Make the pain go away. Keet, wake up. Don't leave me alone with them.

✂ ✂ ✂

Wake up. That's enough. I just won't sleep anymore and they'll leave me alone. The dreams can't touch me if I'm awake; they're just not real; they can't hurt me; they'll just disappear just like the girl. She wasn't real. None of this ever happened. It was all just another one of my bad dreams. Look. I'll prove it. The ceiling is fine. See? Oh no. Stitch! They must have tagged him. How's my scrape. Hardly noticeable... Well, if I hide it with a hat. There. We'll be twins. My comm, my controller, my secure band, and where did Keet leave the... Mashrin. Let's go get some answers.

I wonder what the fanged door keepers are authorized for now, as if trying to eat us wasn't enough. Good. No one is awake yet. According to Keet, getting your biochip slammed with the rod hurts like a mangled scan, not that we know what that feels like either. Anyway, my floormates will be sleeping well past fog lift for sure. Not the most enjoyable way to flip a pass. Whoa, time to plane. Close one. I haven't been on the slick for a while. They had time to shine the floors last night? Crap. Watch out! So the sentinels are trolling the halls now? Ewww. Disgusting. That's not floor shine. How am I going to get down and over, they're blocking the lift too. Think think think. Well, if Keet can... I'm an athlete, you know. Back to the room then.

I'll need a light. Got it. Ok now. Which way. Yes, memories of crawling in the dark under the sliderpad. We used to hide from Father sometimes, when it got scary. Jenny would come too. That's where she'd squeak all those ghost stories. That got us jumping. Silly girl. She still believes all that stuff. I guess some people never grow up. This here. This is where the real monsters are, and slobbering amongst the human population as well.

I'm out. The sky is so beautiful. Look at all those stars. Whoops. Getting dizzy. Look where you're headed, girl. Southwest central branch. Hop. Sneak sneak sneak. And up. Next. Hop. Run run run. And up. Again. Hop. Sneak sneak sneak. And now what? Gulp. Down the links. Here it goes. They're circling the floors so I should be able to slide down the sides and jump down to the next level. And again. And again. And again. And reach down, grab the comm, flash mode, and click. Hmmm. Click. Click. Click. Good. Here he comes. He's opening the window.

"Pica trip! You're crazed, chum! Way. Love the hat." Am I ever glad to see that smile of his.

"Ta, chum." He's not wearing very much. "Ummm."

Very well put there, Eli. Maybe my brows will complete the sentence. He's grabbing some pants. Well, something like pants. And is that a hint of his....? Ugh!

"I didn't expect someone up this high, or down this low from your perspective. Told you I had nothing to hide, yeah?"

What a dweeb! Couldn't hate him if I tried though. Don't just stand there, pass him the slip and start talking.

"There's something missing here." Oh yeah. The tag. "Does it hurt?"

"The tag? Neah. It's not the first time."

"Why am I not surprised?" He pulls out the big grin this time.

"How's yours?" Crap. Can't let him feel back there, not yet. Take a side step and change the subject.

"Juicy. So what about the history here? I think it's crap!"

"Flyer mud, ya fig? Let's sleuth, yeah?" You read my mind, chum. Flash him a smile.

He pulls up a crabseat for me, oh joy, and starts sketching through the maze. I just realized it's the first time I've been to his room. Better keep this between us, not proper for the highlands.

"Stop jumping around!" My brain's still slamming away. What's the story with these things?

"Slap me, chum. It's got the hiccups." You asked for it. "Ta." Hehehe.

"I think I'll just stand. My head."

Look at all these gadgets! He sure wasn't kidding about the "taking stuff apart" fetish of his. There's the frequency thrower he duped the guard with, which reminds me...

"How does the guard know you? You only just got here the day before I did."

"Apparently, I make quite the first impression." No argument there. "I tested out this new invention on him and he wasn't too impressed, neither were the girls in the lobby, yeah?" I even know what that smile means.

Let's test it on him and see, not that I want to see that of course.

"Hands off, lass, yeah? This one you have to see in action. Still a little drift in it. It'll be a few hours for the trace. What's so crit?"

"We need to break into Osler Hall. They took her there. I can't explain yet. It's pica crit!" To put it in words he can relate to. His hair is wiggling. He's apprehensive. "Ziga pica crit!" That should do it.

"Crazed!" He's shaking his head then lights up. "Trip. We'll need Keet. Two won't go. The only way is through the sunshaft and ride the tunnel down. We need to sling from your tower, and then once inside, hold the sentinels, and if the second line defenders sniff us... We need a watch on that too. What pod is she in?" Up go the eyebrows. "No panic."

There is a lot more to this guy than he is letting on. Look how fast he's pulling up the grids, the shaft lines, the sentinel stations. Wow. He even has the hardware; ropes, harnesses, pulleys, spring board? Is he bent? No, he is *completely* insane!

"You've done this before." There's that smile again.

"Let's get Keet, yeah?"

"How are we going to get passed the lockdown scanners? Your tag will set them off." Crap! Oh, I hope he missed that.

"No more than yours, yeah? Here. Wear this."

He's toying with me, he picked up on it. Ok. I'll play along. "A bracelet? Is this some sort of chumbud blood bond?"

He's jumping in. "Yeah. Trip, ya fig? Now we must run naked in the maze together till our dying years." He leans over and whispers in my ear. "Juicy." Ewww. Him and Keet. I'm flanked by post-pubescent toddlers. "Ease, chum. Poked a rib. It's a narrow field rubber. The scanners are stupid, they won't know what hit them."

"Meaning…"

"It cancels out a very specific range with very little power so the drop detectors can't spot it. I can't explain yet." Zapped. That's fair.

"Don't forget the frequency thrower." There are still protectors at the perimeter.

"You're learning, yeah? Here, catch. Your turn."

Juicy. Time to have some fun.

The only way out is how I came in, then straight down. I can hear them pace back and forth in the halls so the links should be clear. Don't look at it, just lean over and grab the edging. Yes. Down to 4. Breathe, 3. Breathe, 2, Breathe, 1. Slide. Oops. Watch the lobby guard. Grass. Oh yes! I do want to kiss you. Sorry. Have to run. Stitch is on the comm with someone. There's the perimeter protector. Fling him something in the ivy. Juicy. I like this thing. Finally the woods. He's fast. He's definitely done this more than once. Well, look who's here. I'll pass on the rot fingers and toe jam thank you.

"Busy night, Zaf? And Elize." He nods so graciously. We're getting the head-to-toe look. "A little dark for rock climbing is it not?"

Feeling a little sheepish right now, but Stitch banters in.

"Well, Odwin, you know me, yeah?" And I wouldn't mind knowing a bit more myself.

Did he say *Odwin*? Looks like he noticed my squashed frog imitation.

"Answers in time, my young princess."

Oh, I like him. A princess! The Gadlins are so chivalrous. And a wink as well. Juicy.

Finally, some time to relax. Away from the prison. Strange that I would think that word. Prison. I guess it's not the size that matters. It's the freedom or lack thereof. I spent months planning to leave Father's just to end up in a bigger one. How bent is that? But still. What is it about this free-spirited hip-wiggling hair-squirming lowlander that has me so agitated? For over three weeks he's played his social misfit role so well, and then overnight he's a different person. Could Keet have sensed something from the beginning? He's smiling again.

"Look up, chum. The stars are calling. Make a wish."

And I do.

Day 26: early evening

"A dreamless sleep awaits her."

The notion that those beautifully penned words could represent such a foreboding end disturbs me. According to Eli's interpretation at the Snack Shack this evening, the message signals an end to her relentless nightmares, something she has been longing for since childhood, but Stitch offers a vastly different perspective. A dreamless sleep can only mean one thing, death. But for whom? My fear is that this cryptic warning in my journal is directed at Eli. Predictably, her reaction was a prolonged snare and an emphatic "you're both bent," but nonetheless, a twisted knot still grows inside me. Surely this morning's discovery was related. Someone is watching, and I shudder to think that they could have been rummaging through my belongings while I was there, in my bed, traveling to places only my mind has visited.

I was so exhausted after last night's surreal adventure that I was forced to cut our conversation short. By the time I had finished recounting the first part of the evening, the adrenaline crash from my unnerving escape had caught up with me, leaving me barely conscious enough to see clearly, let alone put to paper any manner of coherent thought. I'd like to believe that you were there, a third pair of hands entwined in the dark, creating a protective field around us, like our own personal biowall, while the operatives swarmed the floors, injecting everyone in their path with invisible restraints. How else could they have missed us? But I must concede to good fortune. Scanners are not infallible and drifting does occur during meteor showers, of which the skies threw us plenty last night. Whatever the source, I am grateful.

I sense I am at a crossroads, as does Eli, although she refuses to admit it. She was convinced I would succeed, even amidst overwhelming indications to the contrary. She might be all science and numbers, but she still has faith. Faith in me at least, something I have yet to embrace. As I recoiled at the edge of the tower, re-ingesting the contents of my stomach before committing to the task, I remembered the incident with the dark figure and found the courage to leap onto the first link. Once balanced, momentum and urgency carried me down the levels until I heard it again, the ominous flutter, so easily mistaken through a comm as the innocuous wings of night flyers. I froze on the last level, just in time to avoid falling into the path of the cloaked stranger and the pursuing pack of fork-tailed creatures. As the howling continued along the gap between the towers towards and around the center back, I regained control of my body, focused on my accomplice waiting beyond the ivy wall, and made a run for it, trusting that the hounds and their prey were suitably distracted. As I curved left towards the open gate, its protector slumped against it, my gaze was drawn to the absence of noise behind me. The stranger was gone and the hunters lay unconscious on the ground.

Yes, our paths are indeed becoming more entangled and our self-reliance is no longer enough, but inviting an outsider into our private pursuit was never part of the plan. Stitch's attentiveness towards Eli has clouded her judgment, and now she has wedged him between us and opened a door he immediately took advantage of. Although I appreciate the resourcefulness of this Zafarian character, if that is in fact his real name, I will continue to question his intentions until he divulges his true connection with the outlanders. But until then, I must choose to step out of my skin, to take an uncomfortable chance with him and open a door of my own.

It was not even hinting at dawn when I heard them knock. My brain must have still been processing yesterday's emotional whirlwind, because I shot straight up, covered in sweat with my heart trying to bust through my ribcage. I sat with my feet bolted to the floor by the edge of the bed until I recognized Eli's voice through the keyhole. "What's with the hat?" is all I could muster in my confusion, as she muttered something witty about my room protector, while Stitch attempted to restrain himself from bursting. She hadn't yet met the tiny yet effective addition to my crypt, since she hadn't been back here since my first day. Just try to go near my journal and you'll see how fast fingers can disappear. Nonetheless, I have to admit that it is difficult to imagine him expressing any wolf-like qualities when he's lapping up the pats and cuddles Eli is spoiling him with.

Suspecting that my new pup wasn't the reason for their impromptu visit, I bypassed any formalities and demanded some answers. After I had calmed down and essentially accused Stitch of corrupting my "cousin" and putting her life in danger by making her skulk around in the dark with a concussion, Eli rolled her eyes and started laughing. Evidently, she found my outburst entertaining, which irritated me even further, but I think Stitch got the point. He pulled himself away from the discussion and let her explain.

She had been thinking about the events which had happened since the medi clinic and my suggestion that her involvement was not accidental, and she admitted to feeling watched even before we left home. Her analytical self had rationalized it as being the result of emotional adjustments to a completely new environment, and in light of the circumstances of our departure, it seemed reasonable, but the compounding evidence is causing her to question her initial assessment. She was the one who enlisted Stitch for the lunacy they were contemplating.

The sun would be rising shortly and that meant the fog was not far behind, a perfect cover for breaking into the medical lab, she continued. After she filled in the details of their grand scheme, the only thing I could think of was: how hard exactly did she bang her head last night? The mere concept of attempting a breach was completely bent, let alone catapulting onto a roof through a blinding cloud. That was suicide. As I attempted to emphasize the fatal consequences of the slightest error in the plan's execution, she pulled me in close and whispered very deliberately: "I saw *them* take her."

At this point I realized that whoever *they* were, she had been keeping her encounters with them secret, so I pressed her for full disclosure, keeping Stitch well within my periphery and away from earshot. Her blood was already at the crime scene, and it was only a matter of time before they assumed her responsible, declaring her sick and dangerous so that

Father could sign her away, just as he did you. Our choices were to flee and seek shelter with the Gadlins, remaining fugitives for the last half of our lives, or search Mashrin for clues that could lead us to the real mastermind behind these apparent coincidences and ultimately discover what they are looking for. Eli was right, we must leave at first mist and follow Stitch's lead, although watching him bopping around in the corner captivated by my magic books did not really instill in me a great deal of confidence.

His interest in my selection of literature of mostly myths, legends, lost civilizations, unsanctioned historical accounts, and biographies of great explorers, annoyed me, mainly because it implied that Eli was right again and that I have more in common with him than I think. He even ranted about your favorite game, the one we used to play when we were allowed to visit you, telling us about how his grandfather was unbeatable, and showing us a few of his best moves. When both Eli and I grew quiet, sensing that there was some emotional trauma attached to my memories of it and trying to lighten the mood, Stitch steered the conversation onto my crystal, which unfortunately had the opposite effect. He said he had seen something similar before, but couldn't remember exactly where, to which Eli stoically responded that it was my mother's who died when I was a child, adding credence to the story that we are just distant cousins who ran into each on the hovertrain several weeks ago. After a brief moment of silence, we spent the rest of the early morning rehearsing the break-in procedure and refining our exit strategy, and as soon as our fog cover rolled in, we were out the door.

The campus was unusually quiet. The regular clicking of heels between the Nook and Van Billund Hall as students grabbed some sweets before classes was missing. In fact, there was very little noise emanating from inside the buildings themselves as most students were still suffering the after-effects of last night's tagging frenzy. There hung an eerie stillness in the mist. Once we had made it along the orchard pathways, Stitch switched the frequency thrower to reflect mode and lowered its setting to below sentinel hearing range. He then handed us each a noise cancellation emitter to keep clamped to our wrists from now on and a set of gloves for prints, and we started our approach. Arms locked, we ventured step by step across the clearing and under the eastern links. Having seen them from above, the thought of climbing them without the benefit of my sight rattled my nerves. Stitch seemed to be the only one of us whose hands were steady and dry, so we shadowed him.

Once on the roof, I immediately switched to canine task force mode and crawled, sacrificing my fingers to the front line instead. From the northeast corner, Stitch hooked one end of a rope, attaching a fourth emitter to the other end, along with an autograbber. He then pointed himself in the direction of the western helix, shot straight into the fog, waited a few seconds, unhooked the rope, slipped a slide on it, pulled it back taut, clamped it, and told us to hop on. Just like that. Ok. So it wasn't a catapult sending me screaming through the air, which of course no one would hear because my emitter would cancel out the incessant wailing as I plummet to my death, but just the same... Being captured and sent to work the mines was looking pretty good just around then, but the gentle squeeze from Eli as she lovingly eased me onto the canvas hoop restored my spirit. "Fly like the wind," she said. And never look back.

Stage two was complete. He released the rope's grab on the spire and fired it back to its origin, for pickup later today, collapsed the slide into his bag, pulled the next set of gadgets out, put them on us, and triple tested them. Spiraling down a shaft across eighteen levels might be thrilling, but erupting out the bottom into a lobby full of GMU operatives because of a containment issue would be anticlimactic to say the least. The brakes had to control the descent and stop us at the right pod, and they did. Stitch was the first one at the panel. He punched a long sequence of numbers into the frequency thrower, camped on the controller channel, hacked the lock code and swung through the opening. Just then, I felt a vibration through the walls of the tube, and voices snaking upwards. Stitch's ingenious wrist clamp all of sudden lost its appeal as we could not hear what was happening in the cell. If the sentinel had him within close range, we would be deaf to it. They had called the lift and were heading our way and Stitch was nowhere in sight.

All of a sudden, my whole body flushed with blood. What if this was a trap? What if he was an undercover operative and had lured us into a false trust? He certainly has the right skills and the stone resolve. He wasn't going to take us that easily. I would rather die than have him take Eli from me. Just as I had decided to fly through the open panel, Stitch poked his head out and pulled us in. My fist was clenched so tight it exploded on its own, while he ducked and deflected its force with a chuckle, and I went stumbling into the belly of a gagged sentinel. Well, at least I didn't get slobbered on. Eli shook her head and mumbled something about post-traumatic stress and we put the incident behind us, for now. Mashrin was waiting.

There she was, covered in a silver shroud. Eli reached her first, pulled off the sheet, and searched through her clothing, while Stitch went straight for the base of her skull, rubbing his fingers against it, and I, well, I supervised. I prefer dead things without the juices intact. Besides, someone had to make sure the defenders stayed in the walls. As the pat-down continued, I saw Eli take something from the girl's pant pocket, then instantly put it back, oblivious to my questioning eyes. It looked like a rock, but I can't be sure because I only caught a glimpse of its reddish hue. Then Stitch called me over and together we carefully rolled Mashrin onto her side. They were keeping her warm. But why? Eli purported to lean into me to get a better view of what Stitch was revealing above her hairline, but what she was really doing was digging into my shoulder blade with her trembling nails. We recognized the mark and stood back in horror as Stitch proclaimed: "Part of her brain is missing."

Our time had run out. After repositioning the body, we jumped into the shaft just as the gag dissolved and the beast reanimated. We hitched a ride to the first level, where a cloaked acquaintance of Stitch's was waiting to escort us to the roof terrace, just a six meter drop to the ground. Just! As recent as yesterday evening I would have sickened at the thought, but after swinging like a monkey between the residence towers, I'll take the six. Off the terrace we rolled, then, hands joined, we raced the rising fog through the clearing towards the J branch, threw the guard another bone, and maneuvered our way through the pacing sentinels until we reached Stitch's room, where we stared at each other and beamed. What a trip!

It is just past nine now and I'm rushing to recap the day before heading back out with Stitch again. Between the wake-up call, the lab, his room, the crime scene, the archives, and finally our morbid speculations at the Snack Shack, I have found his company surprisingly pleasant, aside from the little swipe at the west tower of course. I still have reservations about divulging our true objectives, but as long as he honors his word with regards to protecting your little girl, I am willing to share some. Which brings me to: why the rush? When I was on hush with Eli at the medi clinic, I overheard her secretly plotting to attend a daze with Caroline, and in sharing that with Stitch, we both agreed that given her head injury and the current manhunt, we should follow her. But let me backtrack to Stitch's room first while I wait for him.

The results from the sketch were in. His chumbuds network had extracted more than any of us could have imagined. As suspected, the medical slips Eli had fortuitously acquired at the clinic were a fraud, not unlike our own, come to think of it. Since her parents' death, Mashrin had been hearing voices, suffering debilitating nightmares, and experiencing memory lapses. I looked over at Eli fidgeting in her chair as the facts poured in. There was no emotional drifting. Mashrin's biochip was malfunctioning and she was no longer traceable, which made the Ministry very nervous. Our eyes locked, while Stitch, glued to the board, kept drilling deeper into the maze, and I knew in that instant that Eli had been hiding her blackouts from me. But why just her? The scanners can't trace me either? Why aren't I living in her hell?

At that point, I noticed Stitch becoming extremely tense. There was no more head grooving at his seat, he was perfectly still and fixated on the next packet. He had just read that someone had stripped Mashrin's brain to remove the biochip and was studying her body's reaction to the procedure most likely to perfect a living transplant, the motive unclear. "Collateral damage?" Stitch was furious. Furthermore, the network had correlated the procedure against other medical entries, and discovered a rash of drifting as far back as some forty-five years ago. Stitch started frantically picking through high council packets, from the Pramam's personal advisor himself. The boy's a genius.

Three weeks ago, another girl had bled to death and a guard was murdered, complete organ failure, no puncture wounds, but they have a suspect. Whoever is responsible, they want him alive. The GMU have strict orders to that effect but no access to the truth. They are looking for blood? We both stared at Eli, but she was somewhere lost in her head. We had to get rid of the evidence. Stitch and I grabbed Eli and we hurried to the arcade, only to find the area wiped clean, no blood, no muddy footprints from my shoes, no night flyer crap, nothing. It's as if it never really happened, but there was no mistaking the expression on Eli's face; she was reliving a terror words could not express.

You know what she is facing, don't you? If only you could speak to me and tell me what is happening, or perhaps Dr.

Tenille can. He took care of you, remember? He's teaching now and Eli applied for his study group today. She's holding it together still, just as you warned her. You'd be proud. I know I am.

Stitch is here. Tomorrow, I'll summarize this afternoon's findings at the archives.

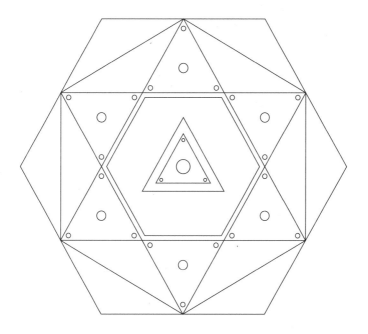

CHAPTER FIVE

NATHRUYU

Day 26: midday

With surgical precision, she transfers the precious seed from the latest victim to an incubator on the windowsill. She had sheltered it against her flesh, her feathery arms draped across her shoulders in the underwater refuge as she awaited the vibrations of the trio's departure. The smooth cloth she presently wears hangs limp from her frame, imbued with the subtle scent of her new champion. The metamorphosis has started, and soon Keeto will shed his cocoon and vanquish his self-inflicted oppression, forsaking the unconscious, whilst the faithful few bask in the aura of his greatness. And she shall dance amongst them, unbounded and free.

Stroking her fingers along the rich linen panels of his chemise, Nathruyu imagines the exalted rank this "borrowed" piece must hold in his wardrobe. She chose wisely since he is unlikely to notice the theft, unless an exclusive engagement calls for it. In the interim, she savors its luxurious weave, as she considers it payment for her loss, a small price to pay for what she dropped on his account, for there was nothing commensurate he could have tendered, except that which he has sworn to protect, that which, in due time, will be forfeit as well.

As the sun works its magic upon the slice she acquired, she loses herself in the crystalline vase where it rests suspended in a blue nectar and recalls her early morning swim with it in the cool pool engulfing the museum generator.

▼ ▼ ▼

Her invisible footprints on the tumbled stone shadow her movements inside Keeto's crypt, where she scouts for the journal to which he confides his daily reflections. The antiquated lock, like the keyhole on his door, did not offer much resistance to her intrusion, nor did its canine custodian provide an effective defense. Instead, he preferred to shiver in the corner by his toys after a brief struggle to avert her strike. She quickly inhales the pages of Keeto's life, looking for shades of a weakness to exploit, and finds one in his impressions of her and the confusion it creates. Her delight is short-lived. It fades to sorrow when, at the end of a recent memoir, she sullies the words with a lone tear as she succumbs to her troubled conscience through a name: "Mashrin Tamehr".

The remorse stoically suppressed, she initiates the dialog by scripting the ink with artistic finesse and gently lowers the book onto the head of his bunk, leaving the journal open for him to see before his subsequent entry. While her exposed skin seeks coverings from his armoire, her eyes wander to the makeshift library resting in piles and boxes bordering the northern wall. Despite the ridicule of his agnostic twin, his taste in literature has persisted, and she stalls her return for a journey through time.

The line between history, myth, and legend had been blurred throughout the ages, and what has materialized is a single man's sanction of fact or fiction in the halls of the official archives, but there, in the private quarters of an apprentice curator, the uncensored truths of remote civilizations congregate, lovingly preserved. From one gem to the next, she dives, thrilled with the diversity of narratives, perspectives, and styles, non-existent in this age of Unification, until her desirous fingertips linger on the fateful romantic tragedy that forever imprisons her soul.

The thinning air cautions her that the mist will soon clear and that a commotion over her scant attire could ensue, so she gathers her treasures and emitter, speeds home along the smoky catwalks to the Victory Bridge hatch, and stealthily slips into the deserted labyrinth. As she strolls underneath the floating causeway bisecting the primary canal, the ignorant pedestrians above her continue their blissful pace, oblivious to the hibernating poison beneath them. That has not always been the case.

Many humans had perished during the initial attempts at resettling the coastal cities, drowned in the planet's wrath when the intricate network of cooling ducts and vents originally operated. Similar to the gargantuan plants filtering the limey sea throughout the islands, smaller generators interlinked the imposing structures and pristine footpaths around them and kept the deadly gases at bay. Accidents had been frequent. One day, in spite of expertly documented and rehearsed evacuation procedures, the people working in the lower levels of the older office towers had collapsed beyond resuscitation, and their bodies had been sealed in the virulent cesspool that became their grave, turning the east district of this illustrious metropolis into submerged catacombs, where today only the lawless play.

Decades passed, and the memories of the dead fed the ghost stories of the living. Rumors abounded of creatures swimming in the depths, immune to the hydrogen sulphide sludge collecting on the ocean bed, whilst the Ministry revised the endorsed GHU statements to suit their own insidious needs and declared the zone restricted, pending further investigation. To the detriment of the current and future generations, the token surviving elders, who had witnessed the true potency of the disaster, no longer speak of it for fear of restraints, and the unwitting masses foolishly accept the fabrications of the misguided leadership.

▲ ▲ ▲

Her illegally extracted specimen is sufficiently replenished as she sighs with relief and attends to her encroaching fatigue. She proceeds to the roof to recharge her energy in the warmth of the afternoon rays and pauses to admire the landscape through the veil of the deluded. As she explores their naive viewpoint, her observations suggest a different interpretation of the fragile ecosystem in which humanity engages. She is alone, enjoying the calming bouquet of the swaying flora, while a temperate breeze caresses her bare thighs. Across the fluid horizon, lavender channels abound in petals of white, rose, violet, and blue, flawlessly arranged in silky blooms that flow to the rhythms of the circadian cycle. By nightfall they sleep and relinquish their dominant presence to a twinkling display of bioluminescent organisms that thrive on the veneer of the aqueous stillness. Between deep flexible green stems sings a whimsical symphony of light, color and sound. The structural eloquence, fundamental to the walkways, bridges, scaffolds, and sajadums, marries function and form to communicate their creators' passion for serenity to everyone treading their path. No aspect was left untouched by the detailed hand of the Gadlins, who, below the surface, skillfully concealed the slightest indication of vulnerability to the delicate chemical balance of their synergistic design. The breathtaking Central Core, with its immaculate gardens, ancestral monuments, and sophisticated mandalas, prevails, nonetheless, as their crowning achievement. Furthermore, were the oceans safe for leisurely crossings, the worldly traveler would undoubtedly revere the unparalleled ingenuity of the enveloping biowall. As the titanic tide comes crashing into the rugged shores, the imperceptible shield repels the toxins and balances the architectural masterpieces upon Eadonberg's liquid foundation, proudly showcasing her to admirers, as she stands majestically perched atop a watery cliff. The city skyline is simply stunning.

Nevertheless, this grand illusion does not beguile all. Without the tinted lens of the common resident, the utopian image transforms substantially. As the swell recedes, the fouler persona reveals itself. A mangled jungle of organic debris excretes noxious compounds that sink to the ocean's floor and invite symbiotic bacteria to aggravate the pollution.

They exist as a grim reminder of the real purpose of the pretty and seemingly innocuous milky lilac hue of the expansive aqueduct system. The conduits hanging off the lips of the buoyant pathways, with their thousands of exhaust shafts boring into the platforms like tumors stretching their bloody roots to the heavens, lie dormant as an ominous threat. Only the eastern sector of the city, caged within a growing fortress, dispenses with deception, and plainly illustrates the dangers of forgetting.

The buried past, unfortunately, has a habit of resurfacing, and judging by the changes in activity evident on the campus oval, the digging has already begun. Keeto and his friend have managed to escape the quarantine and are marching with determination through the bustling foot traffic. She sharpens her focus and maps a visual facsimile of his curious sidekick opposite yesterday's encounter at the ivy wall, then afterwards in the arcade, and unequivocally identifies him as one and the same. In the dark, his features were generally obscured, but the mannerisms are an absolute match, leading her to the disquieting suspicion that his involvement with the twins is not altogether accidental. Exactly how much they have confided in him at this point is unclear, but the unusual joining of minds with Keeto warrants some probing.

She traces their hike over the Victory Bridge and through the marble gate, as she formulates an inconspicuous plan to gain access to the archives. First and foremost, her adopted outfit poses a problem. Modesty permeates the cultural norms, and even though there are occasions when nudity is encouraged, such as during certain Unification rituals, daylight exposure is rare and tends to cause considerable upset. A ploy to enter the museum as a typical patron, clad in a pastel colored garment and carrying a mid-sized slippad, accords the best chance of success and requires minimal provisions. Winding back down the spiral staircase to her studio, she browses the area for her most demure ensemble. With several swift twirls of her wrists, she fashions a simple headdress, threads her impatient arms through the wide sleeves, collects her stage prop, and whirls down the steps to the main entrance, attaching the front panel of the robe across her right breast and knotting the belt, as she emerges from the building.

To embark upon the southbound hovertrain becomes her immediate mission. She competes for the nearest vacant marker and secures the back of the wrap, flush to her hairline, in anticipation of the boarding surge. Once seated, she registers the Central Core as her drop location and brings her breathing into alignment with her pulse, while the sequence controllers rearrange the exit queue. Amid the passenger shuffle, a distinguished individual, whom she recognizes as the administrative counsellor, fixes his eyes onto her as she is swept to the rear of the cabin in preparation for the plunge. Her heartbeat races and her face betrays her worries. He knows but somehow elects to remain unnaturally silent, perhaps counting on more compelling evidence to denounce her. Paralyzed by his implied attack, her brain tries to concentrate on her tactical concerns and to ascertain whether signs of her offenses have been wiped clean. Meanwhile, his disapproving glare burrows a hole in her armor, forcing her gaze to shamefully withdraw to her sandals. The short ride to the marble archway is unpleasantly tense.

As the craft closes in on her destination, she again glances at the pensive gentleman. To the casual observer, he would appear to be preoccupied with a mental conversation of his own; however, her intuitive skills are in no manner underdeveloped. Behind his aloof facade, he absorbs her thoughts, surely contemplating the most judicious timing to his ultimate reproach, and exudes an unspoken warning that leaves her rigid and moist. The importance of finalizing what the boys had interrupted last night is not to be undermined. But beforehand, she must learn the gist of the results from their medical lab caper, regardless of the judgment she is risking once the counsellor detects Mashrin's tragic state. Sensing the impending stop at the city center, he folds his arms as he scans the length of her figure. Her lungs compress with guilt. A nervous head check following the drop confirms the integrity of her disguise, and she resumes her anonymous venture into the round room, where she expects to spy the youths covertly sleuthing for leads.

By the Fountain of Bardo, the curator is entertaining a group of novices who have come from the settlements along the coast to conclude their training, under his esteemed tutelage. As she saunters past the arched entryway, flanked by the likenesses of famous historians, the attendant in the Great Hall signals her to advance briskly, so as not to disturb the session in progress, and inspects her permissions. The time elapsed since her previous visit has seen the entire staff and management replaced, which allows her charade as a spiritual sage to proceed unquestioned. Polishing a respectful bow, the young guide escorts her to the rim of the library, where a mute gathering of others of her pseudo status enlighten themselves. There, he lends her a personal automated librarian, which will safely fetch any ancient texts she wishes. She presents her gratitude in kind, quietly joins the other masters in the learning circle, and orients her position for an unobstructed view to the space in the middle, where the boys have carved out their research post.

Feigning an interest in the ecclesiastical ceremonies of the Ming Dynasty, she programs her PAL with a series of publications and releases it to the towering racks. While the loyal retriever is busy sniffing the shelves, she leans her recording tablet against the onyx counter before her, and convincingly directs her hands through the motions, whereas her actual business hovers just above the edge of her slips and straight down a constricting gap, angled akin to the spoke on a huge wheel converging toward the amateur detectives at its hub. Since the transport in from the highlands, she has been watching Keeto, waiting for the opportune moment to entice him into her world, and this very day, extended by last evening's audacious exchange, she seized it. His nocturnal sessions in the artifacts vault has sequestered him adequately from *them*, suitably engrossed as he is in his imagination and blind to her regular appearances. Captivated by the irreplaceable items he has been cataloging, he has exhibited the dreamy enthusiasm of a child, awed by a land full of adventure and intrigue, but today, he seems veritably focused on his task.

As he huddles over layers of periodicals in his usual seat at the broad circular table, occasionally nudging his unconventional colleague as he unearths fragments of relevant information, she studies his facial expressions for visible clues, while her PAL flies amidst the bookshelves and drops each manuscript in her lap as it grabs them. She pretends to read the documents, page after page, and monitors the pair diligently tackling their discouragingly tall mound until Keeto's pupils shrink into two pin-centered brown saucers. Of all the volumes painstakingly restored in this vast collection, he has coincidentally stumbled upon the pivotal editorial in their crusade and is feverishly devouring its contents, raising the eyebrows of at least one nearby onlooker with his hushed excitement. His partner, she senses, is reacting to the discovery with higher than average emotional attachment, in contrast with the intellectual detachment Keeto has assumed, yet the connection is intangible. He is a stranger to her and an unwelcome obstacle to circumvent.

Her next maneuver hinges on their staying immersed in the accounts they have assembled. She must approach them from the rear, masquerading as a humble philosopher aimed at the antiquities section in search of supporting elements for her dissertation, and as she drifts by, ingest the headlines on the news reports they are scouring. The crisp cerulean fibers beneath her modest robe threaten to expose themselves when her stride loosens the knot in her sash. A fleeting hint of her naked thigh catches the sunlight streaming from the crystal dome as she breaches the inner circle. Distracted by her efforts to conceal the clothing malfunction, she ends up on a collision course with a youthful academic walking towards her. He artfully avoids releasing a thunderous mess of parchments onto the tiles with a nimble leap to the side and acknowledges her with a courteous nod. She duly regains her composure and targets the large shimmering print as she veers left behind Keeto and his companion: "Rash of disappearances haunts parents of 9 year olds", "Missing child found with a slice of brain removed", "Common mark links all abductees, parents urged to contact GHU".

Keeto remembers, although she is not surprised. As a youngster, he had displayed the same reflective traits as he does now, cautiously assimilating wisdom beyond his years from the safety of his bedroom, while his sister grew bold and adventurous by overcoming increasingly punishing battles with her internal demons. Nathruyu remembers as well. The captions are as chords plucked on a timeless instrument in near perfect harmony with the ongoing melody, bound inside the void by the cyclical nature of the universe. Her awareness travels there for an instant as she analyzes their significance in the larger context. To intercept the process that will lead him to an ill-favored conclusion has become her highest priority. As Keeto finishes the article transcription and re-shifts his attention to his surroundings, she slides into the adjacent aisle, retreats to the perimeter and arcs her way behind the stacks and towards the exit, shrouding her profile with her sleeve, as naturally as possible. She must retrieve the girl.

Back on her rooftop terrace, she stares wistfully into the sunset. She currently finds herself faced with diminishing alternatives and is reevaluating the soundness of her decisions. For the latter part of the afternoon, she has been consumed by a visceral need to reconcile her doubts with her convictions, but the turmoil persists. She had opted to sever the ties with the father and withhold their whereabouts, thus breaking her precarious bond of trust with him and alienating a useful government insider. Tonight, as her hopefully enlisted ally shares the message in his journal with his sister and their cohort at the Snack Shack, she surrenders to the circumstances and prepares to reclaim the body, lest the GMU order its release to the Special Investigation Force. This particular transgression cannot be contained, as there are three civilian witnesses, two of whom are intent on dodging entanglements with authorities, but the third has yet to reveal his complete saga. Eventually, he will falter, and when he does…

E L I Z E

I can feel him watching me. We're back. Turn around and say something. The floor is clear.

"Here, Stitch. Your thrower."

"No. Keep it, just in case. I have another one." You can let go of my hand now. Why is he so serious?

Caroline! She'll be waiting. Quick, an out. "Lockdown in three. You'd better get back."

He's not leaving. What is wrong with him? They're hiding behind his head and peeking around the sides. Are they? Yeah. They're shy. Wait. They're squirming. Is he nervous?

"I can stay with you tonight if you need me."

For what? Seriously. "I'm fine. No one can bust through the fuzz patrol anyway."

"I can." He has a point.

Oh, enough. I have to get to the daze. He doesn't suspect, does he?

"Who'll protect me from *you* then?" Nudge. Not even a smile. This new Zafarian is morose. Now it's my arm.

"Be careful. I won't be far." He's actually worried. Sweet but unnecessary.

Crap! "They're waking. Clip." And so should I.

No time for much. What to wear. The purple one. The blue. Juicy. A bit of skin glow, some lashes, and... No biting! I'm your owner, remember? Mother's jewel. No. I'd better not.

Now don't you start with me. Stop talking! Silence? That was fast. Maybe the bump on the head fixed something up there. Oops, the hat. Have to ditch that look. I'll need to cover... Hey, it's... I'll deal with that later. Focus. Ok. I'm missing something. Yeah. Caroline's medical slip, and I'll chew on the way.

Now where's that dribble dropper. At the lift. Grab the handy frequency thrower and... How about a door slam? Stitch is right. It's just too easy. Quick. In the lift. Wait for it...and now a thump. Perfect. Time to clear the lobby. Good. Outside at last. It's so dead with this curfew. That's strange. The lights are out in the orchard. I'd better watch where I'm walking this time. What was that? Freeze! Nothing. Just head for the front gate and stop scaring yourself. Brrr. Did they forget to turn the blowers off? Ok. Now, to get past the... Juicy! The gate is unguarded. But why? Something's not right. He should be right... Oh, no. Don't look. Ahhhhhh!

The protector he's... Crap. I'd better get out of here before someone comes looking for him. Creeps. What if it's... No. Enough already. Just get across the Victory Bridge and head north. Caroline is waiting. Where did I put those directions? Hick. Forgot them. Over there. That man probably knows.

"Excuse me. Can you point me to Almedina Square?" He's frowning at me.

"Almedina Square?"

"Yes. Is it far?"

"Not far enough. Are you sure you want to go there? Alone?" What does he mean by that?

Feeling a little anxious now. "I'm meeting a friend. Is there a problem?" He's acting like he's checking for GMU taggers or something.

"Nobody goes there. It's not safe."

Oh oh. What is Caroline into? Well, I can't turn back now. He's reluctant. Think of something compelling.

"Then I need to get there fast to warn her." Good. He has a slipmap. He's in the maze.

"Of course. Let's see. Ah, yes. Here, take this slip and just follow the blue dot. And be careful. If you start to feel weak, run. And don't look back."

"Thank you."

That was a little disturbing. Can't be worse than last night. I think. Don't quite remember actually. It looks close enough. A bit north, then east near the shores. There's the hovertrain. Whoa! Gets me every time. Now I can relax for a bit until I reach the junction. There it is. Fast ride tonight. I'll just switch to the east-west line and I'm juicy. Destination Almedina— five drops. Phew! Almost there.

"Hey lo, girl." I recognize that giggle.

"Hey lo, Caroline. It's been crazed. I wasn't sure how I'd get out. Everyone got tagged last night."

"No rib! That explains the graveyard today. Hurts, yeah?"

"Eh?" She's pointing to the back of her head. Right, the tag. "Oh that! Like a mangled scan! But it's bearable."

"Not that you've had one though, yeah?" She's looking for my reaction. Don't get baited into it. "So...you solved the mystery then." Stay calm. Try not to look nervous, just puzzled. "The exception." The exception? Oh right.

"Expired program. Quick patch." Pass her the slip. "It was

stuck to mine." Not a flinch. I'd better keep my voice down. "I think you're being tracked." Maybe she didn't hear me. "I think..."

"Shhh." She leans into me, grabs my sleeve tightly and points her eyebrows to her left. "The guy, three seats over with the black hair. Don't look!"

Well, it's a little late now. Crap. He's staring back. Act normal. Slowly look at someone else. Caroline. She's starting to tense up.

"Have you seen him before?" She pulls in closer to me, but I can barely hear her reply. She's not breathing. This is not good. "Caroline? You know him?"

"No. But wouldn't mind a piece though, yeah?"

Oh, the little punk. I fell right into that one. "You're bent." She's laughing now.

"We're going to have fun tonight."

"You mean *you're* going to have fun." I think I need a wipe.

"Oh, ride it, girl. You're in the big city now. After tonight, you'll be back for more. Trust me."

Trust? Right. You first.

"Why is the GHU so interested in you, Caroline?"

"My temperature often drops below optimal. They're always looking for viruses. Afraid of a spread." A mischievous smirk. "They haven't caught me yet." She and Stitch would get along I'm sure. "And you? How did you break out?"

"I can trust you?"

"Of course. The drop's coming up." Here we go.

She turns to me on the platform and giggles, then proceeds to muss my hair into an organized mess. "Thanks. Forgot the hat head syndrome."

"And..."

"This thing is a frequency thrower, and the bangle rubs them out, kind of like a noise maker and a scan jam." She doesn't need to know where I got them.

"Trip. You won't be needing them where we're going though. Best hide them." She's distracted. "Nice skirt. Looks like a VLine." She's checking the courtyard exits. Am I missing something? "And you've spent some time on the slick. I know a few regulars who are going to like you." She winks. Her legs are pretty strong as well. "Have you competed?"

"Been planing since the age of three. How about you?" My hair roots are stiffening.

"On and off. There's a rink on the west side by the transport station. You can't pass it."

"That's great! I've been missing the workout." And the freedom. It's like I leave the whole world behind and enter a new dimension where every part of me resonates in harmony with the universe. I used to dance for hours. Father had to drag me off. I hated him for that. I've never admitted this to Keet, but after the accident, I would go there to escape the voices and be with Mother. I miss that. I miss her.

"Just the workout?" She's smiling softly at me. Sigh. I wish I could talk to her. All these secrets. All this hurt bottled up inside. But I can't risk it. Hold it together. Rub the hair on my arms down. Take a deep breath. It's just your imagination.

"Let's daze."

"That's the spirit. Just through the east corridor. Follow close. We have to be quick." She's on edge. Pay attention.

It's a lot warmer here, being closer to the land. There's some mist forming on the ground. The cooling vents must be blocked, I can feel the heat rising up my skirt. It must be too hot to bear during the high sun. She's really blistering. Any faster and we'd be running. I am having second thoughts about this. I can't see where we're going. I really don't want a repeat of the arcade. Night flyers and a light. Good. She's stopped.

"Over there. There's an opening we can slip through." She *can't* be serious. That's the restricted sector and a living wall. I'm not a believer, but what if there is some shred of truth in the stories... All myths have some basis in fact, right?

"Wait!" Crap. She's gone. Footsteps. Panic. Ok. I've come this far.

"Grab my hand." Got it. Ugh! What's that smell? Gag. "You'll get used to it soon enough. It won't kill you unless you're boxed in. No pretty lavender in these waters." She's right. The channels are disgusting, and there's yellow soot everywhere.

Are those people? "There are actually people living here?" Why would anyone want to live here?

"If you want to call them that." She points to a group leaning out the shattered window of a tower, the scaffold half-rusted and dragging into the sludge. "They don't remember what being a person is. Most of them have been here too long. They're off the scan, so no one knows they're here, not even the GHU. It's freedom. Everybody is running from something. Or someone." And so is she, I sense.

She leads me towards a narrow beam wedged into the side of a small structure a few buildings away and starts walking across. I should be used to this by now. Ok. Here it goes.

"You ever been in one of these?"

"What is it?" All I see is a door.

She pushes a button and the door opens. "An ancient lift. It works on a cable system, so it's a bit slow. Jump in."

Surprise! The back wall is glass. Look at all that junk. Everything is just suspended and there are things moving around in there. It must be the currents. There can't be anything living in there. Eek! What the…

"You see them sometimes, floating around, the ones that haven't been swept. Most of them still decomposing. It's a slow process in these waters; there are no scavengers except for bacteria."

"What happened here?"

"Explosions, I think. It happened before either of us were born. The newer ones like that one." Jumpers! "Yeah. They say they were workers hired to clean up and seal the buildings again. No one can trace us in here, you see. We're too far down. No one can find us if something happens." Well, that's not very comforting.

The lift opens onto a long hallway leading to another door. I follow her through and just stand there in disbelief. I don't know what I am looking at. There's a ledge, then a ditch with two steel beams running through and into tunnels at either end. Is it some sort of transport system?

"It's called a subway. We're under the ocean floor. This one is safe, but not all of them are. An air vent goes up more than three hundred meters to the surface. Hop down. We need to walk to the next station."

How am I going to explain this to Keet? I wonder if Stitch knows about this. Or should I say Zafarian. I'm sure he does. I regret not telling them.

"Through here, Eli. Shhh. Let them pass."

Who? Heart, stop pounding. Hands, hold steady. Just close your eyes. No. Open them. Figures. Scream time.

"Eek! Eli, you little—"

"What are you doing here, Keet?"

Stitch is really rolling in it. "Pica trip, chum. Priceless." Hehehe. "You're head. Healed already?"

"I gave Eli a bioskin this morning. Works fast, eh?" Keet and I lock eyes. We'll need to talk about that later.

"You *know* these people, Eli? They've been following us since Almedina Square."

"I *thought* you were a bit preoccupied. That's my cousin, Keet, and our friend, Stitch."

"Trip. I'm Caroline." She's giving Keet the standard cheek to cheek lowland greeting. Hmmm. Holding the back of his head? She's flirting with him. "The juicy one."

Keet is actually blushing. Catch her.

She's dizzy. "I'm fine, just leaned over too far." Right. I don't believe that one. "And Stitch you said?" She's in for a treat. "Crazed!" Hehehe. That hair will do it every time.

Oh please! Stand on your legs, boy! She's not *that* mesmerizing. "Boys!" My giggly friend turns serious on me now. How I'd like to know what her voices are telling her.

"Ok. Just act like you've been here before, yeah? And there shouldn't be any scuffs." She's staring straight at Stitch. "Just ahead. Through that red door. I'll have to make up some story to get you guys in, so just let me do the talking, yeah?"

"I'm trip with that."

That's some huge door. It's so cold here. Caroline's the only one not shivering.

"You get used to it." Stitch is not looking good at all. His hair is out of control. Loosen up. The door's opening. This is it. You wanted a party. "Way, Banique." She is quite the charmer.

"Sweet sweet sweet Caroline. Lend me that soft cheek of yours. You break my heart." He's looking at Keet and Stitch and being quite dramatic.

"Eli, Keet, Stitch. You trip, Banique?"

I do believe this guy is in love with her. How does she do it? "Oh, the shards! Be good." He hands her four small tubes and she puts them in a hidden pocket.

"Always." She winks at him and strokes his shoulder as she slinks by. Impressive. We're in, but she's looking concerned. Keet gets the up-down. "Keet, take a look around." Finally! He might listen to her. "You need help in the style department. Stitch? Can you do something about that?" I'm going to bust.

"Da Ya. To the bang-o, bud." I can't wait to see what Stitch is going to come up with.

"He has a language of his own, your friend." She has no idea. "He shouldn't be here."

Well, I certainly didn't invite him or Keet. Who is she looking at? In the corner, that man. I've felt his eyes on us since we walked in.

"Who is he? In the corner."

"The Pramam's advisor."

"Whoa! For real?"

Yeah. She's serious. "He's a regular. How do you think this place exists? Want to meet him?"

"No, thanks." Crap. I have to get out of here.

"It pays to have a friend in the Ministry, yeah?" All I can do is shake my head. She must smell the fear. I want to go now. "Ease, girl. I was scared the first time too. Next time." She waves at him and blows him a kiss.

Someone's coming over. And the advisor keeps staring at us from the corner.

"Way, Caroline. Who's your new friend?"

"Mine. Now trip out." Wow! That was rude. "You'll want to stay away from that one, he has poor control. You'll need to build up to him."

I'm confused. "What exactly is this place?" The music is earthy. The rhythms are good, and everyone seems into it, in a trance-like way.

"Sit with me. Feel the energy. Close your eyes, it helps get you connected. Do you feel it? This is the world they don't want you to see. It's pure sensation. That's why he comes here. Do you feel him?"

What's happening to me? I'm feeling so...everything is so... My heartbeat... I'm so hungry, thirsty, I want to just...take a piece out of someone. Stop it! They're pumping something in here. Open your eyes. I'm burning up all of a sudden. It's just so hot in here. What's happening? What's everyone staring at?

"Caroline? What?"

"Stay here."

Why are they taking so long? Here they come. Hurry up,

boys. They're getting distracted. What's Caroline doing? The other girls don't look too happy. She sure means business. She's doing the up-down on Keet again.

"Good job, Stitch! Have a seat." I wish I had a flash of this. "Everybody just…stay calm." She's keeping Stitch especially close to her.

Ooo, I think Keet is jealous. Have to use this one later. Yes.

It's the creepy officials! I can't let them recognize me. What are they doing here? We're jam. They're trotting over to talk to the advisor. Everyone is afraid of them, they're sweating. I'm soaked. Keet's sensing something too. I need some answers.

"Caroline?"

"They won't touch us. Not while he's here. We're safe." She looks over at Stitch. "But he's not. We should go." What does she mean by that?

"We just arrived, Eli, I like it here, it's pumped." I don't believe it. The pup is hyped for the daze while Stitch is hanging low.

They're looking over. Oh no. They're heading this way.

"Now!" Caroline's right. She waves to Banique and we make for the back while he intercepts their pursuit.

"I thought you said we were safe, Caroline."

"Well, maybe there's something you need to share, Eli?" She pulls out the tubes Banique gave her and hands one to each of us. "Here. Put these masks on. No time for questions."

Keet is glaring at me. I'm the one who should be angry. If it weren't for him and Stitch, we wouldn't be stuck skulking around these shafts in the dark. Or maybe it's me, skipping off campus. Good. There's a partially lit opening. A way out?

"Don't look up. I'll go last. Keet, you first. Stitch, you're next. Lock your arms in the rungs if you feel dizzy. We'll support you. Then you, Eli. Slow and steady on my count. Keet, stop at nine hundred. They can't follow us in here, but they'll be waiting for you at the Victory Bridge."

Breathe in. Breathe out. Breathe in. Breathe out. And again. Deep. And let it all out. You can do this. Don't think, just move.

✄ ✄ ✄

"Here. Put your wet clothes over there. Stitch, grab those sheets."

I'm drenched. Where am I? There's Sparky. We're in Keet's room. "Where's Caroline?"

"She kept west once we reached under the central corridor. Dry off your hair with this. You two can sneak back to campus in the fog. Your decoy good for the night, Stitch?"

"Yeah. Trip. It'll scan right, but Eli…"

"They can't scan my room." It's time to trust him.

"What? And what just happened down there, chum? Did you see the bodies?"

Keet's quiet. His eyes are searching mine for answers. But I have none.

Day 30: late evening

We've made some progress over the last four days, mostly due to Stitch's efforts. Ever since our trip to the restricted sector, he has devoted every free minute to sinking his probes deeper into the maze, even while his drained energy levels were working against him. It took him a full three days before he could regain complete motor capacity after that night. None of us have been able to determine what afflicted him and spared us, and the only person who might have some answers has disappeared. Caroline is not responding to any comms, and she is nowhere to be seen on campus. In fact, I don't even know if she survived the ventilation shafts after we split up. Eli has been concentrating on securing an interview with Dr. Tenille, completing extra assignments and staying late after class to prove her commitment, and I have been overcompensating for my unauthorized late start at work the following morning in order to regain the curator's favor after explaining my delinquency with a fictitious post-tag headache. So you see, Stitch has really taken the lead.

It's a mystery though, how Eli's gash healed so quickly, and even her episodes, she tells me, have been less frequent. If a bump on her head was all she needed, then I would have gladly obliged on several occasions. A specific instance when we were fighting over your board game vividly comes to mind. Perhaps it is related to her malfunctioning biochip, or conceivably whatever is blocking scans into her room could be affecting her space and her in it. Well, from the physical perspective at least. The voices may have decreased, but the extensive lapse she suffered in the shafts clearly indicates a partial recovery at best. I imagine that is what is driving Stitch's intensive research, even though he is only aware of one aspect of her sickness. According to the packets he has managed to intercept and decode, every single case of memory loss has led to an MPD diagnosis and subsequent permanent GHU hospitalization or premature death.

My conscience struggles with continuing to withhold information from him, especially given his genuine concern for Eli. He could easily dissect her medical history just like he did Mashrin's, if he has not already done so, and expose our true family history. All he needs to do is investigate far back enough into the GHU records to find you, and ultimately draw the connection between us, providing the details are still present. I fear that not revealing ourselves to him is actually endangering Eli beyond my ability to protect her, slowing our progress while the hunters regroup, yet part of me will not trust, not even myself. In his desperation to hide the truth from us, Father has groomed us well. As with any gifted apprentice, we have surpassed our grand master in his craft of deceit and have built relationships on a foundation of lies, including our own with each other and ourselves. But not with you.

The reports are conclusive. A common mark, disclosed only to the parents of children detected with it by the GHU, connects the victims with their fate, a fate that by association would befall Eli and similarly myself. However, through a fortunate yet traumatic chain of events, we are coincidentally in possession of the precise knowledge that can alter the course of a sinister destiny we were not even aware of. This ignorance began, as expected, with another one of Father's lies. About a year after the accident, Eli was in her room stroking her hair with your hand carved brush, just like you used to. It had become a daily ritual for her, at first light, to soothe her weeping, and it lasted until she heard Father stir. One morning, after a particularly intense night, I found her sitting at her vanity, brushing and brushing and brushing while tears rolled down her face. She was trying to make a ponytail, but her hands were still too tiny, so I gently took the brush from her and started at the back. That's when I saw it. The mark that sent Eli's nails digging into my arm at the medical lab. Alarmed, I called for Father who chastised me for frightening my sister and told us it was just a birthmark, and that because we were twins, I had the same one. He then forbade us to discuss the matter any further with anyone, or the GHU would take us away.

Since the daze, almost as a means of survival it seems, we have been avoiding any meaningful conversation about our increasingly precarious circumstances, preferring instead to occupy our minds with the day to day and foolishly expecting that by some miracle the nightmare will vanish. Was a reprieve what Eli needed in order to restore her shattered spirit? She certainly was more open to listening to our theories earlier today, especially considering the GMU secret bulletin Stitch uncovered that listed a third defender murdered at the main campus entrance on that very evening. I also confronted her directly about the three officials who chased us, and she admitted that they were in fact the ones who have been sniffing around since the first day at the transport station, a confession which aggravated Stitch's already resentful attitude towards our apparent distrust of him.

Fortunately, Eli adeptly diffused the situation by accepting full responsibility for her fears with respect to close relationships, without belaboring the effects of her oppressed childhood. She explained that it has been in no way a reflection of his character. I don't blame him for his outburst though. We had accepted his unconditional trust, at great personal risk to himself, and had offered nothing but lies in return. I could see the shame in her eyes, so I grabbed her hand and squeezed, further exacerbating the exchanges and gave my consent at last.

He already knew about how the sweep had bypassed Eli's room and her lapses, having witnessed two already, but the nightmares, the voices, the officials, our flight, and our true connection as brother and sister were a total revelation to him. We apologized that there was too much detail to convey all at once, and that we had probably overlooked key components that could provide a better grasp of how our accidental involvement in these crimes could impact the future. The two significant areas I personally avoided mentioning, other than your own affliction and its pivotal role in our lives, were the marks and malfunctioning biochips that each of us carry, although from our description of Eli's delicate mental state, it is not difficult to imagine that he has already inferred a direct link to her malfunction at least. Highlighting the mark would only have served to raise his level of anxiety beyond what is necessary to stay focused on our mission to save her.

Having patiently listened to the agony of our plight, Stitch graciously reciprocated with a tortuous tale of his own. His mother's brother and sister-in-law had perished on a barge crossing of the Magyar Sea, and their infant son was found floating near its shores, amazingly alive and conscious. The next of kin was swiftly traced and a sweet woman arrived at their doorstep with his cousin lovingly wrapped in her arms. They were born just one month apart and immediately formed an inseparable bond, which he fondly recalls as "the unified front against Jicaro the Tyrant", his older brother. That's where all the mischief began I'm sure. Shortly after Zbrietz's third birthday, he developed a second personality that the duo adopted as their imaginary friend. But his parents became concerned and the GHU became involved. There were months where he would lie in his cell, listless, sedated and restrained while they ran their series of tests, always claiming to find nothing, then releasing him to his heartbroken guardians. Then one day, after his ninth birthday, he simply disappeared. His body was discovered a few weeks later. Since then, Stitch has been searching for answers. He finally laid his cousin to rest that afternoon with me in the archives. The child with the mutilated brain was undeniably Zbrietz.

By the time he had finished his story, all was said that needed to be at this juncture, and we bowed our heads in quiet meditation. We then improvised a group chumbuds salute and recommitted our energies to the present. I had a shelf to buy, and Stitch knew the perfect shop to suit my peculiar tastes.

A few buildings west of the hostel where we'd spent our first night in the city, there is a glass courtyard centered around a jade fountain and bordered by quaint shops, tightly stacked side-by-side. An ornate white boutique with a patched clay roof lies on the western edge of the square, with an enchanting view of the mythical horse of Tir-na-nog reenacting the last voyage of Oisin, hovering on the mirrored surface of the wishing well. While Eli and Stitch attempted to distract the holorider with a water fight, I captured their childlike enthusiasm with my recorder. It was the first time in recent history that I had seen her truly enjoy a carefree moment, and I wanted to ensure I could rely on this feeling to lift me above the challenging trials that lay ahead. This afternoon was dedicated to whimsical exploration, but on my personal agenda was digging for treasures.

An attractive gentleman sporting a white fedora greeted Stitch with a thunderous laugh as he toyed with Stitch's hair. Apparently, Mr. G had introduced him to the wriggly mess, which Stitch promptly adapted from its original purpose of sensing harmful frequency waves, to key off emotional vibes instead. Eli, I noticed, was quite taken by his lean physique, long neck, and sharp features, as she commented on how he reminded her of a beautiful gold statue she had seen in the Museum of Antiquities. Much to her embarrassment, she started to blush when she realized how audacious her comment must have sounded, but his good-hearted response rapidly put her at ease. I must concede that he does have the stoic appearance of a Roman emperor.

I must also acknowledge Stitch's keen design sense, for

at least half of the items in this store were physically crafted ages ago, many having the perfect decorative touches for my faux marble walls. While I deliberated between the various book display units, refreshingly devoid of sharp teeth may I add, Stitch browsed the small bioclothing section, while Eli terrorized an early model crabseat. She has never forgiven the species for her sudden dunk in Bermuda Gorge, as we used to call it, when her reclining model instinctively scampered into the waters taking her along for the ride. Hybrid architects have the best jobs. There never ceases to be a playful side to their creations although it is always more amusing when the "special" features have their fun at someone else's expense.

As Mr. G was congratulating me on my eventual choice, his entire body suddenly began violently tossing back and forth to the rhythms of his breathing. I clamored for the nearest counter as I noticed myself writhing in tandem. Stitch snatched Eli from beneath the collapsing mezzanine and hollered at us to "Clip out!" By the time we reached the fountain, the tremors had stopped, the entire loft had crumbled, the back wall lay open to the neighboring waterway, the courtyard had transformed into a random mosaic of transparent shards capriciously held together by a thin protective sandwich, and the sky was filled with shooting stars flying past the blinding sun setting in the east. The channels comprising the perimeter of the square had spilled onto the adjoining walkways, leaving them slick with lavender and green, covered in stray petals of white, rose, purple, and blue, but the structures intact. The quake had only compromised the commercial sector.

As the skies continued to rain tiny balls of fire, I shadowed

Mr. G's enraptured gaze towards the falling meteors. "Isn't she beautiful?" he sighed to me. When I asked who he was talking about, he replied: "My sky, her tears caressing the earth with such passion," but through the shell-shocked crowd, I could distinguish a female form fading in the distance. Eli, quick with the rib as always, teased me about him being afflicted by the same virus I had caught on the hovertrain platform our first day in. "He may look like a warrior," she commented, "but he whimpers like a pup," no doubt referring to my formidable canine guard.

The emergency crews would soon appear to attend to the injured, so we trusted our safety to the integrity of the platform, ran back into the shop to gather our purchases and fled to the central corridor as the red crafts arrived. After we had dropped off the two shelves at my quarters, we continued on to the campus oval for a meal at the commons, where Stitch proudly modeled his blindingly bright new coveralls. I honestly do not see the logic in owning a wilderness suit in the city, but somehow I am sure he will find a use for it, or otherwise create an entertaining opportunity to wear it, but after the freak seismic activity we had just survived, a lifeshield would have been a wiser investment, in my opinion. Regardless, the city secretary was likely already fabricating some semi-plausible fiction about the event, and Stitch wanted to be the first to debunk it, so he packed down his food and assalammed.

Eli and I retreated to her room where we could safely resume our earlier discussions. The altercation at the club still troubled me. The three ministry thugs were getting too close, and with another colleague eliminated and Eli's porous alibi, I feared they might consider her suspect. They could have already scanned through the student roster, matched her picture against their internal flashes, and tracked her to this floor, making her vulnerable to detainment. A quick comm to Stitch calmed my nerves, as he had already doctored her registration records the morning after the daze with a credible alternate image. With that exposure eliminated, we delved deeper into their obscure interest in us from the start, prompting Eli to admit their role as the voices outside our kitchen window.

They are looking for something important and the clues may rest in the flashes we took from Father's office. Eli had already reviewed them soon after we arrived here and had found nothing out of the ordinary; however, given that we had gained so much new awareness since then, we decided to inspect the images within a different context. We also chose to interact with the main viewing room instead of one of the thirty-six satellite offshoots around the center branch perimeter on level zero, which would give us more than enough space to accurately recreate most experiences on a one-to-one scale, especially the ones recorded inside the rooms of our childhood home. Although usually reserved for group communications and motion capture productions, the ongoing lockdown confined the use of shared facilities to a restrictive schedule, making them conveniently accessible to wily participants like ourselves.

Thanks to Stitch, getting past the sentinels was no longer much of a challenge. While Eli sealed the doors, I hurried to the console wall and snapped the flashpack in. We had taken the audio headsets from Father's study as well, so we could still immerse ourselves in a complete sensory recreation without tugging the ears of the gob-happy sentries. We then boldly stepped into the first frame and let his world unfold. Since I had not actually navigated these memories before, I was relying on Eli's interpretation of what partial images she was able to detect mirrored in the cabinetry behind him, as his eyes followed them on the board. When we reached the section where Father's jaw would tighten, she looked over and nodded, then we each took a different vantage point to get a combined panoramic view of the scene.

Over and over again, we followed Father's lens, desperate to catch a glimpse of anything disconcerting, but it just did not make sense. What had changed for him the last time he had played this? There was nothing happening at our ninth birthday celebration which could worry a parent, yet according to Eli, every time he reached this scene he would tremble until it was over, almost as if he was expecting something other than the joyous sound of children playing their favorite indoor games. I concluded that the flashes were not the object of their quest. We each had filled a large transfer chest, and in my case several, with items of varying financial value, some of which may even be priceless, but what would the Ministry need of riches?

There was no denying that we had been avoiding the painful task of digging through our baggage, although I seem to have no issue doing so with the museum artifacts. Since Eli's morning was free, we committed to starting tonight with my effects for as long it takes. I also reluctantly agreed that we could no longer risk traveling together, in case she was identified, so while she checked in with Stitch's progress, I would head back and journal until she arrived. But before we parted, we decided to switch to spectator mode and restart the viewer.

In doing so, we were able to stand behind the recorder and look beyond the living room where our younger selves were laughing, and down the hallway supporting the staircase. And on that wall, there was a mirror, reflecting our lives through the kitchen and out the window, where a solitary figure stood, watching. My heart stopped. I froze the scene and walked towards the reflection, with Eli clutching me as we approached. We knew those gemstone eyes.

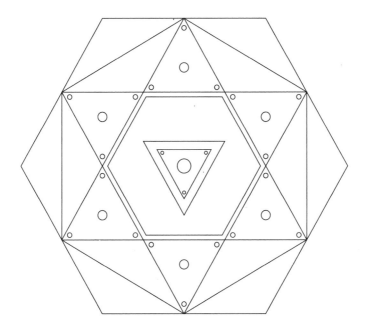

CHAPTER SIX

N A T H R U Y U

Day 31: early morning

As her shoulder casually leans against a manicured replica of Manetho, Nathruyu eagerly awaits the arrival of frantic footsteps. Five days ago, on the evening Keeto had disclosed her entry in his journal, she had re-infiltrated Osler Hall desperate to redeem herself and recover her abandoned charge, only to find the innocent victim missing and the observation cell immaculate. Unfortunately, a third sentry had succumbed to her craft in the attempt. Since then, her patience with the unwitting Zafarian has endowed her with transparent access to their undercover resources, an impromptu rendezvous with his Gadlin mentor, and timely updates on how their investigation is progressing. Specifically, with Odwin's reluctantly surrendered identity, she can sketch through the tightest and most secure layers of the maze to manipulate any history she may deem necessary to fulfil her objective and to navigate by floating between the packets. The hapless hunted has reclaimed her role as a skillful hunter.

Immediately after the failed retrieval in the medical lab, she had reverted to the ventilation shafts and had shifted her attention to the Social Studies sector. While skimming Keeto's diary pages that morning, she had formulated a general picture of an encroaching nuisance she was impatient to eradicate. Elize's first true friend, excluding her immediate home circle, posed a plausible threat, and his poorly concealed and impassioned reaction to the news reports in the round room, coupled with his keen affection for parapsychology and the paranormal made him exceptionally unpredictable. Fundamentally, Nathruyu questioned Zafarian's grounding in this world and feared it could cause some instability, impelling her to address the issue. Knowing that most of his curriculum was concentrated in Bleuler Hall, directly opposite Rubrique Court's principle archway, she had camped alongside its cooling generator that night and had entrusted her worries to the warmth of the blue flame.

As the hazy version of Nathruyu's mirrored self slowly surrenders to fatigue, she recalls her last waking thoughts preceding the visit with the young sleuth. No manner of imagined retribution must ever again sway her course, and whatever thread of compassion had existed leading up to this renewed commitment no longer serves her purpose. She must continue the work.

▼ ▼ ▼

Such unnecessary suffering for the glory of one is unavoidable. The mark chooses the child and the choice seals their fate. As she cradles the fragile frame next to her breast, the impulse within her that forces her hand cannot be contained, cannot be smothered, and cannot be rationalized. From the supple skin of a girl's skull, the sparkle is reaped, the fortune is sown, and the confused years in limbo are sacrificed. Nathruyu weeps, for sequestering her body decisively yet involuntarily is essential to their ultimate survival and leaving her adrift in the chaos is a risk she is not looking to bear.

▲ ▲ ▲

Nathruyu's anxiety gives way to calm, and clarity regains control of her doubting voices. There was no concrete evidence linking her to Mashrin, and regardless of enduring residual imprints, she is not traceable in the records of the GMU, of the Ministry, or even of the Pramam himself. She has been so fastidious in erasing her trail this time that just a single individual can unequivocally identify her, and the possibility of facing him excites her in ways indescribable.

She loiters, invisibly tucked inside the fenced museum property, and replays her latest visions on an indigo cloud in the fog, as the curator brushes by the adjacent columns, oblivious to the entity lurking beside the carved relief. His passage momentarily pulls her out of reflection before she plunges deeper into the drama.

▼ ▼ ▼

When the groggy shuffling of students congregates at her section of the square, she flattens the wrinkles in her coat and rises from the sombre tunnels. Her spatial acuity guides her exactly to the enclosed landing of the auditorium. She proceeds to the air lock and orients her face away from the beveled glass, while the heat exchangers evaporate the misty puffs that followed her in. Once her silhouette is plainly visible from the interior of the building, she rushes through the second set of doors and to the sunken room on the left. Pacing back and forth at center stage, down the steps of the lecture theater aisles, a dowdy professor is pontificating on his seminal theory of the id, the ego, and the super-ego, shamelessly plagiarizing the ancient dissertations of Sigmund Freud, whereas her target is gainfully preoccupied with the pink of his eyelids. She hides in the shadows, patiently waits for the mass dispersal, then swiftly tags his dragging collar as he ambles amongst the horde.

Puzzled, she tracks his clumsy gait prematurely retiring to the south central branch of Van Billund Hall, and realizes that he has been afflicted by an all too familiar sickness. She knows what he did last night. She knows whom he saw. The fool has faltered, and the forecasted lapse of alertness has occurred, ripe for her to exploit his vulnerability as she wishes. She revels in the prospect of it and quickens her pace through the arcade. After curving around the west side of the towers, she cloaks her distinguishing features with her hair, darts past the scanner, immobilizes the presiding guard and flies up the lift to level five. Determined to eliminate the thorn she perceives as the lone obstacle in her path, she summons the surrounding energy to steady her nerves, and squeezes, undetected, through the crack in his door, where she finds him slumped in front of the board, his query in mid-sketch.

The stroke that was to be his climactic twitch becomes the gesture that saves his life. The request is complete and a packet appears with the secret seal of her double-crossing nemesis. What agency lies dormant at his beckoning? Does this character seriously comprehend the total magnitude of his power? Confident that the boy will be unconscious for a good hour, she wiggles her prying fingers along the slits of his clothing and studies his intimate details as the results from his research trickle in.

The gadgets and covert equipment that this singular young man has strewn across every conceivable surface are only eclipsed by the mastermind web he is connected to. Whilst she forages among the clutter assessing the extent of his technological genius, her focus abruptly switches to an incoming communication from the maze, confirming an appointment for a therapeutic intervention, to which she forges a reply. She will attend in his stead. She replaces the content of the message with a benign herbal prescription, which will keep Zafarian occupied once he awakes and will give her the leeway she needs to handle the new situation. Satisfied with her clever pretense, Nathruyu redirects her aggression to the coastal shores. Zafarian's connection to the itinerant merchant could prove monumentally advantageous.

▲ ▲ ▲

Many people have been entering the gateway, but none have emerged, and the hushed apprentices, assembling in the vestibule, suggest that their mentor is preparing to resume his teachings by the Fountain of Bardo. The squirmy-haired Gadlin descendant, however, has had his lifelong mentoring unexpectedly terminated, yet deception has him believing otherwise.

The swirling fog captures an auspicious scene in the sulfur dusted escarpment flanking an overgrown roadway.

▼ ▼ ▼

The entrance is barely discernible, and if it were not for the lingering memory of this place, Nathruyu's nimble limbs would have missed a chance to challenge the integrity of the steep incline. The onshore breeze keeps her scent obscured, while she traverses the narrow lip, above the jagged slabs in the putrid sludge below. As she hesitates, with her palms gingerly spread along the false bluff, Odwin slides open the sandstone decoy and thwarts the ambush. Her rendezvous is stripped of the element of surprise. She must therefore shrewdly negotiate the altered terrain using her signature smile and deceive her host with pleasant posturing. Defeated by her unspoken words, Odwin stumbles backwards inside his uncharted shelter off the remote passage to the strongholds and regretfully submits to his destiny.

Nathruyu steps into the rustic den and surveys the walls for disguised chambers, then turns to her old acquaintance. He sits, despondent, on a wooden chair beside a colorful map etched in the rock, representing the continents as they were ages ago, prior to the Great Ocean Swell. He knows why she has traveled the broken road to seek him, and, more importantly, he also knows the sole recourse available to him if he treasures a hope of delaying the demise of his dead friend's nephew,

Zaf. He is ready.

Zafarian must remain ignorant of Odwin's disappearance, and Odwin's contacts must become accomplices to her devices. Solemnly, she crosses the dusty floor, extends her reach to the ceiling and back down again to her heart, and when he stands to welcome her, she graciously bows, as she lets a solitary tear shatter on the naked earth, grieving his farewell sigh and his languid drop. He has honored his explicit promise, in matter, and is destined to do the same, in spirit. She can now assume his identity.

Shortly, twilight will bring the tide and centuries of decay will flood the exposed cave. She lunges for the slippads, sketches and boards on his desk and rips the emitter from her innermost pocket as she stows them securely between the fabrics. Shrouding his empty stillness with a silky white cloth, she springs to the outer ledge and seals the doorway to his eternal grave, while the virulent surf crashes into her spine. As the sea retreats to regroup for a mightier surge, she fills her lungs, stretches her arms as high as her toes can raise her, and rifts a grip in the cliff. The cyclical waves repeatedly come smashing down on her, thrusting themselves upwards with each strike, as she races against its thunderous sweep, rifting and climbing until she attains the plateau. Regal before the burnt orange sun, she sheds the noxious assault from the watery depths and anchors her resolve for the demanding return.

▲ ▲ ▲

NATHRUYU

The distant frames of her past, it seems, have faded, layer upon layer beyond recollection, along with those who have deeply touched her, now mere fossils in her mind, forever trapped in the calcified sediments of her emotional debris. Her most recent experiences still churn in the fluid fibers of her consciousness, advancing and receding behind her eyes as a muddled pool of images, and arbitrarily bursting through the illusionary tranquillity of the aqueous veneer—transient apparitions dissolving in the mist. In time, they, too, shall harden and descend, and the present shall scatter its droplets to the atmosphere and drift to the future, only to merge and plummet anew, fused as one in the brittle shale of her soul. On occasion, a slender shard will splinter free of the cluster and stubbornly implant itself in her tender flesh, creating a wound that does not mend and oozing a thick, toxic, syrup prone to envelop and infect all who dare to come close. Such is the darkness consuming her, as she yearns for healing, the cravings growing stronger and stronger every time they cross paths. But soon...

The enchanting floral perfume that bewitches the patrons is evident in the delicate carefree tap of the heels waltzing to stringed instruments and seeds joy under the concave canopy of the Great Hall. A few pardons and forgive-me's thrown into the brume, as they test the trial proximity detector program, adds a little humor to the mayhem as well.

The morning socials at the Museum of Antiquities are the brainchild of the current administration, who always strives to increase the ranking of this renowned facility, in order to attract more exclusive and expensive artifacts, and consequently even more supporting members. The concept of converting the gardens and vaulted spaces into a playground of sound, smell, taste, and touch during the blind hours of the day has been universally praised, and so well-received, in fact, that many betrothed couples elect to consummate their love, via the Unification ritual, with a blanketed banquet of culinary and musical delights. Sadly, for her this shall never be. He had been seized from her, and she from him, by the winds and the torrent of a freak summer storm.

▼ ▼ ▼

Their children are playing, the boys scrapping and their sisters granting favor to the darker one, whilst the other denies having bent the rules of the sport. From their private chamber, they hear the teasing, as their glistening contours writhe in the midday heat. The clever one twists the pointed comments of the other and stings with his own, methodically degrading the discussion to an argument and ultimately a whipping contest. Immersed in the sensual rhythms of their unrestrained passion, they abandon their ears to their ecstasy. As they crest the peak of their mountainous drive, they aimlessly drift between the stars and the dust and release their cares to the void.

The shrill scream of their youngest announces the squall on the horizon. Scrambling for cover, the brood runs to the sanctuary the family has dug in the mound, while the darkest beseeches his parents to join them. The sun deserts its post, tugging daylight behind it as a colossal funnel sucks the air from the heavens and consumes everything within its grasp.

The deluge gushes first and floods the escape route they have designed, burying their progeny beneath a murky river, and assuring their death if the enclosure were to be compromised. Next coils the infinite spiral, which expands its girth across the land and cleaves the sky from the earth. As bonded as their minds, bodies and spirits are, the forces conspiring to split them cannot be diverted. Their gaze locks in wanton embrace, one last time, as they brim with gratitude for their bliss and tears for their loss, in what seems an eternity of lament, for they feel the chasm forming. She is plucked from his hold and lost to the currents of obscurity.

▲ ▲ ▲

Nathruyu has been standing too long at the edge of society, her frivolous fantasies gambling with her sanity. Perhaps her reality is not reality, and the realm she abides does not presently exist. It is odd that the mornings stay hidden from sight, and later they rouse to welcome the light. Are there reasons besides reason that fuel their decisions? Or is the Ministry earnestly heeding the cautions of the Gadlins, the outlanders, the ones the Pramam banished and persecuted? If the blowers were started at the break of dawn, would the Unification be caught unawares? The GHU, the URA, the GMU, the Ministry, and even the illustrious Pramam? Would they slink under the pathways and crawl the poisonous ducts to hide, justifiably condemning their own depravity? Only the ears and the nose of those who make the effort to hone their senses are able to see with the invisible eye, but their dependency on technology to guide them in their activities hampers their sensory evolution. The biochip, in essence, separates them further from their humanity and veils the corruption in full view of the enlightened.

The laughter mounts as the proximity readers confuse the pillars for dancers, although the participants forcefully kissing the marble have a different perspective. Witnessing the confusion from the fringes has provided an appropriate amount of security and has also promoted a semblance of belonging, which has been sorely lacking from her alienating lifestyle. She had forgotten the spontaneous release that emanates from basic pleasures, especially considering the strain her conscience has withstood as of late. Nonetheless, the simplistic distractions of this gullible nation fill her with disdain for their stupidity. Her deeds have pushed her outside the accepted norms of behavior; hence, she must journey alone, albeit devout in her belief that they shall unite before the voyage.

The music stops, and the troupe falls silent. The shoes are vacating the Great Hall and herding toward the white gate, making it difficult for her to recognize the precise click she has been searching for. She slides her head sideways and listens for a unique cadence competing with the random clomps. Nathruyu is starting to wonder whether Elize has already left, or maybe she has echoed the movements of someone in the crowd and walked square past her. Amidst the clanging dishes, the rolling trolleys, and the curt directives of the senior service staff, she gleans a faint hint of motion emanating from the far corner of the main hallway, a quick, solid tempo beating against the granite tile. Her moment is finally here.

No one can prevent her from collecting that which has

been marked, and certainly not a self-assured half-breed from the lowlands. She now exercises dominion over the Gadlins' diminished influence on civilization, as aliases inside the maze, and plans to take thorough advantage of her new high-ranking outlander status. She will leverage Zafarian's relationship with Odwin, until his usefulness expires or the network exposes her treachery, and, in the process, crush the arrogant taunt of the Pramam's advisor once and for all. Zafarian is merely a pawn to her, whose agenda happens to mesh with hers in regards to keeping Elize away from authorities and her father, and, in this particular game, pawns are expendable.

Watching him yesterday afternoon, as the trio enjoyed a playful reprieve, resurfaced intense feelings of longing and reignited the desires constantly haunting her loins. She closes her eyes, and casts the sentiments from the latter four days into their dark pools, replacing them with fervent anticipation. The scarcely palpable vibrations from the masonry signal the blowers stirring below and warn her that the opaque curtain will soon lift. Her hands curled tensely around the edges of the cold stone, elbows and knees slightly flexed and feet firmly planted on the ground, she waits, poised to spring from her fanciful musings, while the scurrying becomes louder and louder. Nathruyu rewarded at last, Elize emerges from the foyer.

E L I Z E

Day 31: late afternoon

Now, my turn. Brush, tresses, dreamcatcher, jewel? Jewel? Jewel?...

▼ ▼ ▼

What's taking Keet so long? Juicy. I can see him through the keyhole. Hehehe.

"Hang, Eli. Almost done."

Ah. The mouthy yet ineffective little protector strikes terror in the unsuspecting visitor. Here comes Keet. "It's about time, pup. Whoops, slap me." Ouch. He's annoyed. "Stitch is looking for her."

"Who? Sparky, sit."

"Impressive. He can now sit on intruders' feet." Time to cuddle the little yapper. "The woman in the mirror. I gave him the frame from the flashes. He put a sketch out."

"But you already know who she is, don't you, Eli?"

Part of me does, but secretly hopes I am wrong. "Then why hasn't Father shown up?" Keet is scrunching his face. It doesn't make sense to him either, unless... "Do you suppose he *knows* her?"

"We have no proof either way. We'll need to see what comes back from the maze."

I agree. We must focus on getting through all these... What

the! "Did you transport your entire bedroom here?" There is no way two shelves will be enough. "I can't believe you brought *more* stuff. How did they get past Father?"

"It was worth the risk. I was bending in this empty space." Empty? He already had enough books to make furniture.

Just have to shake my head. "Sure. I see that all of these are absolutely essential, especially this one. *How To Survive an Avalanche*? In case you haven't noticed, it's a little warm out there." He snatches it from my hands and sneers. "Stitch says all the missing children were the same age. Nine. Just like Mashrin. He's still looking for details on their families, but nothing so far."

"I know, Eli. He commed me the day after we went to the restricted sector. He also discovered that Mashrin's body is now in GHU hands. I assumed he'd told you already, otherwise I would have—"

"Well, he didn't!" Oh, don't be a baby. It's a good thing that Stitch can trust Keet now. Better ease a bit. "Just make sure you check with me next time, eh?"

He nods apologetically. "What about Caroline? I'd rather like to know how she came across those shafts."

"So would I. I forgot to tell you I ran into her the day after. She was leaving O'Leary Hall, crying. She said she was expelled but wouldn't tell me why. She just assalammed. The counsellor was watching from his window. When you and Stitch were in the washroom, she told me she knew the Pramam's advisor. He was the redhead the officials were talking to."

Crap! I should have kept that one to myself. Here it comes.

"Are you bent? Why didn't you tell me? He's seen you now and—"

"Ease, Keet. Caroline doesn't know anything, and Stitch took care of my picture. Right. Let's get focused." He still needs to get up for work tomorrow. What a mess!

"I still don't see why you think we need to go through all of these. They're just books, Eli."

"Well, maybe there's something Mother hid there for us to find. Let's start with the ones she used to obsess over in the hospital." I have to believe that she wasn't crazy, that maybe now that I'm starting to drift as well, it might trigger something. He's complying, which is better than resistance. "I'll take this pile. Look for scribbles, notes, missing pages, creases, anything."

This may look like a heap of random literature, but he's organized it in sections. Here we go: Chopra, Tolle, Hicks, Braden, Zukav, Vitale, McTaggart, Gardener, Hoff, Emoto, Cannon, Klemmer, Schwartz, Eden, Tonay, Ming-Dao, Ali, Mathers, Griffith, James, Carus, Chamberlain… Mother read each of these too many times to single one of them out. I wonder if she found what she was looking for. The Ministry would not likely approve of these.

"Does the curator know you have these?"

"No. The philosophies aren't exactly condoned. You think that's what they are after?"

"I doubt it. Mother would have been stripped of them." The shelves are almost full. "What about your stack? Anything suspicious with your favorite historians, except that one's whip of course? Ancient civilizations? And those?"

"Nothing either. Just some water damage. The transfer chest must have had a weak seal."

Odd. That would be so unlike the Gadlins. "Well, then, what's left?"

"Just random fiction: Tolkien, Rowling, Shakespeare, Stevenson, Rice, Christie, Verne, Lucas, Whedon, Stewart... All clean. And then our board game over there in the niche. My clothes. Hey, stop shaking it."

Nothing in it anyway. Even the drawers have no unusual markings. Something is missing I can tell. He keeps checking his tunics.

"I was positive I packed it. The one I wore at graduation?"

"Maybe you gifted it to your date as a keepsake." Hehehe.

"Very funny. And you?"

"I *had* one."

"A stretch rodent?"

That deserves a snare. At least Squiggles was sentient. Keet brought a hologirl. Come on. Hold it together. No more tears. It's not your fault he was snapped up by a predator. Yuck. This puppy is like a mini-sentinel. My face is soaked. I should have a wipe in my pocket right... What?

"Where did you get that?"

I've seen this before, but where? Oh no. This was in her pocket at the medical lab. But I left it there, didn't I? "I don't know. It was in Mashrin's pocket."

He has saucer eyes now. "You took it?"

"Of course not. I didn't want any evidence pointing to us. If they find me with this, then I'm jam. They'll think I did it. And the guard? I have no alibi. They saw me at the daze."

Calm down, girl. It's all mere speculation. "It wasn't in my pocket this morning. I'm positive."

Keet is squinting at me like he does when I'm having an episode. He doesn't believe me.

"I did *not* take it. Don't you think I would remember?" Maybe not the most persuasive argument. I'm confused. Who's talking?

"Eli...Eli. It's juicy. Let's think about this. If that's in fact the case then—"

"It is."

He's annoyed I just cut him off again. "Then, the only plausible explanation is that someone put it there in Tir-na-nog Square. It could have been anyone, especially with the chaos."

"Well, it had to be someone who wants me trapped and who saw Mashrin after we broke in. Or ..." I hope he's not thinking what I am.

"Let's not jump to conclusions." But he is.

A sinking feeling is coming over me, and Keet is looking demoralized. "I'll take another pass through the books. You get some sleep, Keet." I have the morning off. "Come here, Sparky." We can cuddle in the corner together. I miss my Squiggles.

"Good night. Eli. Don't stay up too late."

I can use the moonlight. I'll start with Joe, it's slightly more worn than the others: cleaning, cleaning, cleaning...

✂ ✂ ✂

I'm here. Don't leave. Mother. "Noooooooooo..."

"Eli. It's just a dream."

I thought I was getting better. They're back. "Make them stop, Keet." He would if he could. I feel so helpless.

"We will. Dr. Tenille will have some answers. Here, dry your eyes. Did you get any sleep at all?" He leans over and walks me to his bed. "Get a little more rest. I'll comm you before the fog lifts." It will do me good.

✂ ✂ ✂

Oh right. Keet. "I'm awake. I feel much better."

"That's a relief. The social is over. You can come through the back, fewer people to bump into. Good luck with the interview."

"Thanks."

Quite honestly, I am nervous. Am I absolutely prepared for the answers to my questions? What if there is no cure, what happens next? Ridiculous. I'm sitting here paralyzed by negativity. Where has my boldness gone? Pat my little friend, out the crypt, and through the archives, quick. I seem to have a feel for this place now. Juicy. No more bruises in the mist. Ouch! Spoke too soon. That's going to leave a mark. Strike that thought. I don't need any more of those. I feel the openness. I'm in the Great Hall and almost out. Is something behind me? Turn around. Those eyes!

▲ ▲ ▲

Ouch! My head. Where am I? It's so bright. The window. The

sun is out. Creeps! Oh good. Just the shag. Will you leave my toes alone? Why did I take my shoes off anyway? I think I've been daydreaming. Snap back. Oh right. My turn. What did I bring from home? Brush, tresses, dreamcatcher, jewel? Jewel? Jewel? Anything but that. Where is it? I can't find it anywhere. Stop snapping, shelf! Did I wear it to the daze? No. I thought about it but I left it. I am feeling very faint right now. But how could anyone get in here? Stitch did a scan on my room and said there was some sort of field around it, that no one could see or get inside it without my secure band. I'm getting that sinking feeling again. I have to comm Keet.

"Keet. I just...I just...I can't find it." I can't help it anymore. It's just too heartbreaking.

"What? Talk to me. Everything will be fine. We'll find it. Take your time. Just breathe. So, what are we looking for?"

I want to believe, but I just can't see. "Mother's jewel."

Dead silence.

Here I go again. Mother, I feel so guilty. I should have left it with Father. At least no one would have found it through the clutter in her room.

"Eli, I am soooooo sorry. I know how precious it is to you. To me as well, and to her." I can hear him trying to hide his pain. "Let me see what I can find out. We might need Stitch to sketch it as well."

"But—"

"We don't know for certain. Don't mention the granite piece and—"

"I saw her. I saw her eyes in the fog."

"You mean...today?" He is quivering.

"Yes. Just outside the Great Hall, by the arch, on my way back. I don't remember how I got here. I just ran. She was waiting, I know it."

I can almost hear his heart pounding. "You blacked out again? Be extra careful. We don't know what her motives are yet. Keep your rubber on. There's a beacon on it."

Oh, the little brat. The bracelet. That's how they trailed Caroline and me.

"Stitch is tracing us?"

The notion doesn't seem to be disturbing him much. "He's not hiding the fact. Well, not from me anyway. Besides, we can trace him as well. We're all linked."

That's no more comforting to me, but I guess it does have its advantages. I'm yay with it then. "Juicy then. Oh, crap. I'm meeting my study partner, Jacinta, in a few minutes at the Nook. I'm off."

"Comm later."

I need a zapper or something to keep me on track with my schedule. What do I need to bring? My slippad of course. Oh and Mother's constellation charms, to spark Dr. Tenille's memory just in case. I remember he used to hold her hands to stop her from rubbing them all the time. He was worried she would cut herself. She used to stroke so hard she would bleed sometimes. A deep breath in, then out again. I have to plane like I'm on the slick.

The pond's looking pretty in pink today. Those flowers really do lap up the rays. I wish I could sleep as peacefully as they do at night. The morning dew might look like tears on them, but they're not sad, they shed joy instead, welcoming the brand new day. I need to cut through the grass. I could lie underneath these trees forever, the citrus is so soothing. Sigh. Another time maybe, Jacinta is probably parked already. I can see her through the archway sitting at the sweet counter. Almost there. I truly have been slacking. My recovery time is sliding.

"Hey l... Um. Way, Jacinta."

"Way. Nice bracelet."

"Thanks. And for saving me a seat."

"Wasn't the sweep a jumper? It took me three days to chip down. Intense! How about you? Shaplo says you were bouncing."

Try not to look stunned. Make something up. Fast. "Off the walls, yeah? I think the tag had the opposite effect on me. I couldn't sleep for three nights." Nice to know my pretentious neighbor is spying on me. I'll have to feed him something scandalous to keep him busy. "So. Let's compare slips."

"I found a case study for kidney transplants, no detail spared. Dizzy, yeah?"

"I found a brain transplant, just behind the eyeballs. I'll never look at a reflector the same way again, eh?"

That caused a shudder and a show of tongue. The poor girl is going to have to toughen up if she wants to be a medical lead.

"I'm not sure why they make us study these barbaric images. Technology is far past the blood, guts, and gore now."

That's what you think. Not from what I've seen recently. "Maybe there are GHU procedures only select medics are aware of, and they test our digestive systems as part of their evil grooming process."

A gasp! This is fun. What a nervous lass. She's been tapping her foot under the table the whole time.

"Whoa! What's with the sudden shove?" She just slammed herself up with her eyes glazed. "Way! Hey lo! Planet earth calling Jacinta. You awake?" I didn't mean to terrorize the girl. "It was just a rib." Oh, I get it. Rib's on me. "Very funny. Good whip! You can stop now. Come on, people are watching us." She's non-responsive, and actually people are...

Let go of your breath. What are they all doing? Creeps! Did they just all stomp their left foot and pop their jaw in unison? The courtyard was almost empty a few minutes ago, and now look. Row after row of vacant bodies, twitching their right shoulders and marching. Am I the only one who is sane here? Did the Gadlins neglect to mention something in the water?

"Jacinta, you..." Where did she go? She left her things and just assalammed.

Eek! Hands off, you wack! How am I going to get through this mob? Quiet! I can't hear myself think. All of you. Out! Out of my head! Stay loose. Breathe. Count them out. One. Two. Three. Breathe. Four. Five. Six. Breathe. Seven. Eight. Nine. Good. Now clip!

"Get out of my way!" Ouch. Get up! Watch their legs again. There. Between the slides. Dodge their arms. Almost out. Finally. Head for the clearing. More? Eek. Behind me.

"Hey lo, chum." Smack right into Stitch. At last, someone normal...ish. Oh no! Not him too.

Keep running.

"Let go! You're bent! You're all bent!" I can't control the

shakes now.

"Ease, Eli." He is almost falling down in, well, stitches. "You've never seen the thriller dance before?"

"The what?" I am in complete shock. That was a dance? Where was the music?

"It's a 20th century ritual. Pica trip!" I am still puzzled. "You don't subscribe to bioRhythms do you?" More confused. "You're cute."

Ah yes. The smile. Wonderful. I'm back to being cute again.

"What are bioRhythms?"

If he could just stop laughing maybe he would start making some sense. "It's a…"

"Ohhhm gee. You're safe. Both of you. Something is possessing the archives, and everyone in the Central Core. People are acting like demented cadavers and one tried to grab me."

Stitch is absolutely howling now, Keet is struggling to catch up with his lungs, and I am finally controlling my nerves.

"You two are priceless. Welcome to the big city, newbs."

Is it over now? Rubrique Court looks clear from here. Students are heading to their lessons as usual. I wonder if I should return to the Nook in case Jacinta is looking for me. I don't imagine she actually saw me leave. It was all very creepy how whatever program was running in their head, they just followed instructions like some master puppeteer was pulling their strings. Is this perhaps why the Ministry gets nervous with malfunctioning biochips? They obviously weren't able to control Keet or myself, and Stitch even seemed to have a dual presence of mind. But then again, he has all sorts of emitting and rubbing devices that he probably can control incoming signals to a certain extent.

"She's lost in thought."

Are they talking about me? "Sorry. I just drifted for a while." They're looking concerned. Oh. "Not that kind of drifting, was just thinking about what happened. I'm still a bit rattled." Stitch has it down to a giggle at last.

"I found the documents you needed for your anatomy project, Eli."

I didn't ask Keet to research my... Oh right. We can't reveal the theft to Stitch just yet. I hope he missed my momentary flinch.

"Ah thanks, but I have to dash to the interview. I want to be early in case I get dragged to my eternal grave when the salsa zombies start looking for partners." You never know. I have encountered quite a few, dare I say, peculiarities in this city, and I am convinced this is only the beginning.

Stitch is observing us very closely, with the corners of his eyes secretly trying to focus on the documents Keet is obscuring with his chest. I lean into him to break his line of sight.

"You can educate us both later on the insanity we just witnessed. You trip with that?"

"I'm trip with that." And there he goes, wiggling, spinning, shadow beating.

Keet and I look at each other, shake our heads, and smirk. That boy is a walking oxymoron, a dweeby genius with military training and a penchant for practical jokes.

"I'll wait in your room then. Pass me the key, Eli."

"You mean the secure band and the controller, master of antiques."

He fakes a ha-ha and walks away with a honker following him.

"Oh and lose the goose."

My chest is throbbing. This could be it. Off to Dr. Tenille.

K E E T O

Day 31: early evening

My chest is throbbing. This could be it, the culmination of years of hiding, months of planning, weeks of refining. I am hopeful that Dr. Tenille will have the answers that will put your mysterious accident to rest and will consequently expose whatever demons have been trapped inside Eli's subconscious. If she can at least become part of his crew, the gifted few he shares his patient roster with at the GHU, she might be granted special permissions to the observation facilities, like the one you lived in, if that's what you want to call it. But abandoning the safety of her residence to volunteer herself to the probing scrutiny of the very organization we have been sheltering her from as far back as I can remember may be a risk that offers limited blessings in return. As much as I desire closure with regards to your death, my utmost concern is with regards to Eli's life, to keep her from sacrificing the second half of her years to a padded cell.

My calm remains challenged in the midst of this tranquil room as each second stretches into hours. Anticipation has my mind reeling into realms I dare not enter completely. What if Dr. Tenille's involvement with your case was not purely academic? What if he was instrumental in keeping you under his microscope and as such stripped your freedom and kept you from us? We honestly do not know whether he had motives none too honorable; all we know is that his was the name authorizing your release, and that he now represents our leap of faith into a volatile future, which began the first day we set foot in this city. Even the promised stability of my position at the Museum of Antiquities has proven to be vulnerable to a cryptic intruder, forcing me to carry my journal at all times, without which writing to you while sitting at Eli's desk nervously awaiting her return would not be possible. The cosmic order, it seems, has its own hidden agenda.

Slightly past dawn, while Eli lay sleeping in my bed, I had entered the rear of the round room as usual and collected my daily archival duties from the scheduler. The exhibits in the Ancient Civilizations Gallery under the east dome had completed their tour at this location and were ready for travel to the next museum on their circuit. My charge for the day was to ensure the appropriate documentation was in place and that their replacements were properly cataloged; so, I withdrew to the artifacts room for the greater part of the day, checking and cross-checking the incoming and outgoing transport chests. At the back of my mind, I kept visualizing the unique composition of granite that Eli had pulled from her pocket. Even though its reddish hue was notably rare, I was convinced I had seen that particular stone before, but I was unsure as to whether it was in its physical form. Just as I remembered where I had come across a similar rock type, Eli appeared on the comm, her panic causing me to immediately abandon my dig and switch to the stacks.

Fortunately, my sketching skills have immensely improved since accepting this position of apprentice curator, because little did I know that within less than ten minutes I would be running from my research terrified for my life, and the only reason I escaped ridicule from my favorite twin is because she had made an even greater spectacle of herself than I had. Just as the patrons were struck with madness, the PAL had completed its preliminary pass through the volumes and returned with a sleeve matching the exact likeness of your jewel that I had etched in my brain. Since everyone else was intently committed to being the walking dead, the staff paid no attention to the security scanner gesticulating wildly as I rushed the exit with the documents in hand. Understandably, I wasn't entirely worried at the time about the consequences of blatant theft, but tonight I will no doubt be testing my powers of persuasion by imploring my supervisor to forgive my highland naivety and keep the incident between us. In any case, the contents of my booty did not turn out to be especially threatening to the Unification and raised more questions than gave answers about who you really are.

When I finally reached the campus oval, panting and visibly shaken, I found Eli at the pond, obviously irritated at Stitch, but that time the tremors came from within, while I wrestled with my tongue and strove to conceal the stolen goods from him as he gradually tempered his hysteria. Eli was no doubt sensing, as was I, an impending repeat of yesterday's confrontation regarding trust issues, so she sliced through the tension and cleverly redirected us in separate directions, while she focused on the interview. That is how I arrived at sitting here, at Eli's window, massaging my temples, my head pounding and confused by the story I had just read.

It is not clear to me whether the tale is fact or fiction, but the astonishing narrative alludes to possibilities I had never considered. Trusting the validity of the account, how you came into possession of such an elusive treasure is a curiosity, for according to legend it was last seen in the hands of a Gadlin sage, centuries before their flight. The text continues to describe nine gold and silver domed spikes evenly spaced radially from the center of a hollow crystal bulb, protecting the heart of the jewel with its nine delicate rose petals. Although the actual gem had never been revealed, rumors abounded concerning the existence of a flawless diamond the size of a human eyeball resting at its core. Ordinarily, I would uphold Father's version of its origin, as a family heirloom gifted to you through him on the day of our birth, a longstanding tradition, but my intuition in light of recent events and his questionable honesty invites alternate interpretations

A theory still plausible is that the brooch Eli adopted was merely a replica of the artist's rendition I discovered, its worth is nothing more than a sentimental link to a long line of highlanders, and the thief was enamored with a childhood fable; however I trust the Ministry with due diligence in all matters of state. No, this act of piracy is not the result of a childish fantasy. Whoever breached this space and muzzled the privyshelf is fully aware of its prophesied value and is quite possibly linked to the three officials and ultimately the Pramam's advisor. The question that remains is why now? How could you, our supposedly mentally unstable mother, a common orphaned clerk, have managed to shield it from authorities while tenanted inside a GHU asylum?

As I pulled the second and last page from the folder, the

lighting started to flicker and I was unable to continue reading. I was forced to investigate the source of the malfunction. Taking the secure band and controller with me, I sealed the room and peeked around the corner to the central shaft. The solar storage cells on the mirrored inner surfaces of the tube were very dim, almost as if they had been drained of the day's sunlight, and the whole branch was affected. With previous releases of this technology, the cells were attached to separate storage collectors which relied on a dual feed system that was susceptible to cosmic variances, like the storms we have been experiencing recently, but this latest advancement keeps the energy locked in each individual cell, releasing it gradually when required. For thousands of these units to empty all at once would require a load far above their intended capacity, which the architects of the residence complex had generously compensated for. The sentinels were also strangely absent, and unless my memory fails me, the curfew was still in effect, which also contributed to my anxiety over Eli's lengthy meeting with Dr. Tenille.

I could hear another student fumbling in the dark, so I returned to the room in time to avoid any raised eyebrows and activated the bioluminescent frames. Then it dawned on me. What if the sudden plunge was a manifestation of someone's intentional design and the scampering in the hallway was not caused by one of the neighbors. As the footsteps neared, I was catapulted backwards to the night of the sweep when Eli and I were cornered and I was silently calling to you to somehow protect us from what lurked outside. But this time I am scribbling in the dark, recording my thoughts as they appear, a voyeur into my own consciousness.

The lift is opening and there is a chase, and some… what? I must be acoustically challenged. It actually sounds like…I'll finish up later.

Boy, did I feel brainless. A short episode with fake zombies and I fell right into a state of paranoia. When I finally heard her voice calling me, I realized that the lobby guard must have escorted her up the lift, which was running on emergency power. To my surprise however, when I finally opened the door, she was carrying a goose. A big white goose, still honking. Trying as I did to act as if she had just interrupted an intense journaling session, she saw right through my charade and exploded with laughter. I will never live this one down.

With the waddler on her lap, she proceeded to recount the main highlights of her encounter with Dr. Tenille, minus the ocean-faring sailor analogies he is fondly known for, of course. His nickname is Captain Hook for precisely that reason. Since he has been lecturing, coincidentally shortly after your accident, he has been obsessed with creating a 16th century galleon to explore the uncharted waters of our glorious planet, as he puts it. No one has dared to inform him that all the waters are accounted for, and that the mighty vessel would never survive the seas, virulent as they have become. So it is with this incidental information that we had to evaluate the sanity of what he chose to divulge to Eli concerning your own state of mind under his care. She did succeed, by the way, in securing an envious assignment as part of his courageous crew, code name Tinkerbell. Utterly fitting.

At first, he simply recognized her as an industrious

freshman, but upon presenting him with your charmed ribbon, his demeanor changed. The frown on his face, as he scoured his internal flashes for an image to match the sudden emotion he was attempting to conceal, took a more serious turn. His eyes grew wide, his shoulders rounded, and his voice weakened, searching for the right words. The girl sitting across from him in his cabin, I mean office, was none other than the twin child of his most psychotic patient and represented evidence of a past he had vowed to forget. Perceiving his apprehension, Eli opened the discussion with a heartfelt thanks for his compassion for you and the family during your last three years, and kept the conversation light and playful, reminiscing about a few joyful visits we had experienced. Once his fear had subsided, she broached the subject of your death and explained to him that all she wanted was to know what really happened so that she could attain closure. With her genuine intent succinctly articulated, he agreed to comply as best as he could recall.

As I write these words, comforted by my loyal foot warmer, I wish you could send me a sign, to either confirm or deny the verity of his statements. Even though Odwin, our trustworthy Gadlin contact, had produced a slip distinctly showing Dr. Tenille's signature on your release permissions, he staunchly denied having ever entertained the idea of discharging you, especially after finding his colleague Dr. Yarkovsky dead in your cell. Following the incident, you were promptly declared exceptionally dangerous and slapped with level three restraints for the remainder of your days at the hospital. There was talk that the Ministry's Inner Council had ordered the GMU to assemble a contingent of operatives to sedate and move you into a level three lockdown facility just outside Ministburg, but the transfer never materialized. The day after the murder, you vanished, taking Eli and me with you, and none of us was ever seen or heard of again, until now.

You see, Dr. Tenille had presumed that we, like many children our age at the time, had fallen prey to a rash of serial killings which inexplicably ended with your disappearance, but how can that be true? Stitch and I pulled every existing news article from the archives and found nothing about twin sibling victims, and if we were indeed kidnapped, there was no historical record of that either. Obviously, there was a veil of deception obscuring the facts, and Dr. Tenille was either wittingly or not involved.

When prompted about the specific nature of your illness, he described frequent hallucinations as of yet foreign to Eli's mix of symptoms, according to her confessions; however, as she has been known to downplay the severity of her syndrome in the past, I will closely monitor her lucidity in light of this development. His tone became resolute as he attempted to steer the conversation towards Eli's internship application. For reasons he had no access to, you were secretly protected from the surgical treatments his other mentally disturbed patients were routinely subjected to, which implies, from his assessment, that someone influential within the Unification wanted your brain intact. He warned Eli that she must actively protect her identity and promised to do the same while she remains under his tutelage.

The suggestion that Eli was in danger from not only herself as her affliction worsened but also from some faction in the Unification was no surprise. She sat there overwhelmed. The soothing effect Squiggles had had on her grief as a teenager was evident as the poor goose squirmed to break free, apparently annoyed by the tears coming from above. I must admit to strong feelings of my own, although they were more akin to anger than sadness. How dare he insinuate that you were in some way connected to these horrid crimes? I refuse to believe it.

As we struggled with the ramifications Dr. Tenille's testimony implied, a puzzled Stitch appeared at the door, markedly distressed by Eli's emotional state while at the same time quietly amused by the honker waddling around the room. He had logically assumed that the doctor had decided against adding her to his crew and was further befuddled when she showed him the official pirate eye patch. Captain Hook does enjoy living up to his student's expectations.

As we were on the verge of disclosing this morning's loss, Stitch crooked his neck and exclaimed: "The Jewel of Airmid!" At last, in plain view, he was able to see what I had been guarding so closely. Less than a week ago, I would have been shocked that he even knew what a jewel was, but now, I almost expect him to know what color underwear I wore five days ago. He was stupefied, however, when we admitted the burglary, and went on to say that it was a piece of folklore his grandfather learned from his grandfather who learned it from his grandfather and so on, but that he never thought it was actually real. Judging by his tone, or more specifically his hair's reaction, he could have been telling the truth, but my inclination was to continue keeping your history private until this nagging knot in my gut dissipates, so we passed on the lie Father fed us and withheld Dr. Tenille's significance in your life.

Eli was showing signs of fading, so I collected the museum's property and lead Stitch towards the exit, almost relinquishing my own personal chronicles. I grabbed the goose just in the nick of time as he was beaking his way through my journal, which was lying victim on the floor in the corner. Eli giggled and made some snide remark about the dangers of him spreading all my secrets around the whole flock. When I told her he could be a goosebot, she just rolled her eyes and pointed to the fresh gift our illustrious Mr. Goose had left on the shag, which was clearly repulsed. Yes. Definitely getting paranoid.

Thanks to Stitch's offer to change the scanner records and consequently remove the out-of-bounds tag on the shelf slot, I was able to sneak the folder into the stacks without creating an exception and thereby avert an uncomfortable discussion with Madame Beaudoin. When I reached my quarters, however, I found several of my effects out of their assigned places. Annoyed, I automatically concluded that Eli's haphazard filing skills were responsible, but something about the manner in which they were tossed struck me as intentional, almost as if they were pointing to something. My gaze followed what I gathered was their alignment and ultimately rested on the niche in the back wall. A challenge had been delivered.

As I advanced towards the object of focus, picking up the bread crumbs along the way, I noticed Sparky trembling in his blanket. The room was cooler than normal, although not enough to induce hypothermia; however, the poor puppy was indeed suffering from an unusually penetrating chill. I cradled him inside my shirt and consoled him, massaging his quivering shoulders. Eli was right about his being combat challenged, though I wouldn't admit that to her, since based on results or lack thereof, he has yet to exhibit the territorial behavior I was assured was innate, as evidenced by the current breach.

Peeping from the gameboard's drawer, there was a second message beautiful penned on an old piece of parchment, and the alabaster pieces were placed in perfect formation for a sleight of hand. One final throw could either end the game or change its course. The next move was mine to make.

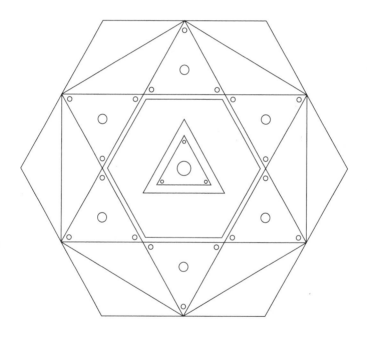

CHAPTER SEVEN

NATHRUYU

Day 32: early afternoon

The city is brimming with wary travelers from diverse regions of the Earth, some risking a treacherous voyage across the waters for the coveted opportunity to share ground with him. Seldom does the Pramam speak in a public forum, generally preferring to communicate the Ministry message from the safety of Inner Council chambers via scheduled daily meditations broadcast to the local sajadums that are strategically interconnected within each municipality. She expects that his advisor will have reported the recent disturbances on the campus oval and anticipates an animated exchange at Rubrique Court tomorrow when he addresses the student assembly. With her newly acquired persona as Odwin in the maze, she is in direct contact with the subculture loyal to her Gadlin predecessor, and, thanks to his unsuspecting protégé, Zafarian, able to covertly navigate the encrypted layers of the Unification. Her influence is the knife that shall peel their vile onion of deceit.

The strife resumed approximately a century ago, during a period known as the Second Great Water Wars. Due to the tremendous success of the cooling stations, the rampant plague of global misery had shifted from environmental to psychological. The impending threat of cataclysmic annihilation had united all cultures in their mission to rescue themselves from certain extinction and had given rise to the Great Age of the Gadlins, but as the atmospheric climate slowly recovered, the ego resurfaced and plotted to divide once again. An insidious affliction, called scarcity thinking, spawned by the diminishing supply of land and potable water, had gripped the inattentive minds of the complacent masses. People were packed into the cities, as governments expropriated more and more terrain for agricultural rehabilitation and processing plants. A tsunami of lies and treachery, solely rivaled in its destructive capacity by the Great Ocean Swell, brought with it insurrection and disease, as the wealthy few, who controlled and apportioned the livelihood, reverted to their hoarding habits. The populace grew increasingly malcontent and organized itself into violent mobs. One by one, the unsanctioned captains of each territory were assassinated.

From the anarchy, arose a multi-faith federation of religious leaders that championed a grassroots movement, bringing peace and stability to the remnants of the crumbled houses. They elected a charismatic politician, who consolidated what was left of the population under a single planetary government. Anabelle, the Pramam's mother, as a respected spiritual being and chair of the coalition, was instrumental in mediating disputes on behalf of the various doctrines and in maintaining a healthy separation between church and state. Sadly, eighteen years after the birth of her only child, humanity mourned when the whole fellowship perished in an explosion that destroyed the greater part of the holy retreat where they held their quarterly summit. A unanimous urge for her son to extend his mother's legacy ensued, and that movement became the seed for the current dictatorial system.

That fateful day, forty-five years prior, the cherished luminary who had marched the globe wearing the armor of love and wisdom, shed her broken shell and bequeathed her enterprises to the misguided ambitions of her progeny. Abusing the trust she had spent a lifetime nurturing, he sanctimoniously dismissed the supreme director as superfluous. He then concocted a divine book negating all previous ecclesiastical teachings with his supposedly anointed, incontestable, and exclusive trinity of Jesus, Mohammed, and Abraham, and appointed himself Pramam, the lord over every living thing. The Unification, as it exists today, is the result of an individual man's prophecy or sanity, depending on whose perspective prevails, the melding of clerical and secular responsibilities, and the corruptive power that they breed.

The procession glides southwards on the principle artery and onwards to the Central Core, where thousands of citizens are gathered to welcome his arrival. For the vast majority, it is their initial physical interaction with him, albeit behind a fortress of GMU bodyguards, but for Nathruyu, it is a deliciously intoxicating experience. She casually leans against the base of the Victory Bridge, primed to escape through the hatch at a moment's notice, as the Pramam ceremoniously descends from the escorted convoy in the distance. The wide pathway bisecting the district and the festively decorated catwalks are buzzing with expectant bystanders, straining their necks to glimpse the colorful parade. While the heads bobbing in front of her busily compete with their peers for the choicest view, her thoughts sizzle in the heat of her own excitement.

The advantage is almost too tantalizing to resist. She could quite easily terminate the contest right there, without engaging the surrounding militia, by simply retreating to the underground labyrinth and tracking the Pramam underfoot, till he heedlessly pauses his promotional strut and straddles a hidden vent. But that is not her duty to fulfill.

Staring at the furthest table on the Snack Shack patio, she sees the meddlesome trio absorbed in conversation and swallows a million butterflies. They, also, are within her ominous reach, but the challenge has not yet been answered. She must wait for a sign that Keeto is ready to partake of the game, as opposed to vacillating on the sidelines, and until such a critical juncture occurs, her anonymity must persist.

Her focus returns to the throngs of cheering spectators embossing the petal strewn avenue. Although his well-trained entourage effectively shields him from a clean line of sight, she gapes in shock as they stroll to greet the proud chancellor, who is honored with the task of officially welcoming the preeminent delegation. The two faces flanking the Pramam ram her chest against the stone foundation. Her nemesis, the fair-complexioned one predictably glued to his hip as the devoted guardian, she expected, but the second, anxiously scanning the hordes, elevates the stakes. Her lungs collapse with the dense fear that he might recognize the twins, or perhaps her, dwelling in his periphery, and she hurries to blend into the background by joining a group of enthusiastic tourists engrossed in a holopost advertisement. As soon as the exalted guests cross the island gate, she regains her composure and vanishes into the dispersing crowd, flirtatiously locking her defiant eyes with those of the elated advisor, as he veers eastward on the way to O'Leary Hall.

Back in her studio, she checks the packets she had requested from her defrauded accomplices in the maze and notes the overnight accommodations reserved for the Ministry contingent. Their father's coincidental presence alarms her. According to her observations, the risks to her freedom are substantial, even though they pale in comparison to the irreversible damage his interference could produce. She does not appreciate having her plans sidetracked by yet another prying nuisance, for she is on the verge of rekindling the trio's interest in Mashrin, so that unbeknownst to them and using their keen investigatory skills, they will guide her to the girl's precise holding area. An unofficial appointment at the Ministry House where he is staying should aptly handle the situation.

She fakes a status update by pirating Odwin's nickname in order to appease any suspicious members in the community, and dissects her emotions, combing for conflicts that may jeopardize the most exacting task she has, to date, been summoned to perform. The winds of her imagination snatch her and she lands, dejected, an ailing outcast in a different world.

▼ ▼ ▼

Cut, bruised, and bleeding, her mangled form hangs from the barren branch of a desolate tree, her torn flesh desperately yearning for his healing touch. The garden, at one time replete with stimulating bouquets of mulberry bushes and quince trees thriving under the loving care of their master, has endured unrelenting hardships at the hands of creation. She is dropped in the midst of a dying landscape, naked and afraid, her memory stripped of who she once was, yet filled with visions of what she has become, visions that will her to survive and pursue that which will save her from an agonizing eternity. As the arid scent of impulsive brush fires snakes towards her in a black ribbon of smoke, her heart chokes with regret whilst her deafening anguish echoes amidst the void of the blazing hills. Sensing herself being dragged deeper and deeper into the nightmare, she tears her lacerated skin from the smoldering thorns and plummets into a dark chasm of despair, tormented and throbbing, until she surrenders to her beckoning destiny.

▲ ▲ ▲

With immutable conviction, she eradicates any hint of uncertainty and pulls her consciousness from the waking trance. She concludes that no earthly reproach can compare with the fiery hell that dominates her hungering hours, and boldly aims for the king of deception, with the speed of a shooting star.

A GMU unit is stationed around the facility, validating her assumption that the visiting dignitaries have retired for the evening. As the sun sets on the horizon, behind the sprouting wall of the restricted sector, the sentries stand erect, bronze trophies on a floating mantle serving the abject vanity of a self-proclaimed prophet. The disdain she harbors for the

Pramam's arrogance momentarily detracts her attention from the job and impedes her ability to improvise an efficient and invisible approach from her revealing position at the Central Core drop. Based on her recollection, a duct hangs underneath the footbridge and connects the main corridor to the entrance, but she is unsure as to whether they are also surveying the access panel to the submerged levels of the building.

The slight hum of the hovertrain arriving from the north allows Nathruyu but a few minutes to co-ordinate her descent with the passenger grab. Pressed for time, she targets the operative nearest to her, examines his uniform carefully, and notes a series of cleverly disguised sensors, looking more akin to decorative buttons than frequency transponders. The entire brigade is linked as one, probably in response to the isolated attacks on the university property. Were she to subdue an unlucky guard en route to the residences, the others would be immediately hailed to the crime scene; therefore, her usual tactic of disabling human obstacles, if warranted of course, would clearly be ineffective against the solid blockade. Alternatively, a diversion that pierces their fence formation may succeed in ushering her through the facade, but once indoors, the element of surprise might not be guaranteed, for she possesses no intelligence on the security forces assigned to the cavernous conference room. Her best option is to infiltrate from below and borrow a secluded nook, where she can secretly scour the interior squad for weaknesses.

The red circles on the platform light up, announcing the imminent boarding. While the commuters hustle to assert their claim on a marker, she readies her emitter for the oncoming shuffle, and, just as the cylindrical shoots at the bottom of the craft materialize, she drops into the subsurface passageways and seals the breach above her. The footsteps reflecting off the sides and ceiling invade her nerves like a thousand termites, for they imply that he must have indeed found evidence of a trespass at Osler Hall. To carve a slit out of the structure for easy entry then fuse it behind her would have been a complete bore, but encountering a protector at the site, and reinforcements instantly available from a quick pat on his lapel, makes the intrusion eminently more entertaining.

As the systematic vibrations emanating from around the bend continue, the shivers that tickle her spine dissipate. Acrobatic stealth still graces her. The delicate landing has afforded her a perfect vantage point from which to analyze the lone opponent, and the regular influx of carriers flying above provides cyclical breaks in the stillness, and creates a suitable cover for her chosen distraction. Arresting her breath between bursts of boisterous activity, she calms her inner voice and maps the methodical trudging of her mark. She counts the thuds interrupting the silence, records the amplitude of the noise, and calculates the matrix of dead space interlacing the rumbles up top.

Once he is beyond her visual field from across the channel and is patrolling the tunnels attached to the perimeter scaffolds, she turns the corner, veiled by the commotion overhead, and swiftly sneaks toward the fortified opening. During the next discordant interlude which drowns the boots robotically treading away from her, she rifts through the barrier, and promptly reseals it. Since the acoustics in the shafts bounce sound from here to there and muddle its origin, her sequence of well-timed advances progresses, undiscovered.

Nathruyu squirms her way along the sombre narrow tubes on the generator level and trails her ears to a hushed dialog drifting down from the south wing. As it was at the triple helix, her supple limbs ease her up the spiral air conduits buried in the staircase and into the mezzanine grid, where she hesitates. Beneath her crowded refuge in the palatial foyer presides an additional GMU unit, poised to swarm and apprehend. As the murmurs meander the ductwork, she spreads her body more thinly, so as to avoid dotting her passage with bulges, and outstretches her arms to funnel her slender frame in the direction of the chatter. The identity of the whisperers confirmed, she stops at a grate on the outside wall and witnesses a photographic account of the ongoing discussion.

The question is unambiguous and blunt. Nathruyu detects impatience in the Pramam's tone as their father stammers through a litany of detail concerning the latest transgressions. Was he not responsible for the URA? How could such a blatant disregard for protocol have taken place under his very leadership? The fierce reprimand eventually tapers, and the subject migrates to the whereabouts of the twins, as Vincent endeavors to con his superior with a fabricated story. Rather than admit that they have escaped his vigil, he declares that he has resettled them elsewhere, at a location where she would not find them. From her calf-height peephole, she cannot discern any facial cues that either support or deny the Pramam's acceptance, but the subtle clue from a mysterious third party, discreetly tapping his toes, suggests that someone important may doubt his honesty.

As Vincent's feet turn to leave, she squeezes backwards, selects an obscured recess of the gallery to emerge from, and shadows him past the glassed-in rooftop courtyard that crowns the colossal mural on the lower tier and on to the far end of the north block. Her heartbeat hastens as she assumes a shrouded setting inside the bulky window coverings across the hall from his quarters. He is not alone. The advisor and his faithful hounds, attentively sitting at the pedestal of a crystal fountain and angling their ears in her direction, have trapped him first. With a beam of sweat strung from his brow, Vincent informs him that the siblings have, in fact, disappeared.

An eruption of sensations consumes her as her faculties abandon the present, and all that she hears are these biting words.

"You lie."

"No."

"Yes. Tell me where they are. She must not find them first."

"They left at dawn after our last meeting. Please. I beg of you. It's the truth."

"We shall see. My loyal friends possess a special talent for sniffing out deceit."

"Ahhhhhhhhh. I know nothing. Please. Stop. Ahhhhhhhhhhhhhhhhhhh."

"Perhaps, but your lack of wisdom seals your fate. Come, my friends. We must leave him."

Elize has wasted no time learning to walk, an adventurous little soul from the start, whilst her brother crawls as fast as he can, boring holes in the third set of knee patches in as many months. Pausing at the cusp of the threshold, Nathruyu remembers the trials leading her here, how Vincent struggles to keep them from a fragmented notion of family, and how he fails to mask her oddness and shelter them from her. The favor he seeks carries with it a commanding price; nevertheless, he submits in silent compliance, and retreats to his study.

Casting occasional glances at the mirrored hallway, she monitors him closely and catches his shaking fingers adjusting his headset. His lips tremble and mutter a useless prayer. Blocking out the haunting cries of the infants and the unnerving images that follow contributes nothing to absolving him of guilt, and he is to forever remain an implicit participant in their callous branding incident.

▲ ▲ ▲

Reality trickles in at the shrill pitch of his pleas, uttered with futility as they were then. Her eternal adversary has left him for dead, and, now, she is distraught, faced with an onerous decision: to let Vincent perish by a slow and caustic demise, or to grant him mercy and indenture him further to her cause. She flows from the drapery and steadies her resolve for the gruesome creature awaiting his salvation. His eyes, appearing to glow inside a charred skull, still manage to express horror as Nathruyu brazenly enters the suite. She chastises his idle attempts to strip the children from her, demands his future allegiance in payment for his life, and warns him that a subsequent indiscretion will meet with her heel etching an impression in his throat instead of the soft soil by the shrubbery. Envisioning his obsessive pursuit slip beyond his grasp, he vows to atone the ill-conceived betrayal and, moreover, promises to relinquish his role at the URA and hide his unexpected recovery from his assailant, till she advises him otherwise.

The temperature grows cooler, as she towers above his brittle and twisted figure, his blistered torso oozing through the steaming silk pasted against his sweltering crust. Riveted by a sinister satisfaction in watching Vincent convulse at the sheer potency of his suffering, she briefly reconsiders her offer to help. However, once the stinging pain intensifies to the degree that he loses control of his muscles and of his conscious awareness, compassion replaces her contempt, and she holds true to the verbal agreement. Hoisting him over her shoulder, Nathruyu springs for the balcony, and plunges into the stagnant waters below, while the stupefied sentries scurry to uncover the source of the splash.

Elize

Day 33: early morning

Look at my eyes. I can't let him see me like this. They're getting worse again. Cover cream. Crap! Must have left it in the sun; the applicator is all funny. Still works though. There.

"Hey lo." Keet? Did Stitch lend him a frequency thrower?

"Hey lo. How did you get past the lobby guard, and the trolling gobbers?"

"No more lockdown. They must have captured the killer."

What a relief! Our conversation at the Snack Shack yesterday had me worried. Another cryptic message and more speculation about a stalker. "Juicy! It's time to focus on what we came here for anyway. I met with Dr. Tenille after the flyer bakes. I start volunteering at the GHU today." Here we go again. "*What?*"

"Are you sure you can hold it together? The memories."

I'm not sure, but I can't tell him. Honestly, I just don't know what the voices will say if I come across Mother's cell. Be decisive. "Of course. We'll find her jewel, and we'll find the answers. That's all we need to think about. No more worrying, eh?" But it's an affliction of his. He doesn't know how not to.

"They're getting worse again, aren't they?" My denial is not convincing. "You missed a spot." He wipes the corner of my eye with his finger.

Crap! Busted! Don't look at me like that. He knows, just tell him.

"They're getting more vivid, and there's a new one. It started the day after we went out with Caroline and it's been replaying every night since. He is just standing there, watching me, tapping his foot like he's waiting." It's more than just a dream. It's a feeling I have during the day as well. Am I hallucinating? Don't be silly. It's just another bad dream. I should be used to this by now.

"Do you think it's them? The three creepy guys?"

"No. There's only one." But still creepy.

"Wasn't the last time you saw Mother's brooch that night? Maybe it was a warning."

Oh please! Don't start with all that paranormal stuff. "Ohhhm gee! You're right! It was a ghost coming back for his treasure, and come to think of it, he had bird droppings on his boots. Eek! A pirate!" Well, I *am* enrolled in Captain Hook's crew now. Hehehe.

"Very funny. There's more to life than facts and figures you know, sometimes you just need to get out of your head and into your heart." .

Too philosophical for me. "It's just a dream." Keep telling yourself that. "My subconscious is processing the trauma of the past few days and using archetypes to do so. It will pass." He's still shaking his head. "It *will* pass." Enough already.

"Ok, Ms Carl Jung." He rolls his eyes.

"If it will make you happy, we can ask Stitch. His courses cover psychotics like me."

"No. Not the dreams. We still don't know for sure."

What is it with him and Stitch anyway? "I don't think he had anything to do with the theft. You heard him. He's juicy."

"If you say so. Ewww."

Sigh. Let it ride. "He's coming any minute now. We're going to grab a sweet something."

"You're going on a date?" What? He bent? "Stitch is a dweeb. I swear his social skills are lacking."

"He is *not* a dweeb. Seriously, you're acting like a jealous boyfriend." Oh, that's too wrong to even consider.

"You're not—"

"No, fishy! He's a dweeb." A good chuckle. Besides, I don't have time for that stuff. "Soooooo..."

"So?"

"Soooooo, you wanted to tell me something?" He's here for a reason.

"Actually, show you." He pulls a parchment from his journal.

Another note? It says: *Broken and torn shall she reveal herself to you.*

"Then I can join you and Stitch in the commons, eh?"

"Huh? Yeah." *In the darkest hour of her existence. And you shall come to her begging for forgiveness.* "When did you get this?" *And she should say to you there is nothing to forgive being that... .*

"Yesterday. I just didn't want to show it to Stitch."

....you and she are entangled in a dance for all eternity and shall become that which is right and virtuous through no misdeeds of your own. "Whoa! Sounds like you have a demonic girlfriend. You two need to work this out in person. It's all about communication, eh?" Wink.

"I knew you would say something like that. It's another

riddle. She's talking about you."

That is ridiculous. "Me? I'm not broken and torn. Maybe you two just have a '*deep connection beyond the physical'*." Giggle.

"You read my journal!"

Oh oh. Recover. "It just reminds me of the exotic woman on the platform, and how you looked at her. You know. The drama." Even I think that is lame..

"But I never said anything…and as far as I am aware, you can't read minds...so you read my journal." Hands on the hips. He's serious.

Crap. Caught with my fingers in the bake again. How does he always know when I'm pulling one over?

"Well, only one section. The one you wrote in my room. On the upside, I got to perfect my sleuthing skills again." He sneers. "Quite frankly, I was disappointed. I was hoping to find something a bit more steamy." Was that a tiny smile? "In any case, she popped into my head for some reason while I was untangling my dreamcatcher. It's not like I really *wanted* to spy on your deepest most private thoughts. I just hoped there would be clues, some more details that could explain why she was on my mind. I mean, I don't remember ever meeting her before."

"Did it work?"

"No. Nothing." But maybe. "When I zone out during the day sometimes, I get these horrible feelings and then afterwards, I just can't remember."

"Is that what happened to you on the transport then? You keep avoiding talking about it. You saw something. I know you did because—"

"She's in my dream. You know the one. There's something very dark about her."

"Is she the one who—"

"No. I don't think so. She's only there watching. Anyway, I'm not broken and I don't have to be right all the time. You're bending the truth."

"I write what I see. It's getting worse and now you're being careless and—"

"You write what you *want* to see."

"Why do you always cut me off like—"

"I don't *always* cut you off."

"Well, mostly you do." He's exaggerating. "I mean, it's like you're always trying to be right and you won't let me…"

Blah blah blah. "Pup, you just talk so much sometimes that I just can't hear myself think." Which isn't all that bad because then I can't hear the other voices either. Like replacing one chatter for another.

"And for the last time, *stop calling me pup*! Honestly…"

Got it! Loud and clear! And on he goes. I'd better just let him blow off some steam for a bit. He's topped up about something. Oh, good! Must be Stitch. Saved.

"Hey lo." He takes one look at Keet and "Shakes! Making some tea up there?" Still not amused. "Steam out the ears, bud." And he can groove and laugh at the same time. Astounding! Ah! He's eyeing the note. Keet grabs it from my hands and slides it into his journal.

"Let him read it." We're both staring at Keet now.

"Here." He turns to me. "Don't say a thing."

Moi? Hehehe. Don't need to. Stitch's eyebrow is lifting. This will be good.

"So when's the ceremony, yeah?" Game on! "Just a rib. Ease, bud." Stitch and I look at each other. He looks back at Keet. "Ready for something pica trip?"

He takes a miniature frequency thrower out of his sort-of-pocket and points it out the window frame. Keet's mood is still foul.

"It's finally working properly." Pay attention Keet. "I call it the O2-Line." Hmmm? "Watch. See Cherry over there? I happen to know she wears VLine exclusively, and I do mean *exclusively*." Keet's watching now, disinterested, but... Oh honestly!

"Stitch! That is brilliant! I'm peeing myself." That got Keet's attention.

Leave it up to a boy to think of a holocloth jammer.

"Oh oh! Ta, bud."

"Rip. I get it. 'O' 'O'." Stitch is howling. Give Keet the snare face, and then both of them a look of disgust... "Oh, grow up, you two. And flick her clothes back on, please. Thanks."

"Do it again. You're a genius, bud!"

Right. He's not a pup, he's a dog. "So that's why the J-branch guard hangs his slippad front and center." And why Stitch left such an impression on him his first day here no doubt.

"Yeah. Gotta hide the little thingy from you girls."

Keet's beaming. "How'd you break the frequency pass code? It's like *The Emperor's New Clothes*. Juicy!"

"That she is."

Ugh! Boys! Keet's right. No social skills. I'm starving. "Ok, boys. Let's go before they run out."

I must say, getting around is a lot easier without the slobber. Here's the lift. Keet's blabbering back to normal now. I'm done. If he calls Stitch a genius one more time I am going to scream. Good. Out of the box. Now I can get some distance on them. There's the protector. I can't help it. It's too funny. I wonder if the GMU uniforms are VLine as well. A sweep would look pretty special. Mmmmmm. Sweet somethings. My favorite, and no queue.

"Thanks, Patty." They're still talking, or rather Keet is. "One for each of you."

"Thanks, Eli."

"Ta, lass."

I'd better keep hush. "Find anything on the gemstone eyes?"

Stitch frowns for a moment. "No. She's completely off scan, not even a fake nickname. Could be just shadows."

"With eyeballs?"

Keet shrugs, and Stitch starts with his conspiracy theories again. "I think the whole tagging frenzy was a scam, an excuse to clamp the students. Now the Pramam looks good for lifting the lockdown. Flyer Mud! The GMU had a suspect already remember?"

He's right. If they had a suspect, the whole security hike makes no sense. Well, it's over now, so just move on. I find the eyes more haunting, especially since they tried to grab me. She's watching. She's always watching. In the mirror. In the fog. Those deep gemstone eyes. I don't remember ever meeting her before, but... Heart, slow down. Not here. Not in the commons. Breathe. Too many people. Breathe. They're staring. Stop shaking. Shut up! It's not true. It can't be. It is! Those eyes! Calm down. Breathe. "But…"

"Eli? But what? Shhhhhhhhh. Count with me. One. Two." Who's counting? Where am I?

"…but she apparently knows us." Did I just yell? Why is everyone staring? Keet is mortified. He knows who I am talking about.

Stitch is confused. He leans over and speaks softly. "Remember. You're here on this chair, safe with us. Come back to the room." He grabs Keet's arm. "Don't touch her. You don't want to anchor this."

Quiet. It's very quiet. Is he waiting for me to say something? Deep breath in, then out.

"I'm back. Ta, chum."

"Where did you go?"

Keet gives me the don't-you-tell-him look. Certainly, not here anyway, but Stitch really looks so sad. His hair is droopy. He's hurt. He's hurt we don't trust him. I give Keet the don't-you-think-it's-about-time look, and he sends me back the don't-you-even-*think*-about-it look. Meanwhile, Stitch is retreating.

"Trip. When you're ready then, chumbuds."

Everyone's up at once. Don't tell me it's the zombie thing again. They're all leaving and so is Stitch. Better call him. "Hey!" I don't like that smile. Too cocky. What's he thinking?

"You'd rather stay here? You're going to miss the inauguration." Oh, he's covering for us. Let's go. He follows behind and whispers in my ear. "No bioCal either, yeah?"

"Who needs bioCal when you have a gooseberry. Right, Keet? Honk honk honk." Hehehe. A smirk. It bugs him when I rib his toy. And the goose dig? Clever. But Stitch isn't slow. Anything but. It's time I stop making up stories. I whisper back, "It doesn't work. But you already knew, eh?"

Finally a gentle smile. "I know lots of things. Try me some time."

Ok. That's a challenge. "So where are we going?"

"The Pramam's speech, tough one. Starts in...nine minutes in Rubrique Court. It's on the student calendar, so the bioCal program makes the biochip talk." He leans over closer. "I hear voices too." Poke. Big smile.

"And bioRhythms?"

"Pica Trip! I have it on all the time. My favorite station is Oye Amigos!"

Aha! That's why he's always bopping.

"Doesn't it get noisy in there? How do you hear yourself think?"

"Only listen to one station at a time. Not like you, yeah?"

How true. And my voices aren't nearly as fun. That's a fact. Crap! They have a portable scanner at the arch.

"You have your rubbers, Eli?" Phew. Yeah. I forgot. And Keet? He's good, but he's giving me that what-exactly-did-you-tell-him look. Send him back the don't-worry look. This is silly. We're playing eyeball telepathy.

Stitch throws a pant rip at the operator. We enter the sector together. Juicy. We're through. Everyone's so quiet. I'd better keep my voice down.

"Stitch, why the mutes?"

"Announcements."

"What are they saying?"

"Propaganda. I'll debrief you later." The people around us are staring. Keet kicks my shin. He's right. I shouldn't draw attention to us.

It's an eerie feeling. I can hear yet I am deaf. It's like I am living on the edge of an invisible dimension that I never even knew existed. And now that I do, I feel ever more disconnected than before. Look at them all. They are all in their heads but listening to the same voice. It's unnatural. How am I going to fake this when I start my first shift with Dr. Tenille? Perk. Here he comes. His mouth is moving, but... Crap! Is he going to talk as a bioApp as well? Oh good. Just a volume malfunction.

"Welcome all and may They grant peace upon you."

"They are One."

Better play along. Mumble and point the number three to the sky with my left hand. Then back into a fist. And my turn to kick. Frown at him. Stop playing with the stripper and pay attention.

"Chancellor Vitalidad? Approach the Mount. Blessed be your Trinity in this new assignment. Gracious be They unto you and your community. Perfect are They."

"They are One."

"And finally, please join me in a moment of silent meditation to pay tribute to an honorable guide, Chancellor O'Leary, as he passes through the darkness and into the light where They wait for his Unified spirit."

I know I should look downcast, but I can't help feeling

watched. Almost studied. Shouldn't the counsellor be here? I see most of the teachers in the crowd. He's not on the stage either. Crap! Eyes back down. It's the Pramam's advisor. He is staring. He recognizes me from the daze. I'm positive. And Keet? But surely Stitch. I wish he had worn a hat.

"Perfect are They." Good, it's over.

"They are One."

Ok. So now tell us why you are really here Pramam.

"I have come to offer you my deepest regrets as a fraternity and to address the unspoken terror that has marred the serenity of this venerable institution. Misleading rumors have assumed the responsibility of open communications, and for this They apologize. Recent violations of personal liberties under the authority of the GMU have challenged your trust in the messenger of the Unification's divine mission, and for this They most humbly apologize. Mysterious are Their ways, but Perfect are They."

"They are One."

"Yes. The Truth be known to those who seek it. The atrocities in your very midst have caused the illustrious Pramam to seek Their counsel. The restrictions were necessary during the initial phase of the investigation, but rest assured that as a result we now have a suspect under close surveillance, and the matter has been transferred to the accomplished disciples of the SIF. Perfect are They."

"They are One."

"They, through the word of the Pramam, have lifted the restraints so that you may continue unhindered in Their work. The crimes which have returned to this great civilization after nine years of dormancy shall not persist unpunished. The suffering experienced by the two young girls who have recently perished through the hands of this twisted killer shall be avenged, and on that day, Their children shall be safe again. Perfect are They."

"They are One."

"Let us bow once again in silent meditation for the Trinity in the protectors and the girls who are now United."

The killer is still free? If Mashrin is dead, then why did they move her to the GHU. There should have been a ritual for her. We need to dig deeper into this. Maybe they're using her body as bait? What are Stitch and Keet up to?

"Perfect are They."

"They are One."

"And now for a few announcements from the Inner Council…"

Crap. He's staring this way again. Look away. What *are* they doing? He's not about to… Oh oh.

"*The Emperor's New Clothes*. Juicy!" Keet? No. He didn't! Stitch is having an influence on him. Love it!

That broke the advisor's concentration. I think it's a good time to leave now while everyone is hysterical. They've adjourned the assembly anyway.

"You're crazed, bud. Pica trip!" They just bonded. Good sign. "Perk. Where's the third guy?"

"Who?"

"His second-in-command. Here. I have a flash of him on a slip somewhere. I grabbed it from the morning news. It was taken at the parade yesterday."

"Show us. Over there in the orchard."

He hands me the slip. Keet and I squeeze in close. Don't panic. He's not breathing. I'm not breathing. What the!

"Father!"

K E E T O

Day 33: late evening

Beyond every apparent impasse awaits a tremendous breakthrough, and today proved to be one such threshold, a critical test of absolute trust and exceptional courage. Trust on my part for the sincerity and commitment of a boy who has become my best friend, and courage on Eli's part to willingly deliver herself into the realm of her greatest nightmare. And as for the closing part of my particular day? A whole new level of trust, which I'll get to later. But first...

There was no denying the disparate choices that lay before us. On one hand, we could let Father defeat us, as Eli's mental state continues to deteriorate and to become impotent with fear. On the other, we could thrust ourselves passionately into the psychological battlefield that has become our reality. His privileged position on the Inner Council as the Pramam's favored puppet endows him with an arsenal of powerful resources to wield for whatever campaigns he elects to support, such as maintaining a veil of secrecy around the real significance behind a young girl's tragedy. It was due time for me to give Stitch the much belated honor he deserves, so that, as one, we could support Eli in the dangerous assignment only she can complete.

After we had recovered from the shock of Father's secret identity, we retreated to Stitch's room and initiated a candid conversation. Eli bared her heart to him, releasing years of repressed anger and frustration in a gushing flood of emotions. It was as if her delicate dam, precariously patched with years of sheer will, had finally succumbed to the fissures that the voices and nightmares were constantly forming, and had suddenly burst from the added stress of the past month. As best she could, through the tears, she divulged the most intimate details of her inner struggle, the likes of which she had been protecting me from until now. She admitted to having consciously neglected certain facts in order to avoid arriving at conclusions that she could not reasonably accept. Today marked the end of Eli's intellectual prison.

Stitch was visibly moved. All three of us had become fully vulnerable to each other's motives and ultimately responsible for each other's lives. He embraced Eli tightly and simply allowed her to soften in his arms. You can well imagine the displeasure I was experiencing at this foreign physical display, but my decision to trust, unconditionally, tempered my reaction. When I reached over to caress Eli's shoulder in sincere adoration, she jumped into my arms and gave me a big kiss on the cheek, inadvertently dragging Stitch's head with her. His hair had chosen to join in the fun and had wound itself around a lock of her hair, which prompted a much needed laugh. Out came the hands, and down came the fists, as we sealed our unbreakable bond with the chumbuds salute.

Our hopes had returned, and our next task did not seem quite as daunting. At midi, Eli was to meet Dr. Tenille, so we had to sketch quickly through the maze for as much information as we could gather about the security and the exact location of Mashrin's body in the GHU complex. While the packets were building the access instructions Eli would follow, we reanalyzed the possible significance of my informant's latest two-part note in light of Father's suspected role.

Let's start with the shorter statement: "She still exists in her mind." What if "she" and "her" did not represent the same person? Could Mashrin still exist in Eli's mind? If "she" were referring to Eli, at this point, we concluded that it was no longer accurate, since we had just witnessed a very dramatic vertical shift in her awareness, which implies that her perspective has started to expand past the limited intellect. Besides, all three of us know Mashrin exists so that interpretation does not make any sense. On the flip side, perhaps it is Mashrin who still exists in her own mind, a highly unreasonable scenario for a dead person. I must side with science on that one, unless we are open to entertaining the improbable. Maybe you can tell us.

The second part I include here for the record.

"Broken and torn shall she reveal herself to you in the darkest hour of her existence. And you shall come to her begging for forgiveness and she should say to you there is nothing to forgive being that you and she are entangled in a dance for all eternity and shall become that which is right and virtuous through no misdeeds of your own."

This one is clearer to me, although I have been proven wrong before, by your lovely daughter in fact, to her invariable delight. Is this a prophecy of this morning's breakdown, or unimaginably worse, a warning that more suffering is yet to come and that I am somehow unwittingly responsible for bringing her to the brink of despair? I fear the hallucinations have already begun. Certain aspects of Eli's testimony were contradictory. Furthermore, except for the three officials chasing her from a publicly declared restricted zone for illegally skipping curfew, finding a body on campus, and running into an exotic beauty from time to time, she is the only witness to all other accounts. Even your missing jewel and the exchange she claims to have spied outside our kitchen window play into a paranoid delusion. I remember what you were like, talking to the void, and frantically searching for items you claimed "they" stole from you, just to find them turn up later in your hands. And what about the messages? Has her passion for adventure become an obsession and needs to seduce others in its game, culminating in the ultimate thrill: engulfed in the belly of the GHU?

Between the Ministry conspiracy argument, Father's appearance, and my own private theories, I was apprehensive about letting her follow through with the internship, but Stitch appeased my worries somewhat with another ingenious trick, and I opted to reserve my final judgment until the return. Allegedly, according to Dr. Tenille, there were vaults on location where each physician maintained unofficial patient logs, notes, thoughts, and the like in personal journals. Borrowing your entries in his past records and those of your previous medic was our best chance of grasping the full extent of your disability and saving Eli's sanity. Alternatively, I figured that if this were indeed solely another fabrication within an elaborate fantasy, then her being discovered and hospitalized may be the safest path for her in the end. Of course, this latter thought is between you and me.

KEETO

Before we parted, Stitch gently untied Eli's ponytail and adjusted a band over her ears, fluffing her hair with the pomp of an expert coiffeur. He explained that since there was a plausible chance that Father might be at the GHU, this device would keep her abreast of any sudden security broadcasts. The imbedded earpiece in the fabric intercepts bioApp transmissions, cracks their frequencies, decodes the contents, encodes it back onto the audible frequency range, and focuses an amplified signal directly into the ear canal. I wouldn't mind one of those myself, but it would have taken Stitch a few hours to make a more masculine version for me, and he wanted to continue hacking the advisor's communications. As I had been given the day off in response to the Pramam's request for exclusive access to the archives during his visit, I too had other priorities. I needed to spend the afternoon in the commercial sector, shopping for a formal linen shirt, a space heater for my little buddy, and most importantly, another bookshelf. We all took a deep breath and agreed to regroup back at Stitch's after her shift.

I found my way through the fog and onto Tir-na-nog Square surprisingly fast. Even though the frequency thrower Stitch lent me works brilliantly in reflect mode, acting like an echo location device, I would have preferred that the blowers had been left operating after the chancellor had temporarily ignited them on the island for the speech. Instead, I had to contend with the disturbing notion that the Pramam, his advisor, or even Father could be lurking in the mist, which likely was the source of my shivering along the entire route. Without a biochip, it was futile trying to pinpoint the particular shops I was interested in, since their bioIntro announcements fell on real ears, so I entered each establishment in sequence, pretending to browse.

The first establishment on the left, belonged to a speciality clothing boutique, selling none other than Stew Uber's latest VLine collection, Naked, touted as being so comfortable it's like wearing nothing at all. He has no idea! I couldn't help but snicker, drawing disapproving glares from the sales clerk. I bolted straight back out into the courtyard. A few stores down, I found a more traditional tailor, purchased a bright purple tunic, feeling a little adventurous myself these days and continued down the row until I happened upon a sweet shop. As I indulged in the variety of free samples, I felt a tingling behind my neck. I had been so enthralled by the glucose buffet that I hadn't noticed the owner's assistant following me, sensually teasing me with her warm breath. It was Caroline.

You can imagine my dumbfounded expression when I turned around and dropped the dribbling bonbon onto the floor. She watched as I slowly reached down for it past her long curvy thighs. Her hands on her hips and her head slightly cocked, she stood there giggling at my obvious embarrassment. After I had snapped back into my body, and she had playfully squeezed the juice off my fingers with her glove, the questions shot out of my mouth faster than my brain could properly formulate them. Where had she been? What had she done to get expelled? Why didn't she comm? What's her connection with the Ministry? And most importantly, how and what does she know about the tunnel system? But all she did was smile right into my eyes, and casually slide the soiled protective sheath off her hand, one finger at a time, deliberately stroking the shaft of each digit as she winked, then nonchalantly casting it into a bin behind the counter. Juicy!

She was thoroughly enjoying my discomfort, as we lingered there in awkward silence, the suspicious owner squinting in our general direction. Once she decided that she had sufficiently tortured me, she grabbed my hand, led me to the stock room, and leaned invitingly against the closed door. She had been here in this shop, working for peanuts she said, if there were such a thing anymore. She had ignored the counsellor's reprimands one too many times, according to his godliness, and willfully corrupted an innocent young freshman. She didn't comm because his holier-than-the-Pramam forbade her further contact with us, under pain of GMU restraints. Then shedding the sarcastic undertones, she added that the Pramam's advisor is a regular patron of the underground club who can give her what she craves better than anyone else there, so he has become a special friend of hers, whatever that means. And as for the shafts, she enticed me closer, beckoning me with her left index finger and, with suppressed excitement, lowered her voice.

Since frequenting the counsellor's office had become a habit of hers, she often relieved her boredom by staring listlessly into the garden until one day she noticed a person disappear into the back corner. As she left detainment that evening, she hid beside the limestone structure and waited for the counsellor to leave the building, before cutting through the trellised garden and into the carefully disguised access vent, the sun catcher in the far east corner. She discovered that there is a dangerous labyrinth underneath the entire campus oval, which would explain how easily the dark figure from the arcade had escaped the hounds' swift pursuit. She cautioned that at a moment's notice, these tunnels, like the separate network under the rest of the city, can saturate with deadly gases, and she very nearly turned victim to such an exposure once. And here comes the most fantastic bit of all; she announced that as she was searching for a similar grid under the main corridor, she spotted that same stranger entering the base of the Victory Bridge and followed her northwards to a tunnel on the right leading to a rusted metal door with a circle etched into it.

Before I could even digest what I had heard, there was a loud impatient knock. While her employer was forcefully verbalizing his irritation, Caroline grabbed an entire box of jellies, lead me to the credit counter, swiped it, and smiling courteously, thanked me for my patronage.

Vastly behind schedule, I was glad to see the sun poking through the haze. I went directly to Mr. G's to pick up the remaining two items on my list, where I was met with quite a cold reception. The quake had essentially damaged only his place, since it was made of antique construction, but I sensed that his almost resentful demeanor was aimed at me personally. I really was too rushed to confront him, so I paid for the goods, ran back to my quarters, dumped them off, took care of Sparky's needs, and ran back to Van Billund Hall, where Eli and Stitch were already discussing their individual findings. My skull was exploding, however, from the whirlwind trip to the commercial sector, so I flopped into a virtachair, physically, mentally, and emotionally drained.

Stitch looked at Eli, then they both looked at me, and in unison they blurted: "Share, chumbud." I improvised a brief synopsis, but all I needed to say was the word "Caroline" and Stitch leapt for a slip and highlighted a series of images showing her virtues wantonly compromised. Evidently her relationship with the Pramam's advisor extends into his private residence as well. He fancies himself quite the amateur holographer, but Eli's interest in Caroline centered on the rusted metal door. Despite our repeated attempts to reason with her, she was relentless in her belief that we absolutely had to determine who or what was behind it. The allusion that doing so might fling us into the den of a killer only increased her resolve. The logic was bent, the risks were horrendous, and the benefits questionable, but her stance was firm, so with a few gas masks, some frequency throwers, and an anonymous tip to the SIF, we could send the Ministry goons, including Father, back to Ministburg where they belong. Her report from her first day at the GHU and the rest of Stitch's research results would have to wait.

I recall dancing inside my pants outside the entrance, thinking that I would rather be tracking Caroline's twisted fixations than someone who has an affinity for slicing brains, and judging by Stitch's quivering hair, I'm sure he would have concurred. Eli, on the other hand, was transfixed on the doorknob and unintelligibly mumbling to herself, making me even more nervous when I realized that one of her episodes was not a solution to our immediate challenge. Fortunately, I had mistaken her focused meditation for lunacy, and we soon entered the dank lobby, gratefully alive.

Pausing at the base of a dimly lit staircase, we listened for movement from above while Stitch sent a crabbot to investigate. With our focus locked on the receiver, we agonized over every floor, room, and hallway, expecting to see ceiling at any moment as the villain rips our brave explorer in half. We eventually viewed the top level, which appeared to be the main living area. Satisfied that the home was vacant, we ascended all the way and scoured the studio for clues. While Stitch recorded the visual contents for future reference, and Eli followed her ears, my stomach convulsed as I recognized the faint scent of myrrh coming from the sleeping area. A chronology of internal flashes flew by my eyes, landing with a heavy thud on my heart. The penetrating gaze, the sweet smile, and the silky black coat whisked me back to our first day in Eadonberg. Surely, the beautiful stranger was no psycho, but Eli's muted scream by the window suggested otherwise.

As Stitch and I ran to her aid, she motioned him to take at least a dozen flashes of the specimen. We couldn't be sure, but it looked like a piece of brain with two tiny holes in it, and it was suspended in viscous blue goo with strange luminescent properties. As we stared and stared with a mix of horror and amazement, we watched the slime swim towards us through the crystal vase and hover. Eli had the foresight to take the recorder from Stitch's awestruck hands and capture his priceless expression, so that we could both rib him later, then she swiftly tucked the vessel into her satchel and ushered us through the surface entrance. Once outside, we noted our surroundings and hopped the next hovertrain southbound.

If there was an ounce of energy left in me by the time I

reached my quarters, I was oblivious to it. Even the idea of writing to you tonight seemed like Mount Everest, but once I walked through that door, everything changed.

The scent was unmistakable. Neatly folded at the foot of my bed was my missing shirt, and on the chair, a face full of jellies stuck in his fur, was Sparky, sitting comfortably on her lap.

"You didn't make your move yet," was the first sentence she uttered. As she threw the playing sticks, her crystal pendant caught the moonlight through the slit. I froze.

"Don't you want to play?" The words just seemed to roll off me as she pointed to your game, invading me with those gemstone eyes, and finally declared:

"I am the one."

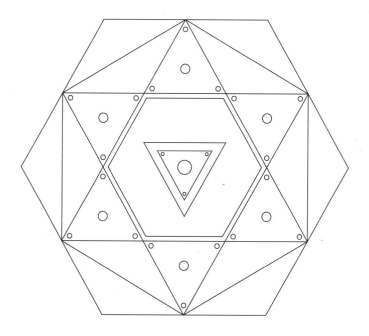

CHAPTER EIGHT

N A T H R U Y U

Day 34: before dawn

Her consciousness hovers in a weightless void, resenting the impending dawn. As nights wash by, her patience grows thinner, whilst those denying her destiny encroach on her territory and fruitlessly prime the perimeter of her cell in anticipation of her imminent capture. They have committed their souls to a dangerous game, one which neither shall vanquish, for although logic would dictate multiple outcomes founded on paradoxical rules, there is only one. The eternal battle between the illusion of order and the illusion of anarchy is nearing a close, and soon Elize will also be drawn into the contest as circumstances heal her mind for the challenge. The sibling ties are still strong and secure a direct path for Nathruyu's agency in spite of *their* recent proximity. Keeto's preternatural feelings will indeed oblige her well as she moves to strike a final time.

An incoming board message addressed to Odwin announces to her that the wild card has been tamed. Her illegitimate portrayal as Zafarian's trusted mentor is presently reaping the rewards of his loyalty as he is keeping Odwin-Nathruyu dutifully informed while their unofficial investigation progresses. Elize has confirmed the whereabouts of the young

Mashrin, has conducted a thorough scan of her skin, and has negated any uncertainties Nathruyu may have harbored relative to her corporal integrity. Apart from the probes feeding various monitors, it appears that the scar marking the primary assault is intact, and, as noted in the medical lab, she remains curiously warm, wrapped in a silver shroud, for reasons none of them can fathom. But Nathruyu knows what clock they are chasing.

As expected, Elize's first visit to the GHU facility since her mother's accident had been trying, and Zafarian is understandably concerned for her safety, especially in light of her father's Inner Council affiliation and his presence within the city. The corners of her mouth curl upwards in smug satisfaction as she recalls Vincent's parting request. She assures the boy that the matter has been suitably handled, and that Elize can complete her internship with the eccentric Dr. Tenille without restrictions. As for Zaf's ongoing standing with the twins, he must abide by his promise to offer them full transparency in order to solidify his position as their dependable confidant, and then report back any changes in Elize's behavior via this secure channel, however trivial he might infer them to be, specifically as it relates to the affliction she seems to have inherited from her mother.

Posing as Odwin, Nathruyu cleverly diverts their communication onto the subject of the enigmatic herald and her cryptic prose. She covertly plants theories as to the woman's authenticity, and asks Zaf if he has accumulated snippets of intelligence regarding her true identity, or if he has attempted to map her penmanship against government employee records, thus hinting that this stranger may, in fact, enjoy an inside perspective on the mutilations, which could lead to the answers they seek, and perhaps even address his private motives with respect to his cousin's murder. Her cunning exploitation of his sentiments for Elize is already sufficient to ensure his cooperation, but this additional seed will assist in cultivating the alliance she has proposed to Keeto, as she packages the mysterious collaborator's history and highlights her plausible access to vital Ministry resources. Having satisfactorily devised a bilateral mechanism for claiming her eagerly awaited prize, she prepares to abandon Zafarian, her naive accomplice, to his research, so that, owing to his sleuthing efforts, she can bring closure to what he and Keeto had interrupted, but his subsequent transmission springs out of the maze and arrests her with its words.

After laboring to regain control of her limbs, she breaks free of the paralysis and rushes to the window where the specimen once thrived. Her anguish quickly turns to anger as she realizes what they have done. Seizing command over her escalating fury, she rejoins the dialog and chastises Zaf for carelessly endangering his life just to entertain the whims of an increasingly unstable girl. She insists that he never again consent to wander the poisonous labyrinth. Furthermore, she warns him that the skills and ruse he has acquired are merely rudimentary compared to what terror lurks in the shafts, to which he acquiesces and solemnly admits to having likely stumbled upon the killer's hideout and stolen a crystal vase that they think may contain the missing section of Mashrin's brain.

As he presses on, spilling the details of their intrusion, she contemplates the possibility that Elize may have anonymously contacted the SIF, that the evidence may actually be in their possession, and that her sanctuary may be compromised. She manipulates his fears and implores him to comm Elize immediately, falsely explaining that there is probably a recorder attached to the vessel, and Elize's portrait will be broadcast to the SIF, who will surely retain her for questioning. While Nathruyu nervously waits for news of her response, she emphasizes that it is critical that they store the perishable organ safely in Elize's room and leave interactions with officials to her well-connected devices, as a respected underground leader. She adds that information on this criminal's location could quite possibly be a highly advantageous bargaining chip for the network and facilitate some much needed favors from allies in the Ministry.

Developing an intimate relationship with Keeto may prove to require a more delicate approach than she had projected, particularly if he has sensed an odd familiarity permeating her living quarters. Fortunately, she has not yet divulged when and where their meeting is to occur tomorrow, giving her freedom to select an appropriate alternative. Thanks to the handwriting inquiry she has suggested, the favorable biography Zafarian will certainly recite to him later on should overshadow whatever suspicions he might carry concerning her guilt, which is, after all, a judgment beyond his usual realm and best reserved for one who exhibits her prescient gift.

Nathruyu's fabricated threat has implanted itself in the subconscious of the thief. Zafarian attests to having relayed the caution to Elize, hence successfully guaranteeing the agenda for the next couple of hours, allowing her time to scheme an impromptu detour en route to the GHU. As the trio belatedly debrief each other on yesterday's fruitful enterprises, the riveting late night guest no doubt occupying the gist of the conversation, she reassures Zaf that the culprit shall be taken care of and that Mashrin will receive the ritual her spirit rightfully deserves. In closing, they agree to reconvene at dusk, in order to discuss how the holistic community can support Elize by recommending natural remedies for her ailment, based on her mother's documented diagnosis in the unpublished patient journals of her allopathic physicians.

She lays her hand upon the sill, where the treasured fragment had lain and releases the tightness in her chest, absorbing the remnants of its existence through the tips of her aching fingers. The last rays of the sun stream between the structures across the main corridor and pierce the empty frame to burrow into her flesh before the thickening sky ultimately engulfs them. All is not lost, but she must recover her stolen property and put the whole embarrassment behind her, as long as time permits her to do so.

The fog, as always, fosters the perfect environment for her clandestine maneuvers. Nathruyu steps out from the sanctity of her refuge and onto the precarious ledge that separates her from the stagnant waters underfoot. Only the saturated air blanketing the surface beneath her shoes can temper her speed.

The eyes tell tales in the mist and, as such, do not serve the bearer, for what prowls the white darkness cannot be seen with blinded sensors. Nathruyu shelters them from deception and summons the sentient field surrounding her physical form. The Ministry pundits persist in their inquest and have appointed the SIF to her case. They also can navigate the pathways, devoid of sight; however, their reliance on technology is no substitute for honing the senses. She comfortably weaves her way through their sweeping grid, as is her artful craft, and glides in the slipstream of the morning rush, flirtatiously stroking their boots with the hem of her silky white coat, as she wisps along under their very noses, numbed by the scent of the powdery clouds. Their numbers overrun the walkways, unbeknownst to the mentally severed pedestrians who, preoccupied with the Unification propaganda which clogs their porous brains, scurry on and funnel towards the hum of the arriving hovertrain and into the diffuse glow of the crimson beams that radiate from the platform circles at their feet.

Nathruyu coasts amongst the glowing columns as they precede the updraft and soars to the seaward end of the promenade on the trail of the sweet orchard fragrance. The static grove is easier to traverse. She sails past the parkette, slicing the brume with her hawk-like intent, to settle her restless hand around the edge of the bottom rung in the ladder of suspended hallways that join the center and south central branches of Van Billund Hall. Between the towers, she scales, harnessing the momentum of each pendulum swing, and propels her legs gracefully upwards and onto the arch of the fifth catwalk. Rifting a transient grip in the siding and hooking her ankles upside down in the hollow, she crawls her sinewy arms down to the window's lip outside Zafarian's room and pulls her eyes over the trim and against the glass. With her long black hair dangling off her left shoulder to the hidden grass below, her pelvis hugs the manmade precipice. Quietly, she hangs, and she watches.

There he huddles, as she remembers him from her aborted attack, feverishly sketching through the maze for the threads she has entwined in its fabric. An image of the latest riddle she penned is plainly visible beside a few textual paragraphs and an understated likeness of her. He imprints on the slips the packets he considers relevant and nudges his crabseat sideways to the flicker at the door to his right. Her heels anchored to the perch, she pushes her face away slightly, to recede into obscurity, while the greetings conclude and the voices regroup at the desk. Her breath blows a fresh puff from the pane, clearing a portal for her to spy through once again, and to witness her official profile being fed to receptive ears. Satisfied with her plan as it is unfolding and amused by the curious mane of her pawn straightening its tentacles in her direction, she locks her penetrating gaze on Keeto's ruminating one and smiles. The player is stirring.

The pressure clamping her arches signals that the rift has expired. It is rebounding and shortening the depth of the hole. She instantly throws her weight forward, grabs the underside of the link, and swoops her falling legs ahead of her, to land soundlessly on the rooftop beneath. Pausing her climb to collect her thoughts, she visualizes the fastest line to the J block, travels it behind closed eyes and rewinds the sequence as often as her muscle memory deems necessary. Five tiers up and an airy hop launches her to the top of the middle tower. She then aims her advance eastward, jumps down to the abutting link, tiptoes across to the subsequent branch and repeats her stealthy exercise to the north.

As it was at the start of their big adventure, Nathruyu lingers at the cusp of a sharp drop and reminisces as a tiny wave beckons her to come and play.

▼ ▼ ▼

She reaches for the giggling toddler, stretching her fingers towards her in the mist and enters the mythical world of a dreamer. United, they travel to distant lands, where sundry sorts of fanciful creatures dwell, some gleefully jumping into the joyful chaos whilst others simply choose to watch. Those lacking the visions fear that which they cannot see, and the child weeps as the fearful conspire to fracture their unique bond, alleging unnatural influence on the part of her new friend.

▲ ▲ ▲

The little voice calling her name retreats to the cloudy distance, leading Nathruyu past the open sunshaft and to the edge of the roof, directly above Elize's room.

Sensing an anomaly in the seal she had meticulously applied, her hands smooth the entire zone and look for signs of willful tampering. They are rewarded by a razor thin break in the consistency of the material, closer to the west-facing wall. Her nails trace a crooked rectangle large enough to enable a slender adult to pass, and she lifts the well-concealed panel to reveal a crawl space between her and the ninth floor ceiling, providing convenient and inconspicuous admittance to any unit on the level, or, conversely, a wily escape. This work was a result of no masterful feat of her own, but accomplished by common etching tools; yet, nonetheless, it efficiently suits her current purpose. She confronts the dark as she readies her emitter for its second assignment today and continues forth on her knees until she encounters that which destroys all semblance of inner peace.

The stupid girl! The immense risks Nathruyu had assumed when she had spent an afternoon in this devious building which is programmed to recognize her return and abduct her, were for not. Any frequency that is able to squeeze through the slit Elize carved can now deliberately invade her dorm, and random entities, adequately adept at locating the obvious breach in security overhead, can pilfer at will.

With the rage still wreathing inside and interfering with her concentration, the simple task of retrieving her cherished treasure becomes an arduous chore as she battles the privyshelf for dominance. After scouring the contents of the shelving, the transfer chest, satchels, clothing, and every conceivable secret nook, she barely holds the fine veneer of calm together, but is transformed into a burning layer of steam consuming her from head to toe as she sinks to the ground in stark realization that it is, in effect, gone.

She drifts in and out of the minefield of emotions shattering her resolve and turns to her freshly enlisted partner for hope. Last evening, her instincts did not betray her. The leap of faith she expressed in revealing her features to Keeto confirmed that he is ripe for one of his own. In the beginning, he had recoiled, afraid of his vulnerability in the company of a suspected stalker, someone who knew where he lived and waited in the shadows for him to relinquish his crypt to her trespasses, but as she toyed with his occult views on synchronicity and teased his ego with concurrence, his jittering nerves relaxed and his heart softened enough for her to slowly mold as she pleases. His sister, she flattered him, did not share his foresight, nor the otherworldly connection with their mother, which ranked his awareness high above that of the ignorant mortal, and that was the reason she had selected him, the sole person she could entrust with knowledge even the Pramam himself had no appreciation for. All this and infinitely more was available to him, in due course, in exchange for his unwavering devotion.

She heeds her wise advice and submits to the present situation, a predicament she has just once previously found herself in and, consequently, has no stable reference point on how to assimilate the disgrace relating to her second failure. With each ill-fated attempt, she jeopardizes her liberation and that of countless individuals, albeit temporarily asleep to her cause, but her preeminence over the feeble-minded detectives, encumbered by a vain pursuit, will expose them to her intrinsic greatness, and the meek shall bow to the sheer magnitude of her selfless nobility when these minor offenses have been forgotten. Her purity will prevail over the farce that purports to be the undisputed messenger and which holds most of humanity captive in a factitious belief system, catering to his delusions of grandeur.

Having internalized her brief struggle with despair, she

emerges victorious and electrified by an invisible force nourishing her blood and charging her synaptic clefts with a limitless source of pure abundance. The strength she has attracted further manifests as both clarity of thought and affirmation of faith. Mashrin has become collateral damage in a quest for enlightenment, an unfortunate victim to her past and a role for which any number of young sacrifices could have similarly been suited, but regardless of how her tragic loss has affected their lives, the righteousness of her condemned misdeeds is indisputable, according to the essence of this grand design. The correct solution to this shortly to be proven insignificant crisis is to let it be. Nothing and no one can stop what fate has preordained, and whatever events unfold are in precise alignment with the intended end, despite how they might display themselves in the moment. The real test will arise on the day Keeto's convictions collide against what his intuition would incite him to believe, and Elize's life lies in the balance.

She honors her vow to attend to Mashrin's body in the proper manner and forgoes the search for the slice. As she resets the storage areas to their original state, repositioning the items she disturbed in the process, she creates a mental inventory of the objects that were under protection, but interrupts the procedure upon discovering an unexpected piece. Her coveting fingertips quiver as she caresses the contours of the polished reddish shard. Desires that she has been forcibly burying resurface. She has touched this peculiar stone before, but what is its significance in Elize's effects? Worrisome speculation could consume the bulk of her energy and would undoubtedly spawn even more provocative questions, such as who else knows its heritage. She subdues her curiosity, rapidly tidies the outstanding disarray, cleans the DNA residues that could incriminate her, and flies out of the attic. Steady and on track, she bears in the direction of the GHU transition wing.

ELIZE

Day 34: early morning

Not again. How am I going to explain this one. I haven't left the room. Enough of that too. I'm running out of cream. Crap. Keet's here.

"Hey lo, Eli. You won't believe what... Have you slept at all?"

"Hush." Grab the journals. "Walk with me." I hope Stitch found something useful. Keep up, Keet.

"Ease a bit. What's the rush?"

Tap, tap, tap. Are we stopping on every floor? Predictable. This lighting is... Eek. I'm a mess! And you over there, yeah, you. Stop staring. Good. On level five. Let's clip across the link. Oops.

"Sorry, Keet, forgot you have no secure band." Zap.

"Juicy. Another one of Stitch's toys?"

"Works on the sentinels every time. Here. Use the thrower on the next one." Almost at Stitch's.

"Hang for a sec. Eli!" What now?

"So your girlfriend left you another love note? You can share that with us in just—"

"No. She brought my shirt back."

"Lucky you. She does laundry too." Hehehe.

"It's her. The beautiful stranger. She was waiting for me when I got back last night."

Was that another one of my voices? Did I hear him say the

stalker was in his crypt? Give it a shake. "She what?" We're here.

"She…"

"Keet, bud, you've got yourself a mole. Hey lo, chum." Don't look at him and he won't notice. I hope. "Grab a seat."

Right. Crabseat? I don't think so. "I'll take the floor." Oh, sorry. Did I offend you? "Ouch!" The nasty little thing. "Fine! I'll sit then. Behave." Yes. They *are* amused.

"What's a mole?"

"A rodent, dear brother. Kind of like your protector." Hehehe. Now where did he learn that snare face from, I wonder.

"Operative term for someone on the inside. The handwriting, see?" I thought he couldn't find any images? Does Odwin have a dust filter? "I used the flash I took of your love note." He grins and pokes Keet. "And this is what came up. The image has dust sprinkled all over it, that's why I couldn't find it using the frame Eli had."

I knew it! Brrr. My energy must be low. I'm going to have trouble staying awake today.

"Perk. She's no shadow in the mist."

Good. So now maybe they won't look at me like I'm bent. What's with Stitch? Has he gone VLine?

"Are you going to an Inner Council meeting or something? What happened to the squirmy guys? I was starting to get used to them, but this look is soooooooooo sophisticated." Actually, the cut brings out the twinkle when he smiles. He doesn't look half-bad, but I'm not going to tell him that of course.

"Not enough sleep?" They're ganging up on me again.

"I've never seen you as a blonde. Ooo. Your shoes are so

shiny. Where did you build the credit for those? Is that silk? Eek! You sold your soul to the devil." Gasp for effect. He does have all the makings of a high official with that outfit. And they are still frowning. Keet touches my forehead. Stop that. Something's not right here. They're looking very concerned. Am I the only one seeing this?

"Maybe you should flip a pass on your classes today, eh?"

"Ya fig? I agree. I don't want to say it but…" But what? Say it, dweeb. Big yawn. Try not to drift. "Right. Let me give you the highlights then. You trip, chum?" Nod. "Her name is Nathruyu. She works for the GHU in catering."

"That's it? There has to be more." Keet looks disappointed, as if he half expected she had a more sinister biography.

"It's pica Tess, bud. It's a great cover. She gets to eavesdrop on all sorts of conversations and socialize with pretty much everyone in a non-threatening way. She's just a servant for the elite."

Keet turns to me, puzzled, and whispers. "Who's Tess?"

Shrug. "I think he means genius."

"Whatever murmurs are floating around at meal time, her ears are twitching. And here, it says she also delivers."

Hmmm. I bet she does. "Well, Keet. Does she deliver?" Aw. He's embarrassed. Hehehe.

Stitch liked that one, but his turn for confusion. "Share. Another note?"

Can't help myself. "A date. And did you know she does laundry too?"

"Ha ha. Let it ride, Eli." Nice tonsils there, Stitch. "She says she is the one. We had a nice chat. That picture really doesn't do her justice. It doesn't capture her eyes…and her smile…and her hair. It's like velvet. And…"

Oh, get a grip, boy.

"You *are* a puddle of mush! She can't be trusted. We don't even know her motive."

"Odwin seems to suggest she is connected to the network somehow. Maybe she's underground."

"But why is she following me? And how did she get in Father's flashes?" Oh, honestly, Keet.

"She's playing with your mind. All these vague statements, these psycho riddles. What exactly is she reading in your journal anyway?" She could be a double-mole and feeding the GHU a little more than just food.

"Shakes! Maybe she watched it all. That night, with Mashrin."

The wrigglers are back?

"She's no double-mole, Eli." Did I say that out loud? "She has a crystal, just like this one. It's a sign."

Sure. Right. Keet's bent. I always knew he was a little off in the spook department. What a pair we make.

"Swish! She's the... Creeps! Not good." Stitch is getting very serious now. "Bud, maybe you need to slack on this new girl of yours." That makes sense to me.

"For the last time, you two. She is *not*—"

"Got it. We're done with that. Right, Stitch?" He's trip with that, and I know what he's thinking. It's in my gut as well. I remember her hanging over me, and the tinted shine. And the voices. They were quiet, almost too quiet, like they were hiding, afraid. It's all coming back, and the words. So confused. I don't understand. Sleepy. Crap. Stay awake.

"Triple-mole maybe. I knew I saw a crystal before. On the dark figure, in the arcade." Stitch can't handle this one. It's not safe.

"You blanked out, Stitch, remember? Besides, lots of people wear jewelry. It could have been anything. It was blacker than black out there. Keet's the one who saw it best. So is it her?" Come on. Help me out here.

"No. Nathruyu is Snow White. She's doesn't murder children." That's a take-charge attitude. The world doesn't only have two crystals anyway.

Good. Stitch is backing off. "Truce, bud. I fly wild sometimes." Chumbuds greeting.

"She said the holding area is like a lab. They have special equipment for the dead."

"I saw the equipment. Does she know what they're for?"

"Something about brain waves. As long as they keep the bodies warm."

"Creeps, yeah?" Stitch's hair is shuddering.

"Does Dr. Tenille know?"

"Didn't ask. I faked a bathroom break and snuck in. But nothing in his notes. Lots of medical jargon I don't understand yet. Mother's entries don't have any real insights either. He calls it an altered state of consciousness. Her previous medic Dr. Kzavier, on the other hand, had all sorts of bent theories. I mean, ghoulish." Boo!

"Jenny's grandfather maybe?" Good whip, Keet. Her and her soul suckers.

"Wouldn't surprise me. But too young. His last entry is

just a big blotch of ink. I think he scared himself to death."
Hehehe. "Not bedtime reading material for the easily rattled."
I guess that's me. The nightmares just wouldn't stop last night.
I felt like someone was watching me again.

"Well, the worm in the blue goo was grody enough, yeah?
Did it jump out and possess you? I mean, you do look like the
walking dead." Snare. "Just a rib, lass." A poke and a grin.

"Ta, dweeb."

More tonsils. Poke back. Keet's rolling.

"We have to fig what to do with the slice. We should hand
it to Odwin; it's too risky for you to keep it." That would be a
problem.

"Is it still...um swimming?"

Here it goes. Just spit it out. "Well...not exactly." They're
waiting. "It's gone." And here it comes.

"Gone? You mean it *did* jump out?" They're both aghast.

"No. The vessel's gone too. It must have happened in-
between nightmares. When you commed this morning, Keet,
I was semi-asleep, and after we assalammed, I went looking
for it."

"How ya fig? Your room is a fortress. In an abnormal way."
Stitch is right, but still they must have... Hang a sec. Oh crap.
The ceiling. Hick. Keet beat me to it.

"The ceiling. They came through the roof. We need to fix
this. That must be how the jewel disappeared too."

Yeah. And where's my apology? "But my privyshelf. It's
sharp."

"They're trip, but not perfect." Stitch should know.

"And the secret recorder? Won't my face be on it?"

"I'll check with Odwin. See what he suggests. Don't crack yet." What if the killer came and took it back? That means... Heartbeat, slow down. "I'm on it, chum."

I know his smile is supposed to reassure me. Just breathe. Yawn. Stay awake. Don't need an episode. Speaking of which...

"...my mother. You find anything on the hack?"

"I can't be sure, but it looks like your mother was an orphan. She was just found one day, a kid wandering the hills not too far from here. Her biochip wasn't working either."

That's before she got sick. Even before we were born.

"Any mention of our father?" I can feel Keet's hand tensing against my thigh.

"It's sparse. A sage master took her in and was grooming her for service, then she just left. She was seventeen. Not a single packet on your man."

"A commit order? Nothing?" Keet is incensed.

Stitch shakes his head and sighs. "No surprise, yeah? He's more slippery than the Pramam's advisor. Maybe her mentor has a history." He hesitates. "There's more, isn't there, Eli, in the logs?"

He found it too. It's stuck in my throat. Out.

"Yeah." I don't have to say it. We all know it. She had the mark. Just like Mashrin. Just like Keet and I. What do I say if he asks? Please. Don't ask. Hold back those tears.

"Lie low, yeah? I'll sketch a bit more before class. Trip?"

Nod.

"And I'll see if I can find out why the Ministry is monopolizing the archives again today. Sweet sleep."

"Thanks both." Yawn. "Chumbuds!" Hands out. Punch

him, then slap.

Yawn. Brain dead. Am I there yet? Even my voices are lying low. Whoa. Yawn. Won't miss much in psych. Know all about that from experience. Anatomy? Saw a piece of brain up close too. Yawn...

✄ ✄ ✄

"What are you doing here?"

Is that music?

"Way! Eli! Hey lo! What are you doing here?"

Caroline? Wake up, girl. I'm in my room sleeping, right? But it's a loud one. Am I at the club? How did I get here?

"You shouldn't be here."

It's her! Nathruyu! In the corner. Quick. Grab Caroline and head for the bar. How *did* I get here? Crap. She's looking for answers and I have none. I should let go now.

"Um. Just bored." That worked. Not sure I'm ready for this. What logic did I use to come here? Can she see me from the corner? No. Good.

"Well, if he finds out... Didn't your cousin tell you?"

My cousin? Oh right. She means Keet. "No worries. I won't tell."

"I'll be in deep." Who is she kidding.

"Not any more than you already are." Shut up. Why did I say that?

"What do you mean?" I don't like that tone. She's not looking very charming right now.

"Where's your special friend? Shouldn't you be riding it

with him on the private?" I'm not sure I like that mischievous smirk.

"Why? You interested in joining us?" What an attitude! She has absolutely no propriety. She's leaning over. "I won't tell." And giggling. She's taunting me. How cocky. Hands off. And guys fall for you? "Ease, pretty. Why not have some fun while you're here." She's looking over at two guys around the counter. "You can start small and work your way up."

What does that mean? Does all that hair twirling really work? Ugh. Apparently so. Ok. I'll play along. But first she'll need to talk.

"So, what else do you service the Pramam's advisor with?"

"Who have you been talking to? What I do in private is none of your business." I have her now.

"He's an amateur holographer, did you know?" Oh crap. She didn't. Loosen the grip! Wait. Girl's room.

"Spill it or I spill you." Not good. I'm trapped. Just calm down. Think. She's just upset, eh? Big breath in. And out. "Well?"

"It's on the maze."

She's stunned. "Pub...public?" She's shaking. I think she's really scared. No. She's terrified.

"No. Boys, you know. Stitch is a hack. Sort of a genius. We hadn't heard from you so he started sketching through secure packets. His private communications."

"He can do that?" Nod. "So apart from your perverted cousin and friend, I'm trip?"

"As far as I know. I'm so sorry, Caroline. I didn't mean to—"

"Well, what did you mean, yeah?" She's really upset, wiping her eyes. Let's just be blunt about this.

"Are you working for the Ministry?"

"You're crazed."

"Did my father hire you? You brought me here the first time to get clamped, didn't you."

"You overdazed, girl? Who are you?" She's telling the truth.

Hick. "You must think I'm paranoid."

"Um...yeah? A little." Sarcasm. I deserved it. At least she's primping again. Hey. My clothes are fine, thank you. "If you're going to have some fun, you need to look a bit more approachable, yeah? Show them off! Look. Like this. It'll get you something sweet." Oh. I'm not so sure. "Trust me. No flashes. And no counsellor. For some reason he was furious about you. No rib! He your father?"

That is too funny. "No, fishy. You see his nose?" She's laughing. I made my point.

"We're trip? Watch and learn." She does have the walk.

Be careful. Nathruyu's here. I don't want her sneaking up on me. Where did she go? Crap. I lost her. Oh good. She's busy with some guy. If he could only shift his head over a tiny bit... there it is. The crystal. Just like Keet's except clearer, a little bit grayish, and blueish too. Hmmm. Indigo I think. Well, well, well. Looks like she has a boyfriend. Quick. Behind Caroline.

"Don't be shy now. I'll make sure they go easy on you, yeah?" What exactly am I getting into?

"Um...isn't that guy over there with the black-haired woman you told to trip out? Poor self control?"

"Yeah. Right. Randy. She keeps him in line. She's like a female Sothese that one. Wonder if he's a star. Wouldn't mind seeing a bit of him." Giggle.

"Sothese? The advisor?"

"Yum. SSSexy SSSothese."

"What about her?"

"All you need to know is stay clear! Randy almost died a few times." I don't like that one bit.

Crap. She saw me. She's coming over. Start talking to someone.

"Is this one yours?"

Caroline is kicking me. Say something. "Ummm. No." Whoa. I feel weak. Caroline?

"Hold on to me. Don't say anything, just let her take him." Take who? Where? "Are you all right? Don't look at her. He hasn't got a chance. We should leave. You don't need to see this. Let's check on Randy first. He's harmless now." I'm bending.

I wasn't here long enough last time to really pay attention. These people are not normal. Then again, what is normal? I certainly don't qualify. Half of them are almost unconscious. What do they serve here anyway? And the guy she took is... is...need oxygen.

"Caroline?"

"I know. Just look away and... The SIF! Eli? Is this your doing again?" Not this time.

"They're after Nathruyu." Oops.

"How do you..?" Bar fight. "Biochip tagged. He's a violent hazer. One shot limit. Does this every time. Banique will take care of it."

"Where is the guy she took?"

"Forget about him. Who *are* you?" I wish I could tell her, but I honestly don't even know myself. "Never mind. We're jam! The SIF are flashing. Sheiss!"

Nathruyu's coming back and Caroline is out of her body. Straight at me. Stand tall. She can't do anything to me. Not in front of them. Caroline can't even stand anymore. Nerves. Look strong. Don't let her see you sweat. Not likely. It's pica cold here. Here she comes. Legs, hold out.

"You know nothing!" Such contempt.

Time to assalam. Grab Caroline.

"Not that way. It's not safe. Clip out!" Caroline signals Banique. He's questioning the SIF now. Oh. A diversion. Smart. Out the front. Fast. In the elevator. She's very quiet. Catch my breath. I still don't know how I got here. She's slumping to the floor. Where's my giggly friend?

"Caroline, what's wrong?"

"The SIF flashes. You really *do* know nothing."

Figure it out later. "I'll take care of it. Stitch can fix this. I'll comm him right now."

She has some color now. "Wait until we're out. Watch your back. Just walk fast until we're through the leafy wall."

Ok. Not looking friendly those ones. Just keep walking. Hurry. With purpose. Phew. In the square now. She nods. Hope he's awake.

"Hey lo, Stitch." Nice to hear her giggle again.

"Way, chum. Some people do sleep. Nightmare?"

"Real one. SIF flashes. You need to del them. All of them.

Caroline's too."

"That girl's trouble, yeah?"

She heard that. She's blowing him a kiss.

"Please. Pica crit. I'll explain later." He's debating. I can tell. "Chumbuds."

"Not sure what I'm on, but it's... You're bent! Is this why you weren't answering?"

"What?"

"It's done." Phew.

"I love you."

"That's Caroline, yeah? Tell her she owes me something sweet."

She's gesturing. Oh, that is lewd.

"She heard you."

"Juicy!" Ugh. Won't that get old?

"Hovertrain's here. I'll ping when I'm back. Ta, chum."

"You owe me too, lass. Ziga!"

"Um...yeah." He's right. Big. But not that way. Back to Caroline.

"You really don't know what you are, do you, Eli?"

K E E T O

I have a confession to make. The past week I have not been entirely honest with you, which is somewhat hypocritical coming from someone who has been touting his breakthrough virtuosity in regards to his commitment to trusting unconditionally. I was afraid that if Eli accidentally acquired my journal again, a further example of my lingering trust issues, that she might turn against me for what I am about to tell you, manifesting my second biggest fear besides the GHU, that of her pulling away from me voluntarily, which I coincidentally had a taste of this afternoon .

Since the day Eli noticed that Mashrin's body had disappeared from the transition wing and her proper ritual had finally made the unofficial news in the maze, life in Eadonberg has returned to its usual pace, and the three of us have been preoccupied with our day-to-day responsibilities, apart from our ongoing investigation of course. While Stitch has been probing for secure packets in the maze with assistance from Odwin, and Eli has been deciphering Dr. Kzavier's private patient records and snooping around the GHU, I have been digging for historical accounts in the archives and secretly meeting with Nathruyu at an inconspicuous hostel near the transport station. The disturbing result of all this is that every single thread and dead end in our research efforts mysteriously seem to point to you. The first documented case of biochip malfunction, albeit penned in a dead medic's handwriting, a large influx of anonymous support for the orphanage you apprenticed at upon your enrollment, Father's covert appointment to the URA shortly after we were born, various other ostensibly disparate events since then, and even Odwin's keen interest in helping Eli discover a cure for her illness, can be traced back to some aspect of your existence.

Once again, the answers exist in a void no living person can enter. If only you could talk to us through my pen. Your daughter desperately needs you, as do I. Please.

I'm sorry. I had to steady my hand before continuing. It is just this overwhelming feeling of helplessness which fills me with anguish, watching Eli gradually shatter, and my constant questioning as to why I haven't succumbed to the voices as she has. I hear yours speaking encouragement and patience, although it is difficult to know where your thoughts end and mine begin. Another one I can only infer is Father's voice, destructive and immobilizing, yet they merely feed my own thoughts, rather than consume them. As for Stitch? I am not sure how his mind operates, but there is definitely some self-talk going on up there, even though his scans label him drift free. Studying his brain might be enlightening, or at least amusing. So the enigma persists, as I become entangled with the possibly treacherous plans of a ministry insider. Why is Eli broken while I remain whole?

Nathruyu has been able to offer me some clues, although with her it is often difficult to ascertain what her vague statements mean. I suspect she is keeping our communications ambiguous so as to safeguard her true identity, or perhaps she simply enjoys the game, one in which I suspect the rules are of her own making. She knows things, and the source of this knowledge is a well-protected entity. Her features place her age in the mid to late twenties, certainly no older than thirty, which implies that she would have at the very least still been a teenager at the time of our ninth birthday, when she peered into the kitchen window. It also suggests that she could have memories of you either arriving at the orphanage after you were found wandering or a few short years later. The only plausible explanation I have at this moment for the uncanny details she shared with me about your youth, which incidentally correspond with the facts Stitch and Odwin have gathered, is your connection with the sage master, whose particular story still eludes us.

According to Odwin's allies and Nathruyu's testimony, when you were seventeen you were seduced away from your training by a newcomer to this city, you had unsanctioned relations with him, and you became expectant with twins. Unlike what commonly occurs with such a pregnancy, disclosure of your condition was withheld from the Unification and you were confined to your quarters until the delivery date. As the gestation period progressed, however, you became increasingly unstable, and fearing that the GMU would respond to neighboring complaints, your mentor transferred you to a hidden facility in the highlands where we were born. In the meantime, Father had tracked you, and through his newly acquired position in the Ministry as the chief director of the URA, he hid all three of us in the settlement we adopted as our home until the accident. The sage has been missing ever since.

Although he had proven his honor as it concerns Mashrin's spirit, Odwin's assurances that he had revealed the criminal's hideout to gain favor with the SIF were not altogether convincing to me. Granted, no more atrocities in Osler Hall have been reported, but that alone is not enough to prove that the perpetrator has been clamped. Furthermore, the original orders to the GMU were quite clear as to the urgency of apprehending the suspect, so if they knew where to conduct their vigil, then why was Nathruyu still freely wandering the pathways? After all, I doubt my senses were playing tricks on me that night, because I distinctly recall a hint of myrrh in the air, a fragrance permanently embedded in my heart even before I can remember, and rare enough to negate the likelihood of coincidence. Unable to raise objections without exposing myself to similar criticism for dishonoring my pledge to full transparency, I automatically assumed that Odwin, our trusted Gadlin contact, was operating under an ulterior motive, until today.

After contiguous double shifts in the round room over the past week, on top of my clandestine late night encounters and the extra research, at last, I had finished reorganizing the utter chaos born out of the Pramam's visit. Judging by the volumes of journals, parchments, books, and folders left in heaps in the aisles, I surmise he was looking for a specific item, because in no way could one person read the entire archives over the course of two days. My diligence merited me a well-deserved early start to the evening, and although I could have slept until fog lift tomorrow, I realized a talk with Eli was long overdue, and not a moment too soon.

As I was about to emerge from the orchard, I saw Stitch and Eli sitting on the glass bench in the clearing, passionately locked in conversation by the side of the pond. His body was slightly turned towards her with his left arm extended behind her on the seat back and his right wrist resting on her right forearm. My initial reaction was to interrupt his advances, but my instincts were guiding me to a different approach. As much as my toes were cramping with indignation and accusations of opportunistic manipulation were flying back and forth inside my head, I managed to control my impulses and, nailing my tongue to the roof of my mouth, I crept as close as I could to monitor the situation unseen. From the new vantage point, I could detect the distraught look on her face and the worried look on his, and despite the pause in their discussion, the dynamic tension between them was plainly obvious. I grappled with my imagination as I projected your plight onto your daughter, fearful that history was repeating itself in yet another way, and focused my attention on their lips, trying to read the words that their eyes were expressing. "We have to tell Keet."

I was not the only one keeping secrets. As I envisioned the worst, it was difficult not to blame myself for unwittingly pushing Eli into his space by broaching the subject of his intentions on several occasions, and by perhaps implanting an idea that would become self-fulfilling. Her posture stiffened as they exchanged a few more sentences that I could not interpret, and with his back towards me, he leaned closer into her, raising his palms to her face, gently cupping her chin and obscuring her with a sideways tilt. At this point, I had witnessed just about enough to send me sailing through the air like a jealous boyfriend, but I endured one additional assault before breaking my silence and making my presence emphatically known. His presumptuous paw then slid up her spine to steady the back of her head, as she timidly pushed herself away from him, while his right one gently reached past her right shoulder to cradle her behind the neck. What felt like an eternity to me as he gazed intently into her eyes, transpired in the matter of a few seconds, and what he said next slapped my ears with such force that I had to grab the tree beside me for support. "Part of your brain is missing."

That was my cue. I burst into the open, surprising them both, and began an embarrassingly long diatribe about the inappropriate liberties he was taking with a trusted friend who is highly vulnerable and confused, to which he started laughing and assured me that I had totally misread his gestures. Eli, on the other hand, was eerily despondent and oblivious to the confrontation, her gaze fixed on the open blue lotus floating in front of her, and rightly so. I was so preoccupied with flexing my overbearing brother muscles, a product of a dysfunctional upbringing I wager, that the revelation which was paralyzing her had not even registered. Stitch was so engaged in poking fun at me, that he too had temporarily ignored the impact of his exclamation. As he had in the commons the morning of the Pramam's speech, he carefully brought Eli back into the present, then explained the basis for his conclusion.

He had noticed the mark at the base of her skull the night we had escaped the daze through the ventilation tunnel network. It was while she was bent over drying her hair after we had swum through the water garden by my crypt that he had glimpsed it, but decided against mentioning anything, in case it was a trick of poor lighting. However, as her symptoms became apparent, as he deepened his understanding of the condition, and as we gradually volunteered pertinent background information, he concluded that his observational skills had in fact not failed him. He had been waiting for the opportune moment to test his theory. Once more, what we had been keeping from him, he had already figured out, which makes me wonder why I bother to build invisible walls between us in the first place. The exercise is futile, and it truly no longer serves our purpose for us to continue this little charade.

This is his theory. The depression in the back of Eli's skull bores a shaft into it approximately one finger wide, but without slicing her open like the first mutilated girl in the medical lab, he cannot confirm how deep it tunnels. Based on the size of the slimy slice in the blue goo we found at the killer's place and assuming that it belongs to Mashrin's brain, he surmises a hole large enough to house the critter. So in effect, what we are dealing with is not a defective biochip, but a lack of any at all. The two tiny holes we noted at one end of the specimen could conceivably act as an anchor for it or a vesicle containing it.

I must admit that the logic he employed was sound, except for the phenomenon referred to as death. Eli, and I for that matter, were alive, whereas the girls were not. When I articulated that technicality, Stitch, with much exaggerated movement and a dramatic flick of his squigglers, swooped his hand behind my neck, and fluttering his lashes, he stared into my eyes and gasped theatrically horrified. "Part of your brain is missing too!" A few giggles from the bench made the whole spectacle worth tolerating. He double-poked us, and we all breathed a huge sigh, ready to address our grim reality.

Confusion was the key ingredient in our emotional soup. We spent the better part of an hour speculating, too graphically for my liking, on how delicate a procedure would be necessary to strip pieces off without disabling certain neurological functions, and whether it was even possible to remove such a large chunk without killing the subject. Wouldn't the fragment atrophy with its root system severed? The tissue suspended in the bioluminescent fluid behaved almost consciously, as if it was aware of us watching beyond the crystal barrier. I shudder to think that Stitch is still walking around with a wormy chunk in his brain with a biochip attached to it. Then again, it would explain a few things.

Evidently, we need more answers. Is the specimen even a natural human organ? It reminded me of something out of a carnival freak show, like the one that used to travel the highlands when we were kids. While most of the exhibitions were oddly defective hybrid products or failed bioresearch projects, there were always one or two random jarred items with alien "soul sucker" slime in them, or so they claimed, whose plans to invade the planet had been thwarted by the very merchants who were charging admission. It always got Eli rolling on the ground when sweet gullible Jenny would run out of the booth shrieking, but she is not debunking this creepy creature, although I half-expect it to make a debut appearance at a sideshow somewhere. If only this were nothing but another harmless childhood scare, something benign that draws you in for the fear factor.

As their medical debate droned on, I caught myself losing enthusiasm for the dialog until Eli proposed staging another Osler Hall break-in for clues, and Stitch slipped in a quip about her recent brush with the SIF, at which point I demanded a complete confession. Neither of them denied intentionally suppressing the episode, but Eli reasoned that the case was most likely closed anyway, and that I would just have added this to my list of worries for nothing. There was not much I could say to argue with that, and certainly no reprimand I could throw at them in light of my unscrupulous behavior, so I used it as a lead-in to the nightly adventures I, in turn, was hiding from them.

They listened in shock while I relayed that Nathruyu was still roaming the city, and how much she knew about you, which, I added, did not surprise me since I had already imagined a familiarity with the family by the jewel peeking through her open coat. The two of them had been entertaining the probability that she was the murder suspect. Eli had taken it upon herself to succeed in our previous attempt at identifying the person behind the rusted metal door. Unfortunately, because of the consciousness gap in her evening, not recalling how she had arrived at the club in the first place, the yellow dust she found on her clothing the next morning could only circumstantially prove that she had actually wandered the underground shafts to get there. She had likely been shadowing the suspect. Together with Stitch's earlier comment regarding the glitter above the obscure figure's chest at the arcade, Eli's new attestation of remembering a similar shimmer, and ultimately, my admission about her intoxicating scent, no more could we deny that the beautiful stranger had a perverted alter ego. She was the one.

While Eli was battering me with countless warnings and specifics on her brief yet intense interaction with Nathruyu, my thoughts drifted back to the last rendezvous I had experienced with her, and why I was seriously considering her proposal. At first, I resisted in the interest of safety the prospect of inviting Eli to join us. I clearly had issues with the dark aspects of this woman's personality, and, due to Eli's deteriorating condition, I had deemed it prudent to exhaust all our other leads before introducing her to an SIF suspect, but given that Eli's resolve held fast when confronted with a face-to-face, the proposition may be our final hope. Nathruyu had effectively convinced me that our intimate chats could not continue without Eli, because what she was to share next would permanently alter our perspective on you, on the murders, on Eli's struggle, on myself, and on life itself. We were the key to everything.

Eventually, Stitch sided with me on the issue, and with a reluctant nod, Eli consented. As long as we agreed to meet with her in a public establishment, with high foot traffic and a convenient escape route, Eli should be safe from whatever unspoken treachery Nathruyu may be devising, especially if she intends on trading her to the GHU in return for absolution. Stitch would hang back and monitor the situation from a distance, so that if a betrayal did transpire, he could assist us on the outside, diligently working to pull us out of confinement. Once someone is placed under psychiatric care, regardless of the final diagnosis, they are doomed to a padded cell until they inevitably lose their grip on reality or physically wither away after repeated useless surgical interventions. That prospect does not excite either of us.

As I wrap up my journaling for today, an uncertain future looms. Nathruyu has confirmed our request to connect at the Snack Shack during the second rush. Although my heart wishes otherwise, this could very well be the last time we communicate through the pages of this book. Our destiny now lies in Nathruyu's hands.

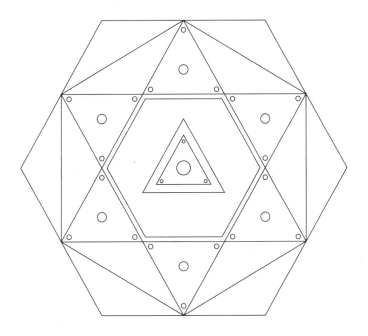

CHAPTER NINE

NATHRUYU

Day 42: late morning

The reflection passes through her as she clears the steam from the fractured glass. Nathruyu's hideout is under surveillance, forcing her to abide in conditions that solely the fortunate few can endure; yet the hardship is no less severe, and the banishment arguably ill-deserved. She had not succeeded in collecting that which she required. Although one such as she might construe the latest oversights as irreconcilable failures, her righteous convictions uphold her stance that the fated sufferings were tolerable losses to incur for the awareness she is cultivating. There will be other victims to acquire, and with either the voluntary or involuntary assistance of her virgin accomplices, her agenda shall overrule.

As she slides an ivory comb through her black silky mane, meticulously parting her hair into three sections, she hears the rumble of the hovertrain overhead and the thunder of the morning rush. Today is a pivotal day, one which will echo throughout the universe, which will secure the foundation for the perfect union, and which will ultimately dismantle the current illusion, for when the scorching sun obediently retreats this cycle to the virulent seas, earth shall meet the night sky, expectant and liberated.

The adrenaline flooding her veins seeks an outlet for its overabundant flow and roosts in a pool at the base of her pelvis, where she savors the intensity she yearns to release. The gathering is scheduled. Eventually, the twins will develop a visceral understanding of the truth, as their faith guides them through the process. Nathruyu would have preferred to involve them earlier, but circumstances were unfavorable under Vincent's watch, and shades of obedience still colored their perception. Now that their distrust of him is absolute, that Keeto is seduced by her challenge, and that Elize has succumbed to an inner drive beyond her intellect, their minds are ripe for the forthcoming transformation. While she exploits their greatest fear and their most intrinsic desire, both intricately woven into their mother's closeted past, she holds them hostage to their obsessions with the enlightenment only she can bequeath them. At last, they are hers to mold.

As her fingertips braid the first long tress, Nathruyu peers intently into the recesses of her shell, explores the urges percolating within, and exhales the weak pressure in her chest. Adjusting the lens in her eye, she laments the absence of natural lighting. She blames her miserable accommodations on everything and everyone but her own carelessness and curses at the yellow dust dulling her lustrous coat. The glow from the generator keeps her from shivering, but the energy is lacking the full range of solar renewal that used to revitalize her spirit as she stood majestically upon her beautiful rooftop sanctuary. Homeless in her beloved city, her present hovel does not do her grace justice, but "just" is not a term she employs in the context of this contrived society. The climate shall soon change, however.

She shakes the poison from her clothing and shines her boots with a discarded rag. From a workman's hook on the wall by her makeshift bed, she grabs the emitter and the false biography she had imprinted beforehand, according her adoption permissions from the Youth Services branch of the GHU. The health history is predictably impeccable, as are her Unified practices. She is an A-class contender for guardianship, and the single decision obliged of her, when she attends the appointment she, as Odwin, arranged at the orphanage, is to select the lucky little soul who will be freed.

The shiny surface of the cooling furnace captures her playful titter as she glides by, mirroring the cleverness of her scheme and the thrill of anointed deceit. With a final snap of her coattails, she threads her way through the underfoot labyrinth to exit by Almedina Square.

The jubilant sound of childhood fun had long been stricken from Nathruyu's memories, and as she pauses in delight by the gated crossway, her ears float above the ocean to the arid land of her origin.

▼ ▼ ▼

It is the afternoon her innocence was taken, and her parents are watching as she is assaulted by a ritual too traumatic for her young years. She feels the swift slash paralyzing her limbs, the warm red fluid creating a river with her blood, the explosion, the intense heat numbing her senses, and the damp crimson sand choking her lungs. Barely conscious and blinded by hallucinations, she hears the neighborhood children running and laughing in the distance, immersed in their carefree existence and ignorant of the atrocities in the valley nearby. The voices will help her bear the tenuous recovery, and if her essence should drift in the nebulous void to live a dreamless sleep for all eternity, then it is justly so.

▲ ▲ ▲

As the gleeful squealing subsides, dozens of small shoes shuffle towards the entrance and wait to be filed and counted, whilst the biodome, which cleaved a fog-free haven during their study break, prepares to disconnect. Nathruyu lingers at the security pillar until the footsteps quiet inside the building. Announcing her arrival to the sage master, she imprints the recommendation slip onto the board at his request and anxiously stands by for the latch to unlock. Even though her face is no longer familiar to this facility, thanks to her backdoor access to secure packets, and the staff is confirmed as fairly recent, the delay in approving the entry unsettles her. A call for additional identification sends her frantically scouring her slipwork for the missing details, as she respectfully apologizes for the poor visibility and claims someone must have stolen her portablower on the crowded platform. Once thoroughly authenticated, she sighs, and over the channel she swoops.

Master Chung greets her with a broad grin, sincerely grateful for her benevolent offer to bring love and acceptance to a distressed child. She bows humbly and follows him to his office, where he openly discusses the particular behavioral difficulties that manifest as a result of their trauma and assures her that he and his team will support her during the transition period while she adjusts to this gratifying responsibility.

As he reaches for the viewer in the cabinet beside his desk, a diminutive apprentice enters the room carrying a sweet snack and a fragrant beverage, and proceeds to serve his mentor and his well-appointed guest. Seizing the opportunity to accentuate her nurturing character and to gain favor with her interviewer, Nathruyu tenderly calms the boy's nervous hands with hers and helps him pour the cool drink, giggling with him as they spy a naughty droplet falling to the ground. The gentleman is visibly pleased, and once the wee darling hugs her good-bye, he plugs in the flashes and introduces the candidates.

Approximately twenty profiles play before the youngster she has secretly preselected attempts his monologue. He is dismally withdrawn, his posture slightly hunched, as if protecting a splintered heart from shattering, and his listless gaze transfixed on his fidgeting toes. She notes a shadow gesturing wildly in the background with what appears to be a canine puppet, trying to divert his attention up to recorder height, but he prefers the comfort of a former reality than the frightful unknown. His condition is so serious, pursuant to Ministry guidelines, that tomorrow his permanent home shall become the GHU psychiatric wing, unless he encounters a qualified foster parent who will give him the one-on-one emotional nourishment he needs. Master Chung's humble staffing is simply insufficient to provide this, which, as projected, aligns itself flawlessly with her plan.

After his allotted segment expires, her facial expression

feigns profound sorrow and empathy for his troubled state, even shedding a tear for the pain she shares with him, further endearing her to the captivated host. The ingenious performance culminates with an impassioned plea for mercy on the part of the Divine Trinity, an appeal for private blessings from the Pramam, topped with the ritualistic "Perfect are They," to which he unconsciously responds, "They are One." Only the legal transfer remains.

Teddy dawdles in, clutching a plush bear in his left and a storybook in his right, the scant items that survived the transport accident he miraculously outlived on the family's journey to a brighter future in Eadonberg. Across his shoulders, he wears a satchel containing a nightshirt, an additional tunic, socks with smiley faces on them, an extra set of sandals, and his wash kit. A fleeting wave of genuine compassion temporarily supplants Nathruyu's resolve and dredges up sentiments inappropriate to the task when confronted with the dejected vortex sucking any remnants of hope bottled inside this tiny frail person, reminiscent of the wavering that led to the Mashrin predicament. Nonetheless, the guilt is short-lived as she pleads the case to her intruding conscience. As of tomorrow, his life is forfeit, for he will belong to the GHU surgeons, an unwitting subject for their sanctioned tests, whereas she, by her graciousness, is granting him another day.

The sun is shining and the second rush shall rapidly be upon them, hardly giving them an hour to reach the Snack Shack. Teddy is holding her hand and gripping her sleeve with the other, his hip glued to hers, as they walk along the narrow passageways to the main corridor. The ride in the hovertrain manages to enchant him, especially the abrupt drop, and, for a moment, he radiates a glint of pure joy that sadly rejoins its source as they arrive in the vicinity of their designated meeting place. Over a month has elapsed since the crash, and his maturity has certainly regressed in response to his parents' death. He acts roughly like a frightened three-year-old rather than his nine years and attracts inquiring stares, which, advantageously, will leave a memorable impression on the otherwise preoccupied patrons.

Turning to her despondent companion, she kisses his cheek with his stuffed pet, and asks what the two would wish to eat. A bashful shrug and a shy smile is the best he can muster, so she points to a fanciful bake and watches his eyes respond with a famished yes. As Nathruyu scouts for a protected corner of the patio, Teddy devours the treat and absorbs his brand-new experiences, occasionally shifting his focus from the food to the landscape, then down to his food again. He then tugs at her coat to signal a vacant table on the second tier which lies behind a glossy panel and backs onto the floral waterway, an excellent lookout with minimal vulnerability to surprise attacks, and coincidentally the trio's habitual nook. She whisks him up the step, installs him opposite her and the water's edge, and awaits the twins.

A sudden fiery display in the heavens causes hysteria to mount. Some instinctively dive for cover and others reach for the personal bioshield they carry with them, just in case, but Teddy sits engrossed in his imagination, unaware of the mayhem surrounding him. The meteor storms have been regular these past six weeks and always cause a bit of a frenzy because of the damage they can inflict on the biowall with a precise hit to the grid posts, in spite of the emergency backup units below water level. Many entertain theories concerning their significance, but to Nathruyu, the speculations are immaterial. In her opinion, the increased collision frequency transpiring this hour are paltry competitors to the explosive anticipation she harbors as the event draws near.

The showers have grazed the top of tower number nine in the east end of the city, impelling the customers to scramble for the round markers and leave their meals unfinished to jockey for spots on the next carrier, their impetuous actions oblivious to the fact that the volley created more noise than actual destruction, and that Eadonberg is not compromised. Nevertheless, they clear the area in panic and convert the Central Core to a ghost town where only the fearless tread.

Perched on a stage for the earth to see, Nathruyu's doubt begins to question the twins' commitment. Surely a harmless pile of pebbles from space could not stand between Keeto and Elize's lifelong pursuit. Their tardiness must therefore be attributable to the unexpected confusion, yet her excitement wanes at the thought that they, too, are meek, or worse, that they have discovered her disreputable identity and have denounced her to the SIF. All is not lost as she contemplates the treasure in front of her and reigns in her scattered anxieties, trusting in the intimacy she has nurtured to deliver on its pledge, and indeed it has, with the late appearance of her commissioned two.

Initially, they do not notice the boy, but as Nathruyu extends her arm toward the empty chairs on either side of him, Elize smiles uncomfortably, whilst Keeto momentarily hesitates before they assume their places. Teddy is squirming in his seat, confused as to which angle he should twist his body, in order to avoid engaging with these intimidating strangers. He starts to wrestle with his bag, looking for the book he stashed away on the trip south. Then, self-conscious about staying hushed, he gingerly pushes his find onto the table, sheepishly checking his periphery for any hasty movements, almost as though he believes he is disobeying a rule. As he mumbles a highland nursery rhyme, he rocks back and forth, hugging his toy, and disappears into the fantastical world of mythical creatures that are coming alive through the vibrant illustrations.

The siblings are mute, for no introductions are necessary. As the awkward silence persists, Nathruyu teases Keeto with a slow intoxicating stroke from his clavicle to the tips of his surrendering fingers, reveling in the cold reproach emanating from her right, and strives to tranquillize him with her penetrating gaze. Much to her satisfaction, their nocturnal rendezvous have evidently become an intravenous drug with the capacity to subjugate his will, making his arteries dependent on her soothing touch to sustain their host. Elize, however, has not been privy to the same indulgences and subsequently is not impressed with what she construes as her brother's lack of discipline, which she boldly exhibits as a swift kick to his shin and a menacing glance directed at Nathruyu. As Elize has previously demonstrated in the club, the girl can clearly conquer her debilitating mental chatter in Nathruyu's presence, even to the extent of tinting the subtle energies with her own and effectively communicating thoughts from her eyes. Her attitude reconfirms that she also is ready for the challenge.

The sharp jolt pulls Teddy from his daydream long enough to recognize Elize sitting to his left, and suddenly, with an ecstatic shriek, he jumps to his feet and throws himself into Elize's arms, excitedly repeating her name. Nathruyu could not have concocted a choicer spectacle. Since the storm has abated, foot traffic has returned to the Central Core, and several onlookers rejoice at the happy reunion, embedding within them an indelible image and a name to go with it. Whatever happens to Teddy from now on, he will be intimately connected with the three of them, and their loyalties bound to her with a threat of exposure.

Nathruyu casually leans back and crosses her long legs as she relishes the tension escalating before her. Keeto knows. With Elize in shock and Teddy on her lap pouring his anguish out and begging her to babysit him again when his new mom wants her downtime, she senses the stiffness underneath Keeto's skin. Elize does not remember, but he does, and likely, he finally appreciates the consequences of responding to the metaphorical throw in her sinister game. He is probably wondering how she happens to pick those with whom Elize has established a relationship, or more accurately, a trusting relationship, and perhaps questioning exactly what sort of liaisons she maintained, and quite possibly continues to maintain, with their father. Nathruyu lured him into this affair with the promise of answers, and by the tone of his verbal eruption, she judges it prudent to diffuse his anger quickly, lest she lose control of him.

"You knew, yet you said nothing." Nathruyu's declaration was indisputable. Keeto had somehow hidden his suspicions, and ignoring them, had willingly endangered himself and his sister by indulging in her deception. But there is still plenty for him to learn. She softens her position, gently reminds him of their stated purpose, and points to Elize, who is distracted by Teddy and his cherished storybook and is concurrently monitoring their power struggle with an accusatory glare aimed at her neckline. The object of contempt comes to light as Nathruyu catches her own semblance off the polished divider and sees the glitter beneath her collarbone. "You're a petty thief," Elize declares.

The words ring partially true, she concedes, but not in the manner in which Elize presumes, and, considering her entanglement with the family, this unenlightened assessment disregards the crucial element of a motive she is not inclined to unveil to them in this public forum.

Testing the substance behind Elize's brazen facade, she strokes the crystal pendant and taunts her with a defiant smile, essentially daring her to defend the inflammatory statement, and clarifying who is really in charge here. The air thickens as the invisible duel magnifies until Elize forcefully retaliates, squeezing Teddy to her chest. "*This* one is mine."

Were it not for the icy tingling down her spine and the approaching silhouettes reflected off the facing partition, Elize's insolence would have met with her commanding fury. Nathruyu's departing quip slices through the pretense and pierces Elize's shell. "We are not complete, you and I."

As she leaps from the terrace in the midst of the startled diners, the Pramam's advisor and his loyal pack commit to the chase, matching her pace from across the western canal. Just as she breaches the Victory Bridge and darts for the shafts, she whips her head around to witness her nemesis lock eyes with Keeto and wink.

Sothese knew.

E L I Z E

Day 43: early morning

"Did they clamp her yet?" Please, tell me some good news, Stitch.

"Neah. Underground, yeah? Slam!"

"Where are you?"

"On the courts. You trip? Flip it over, bud."

"Yeah." He's not alone. Better keep this short. "What about Teddy? If she touches him I swear…"

"Ease, chum. Odwin's on it. Time out." He's walking off. Good. More privacy. "You got her blowing, lass. If you see her, you clip."

"*I'm* not nine. Keet handled her fine in the arcade. She doesn't scare me." If I can do a triple on the slick, then I can kick her through a wall.

"That was luck, yeah. It's all between the packets. The SIF has no clue. Sothese is working alone, along with the creepy three. They're afraid of her, and you should be too."

He's right, but I'm not. It makes no sense. I saw what she did to that guy. And what about those protectors? "I have something she wants. That's why I'm alive. That's why she's using Keet. To get to me." And she *sucked* him right in. Ewww. He'd better not have. Strike that lewd thought.

"Then she'll come for you. You shouldn't be out until fog lift. Where are you, Eli?"

"Whoa!" What was that?

"Zafarian! Such a *strong* name." Crap. She has my comm. I can hear her. On the left. "You will never run fast enough." On the right.

Stitch is running. He's going to get his band so he can trace me. He needs time. Where is she now?

"All I need is one stroke and the SIF is on you." That's Stitch.

It's coming from behind now. Turn around. She's moving. On the left. In front. On the right. She's circling. Focus. She's closer. Hurry up, Stitch. It sounds like wings. If I can just get between... Yell. "Stitch!" She's laughing. "Sothese!"

"Do *not* utter that word in my presence."

Ouch. Something's digging into my shoulder. I feel light-headed. So cold. Is anybody out there? Just laughter. Just Stitch's voice fading in the distance. Where is she taking me? So dizzy. Where did everybody go?

✂ ✂ ✂

"You think you can keep him from me?"

Who said that? What's that horrible stench. Smells worse than partially digested flyer bake. Look around. Crap. I'm in the shafts. A bed? She lives here? Over there in the corner. What is she doing? Creeps. She's so dark.

"Answer!" Go ahead. Answer. Ummm. What was the question? Oh yeah. The kid.

"Like I told you. *This* one is mine." Gulp. Don't let her sense my fear. "I know what you did." And don't give me that cocky attitude.

"You know nothing."

No, you wack! You're the one who knows nothing. You probably siphoned some packets just like Stitch did. You didn't tell us anything we didn't already get from Odwin.

"I know you're a liar, you're a thief, and you murder children." She's scoffing at me.

I don't have to stay here. No restraints, so I'm leaving. Just watch me. Right past her and...

✀ ✀ ✀

What? Crap. Back here again. She's having no end of fun at my expense. Ok. So I can't get through the tunnels without falling unconscious. She must have sealed the area with a biowall so it creates a safe air pocket. I wonder how far down we are, or even which part of the city we are under. I don't even know what time it is. No noises coming from above. We're probably out of the main corridor. My stomach tells me it's around midi. I could be stuck in here for days trying to find my way out. I need a mask. I'll just take hers when she's not looking, if I can find it. In the meantime, I deserve some answers.

"First, you must ask." Sounds like an invitation, or another one of her games. Juicy. Let's play.

"You're a killer."

There's that arrogant stance again. "So it would seem. But that is not a question." She's arguing semantics with me? Shades of Keet here.

"Oh, I'm sorry. Was that too harsh?" Here, have a snare on me. "Why did you mutilate Mashrin and steal part of her brain?" Impressed now? Grammatically correct as well. So enlighten me.

She's smiling. "No child died by my hand." Was that another riddle? How about your blade then? This is flyer mud! She leans against the generator. The blue flame is blinding me. All I see is a silhouette. "How long do you think you have to live?" Is she threatening me?

"Longer than you." She laughs. "The Pramam's advisor has a special interest in you."

"And I in him." Ugh. A memory flash of Caroline just popped in.

"He has that effect I am told." Oh. Not what she meant.

I wonder what her fascination with Sothese is then. According to Caroline, they're like one person in two bodies. No doubt that's why Keet is acting like such a fishy around her. She doesn't have that effect on me, and neither does the advisor. Maybe it's an IQ thing. Hehehe.

She's coming towards me. I don't like her that close. Just stand firm. Remember, this is just intimidation. Circling again. Gives me the up-down. She looks so much paler in the sun, but here... Heartbeat, slow down. She's just drinking this all up, isn't she, and starting to annoy me with all this posturing. Why did she stop back there? Oh no. Claws again. Breathe. Don't crack. Gasp. She has my hair. She's parting it. Not that!

"He cannot stop that which has already begun."

Fight her off. I can't move. She's too strong. Is that her nail scratching the back of my neck? One long stroke. Skin, any liquid oozing out? Concentrate. Phew. Nothing. What exactly is she trying to prove anyway? If you're going to go ahead and slice me, just do it. My fingers are back. I can feel the tingling. Ok, ready? Drop and take her knees out. Crap. Not fast enough. She's hiding behind the cooling generator and laughing. Well, I'm glad someone is enjoying herself. I have no time for hide and seek.

"What do you want from me? You obviously don't want my brain, or you wouldn't be toying with me like this. And where did you get that crystal?"

"Which one?"

"The one around your neck." Is she slow?

"Which question?"

Seriously. I've just about had enough of her. How did Keet put up with this charade every night? It takes forever just to draw one sentence from this woman, and then all I get is nonsense. Honestly. If I'm going to be stuck here listening to her until my dying years, then kill me now. Please!

"That day will come."

What does she mean by that? Wait. Did I say that out loud? I must have.

"Both questions! Do I have a limit? And no, I don't want one." I have you figured out.

Well, what now? She walks out into the main shaft with the fumes and just stands there, smiling. Good. You stay there, and when you pass out, I'm snooping through your stuff. She's walking away. Hang for a sec. Pay attention, ears. Count her steps and wait for the sound of a hatch. Nothing? She's humming. I know that tune; it's an old Gadlin lullaby. I haven't heard that in years, ever since… Mother!

Oh. get a grip, girl. It's just a coincidence. It's not like

Mother wrote the song or we were the only kids who were lulled to sleep by it. What if I hold my breath and peak around the corner to see what's there. That's it! She has a bioshield, and that's exactly what I need to make a run for it. I'd better know where the exit is first, just in case the power runs out in a stink zone. Think. How do I get her back in here so I can somehow take it. It's quiet again, except for a night flyer. Quick. See where it's going. That will be the way out. Let's peek.

Crap. Missed it. There must be some cleaner air up near the roof, but I can't fly so that doesn't work for me. Looks like some yellowish fog settling near the floor, so it makes sense. Where did she go? Other side? Not there either. She just left me here. Head back in. Breathe. I think I can hold it for one minute max and then I'm jam. Time to look around before she returns. There's a bag over there. Let's see what she deems important enough to hold on to.

How exciting. Books mostly. Hang a sec. I know these. They're Keet's. Is he lending them to her? I find it hard to believe he would part with this one though. Mother used to read it to us, *The Myths and Legends of Ancient Civilizations*. And a box? There's something in it. How does it open? Ouch! Something sharp. A privybox! I should have guessed it. Stop nipping at me, you nasty little thing. OK. Fine! Stay in the bag. I'll figure out how to… Hush! What was that? More shuffling, scurrying, and whispers. Heartbeat, slow down. Maybe it's just my voices coming back. They've been quiet since yesterday, and last night I actually slept. Perk. More, and they're getting nearer. Not liking this one bit. Oh, how I wish she were here just now. What am I saying? Well, at least I would know what I'm dealing with, of sorts. It's the unknown that sets the blood pressure soaring. Hide back there and work on this.

How can Nathruyu stand it here? I'm a sopping mess. I was warm earlier, but now I feel like I'm going to pass out from the heat. I need fluids. Stop breathing. There's someone at the entrance. It's a different stride. Someone else. Hold it together. Not a single sound and they'll walk on by. Eek! At the bed, searching. Maybe it's just a vagrant looking for trinkets to sell. No food here, or water. So thirsty. Hurry up, I need some air. Crap. Can't hold it any longer. Ok. And again. Ahhhhhh!

"You bent? You jumped me!" Stitch! It's not funny. Do you have any idea what I've been through? Oh no. I'm going to cry now. Be tough.

"Slap me, yeah?" With pleasure. "Ouch!" Right. A hug. That's good. You can stop now. Ok. A little more? This is getting awkward. You can let go. Wouldn't mind some air. "I thought…" He's puzzled, and are those tears?

"You can take the mask off. You just crossed a biowall over there." This is an awfully long gazing session. Say something before he gets grody on me. "Pica happy to see you. How did you find me?" I thought I'd never see that smile of his again.

"I found your comm and the bracelet near the Victory Bridge. Then I used the Minotaur trick and came in and out of the labyrinth to recharge. I brought a slipmap." Leave it to Stitch to find a way.

"I am ziga pica grateful you are my chum, Stitch. You're my juiciest friend." My turn. Big hug. That feels a little odd.

"Trip! Juicy, yeah?" Giggle. Old rib, but strangely funny

this time.

"Did you see anyone else? The scampering around?"

"Neah. Just shadows. We need to clip out. Put this on. We're near the east side. It's almost sunset."

Wow! I must have been knocked out most of the day.

"Hang. There's a box over there I need to open. I have a hunch. Her crystal is the same material as my mother's jewel. But…"

"Jumper!" Hehehe.

"…watch your fingers."

"You poor sweet soul." Crap! She's back! Don't let her touch you, Stitch. She's kissing his finger. My head is going to explode.

"Get away from him!" You think your glare frightens me?

"Pandora needs a lesson in privacy. I should have taken you when I had the chance." She's distracted. Here's my chance. Ouch! How does she do that? "You stupid girl!" What the! Stitch? No, his knees are buckling. What is she doing to him?

"Stop! Please, don't hurt him."

She turns her head slowly and tilts it. A malicious smile. "And what shall you offer me in return?"

He's weak, but alive. Think of something. I need to stall her until I figure out a plan. Teddy.

"The boy. You wanted him."

She is shocked yet intrigued. And so am I. I am forced to choose between an innocent child and my best friend. This is not a responsibility that I asked for, and I resent her for cornering me like this. Is that what collateral damage is?

"You think I want the boy?"

Did I miss something? Isn't that what she said just a while ago? Sure. Play those head games with me. I'll humor you. "I won't keep him from you."

That was a cross between a giggle and a grunt. "You know nothing."

Here we go again. Just be direct. "Juicy! I get that! What is it you want from me then?"

She is lowering Stitch to her bed. He's shivering. I have this compelling urge to run to him. But she stops me. "I want *you.*"

Me? I don't have any slime to collect. Well, that's the theory.

"And your brother." Sure. Who are you ribbing? She's asking for too much.

Think, think, think. Yes! Two can play at this. She didn't specify how she wants us. Besides, she's had Keet all week.

"What for?" She's staring right into the blue flame. I'd love to know what she is thinking or if she is thinking at all. Her eyes are telling a sad story.

"For the children. They have been chosen. We must save them."

Whoa! Hang there. She is completely bent. Not even marginally sane. I'm building an accurate profile now. She's starting to sound like she has megalomania. I studied that in psycho class. Delusions of grandeur. As long as I go along with the fantasy then we're safe, right?

"Of course, but who chose them?" I hope that was not too accommodating.

"You did."

Did not! I don't even remember them. Does that mean there are more? I'm confused. "I just happened to trip on your choice in the arcade. You are trying to manipulate the facts to paint me as an accomplice."

"It was no accident."

Am I hearing this right? She is the one who chose them. I am the only connection between the murders, and she knew that because she has been spying on us. It's in Father's flashes. She was looking for a fall-girl, and now hundreds of people have seen me with her next victim. If Sothese hadn't appeared... I shudder to imagine. If they take her, she will say she wasn't working alone, and eventually they will trace them back to me. A disturbed and dangerous GHU captive just like Mother. There's that smugness again.

"You need me. And I need you." That's a sick co-dependency.

"And Keet?"

"We are all one."

"And Stitch?"

She's shaking her head. "He is trouble. Like your father."

He's nothing like my father. I can't trust her. Stitch is a witness, and if he's no good to her then... No, I won't allow it! "You can't force me to join you."

I always have choice. I am not helping her destroy life. If there is a nebulous field like the Pramam says, then I'm not going there.

"You will. It is not your choice to make."

That's where you're wrong. "We'll see about that." I'll turn her in and Father will vouch for us. He's important in the

Ministry. They will listen. He'll forgive us for leaving without telling him. I know he will.

"He can no longer protect you."

Ohhhm gee! He knew. He knew about her. He was protecting us? That means she's been planning this for years. We sealed our own fate by running away. I can't bear the thought that I was in some way responsible for Mashrin's death. Don't take on the guilt. It will only serve her and her cleansing mission. Ignorance is not a sin, but now that I can see her malice, standing by and turning a blind eye is. Stitch has stopped shaking. His hair is moving again.

"Cover your ears, Stitch." This kick should reach the surface. Get off me. Run. Kick the other wall. Just keep hitting. The echo in here is deafening. She's on me. Yell then. "Nathruyu is here. She has hostages. Beside the generator. Nathruyu is here. The…" She's choking me.

Juicy! Cough. Gasp. Cough. She's down. Stitch is up.

"Ta, Stitch. Let's clip out." Masks on.

"The vent is on the right." Shadows. Four of them, running fast towards us. I yank Stitch's arm. "I hear them. Left then. We'll find another way. Hold out in here."

We're hiding in a nook, waiting. Some voices. It's them! Thank the little baby prophet! Never thought I would ever be ecstatic about being around those creepy ones again. I signal Stitch to keep hush and perk. Perfect. The ducts act as amplifiers.

"She is not here." No! That's impossible!

"You. Take the box. You. Disable the biowall. You. Secure the exit. I will find her."

That was Sothese. Some banging, clanging, ripping. They're tearing the area apart. This is our chance. The noise will be our cover. Talk hush.

"Show me the slipmap. Where are we?" I nudge Stitch.

"Here. South west of Almedina Square. And a hatch. One minute away, if we clip. Ready, chum?"

"Yeah. Let's clip out!"

We're running low on time. If the map is wrong then... We'll make it. My eyes are burning. They're chasing us. Stitch hears them too. He grabs my hand and...almost there. I can see a glow from the side and a ladder. Turn around. Who are these shadows? They just stopped. All I see is the whites of their eyes. It's too dark. Stitch? A struggle in the nook. No! They're looking past me. No more noise. Whoa! Let go!

"Counsellor?"

KEETO

Yesterday marked the end of an exhausting detour in our personal journey.

It was Unified Day. Although Eli and I do not actually practice, it has become a tradition over the years, mostly because Father insisted we pay respect to the Pramam and celebrate his birth date, so Eli and I gathered at dawn to exchange a few gifts. We had invited Stitch to join us, but, predictably, he denounced the celebration as a conspiracy to legitimize the Pramam's ascent to power and his personal judgments as divine authority. He added that if there were a single physical manifestation in this world which could be classed non-sentient, then the Pramam was it. I cannot say that I disagree with his position, especially concerning his underlying callousness veiled as righteous compassion. In hindsight, I am surprised, yet grateful, that we never attended any meditations, considering how closely linked Father was with the Inner Council. With his insider perspective, maybe he experienced the cruelty first hand and simply kept up appearances for the neighbors by claiming we had a private sajadum in our home. Regardless, it was the only time of year that he acknowledged you, and because of that, for a few brief moments, we were together as a family.

In the end, Stitch did eventually drop by Eli's room, a half hour late and bearing a different kind of present, an imprint of the Pramam's speech scheduled for broadcast at midi. He had been tipped by one of his chumbuds that there was to be a significant announcement regarding the twisted child collector, as she had been dubbed since her highly publicized clamp about a month ago, and what Stitch discovered revealed her intrinsic motive, and reminded us of how close we had come to unwittingly earning a private cell in the Ministburg lockdown.

A thorough diagnosis was finally complete, and Dr. Tenille, the expert assigned to the painstaking task of daily interviewing Nathruyu, had presented his case to the Inner Council last evening. Having spent seven straight days with her myself, trying to decipher her ambiguous and misleading statements, the fact that he was able to pull together a cohesive interpretation of her madness is commendable. Then again, he has made his career out of gaining the trust of exceptionally difficult patients, like you, who coincidentally suffered from an affliction almost exactly like hers. The voices, the hallucinations, the memory lapses, and the nightmares were all similarly entrenched, and even the tendency towards seemingly random violent behavior. However, in her case, the aggressive traits she exhibited were founded on a more intense level of paranoid schizophrenia.

She was obsessed with the notion that the mutilations were simply regrettable casualties in a war against the ills of society promoted and sustained by the current dynasty, referring to the Unification lead by the self-proclaimed prophet. She likened the current government to an incestuous band of puppets acquiescing in unison to the whims of a tyrant, as if all fed into a single string. Except for the method she chose to draw attention to her cause, these are hardly the words of a madwoman. I can think of an entire underground society which shares that view, albeit they have chosen to express themselves in a more civilized manner, through private lobbying and political espionage. The Gadlins understand that the masses need stability more than anything else, and though they do not agree with many laws and traditions ratified by the governing officials, they believe in peace above all else, and consequently they work creatively within the existing system to prepare a successor for the Pramam's inevitable replacement.

The report continued, claiming that the most effective method she had devised for rallying the people against the autocratic warden of the prison they were oblivious to living in was to create fear for their children, to make them begin to doubt that the Pramam was capable of protecting them, and, as a result, to foster disbelief in his claims of prophetic powers, in essence shattering the spiritual bond that stops our fragile society from falling victim to human greed and creating a void for her to fill with her deluded grandness. She had already selected the unsuspecting scapegoat for her scheme and had orchestrated a few chance encounters which would place the accused at the scene of the crimes, even to the point of enlisting accomplices with competence in the art of covert operations and record falsifications. As soon as the ensuing uprising gained enough momentum, she would arise, victorious, with a true prophecy of the murderer's identity to become their savior and newly elected leader.

Despite the fact that there was no mention of names, we

knew who the unfortunate fools were. A warm gush of blood shot up to my brain, causing my skin to flush, and instantly spread to Eli and Stitch huddled beside me. Could we have been that stupid? We were so blinded by our egotistical needs to avenge our own pasts, Stitch with his cousin, Eli with her guilt-driven nightmares, and me with proving Father wrong about you at all costs, that we were easy targets for an unscrupulous manipulator. It was the enemy within that defeated our better judgment and convinced us that it was acceptable to play along with a killer's fantasy for personal gain. Fortunately for us, her tactics failed and her last move became her undoing, as she vainly assumed that I had succumbed to her irresistible charms and at the same time vastly underestimated Stitch's ingenuity and loyalty. There were no conflicted emotions on my part, so I alerted the Pramam's advisor and his hounds.

The official message, on the other hand, does not give credit to the anonymous tip, rather it states that the SIF investigation has been a resounding success. The lone conspirator considered herself anointed by a higher source, who had given her the mandate to remove the biochip implants of children to save them from the Unified monstrosity, knowing full well that it would doom their bodies, and that a local sage from her home town had banished her from training when he noticed her narcissistic tendencies, dutifully informing the Ministry of her objective to advocate anarchy.

I am not sure as to just how much of this transmission actually ended up in the final draft, since a new mission presented itself as a result of the transfer plans. Because of the direct threat to the Unification, Sothese has been stationed in

Eadonberg since the capture, making sure Nathruyu does not endeavor to escape solitary confinement from a customized cell prepared in her honor in the GHU transition wing. As such, we had resigned ourselves to accepting the disjointed pieces she had fed us about your history until we read the second section of the communiqué.

This morning, as I sit here in quiet reflection with you in my heart as always, Nathruyu is moving to the Ministburg penal island, awaiting trial, which means that if we still wanted the answers she promised us during our Snack Shack meeting, we needed to act during his Holy address. Not having disappointed us yet, Stitch had already taken the initiative and made arrangements to sneak me through security, and that day, I was to learn from her fine example and outcharm the charmer.

Under cover of fog, I entered the building with the usual thrower and rubber combination and headed to the underwater level where I came upon the first serious challenge, the second being the actual encounter with the beautiful stranger. The level was in complete obscurity except for a thin ray of natural light I could barely discern, emanating from a hole in the ceiling. The walls deadened the sound of my footsteps as I counted the paces to the unit where she supposedly was held, trusting that there would be a door or some other suitable barrier separating us. As I advanced, I had the distinct sensation that someone was monitoring my progress and would reach out to grab me at any instant. Stitch had recently fashioned a biochip decoder like Eli's, which worked wonderfully for camping on GMU frequencies, but I had to rely on the thrower's display for lighting, which did little more than announce my presence to whoever was lurking in the shadows. And that is when I found myself on the floor, nursing my bruised behind, as I smashed against an invisible barrier.

The angel who had captivated me with that first smile on the hovertrain platform was barely recognizable through the field I had just bounced off. She was crouched in the center of the room, her frostbitten lips shivering in a beam of light, a meek sombre figure whimpering in agonizing pain. Something inside me yearned to believe that this semblance of a person muttering unintelligible verses was not the one I was looking for, but the feeling that overwhelmed me when our eyes met convinced me otherwise. I cannot fathom what torture she has endured at the hands of her nemesis, nor what willpower she has drawn on in order to survive, yet one thing is clear. The benevolent Pramam was anything but, and this woman was being denied the basic human rights guaranteed her in our professedly enlightened legal system. Ironically, the very hypocrisy she was ordained to expose had her trapped without a voice to do so.

As I observed her dungeon more attentively, I could see the walls glisten faintly, covered with a substance that had all the characteristics of ice. The moisture in the air had condensed against the walls, turning the area enclosed by them into a large freezer and maintaining its hostage in a quasi-hypothermic state. A heavy weight on my chest began to crush my rib cage, starving my lungs of oxygen when I realized that the dark layer covering her from head to toe, was not the silk I was so accustomed to admiring on her, but her naked flesh. Had they burned her? They had stripped her of her clothing and her dignity and left her straining to wrap her body as tightly as she could with her arms, to keep its plummeting temperature from reducing her into a corpse. She was using her long black hair as a cloak to preserve whatever modesty she realistically could. To my horror, the creature I had confronted in the arcade had not been a fabrication of the night.

The invisible door between us sheltered me from the inhumane conditions they were subjecting her to, but I still sensed her presence in my core, not as it relates to pity, but more akin to the sensation I had first experienced with her: joy, kindness, and a deep connection beyond the physical. The entire situation felt incredibly wrong. I was convinced that no matter how obtuse her communication style was, underneath it all lay a fundamental truth that I had yet to uncover. I imagined that perhaps, at last, with the two of us locked in silent acceptance, my eyes floating in the void beyond the gateway to her liberation, we could dispense with the game and open a fresh and honest dialog, if only to appease the conscience I am certain she possesses.

She confessed to me then that he was punishing her, that he had the power to release her but had chosen to inflict incommensurate suffering upon her. Such was his judgment and effectively timed ultimate reproach. There were no tears for her to cry, just the caustic pain of an abandoned child, alone, trembling, and confused while she heaved, desperately searching for a way to expel her grief.

As I listened, absorbed in her agony, the sweet scent of myrrh evoked your memory. Or was it the image of her contorted pose that was rousing your scent? Her features may have been different, but the silhouette was strangely familiar. Bent into a ball in the corner of your cell, I recall you warning us to hide Eli's voices from everyone, especially Father, and never to trust, which as children served us well. Now, circumstances have altered our beliefs. There is a sordid past which, for reasons incomprehensible to a young intellect, you shielded us from, and which our sinister stalker alleges to have intimate knowledge of. The question that continued to haunt me, faced with the fear of eternal ignorance as the opportunity for closure was quickly fading, was: does Nathruyu know or does she not know what really happened to you.

She opened with a quip about Eli's carelessness. There was a hole in Eli's ceiling that needed fixing because it rendered the energy shield she had meticulously sealed her dorm with ineffective against intrusions through the roof. She assured me that she was no thief. She had merely sought to recover what Eli had stolen from her, but someone else had beaten her to it, and now, all of her prized effects, as well as Eli herself, are vulnerable to wanton hands.

A flash of a libidinous monster crept into my mind, with Eli struggling to break his hold, then I remembered past conversations where Nathruyu had exploited my anxiety over Eli's health to imply how critically dependent we were on her for help, and conversely how doomed we would be without her, which evidently was not entirely accurate. It seems Eli's affliction is in remission, and for the first time since your accident, she has experienced many consecutive days of dreamless sleep, while Nathruyu at the same time is diminishing, caged in a waking nightmare.

I countered with further accusations, questioning the means by which she had acquired the crystal, which, interestingly enough, is carved out of the same mineral your jewel is. I demanded its true origin. Likely aware that her seduction skills had waned and that her hopes for a spiritual coup had dimmed to a mere cinder, she voluntarily surrendered the information she had purported to safeguard until we were ready to digest it. It was not what I had expected. The brooch was not yours, it was Eli's, as was the pendant she had strung around her neck, which someone had seized from her while she slept on the evening of her capture.

Anger did not come easily for her, since the energy it requires was beyond her grasp, but it was clearly audible when I re-accused her of theft, not only of the crystal years ago, but also of your flower-shaped indigo jewel. She was incensed at my lack of foresight at ever having entrusted Eli with such a valuable object in her fragmented state, an item of such pivotal importance, far above its credit value, that were it to submit to the wrong fate, it would dangerously shift the balance of power and destabilize the entire ecosystem.

A few extra minutes with her, and I would have been able to put your story to rest, but the Pramam's speech was over, and from what I could detect coming through the GMU band, my visit with Nathruyu was almost up. She sensed it as well and left the subtle heat of the stored sunlight to settle her naked body within inches of mine, so that I could use my device to illuminate our faces. There we lingered, divided in space, yet entangled in time, for the longest second of my life.

The order had been given. They were coming for her, and

her eyes fell silent. She signaled towards a controller on the outside beside the entrance and begged me to tap it, so that a small window could open in the grid. Reaching through it, she touched my cautious fingers and thawed her own with my warmth, which swiftly faded as a cool rush traveled up my arm. I could see her darkness lighten and a single tear freeze on her cheek, trying to escape, as she carefully articulated these final words: "The answers you seek are in Elize's dreams."

I wonder who will appear in her defense. I know there is no reasonable justification for her actions, but our legal system was designed to aid victims not destroy them. Centuries of detailed analysis have shown that a cycle of revenge can only feed on itself and grow. Isn't compassion for all what the Ministry has been advocating? Sothese certainly does not adhere to that philosophy. He should be the one paying for crimes against humanity. I saw the way he looked at her, the way he looked at Eli, and the way he looked at me, not a shred of compassion in his blood.

This morning, as I waited for the sun to rise on our fresh beginning, I felt compelled to snap on my runners and head for the orchard, as a means to rebalance my energies, before recounting yesterday's events. I miss the impending dawn in the highlands where I would run freely through the lavender hills, a secret haven away from Father's suppression, while he lay unconscious after disreputable outings. My cares would drift over the mountain peaks and past the neighboring valleys, dreaming that the wind was carrying me across the starry sky to hover peacefully between heaven and earth, with the world sleeping below my feet. Even though the campus greenery did not offer the same weightless experience, it did satisfy a much-needed urge to finally release a good ten weeks of tension. As much as I welcome a return to stability and routine, our harrowing adventures awoke in me a passion I suspect will not be content living vicariously through the volumes in the archives.

Then again, illusion may be coloring my perception. A lone canine mirrored my pace in the orchard today, daring me to a chase, but his stiff forked tail and squared ears betrayed his intentions. Sothese's hunters were still roaming about the city, and the mornings were not yet safe. My newfound boldness returned his menacing stare, and as the fog rolled across the grove, his haunting howl engraved this parting taunt as a chilling thought in my brain.

"Soon."

GLOSSARY

alias *n*
a nickname or user id inside the maze

assalam *v (anglicism from Arabic)*
to say good-bye, to leave

auto... *n*
a sensing device performing a single task (e.g. autolock)

band *n*
see **secure band**

bang-o *n (Stitch slang)*
anglicism of Spanish word "baño", bathroom

bending *adj. (city slang)*
confusing

bent *adj. (highland slang)*
nuts, crazy

bioApp *n*
A program running on a biochip

biochip *n*
internal intelligent chip attached to a human brain

bioclothing *n*
clothing that is alive and often sentient

biodome *n*
a fully enclosed dome shaped **biowall**

bioRhythms *n*
A **bioApp** that transmits a music broadcast to the brain

bioshield *n*
invisible shield surrounding a person to filter toxins

bioskin *n*
membrane to grow skin on wounds

biowall *n*
invisible shield surrounding a city as a unidirectional filter

blister *v (highland slang)*
  to get things done fast, to move fast
blow *v (city slang)*
  make someone very angry or pissed
board *n*
  futuristic version of a computer screen
bounce *v (city slang)*
  to feel unnaturally energetic, hyper
chip down *v (slang)*
  to physically recover from a change in **biochip** program
chumbud *n (Stitch slang)*
  a friend, chum for opposite sex, bud for same sex
circle *n*
  circular neighborhood of homes protected by a **biodome**
clamp *v*
  to restrict someone to an area and track their whereabouts
cleanerbot *n*
  self-guided intelligent floor cleaner and garbage picker
clip *v (Stitch slang)*
  to hurry, to do something like yesterday
clip out *exp. (Stitch slang)*
  get out fast, head to the exit lightning fast
cloaked *adj. (Stitch slang)*
  encrypted, as it pertains to a communication device
comm *n* and *v*
  1 *n* personal communication device
  2 *v* to communicate using a **comm**
crabbot *n*
  self-guided intelligent crawling surveillance device
crabseat *n*
  genetic hybrid between a crab and a chair
crack *v (Stitch slang)*
  to panic

credit *n*
the currency (there is no cash)
crazed *adj. (city slang)*
nuts, crazy
crit *adj. (Stitch slang)*
very important
creeps *n (highland slang)*
a bummer, crap
da ya *adv. (anglicism)*
a double yes; once in Russian, once in German
daze *n and v (city slang)*
1 *n* a party at an underground club
2 *v* to party, to go to a **daze**
del *v*
to delete
dizzy *adj. (city slang)*
gross, disgusting to the point of an upchuck
drop *n*
a stop on a **hovertrain** route
drop detector *n*
detects when something draws power from the grid
dunked *adj. (Stitch slang)*
to be totally lost, to not understand what is going on
dust *n*
encryption to make images look like garbage to searches
dust filter *n*
special type of maze sketch that can find **dust**ed images
emitter *n*
device emitting frequencies to change properties of matter
ease *v (city slang)*
to chill out, to calm down, to take it easy
eh *interj. (highland slang)*
adopted from Canadian "eh?" at the end of a sentence

fig *v (Stitch slang)*
to figure
fence formation *n*
GMU tactic for securing a perimeter
fishy *n (highland slang)*
turkey, silly, dumb-dumb
flagged *adj.*
marked for Ministry investigation
flash *n* and *v*
1 *n* holographic video, moving memories
2 *v* to record a **flash** on a device
flashpack (flashes) *n*
a pack of multiple **flash**es that plugs into a viewer
flatface *n (highland slang)*
a stone faced, unfriendly, or vacant person
flip *interj. (highland slang)*
bummer, crap
flip a pass *exp. (Stitch slang)*
get out of something without permission (e.g. skip class)
fly wild *exp. (Stitch slang)*
to let imagination control you, to go off on a tangent
flyer mud *n (Stitch slang)*
bullshit
frame *n*
freeze frame from a **flash**
GHU *acronym*
Global Health Unit
GMU *acronym*
Global Military Unit
good whip *exp. (highland slang)*
good comeback to a dig at someone
hanging low *adj. (Stitch slang)*
lacking energy, wiped out

hang for a sec *exp. (highland slang)*
  Hold on for a minute, wait a moment
hey lo *exp. (highland slang)*
  hi
hick *n (highland slang)*
  "doh!" when used alone, dumb-dumb otherwise
hide between the packets *exp.*
  to remove your id tag on a **packet** and thus be untraceable
holo... *n*
  interactive holographic objects (e.g. holopost)
hurts like a mangled scan *exp. (city slang)*
  hurts like hell
hush *adj. (highland slang)*
  to be quiet, to not make a sound, to be on **hush mode**
hush mode *exp.*
  comm setting to emit close-range canceling frequencies
hovertrain *n*
  inner city public transit hovering above walkways
imprint *v*
  to transfer media to/from a slip by sticking it to a device
jam *adj. (city slang)*
  used in expression "we're jam" to mean being in trouble
juicy *adj. (highland slang)*
  cool, equiv. to **trip**
jump *v (slang)*
  to scare someone, used in expression "you jumped me"
jumper *n (city slang)*
  something that startles you
knockout stick *n*
  device that knocks people out
lie low *v (Stitch slang)*
  to get some sleep
lifeshield *n*
  a device that creates a field to protect from getting crushed

lift *n*
shaft with elevator platform that materializes when called
loose *adj. (highland slang)*
relaxed
magnoform *n*
magnetic field acting as a raised sleep surface
maze *n*
futuristic version of an internet-like network
mick *n (anglicism)*
adapted from French slang "mec", meaning a dude
midi *n (highland slang)*
midday meal, lunch, adapted from French "midi"
Mount *n*
the holy podium where only the **Pramam** speaks
MPD *acronym*
multiple personality disorder
neah *adv. (city slang)*
no
newb *n (slang)*
a newcomer
ohhhm gee *interj.*
equiv. to OMG, oh my god.
oh, the shards *exp. (city slang)*
you break my heart in a joking manner
one-way portal *n*
see **uniportal**
operative *n*
a stealthy and highly trained member of the **GMU**
out-of-bounds tag *n*
attached to an archive shelf when a document goes missing
overdazed *adj. (city slang)*
stoned, drugged up, out of it
packet *n*
a block of information existing in the maze

PAL (personal automated librarian) *acronym*
  programable flying book retriever, a type of **sniffer**
parked *adj. (slang)*
  to be sitting waiting for someone
pass *n (Stitch slang)*
  an out, an exit out of a tough situation
patch *n*
  an update or fix to a malfunctioning **biochip**
Perfect are They *exp.*
  ceremonial verse used as a lead in for **They are One**
perk *v (Stitch slang)*
  to listen up, perk one's ears
pica *adv. (Stitch slang)*
  super, very
plane *v*
  to slide just above ground with special shoes
plane like I'm on the slick *exp.*
  to hurry, derived from the sport of planing
poke a rib *exp. (Stitch slang)*
  to tease, to play a trick on
portablower *n*
  personal short-range device to blow fog away for visibility
Pramam *n*
  leader of the Unification and head of the Inner Council
privy... *n*
  protective item container with teeth (e.g. privyshelf)
proximity reader n
  echolocation device used in the fog to detect obstacles
red craft *n*
  GHU ambulance
ride it *exp. (city slang)*
  go with the flow
ride *v (Stitch slang)*
  to not show up for work, just ride on by

rift *v*
to change the properties of matter using frequency shifting
rip *v (highland slang)*
to figuratively rip one's pants laughing, used like LOL
roll *v (highland slang)*
to laugh uncontrollably
rook *n (slang)*
a rookie
rubber (narrow field rubber) *n*
undetectable small frequency range canceling device
sajadum [sá-ha-doom] *n*
small crystal building used for meditation; fits three people
sage master *n*
an individual of highly cultivated wisdom through study
scan *n* and *v*
1 *n* result of reading a **biochip** for health/security purposes
2 *v* to read someone's **biochip** using a frequency device
scan jam *exp.*
jamming of the frequencies a device uses to read a **biochip**
scanning wall *n*
a wall that continuously **scans biochips** within a meter of it
scuff *n (city slang)*
a complication resulting in verbal or physical confrontation
secure band *n*
a wristband with clearance level access past **sentinel** posts
sentinel *n*
a hybrid species bred for security duty
señor *n (slang)*
dude, adapted from Spanish
shakes *interj. (Stitch slang)*
used as expression to mean "whoa"
shard *n*
see **oh, the shards** for its use in city slang

sheiss *interj. (anglicism from German)*
shit
shoe will stick to him something fierce *exp. (Stitch slang)*
the boss will get on his case, give him a butt kick
SIF *acronym*
Special Investigation Forces
sketch the maze *exp.*
equiv. to web surfing but with sketching device
slack *v (slang)*
to put something off, procrastinate
slam *n* and *v*
1 *n (Stitch slang)* a scoring throw in a sports game
2 *v* to lightly punch a friend when annoyed at them
slap me *exp. (Stitch slang)*
I'm sorry
sleeper *n*
portable sleeping surface
sleeve *n*
an envelope style folder used to store loose documents
slick *n*
futuristic sports rink based on hovering mechanism
slide *v*
to arrive at a destination by way of a **slider**
slider *n*
a personal vehicle that moves by sliding just above ground
sliderpad *n*
a place to store a **slider**, like a garage
slip *n*
interactive membrane to store/display/manipulate media
slipmap *n*
an interactive map imprinted on a **slip**
slippad *n*
a stack of **slip**s temporarily bound to each other

slipwork *n*
similar concept to paperwork except concerning **slip**s
sniff *v*
to use a **sniffer** to find something
sniffer *n*
device that finds things based on frequency detection
sprinkle dust *v*
to encrypt an image or **packet** to render it unsearchable
stretch rodent *exp.*
sarcastic way of referring to a ferret-like animal
stroke *n*
one single line or gesture when sketching through the **maze**
sunshaft *n*
a lift shaft that captures and stores solar energy
sweep formation *n*
GMU tactic for fanning out and overtaking an area
sweep *n*
a complete search of an area using a **sweep formation**
swish *v (Stitch slang)*
got it, figured it out
ta *n (Stitch slang)*
thanks
tag *n*
location tracking and monitoring device or **biochip** flag
tagged *adj.*
biochip is altered and marked as a suspected criminal
Tess *adj. (Stitch slang)*
genius, derived from inventor Nikola Tesla
They *pron*
The holy Trinity of Jesus, Mohammed, and Abraham
They are One *exp.*
ceremonial response to **Perfect are They**, equiv. to "Amen"
thrower (frequency thrower) *n*
a device that shoots frequencies at a specific point

top *adj. (highland slang)*
so much, as in "top juicy" meaning so cool, equiv. to **pica**

topped up *adj. (highland slang)*
stressed out

trace *v*
to run a diagnostic on a **biochip** to find a defect

transfer chest *n*
a futuristic shipping crate used by the Gadlins

trip *adj. (city slang)*
cool

trip out *exp. (city slang)*
get lost, go cool off

trip with that *exp. (city slang)*
I'm in, I'm cool with that, it's all good

uniportal *n*
a thin membrane acting as a one-way viewing window

unit *n*
a group of military personnel

URA *acronym*
Unification Research Arm

virta... *n*
a virtual object with solid properties (e.g. virtachair)

wack *n (highland slang)*
creep, weirdo

way *exp. (city slang)*
hi, equiv. to **hey lo**

wipe *n*
a membrane typically used to wipe off sweat, like a hanky

whip *n (highland slang)*
a comeback to a **rib**, as in "good whip!"

ya fig *exp. (Stitch slang)*
you figure, equiv. to **eh**

yay with that *exp. (highland slang)*
down with that, cool with it, all for it

yeah *adv. (city slang)*
  equiv. to **eh**
you-belong-in-a-jar look *exp. (highland slang)*
  you're nuts, you're a freak
zapped *adj. (slang)*
  touché, you got me, I fell into that one
zapper *n*
  a wearable alarm device that sends a mild shock
ziga *adv. (Stitch slang)*
  super super, even more than **pica**

ACKNOWLEDGMENTS

I have a secret to share with you and there are no shades or hues to it. It involves making a decision, a yes or no choice, a blue pill or a red pill. There is no turning back.

My name was not always Kaz. That's right. I pulled a Prince, a P. Diddy, a Lady Gaga, a Houdini, then magic started to happen.

You see, it's about letting go of old limiting beliefs and claiming *All That Kaz* as my own personal screenplay. This simple yet monumental shift is what has fueled the new Nemecene™ World and what has attracted the following awesome people to my life, for whom I am eternally grateful.

Bob Proctor, Sandy Gallagher, Gina Hayden, Arash Vossoughi, my PGI Matrixx friends, Amy Stoehr, Glenn Garnes, Jae Rang, Gabriella Morfesis, Sylvia McConnell, RUKE, Eric Christian, Thomas Wade, Cecilie Svendsen, Jelayne Miles, Rachel Oliver, Neil Oliver, Damon Flowers, Jody Royee, Alena Chapman, Jennifer Beale, Greg Reid, my Secret Knock friends, Lise Patry, Marg Hachey, my GroYourBiz friends, Susannah Davies, Nancy Trites Botkin, Mark Shekter, Ana Jorge, Alecia Guevarra, and many more.

I especially want to acknowledge Les Petriw, Jason Brockwell, and the team at NBN (National Book Network, Inc.) for their role in taking Nemecene to the next level.

I'd also like to send a special hug to my dog Lola for NOT eating the manuscript and for anchoring me in the moment that is now.

ABOUT THE AUTHOR

Kaz is not an author in the traditional sense. She creates fictional worlds using any media she can shape into a richly layered vision. Her strengths have always been imagination, design, and a natural ability to connect the dots, which she weaves into beautiful tapestries that engage the senses. Kaz uses the rhythms and nuances of words to successively reveal deeper meaning behind the narrative.

Nemecene: The Epoch of Redress is the first episode and entry point into the greater Nemecene™ World — a place where you can engage in life-changing immersive experiences that inspire and empower you to think, feel, express, connect, and act in harmony with others, nature, and our life source, water.

Kaz has a bachelor in Applied Science (engineering) from Queen's University, a fashion degree from the Richard Robinson Fashion Design Academy, certifications in personal training and hypnosis, a US patent in user interface design, an IMBD credit as director, and has written extensively on environmental issues via WomanNotWaiting.com, LifeAsAHuman.com and her philanthropy mission at Aguacene.com.

When she is not scheming the perfect muahahaha moment, you can find her hanging around some four-legged friends. She speaks English, French, Spanish, and is currently learning Russian. She also strives to be a recovering chocoholic, with limited success, and to look more and more like her standard poodle every day.

THE MISSION

Do you love water? (say *yes*)

So do I.

We love water because we *are* water and pretty much everyone and everything we hold dear in our life is water.

What if every time you read a book, watched a movie, played a game, hung out, or nabbed some swag, in order to dream big with your friends inside a science fiction fantasy Nemecene™ World, you actually could define history for zigazillions of lives — human and non-human alike?

And you wouldn't have to become an activist, a kayaktivist, a slacktivist, or any other kind of -ivist...unless you wanted to juice it up a notch, of course. You can simply be a friend.

The Nemecene™ World immerses us in a future flooded by dead oceans and poisonous gases, but we don't have to manifest that. How we relate to water is the key.

We truly live in an epoch of water that is fast heading towards an epoch of redress. As founder of the Aguacene™ Fund at Tides Canada Foundation, my personal mission is to use all things Nemecene to fund water stewardship projects, starting with the Mackenzie River watershed and the Beaufort Sea.

Philanthropist through fun! And by purchasing this book, you now are one.

Thank you.

Kaz

GET EPISODE 2

NEMECENE

THE GADLIN CONSPIRACY

Day 363: late evening.

... Her blue sapphire shoes finesse a body roll onto the east spiral tower, and, with another fluid leap of faith, Nepharisse emerges from an airy tumble into the north clearing for an unscathed escape through the orchard. The furious echo of pincers, snapping nine stories above her, fades as she approaches perimeter security at the north gate of the Schrödinger University campus island. She smiles her way past the guard to the Victory Bridge and stops. Her heart races.

A soul piercing feeling pulls Nepharisse's focus to the ninth-floor window in the J tower of the student residence complex, the same feeling of dread she had on her first day in Eadonberg, almost nineteen years ago. Elize is staring back at her. The evil has returned...

Available now!

For more information on where to buy Nemecene™ episodes and products go to

www.GETNEMECENE.com

COLLECT CREDITS

Want to earn some currency?

Join the Nemecene™ World — score 9 Nemecene™ Credits.
Enter YOUR unique biochip # (see inside front cover) at

w w w . N E M E C E N E . c o m / r e g i s t e r - b o o k

Creeps!
You've been biochipped!

Want EVEN MORE currency?

Invite your friends to join.
Find out how at

w w w . N E M E C E N E . c o m / i n v i t e - f r i e n d s

Perk! Here's a little secret.

Leadership has many privileges.
Get the inside scoop at

w w w . N E M E C E N E . c o m / l e a d e r s h i p